40 Hits, 40 Stories

40 Hits, 40 Stories

*Behind Top Songs
of the 1960s and 1970s*

RICK SIMMONS

McFarland & Company, Inc., Publishers
Jefferson, North Carolina

LIBRARY OF CONGRESS CATALOGUING-IN-PUBLICATION DATA

Names: Simmons, Rick, author.
Title: 40 hits, 40 stories : behind top songs of the 1960s and 1970s / Rick Simmons.
Other titles: Forty hits, forty stories
Description: Jefferson, North Carolina : McFarland & Company, Inc., Publishers, 2022. | Includes bibliographical references and index.
Identifiers: LCCN 2022039609 | ISBN 9781476683751 (paperback : acid free paper) ∞
ISBN 9781476646909 (ebook)
Subjects: LCSH: Popular music—1971-1980—History and criticism. | Popular music—1961-1970—History and criticism. | BISAC: MUSIC / History & Criticism
Classification: LCC ML3470 .S58 2022 | DDC 782.4216409—dc23/eng/20220824
LC record available at https://lccn.loc.gov/2022039609

BRITISH LIBRARY CATALOGUING DATA ARE AVAILABLE

ISBN (print) 978-1-4766-8375-1
ISBN (ebook) 978-1-4766-4690-9

© 2023 Rick Simmons. All rights reserved

No part of this book may be reproduced or transmitted in any form or by any means, electronic or mechanical, including photocopying or recording, or by any information storage and retrieval system, without permission in writing from the publisher.

Front cover images: record labels author's collection

Printed in the United States of America

McFarland & Company, Inc., Publishers
Box 611, Jefferson, North Carolina 28640
www.mcfarlandpub.com

Acknowledgments

What made this project different was that it finally gave me a chance to bring together interviews I'd done over the last decade and put them all in one book. Of the featured artists and performers I talked to, I wish to thank Archie Bell, William Bell, Jan Bradley, Norm Burnett of the Tymes, Tony Burrows of the Edison Lighthouse and the First Class, Jerry Butler, Bobby Caldwell, Roe Cree and Larry Meletio of Rose Colored Glass, G.C. Cameron of the Spinners, Harry Wayne Casey (KC) of KC and the Sunshine Band, Emilio Castillo of Tower of Power, Lou Christie, Clem Curtis of the Foundations, Ron Dante of the Archies and the Cuff Links, Harry Elston of the Friends of Distinction, Mark Farner of Grand Funk Railroad, Jim Gilstrap, Cuba Gooding of the Main Ingredient, James Holvay of the MOB, Robert Knight, Bob Kuban of Bob Kuban and the In-Men, Tony Macauley, Nick Marinelli of Shades of Blue, Gene McDaniels, John McElrath of the Swingin' Medallions, Bob Miranda of the Happenings, Bobby Moore Jr. of Bobby Moore and the Rhythm Aces, Deacon John Moore, Rob Parisi of Wild Cherry, Freda Payne, Wayne Pittman of the O'Kaysions, Charles Pope of the Tams, Dianne Pope, Jay Proctor of Jay and the Techniques, Tommy Roe, Bobbie Smith of the Spinners, Ammon Tharp of Bill Deal and the Rhondels, John Townsend of the Sanford Townsend Band, Dennis Tufano of the Buckinghams, Sonny Turner of the Platters, Pat Upton of the Spiral Starecase and Brenton Wood. The ensuing decade have seen quite a few of them pass away, including Clem Curtis, Cuba Gooding, Robert Knight, Gene McDaniels, John McElrath, Charles Pope, Bobbie Smith, Ammon Tharp, Sonny Turner, Wayne Pittman and Pat Upton. I continue to hope that that list doesn't grow longer any time soon.

A *really* big thanks to Ricky Saucier and Woody Lynch, who often read and discuss my ideas with me as I work on my books, and to Hank Mabry. I would also like to thank my student editors and proofreaders in my Advanced Composition class: Ella Cheek, Sage Fairclough, Taylor Jordan, Isaac Shumard and Annika Villafranca.

Finally, to Sue, my wife and copy editor at home, as well as Courtenay, Cord, Julie, Matt and Sutton. Without you, there'd be no book. My heartfelt thanks.

I have endeavored to be as accurate as possible in everything found within this book, and if something is incorrect, I apologize. To all I say thanks.

Table of Contents

Acknowledgments v

Preface 1

Introduction 3

#1. "Play That Funky Music" (1976), Wild Cherry 7

#2. "Band of Gold" (1970), Freda Payne 12

#3. "A Hundred Pounds of Clay" (1961), Gene McDaniels 17

#4. "Bad Time" (1975), Grand Funk............................ 21

#5. "Grazing in the Grass" (1969), Friends of Distinction...... 28

#6. "Girl Watcher" (1968), The O'Kaysions 34

#7. "More Today Than Yesterday" (1969),
    The Spiral Starecase 41

#8. "Just Don't Want to Be Lonely" (1974),
    The Main Ingredient 47

#9. "Tracy" (1969), The Cuff Links 52

#10. "Swing Your Daddy" (1975), Jimmy Gilstrap 57

#11. "Susan" (1967), The Buckinghams........................ 62

#12. "The Cheater" (1965), Bob Kuban and the In-Men 67

#13. "Everlasting Love" (1967), Robert Knight 73

#14. "Mama Didn't Lie" (1963), Jan Bradley 79

Table of Contents

#15. "It's a Shame" (1970),
   THE SPINNERS 83

#16. "Oh How Happy" (1966), SHADES OF BLUE 89

#17. "Private Number" (1968), JUDY CLAY AND WILLIAM BELL 95

#18. "Double Shot (of My Baby's Love)" 1966,
   THE SWINGIN' MEDALLIONS 101

#19. "The Oogum Boogum Song" (1967), BRENTON WOOD 107

#20. "Love Grows (Where My Rosemary Goes)" (1970),
   EDISON LIGHTHOUSE 112

#21. "So Much in Love" (1963), THE TYMES 117

#22. "Sugar, Sugar" (1969), THE ARCHIES 123

#23. "What Kind of Fool" (1969),
   BILL DEAL AND THE RHONDELS 128

#24. "Hey, Western Union Man" (1968), JERRY BUTLER 133

#25. "Searching for My Love" (1966),
   BOBBY MOORE AND THE RHYTHM ACES 138

#26. "Be Young, Be Foolish, Be Happy" (1968), THE TAMS 143

#27. "This Time It's Real" (1973), TOWER OF POWER 148

#28. "I Got Rhythm" (1967), THE HAPPENINGS 153

#29. "Mother-in-Law" (1961), ERNIE K-DOE 159

#30. "Can't Find the Time" (1971), ROSE COLORED GLASS 165

#31. "Keep It Comin' Love" (1977),
   KC AND THE SUNSHINE BAND 172

#32. "Could It Be I'm Falling in Love" (1973),
   THE SPINNERS 177

#33. "Baby, Now That I've Found You" (1967),
   THE FOUNDATIONS 183

#34. "Smoke from a Distant Fire" (1977),
   THE SANFORD TOWNSEND BAND 189

Table of Contents ix

#35. "I Love You 1000 Times" (1966), THE PLATTERS............ 195

#36. "There's Gonna Be a Showdown" (1968),
  ARCHIE BELL AND THE DRELLS 202

#37. "Rhapsody in the Rain" (1966), LOU CHRISTIE 209

#38. "Beach Baby" (1974), THE FIRST CLASS................... 214

#39. "Strawberry Shortcake" (1968),
  JAY AND THE TECHNIQUES 218

#40. "Jack and Jill" (1969), TOMMY ROE 223

Works Cited... 231

Index.. 235

Preface

I honestly wish I could remember the details of the conversation I was having in the winter of 2019 with my old friend Hank Mabry, who was once a fraternity brother of mine at Clemson. He was staying with me for a week at Pawleys Island, South Carolina, the marvelous place I call home. My wife and I moved here in the summer of 2018 after more than two decades in Louisiana. We'd met here, married here, and had the first of our two children here before we moved so I could get my Ph.D. and then teach as a college professor. But by 2017, I was tired, tired of the internal politics and craziness of dysfunctional academic life, so we both took early retirement in 2018 and moved back here to the beach. At that point, in addition to my six books, I'd published 135 articles, some academic but most of them not. All in all, I was just exhausted—tired of writing, tired of teaching. I just wanted to kick back and sit on the beach.

But before I'd even moved back here, I had figured out that the reality of the situation was that it wouldn't work. Besides my family and friends, the two things in life that gave me a purpose were teaching and writing, and I really loved both. I decided I would teach again, but find a place where I no longer had to be an administrator, where I could *just* teach. I wasn't interested in the discipline problems I'd face in a public school, and because my wife had taught at a private school and my children had attended a private school, I figured that would work best for me. I got a job at the Georgetown School of Arts and Sciences in Georgetown, South Carolina, a very small private school where most of the faculty members have Ph.D.s; most have taught in college at some level. It's been a great fit for me being somewhere that values education and where I can just teach.

That brings me to the conversation I was having with Hank Mabry. I hadn't written for more than a year. Other than the academic writing I'd done to get tenure and then promotions as a professor, writing has always been a hobby for me, and I've done it because I love it. I had particularly liked writing about music, but again, at that point I was burned out. I can't force myself to write, I have to want to do it, and I have to have a reason to do it. Very matter-of-factly, Hank asked what my next book would be about, and when I told him I hadn't written in more than a year he was surprised and somewhat disappointed. He said that I had a gift and I was wasting it. That night I went home and started thinking about it and realized I *had* missed it and was ready to write again. As I mentioned in the preface, what to write about wasn't too hard to figure out, because I love writing about music and I had a lot of material waiting to be shared.

That led to this book. Despite having to work around a world in lockdown due to COVID, having to learn to teach online part of the time, and a number of personal challenges of different types, I have finished it at last. And I did enjoy doing it.

Introduction

I've wanted to do a book like this for a long time, but before I get into why the book is structured the way it is, let me tell you how we got here. The first articles I ever published were about local South Carolina history, written when I was in my 20s. It was purely for fun, and soon writing became my hobby. I never considered writing about my interests as anything *but* a hobby, because after getting my Ph.D. I worked as a professor and had to do quite a bit of academic writing to secure tenure and get promoted to associate and full professor. But by 2008—and roughly 25 academic publications later—I had reached those milestones. I turned once again to writing for "fun," and my second and third books were about South Carolina history and folklore. (My first book was academic.) By that point, I was ready to write about another of my major interests, music. Over the last decade, I've been writing about music more and more, and to that end my last three books had been about music, mainly old R&B. In 2014, I started writing for *Rebeat*, a fantastic online magazine about the music and culture of the '50s, '60s and '70s, founded by Allison Johnelle Boron. Allison gave her writers a lot of latitude, and along the way I started a regular feature ("The Story Behind...") about particular songs. It was based on interviews like the ones in this book. Allison shared with me that my article "The Story Behind the Swingin' Medallions' 'Double Shot,'" published in May 2016, had been read more than 25,000 times over the course of the year, second only to (and within 600 reads of) an article about the Beatles' Paul McCartney death hoax which had been written two years earlier. That indicated to me that people were interested in the stories behind the songs, as was I. I'd done quite a few interviews for *Rebeat* that had never appeared in a book (Tommy Roe, KC, Mark Farner, Tony Burrows, Ron Dante), as well as interviews with others that I had never published anywhere (Lou Christie, Bob Miranda of the Happenings, songwriter-producer Tony Macauley). I decided it was time to do a book in which I could share their stories. And so here we are.

The Structure and the Charts

But I wanted to do more than present a set of random interviews. I've always been fascinated by songs' positions on the *Billboard* pop chart and other charts, and I thought I'd start there. One possibility I considered was doing an interview-based book about Top Ten hits, but other than the fact that some of these songs wouldn't have made the final cut if I did, it wouldn't have differed too greatly from this one. I guess the part of me that likes everything neat and orderly came up with the idea of having the songs in this book follow a standard "Top 40" format. The question was how to make it work. Of the 40 songs I write about in this book, about a quarter of them hit #1 on some chart, and if you include the songs I don't feature as the "headline" song in each chapter, 26 of them hit #1. Consequently, it wouldn't be enough to simply list them in order. After a good bit of figuring and trying to approach this like I was putting together a puzzle, I discovered that I had at least one song that had hit every position, 1–40, on one of the five major charts I intended to use as guidelines.

That leads me to the charts. The *Billboard* charts have long been the most authoritative measure of success based on record sales, though other factors have come into play along the way. *Billboard* originated in the 1930s, and by 1958, they were running a Hot 100 of the most popular songs on the charts. By the 1970s, the Top 40 became another milestone, as each week Casey Kasem counted down the nation's 40 most popular songs on *American Top 40*, based on the *Billboard Hot 100 Singles* chart. Before long, making the Hot 100 was big, but making the Top 40 was even bigger. While the *Billboard Hot 100* is an all-genre chart, it often has been dominated by and known for popular music, so here I have designated these charts as the *Billboard* Pop charts. A chart that was in many ways very similar to the *Billboard Hot 100* chart was the *Cashbox* chart. Starting in 1942, *Cashbox* (or *Cash Box*) was a music industry magazine that for a time also tracked plays on jukeboxes. While it never had quite the gravitas of *Billboard*, it ran a close second.

As a result, looking at *Billboard* and *Cashbox*, you get a pretty definitive picture of how a record did, sales-wise and plays-wise. Or perhaps I should say "you *almost* get a definitive picture." Up through the 1950s and early 1960s, *Billboard* and *Cashbox* mainly tracked music by white artists, and since 22 of the 40 artists in this book are African American, it's important to make sure that rhythm and blues chart success is also taken into account here. For example, Judy Clay and William Bell's "Private Number" didn't make the *Billboard* Pop charts but was Top 20 on the R&B charts. Conversely, the Archies' "Sugar, Sugar" didn't make the R&B charts, but peaked at #1 on the *Billboard* and *Cashbox* pop charts. Therefore, it's obvious that just one or two charts may not be enough to tell the whole story of a record's success. Apparently the people at *Billboard* felt the same way. The first *Billboard* R&B chart, "Hot R&B Sides," started in 1958 and ran until 1962 when it was renamed "Hot R&B Singles." There was no separate chart from November 1963 until January 1965 when the "Hot Rhythm & Blues Singles" chart debuted. In 1969, the chart's name became "Best Selling Soul Singles" and in 1973, this same chart became "Hot Soul Singles" and kept that name throughout the parameters of this book. Because of the numerous name changes, I will simply refer to these charts as "the R&B charts."

Another chart that needed to be recognized was the Adult Contemporary chart. By the late 1950s and early 1960s, some radio stations' playlists and some artists weren't comfortable fits when lumped in with rock'n'roll music and artists. Given the demographics of the people who listen to certain types of music, it seems reasonable that there should be a separation, especially for advertisers. To illustrate, the top adult contemporary songs of 1965 were by artists Julie Rogers, Dean Martin, Jack Jones, Horst Jankowski, Eddy Arnold and Herb Alpert and the Tijuana Brass. On the *Billboard Hot 100*, 1965's biggest artists included the Beatles, the Supremes, the Four Tops, the Rolling Stones, the Beach Boys and the Byrds. This is not to say that one group of artists or music was better than the other, but clearly this music was often appreciated by very different audiences. Few of the artists in this book had much success on the Adult Contemporary charts, and the groups who did were often singers of a softer-type sound such as the Main Ingredient, Rose Colored Glass and the Spinners. Some people refer to this as "Easy Listening" music, and over the years this chart underwent many names changes such as "Easy Listening," "Middle-Road Singles," "Hot Adult Contemporary Tracks" and so on. Initially *Billboard* arrived at the ranking for this chart by taking out the rock'n'roll songs from the *Billboard Hot 100* and compressing the rankings of what was left. In any event, it once again gives us a broader view of the music that was popular. Here I have referred to these multinamed charts as "the Adult Contemporary chart."

The final chart I reference was the British Hit Singles chart, which is really just a comprehensive list of English records sales. The music that sells in England is sometimes a bit of a mystery, really. Songs such as "Band of Gold," "Baby, Now That I've Found You" and "Love Grows (Where My Rosemary Goes)" all hit #1 in England but not in the States, but sometimes songs that do quite well here don't make their charts at all. Censorship was so rigid in England that sometimes songs such as Gene McDaniels' "A Hundred Pounds of Clay" weren't even played on the radio there. Then in the 1960s, more rebellious "pirate" radio stations emerged, often offshore; freed from any regulatory responsibility, they played anything they wanted. This was especially important as groups such as the Rolling Stones, the Beatles and the Who were playing music that was rawer and edgier. As songwriter Tony Macaulay told me of "Baby, Now That I've Found You,"

> It came out and flopped completely. But what happened was, they had those pirate radio stations [and some of those] deejays got jobs with the brand new station called Radio One. They were told to go back through the last six months' records and find anything they thought might have been a hit [if the "legitimate" stations had played it]. That was the beginning of my career. ["Baby, Now That I've Found You"] went to #1.

The music the pirates played drove record sales. With that in mind, here I have listed "British Charts" as the fifth and final category showing a record's chart success. This list is based on overall sales in England, and so it rightfully takes in music played legally and illegally in England during the period.

For each of the 40 songs I've written about, you can see and compare how it did on the *Billboard* Pop, R&B, *Cashbox*, Adult Contemporary and British charts, in that order. I lead off each chapter with a number corresponding to where the song placed on one of the charts and list in parentheses the chart I am using. Here, for example, is the header for Ernie K-Doe's "Mother-in-Law":

#29
(British Charts)
"Mother-in-Law" (1961)
Ernie K-Doe

Billboard Pop: #1; R&B: #1; *Cashbox*: #1;
Adult Contemporary: Did not chart

In the list after that, you'll see the song name, year and artist, followed by other charts. The song's position on each chart will be listed. If it didn't chart on a certain chart, it will say, "Did not chart."

If nothing else, it's interesting to compare the success (and occasionally the lack of it) on the different charts. How and why a song performed well on one chart and not as well on another is sometimes obvious, but not always.

In the end, the songs in this book were all successful, and all have interesting stories that make them well worth exploring further.

#1
(*Billboard* Pop Charts)

"Play That Funky Music" (1976)

Wild Cherry

R&B: #1; *Cashbox*: #1; Adult Contemporary:
Did not chart; British Charts: #7

Not every song in this book will be familiar to readers, but there are a few it's probably safe to say almost *everyone* knows. "Play That Funky Music" can surely be counted in that latter category. From its opening bassline to Rob Parissi's howl before he breaks into its distinctive lyrics and beyond, it is one of the most recognizable American songs of the 1970s.

Rob Parissi was born in 1950 in Mingo Junction, Ohio, a steel town. He was involved in music at an early age, and by his mid-teens he was working in the famous Brill Building in New York City, around some of the best songwriters in the business. While there, he became friends with Ellie Greenwich, who with her husband Jeff Barry (as well as Phil Spector) wrote or co-wrote some of the 1960s' biggest hits: "Be My Baby," "I Can Hear Music," "Hanky Panky," "Chapel of Love" and others. Parissi also played in bands. After graduating from high school, he set his sights on starting his own band back in Ohio.

Parissi put together his band in 1970. How they came to name the group Wild Cherry is perhaps one of the best-known stories regarding '70s music but it bears repeating. According to Parissi, they coined their name when he jokingly told the band that maybe they should call themselves Wild Cherry after a box of cough drops he had on hand during an illness. "I had just gotten out of the hospital with a week to go to rehearse for our first gig," he told me. Parissi, who as it turned out was suffering from stomach ulcers, had the cough drops on hand because his throat was raw from the tests he'd undergone:

> I'd had tubes stuck down my throat and still had a sore throat. In the middle of rehearsal one day, the guys said, "What are we going to call ourselves?"

> I picked up the cough drops I had on our keyboard player's B-3 and said, "You can call it Wild Cherry if you want. The band's going to make the name famous if it's good." They stopped dead and said. "That's a great name!" I said, "No, there's no way we're going to name this band Wild Cherry!"

Although Parissi himself was less than enthusiastic about the name, he let it stand for the time being:

> They fought with me every day until I gave in and said we could call ourselves that for the first gig, but after that, I told them we needed to look for a permanent name. At that first gig, they brought up 25 girls at a time who told me what a great name we chose for the band. The guys in the band just wouldn't let me change it. And every time I tried to change it, they'd just bring up more people to disagree at the gigs.

So the name stuck, and the band played throughout the Ohio, Pennsylvania and West Virginia corridor. Initially the group played mainly cover versions of rock songs by the Rolling Stones, Humble Pie, Led Zeppelin, Free and other groups. But Parissi was also writing his own

Rob Parissi wrote "Play That Funky Music" after black audience members at Pittsburgh's 2001 club asked the band, "Are you going to play some funky music, white boys?" It became a #1 hit.

#1. "Play That Funky Music" (1976)

music, and the group pressed a few demos that they also sold to their fans. Their first break came in 1972 when they came to the attention of producer Terry Knight, who worked with Grand Funk. Knight heard the band and signed them to Brown Bag records, and the label released the Parissi-penned tunes "Show Me Your Badge" and "Get Down" in 1972 and 1973. Ultimately, having failed to move very far beyond being a club band, they broke up and Parissi got out of the music business and got steadier work as the manager of some Bonanza steakhouses.

For many bands that probably would have been the end of the story, but Parissi couldn't let go of the desire to play rock'n'roll. In 1975, he re-formed the band as a quartet with Bryan Bassett on guitar, Rob Beitle on drums and percussion, and Allen Wentz on bass. As Wild Cherry, the band still had a great local following in the Pittsburgh area, but they were principally a rock band. By the mid–70s, disco was becoming popular and dance clubs were in vogue as opposed to clubs where people just stood around and heard a group play. Parissi had a hard time booking his rock band because people wanted dance music. This was never more evident than when they performed at Pittsburgh's 2001 club and black audience members asked them, "Are you going to play some funky music, white boys?" One night that while they were between shows, Parissi talked to the other band members about the audience's changing tastes in music: Because disco was becoming the music of choice in the clubs, Parissi felt that it was getting to the point where he wasn't going to be able to get them gigs as a rock band. The other members were none too happy about taking their music in another direction. He suggested they infuse rock into dance music, so it wasn't like they were selling out. Rob Beitle made a comment along the lines of "Well, you know what they say, 'You got to play that funky music, white boy.'"

Parissi immediately had the idea for a song. He wrote out most of it on a bar order pad in about five minutes, and finished up "Play That Funky Music" after the show that night.

When the group again had the opportunity to record some tracks, they decided to cut "Play That Funky Music." They recorded it in Cleveland for Sweet City Records, and the story is that the engineers in the studio instantly knew it was a winner. The group's intention was for their cover of the Commodore's "I Feel Sanctified" to be the A side of the single and "Play That Funky Music" the B side, but it soon became clear that "Play That Funky Music" was the hit side.

Parissi shopped the record around and couldn't get a label to pick it up. Many people were scared off by the words "White Boy," feeling that there might be racial blowback; most labels wanted him to drop those two words from the lyrics. But Parissi held his ground, and eventually

Epic Records picked up the song and released it. In 1976, the song went to #1 on the *Billboard* Pop, *Cashbox* and R&B charts, and the album went platinum. Some of the music industry's highest awards followed, including Grammy nominations for Best New Vocal Group and Best R&B Performance by a Group, an American Music Award and the *Billboard* award for best new band of the year. The single and the album it was on, *Wild Cherry*, were certified platinum by the Recording Industry Association of America and the single eventually sold 2.5 million units in the U.S. alone. Parissi remains confident that had he dropped the words "White Boy," it wouldn't have been as big as it was. Oddly enough, Boston radio stations initially wouldn't play the song, and had Parissi replace "white boy" with "yeah, funky music." But after it became a national hit, the Boston radio stations didn't care any more and played the original.

One might think that having their first chart record go to #1 would have made the group more determined and unified, but even in the midst of their success they were struggling to find an identity and to simply get along. According to Parissi,

> The members of the band hated everything, even "Play That Funky Music." Getting them to do anything at all was a day-to-day challenge, as they constantly complained about everything that I wrote but never contributed anything progressive regarding material they thought was better or what they thought was "cool" enough for them.... It was like dragging the people

From left to right, Wild Cherry members Rob Beitle, Bryan Bassett, Allen Wentz and Rob Parissi. (Photo courtesy Rob Parissi)

you need to cut a track toward getting on the gravy train, constantly. I had to push everything out of all of them.

Perhaps the negativity affected their output: Despite Parissi's pushing and his skill as a writer, none of their singles from 1977 and 1978 broke the Top 40 on the *Billboard* Pop charts. Not a single one entered the Top 40 on the *Cashbox*, Adult Contemporary, British or R&B charts either. The albums *Electrified Funk* (1977), *I Love My Music* (1978) and *Only the Wild Survive* (1979) followed, but didn't sell in big numbers. No Top 40 chart success followed, and only a few of their singles even broke the Top 100. They became the textbook definition of a one-hit wonder.

Things reached a boiling point within the group and there was a total lack of cohesion. Parissi said he was fed up with having to fight to motivate the group, and they finally disbanded. "I wish I had a rosier picture to paint for you," he told me, "but the whole Wild Cherry debacle is not a warm and fuzzy memory for me, and I'm quite glad it's a done deal that I don't need to revisit or live over again. But it's all water under the bridge at this point, and I'm grateful for anything good and sustainable that accidently happened along the way." Despite the underlying acrimony, the group finally reunited in 2014 in Mingo Junction for a scholarship benefit started by Parissi.

After the group's break-up, Parissi explored a number of avenues in music, even writing some songs with his old friend Ellie Greenwich until she passed away in 2009. For many years he was involved in a legal battle over his music with his label, and finally was able to settle that and move forward. He has worked as a producer and performer, having moved into adult contemporary music and smooth jazz.

Despite having only one monster hit, Wild Cherry did manage to make their shining moment count. In many ways, "Play That Funky Music" defined the age. Just like the group that created the song, the disco movement was ephemeral and essentially played out by the late '70s. Nevertheless, the song and the genre were important to the development of American music. In 2008, "Play That Funky Music" was listed at #73 on *Billboard*'s "All-Time Top 100 Songs," a testament to its importance in American music.

I interviewed Rob Parissi in August 2011. As of this writing, he divides his time between homes in Tampa and St. Petersburg, Florida, and is still performing and writing. Bryan Bassett later played with Molly Hatchet and is still playing with Foghat. Allen Wentz is an independent musician and writer. Rob Beitle passed away in 2017.

#2
(R&B Charts)
"Band of Gold" (1970)
FREDA PAYNE

Billboard Pop: #3; *Cashbox*: #2; Adult Contemporary: Did not chart; British Charts: #1

There is little doubt that Freda Payne is one of the most talented and accomplished singers in this book. There are artists here who have had longer careers, more or bigger hits, or have even found success writing for other artists. But Payne's career has been much more than a few hit records on Top 40 radio: As an actress, singer, dancer and talk show host, she has found great success in almost every endeavor she has pursued, and even today always seems to be looking for her next challenge. The R&B classic "Band of Gold" may be her greatest accomplishment.

Born Freda Charcelia Payne in Detroit, Michigan, she was exposed to music and dance at a young age. She grew up listening to jazz; among her favorite artists were Billie Holiday and Ella Fitzgerald. She took piano "from about the time I was five until I was 12." Payne said she lost interest in piano because she and her sister Scherrie had a piano teacher, Ruth Johnson, who asked Freda to sing (Johnson needed singers for a recital she was putting on). Although Scherrie was known to have a great singing voice (Scherrie went on to sing lead for the Supremes after Diana Ross left), Freda had spent years playing the piano and had never invested any time in singing. Johnson heard her sing and asked her to sing a solo at the recital, and that was the end of Freda's focus on piano. After she started entering talent contests and won a few, her career as a singer really took off.

This led to work in radio singing commercial jingles. She appeared on radio shows such as WJR's *Make Way for Youth.* Channel 4 in Detroit had a program called *Ed McKenzie's Saturday Night,* and the program had a talent contest that featured a few acts every week. Payne won. A few months later, after a repeat performance, she won again. Then when

#2. "Band of Gold" (1970)

she was about 13, she had her biggest break to date: She appeared on the nationally acclaimed television show *Ted Mack Amateur Hour*—and won.

Although she was still a teen, a number of people in the music business, including Duke Ellington and Berry Gordy, attempted to sign her to recording contracts. Because she was a minor, her mother refused to allow her to sign with any of them. Payne told me,

> I first met [Gordy] when I was around 14. When you mention the name Berry Gordy Jr., you think of a pioneer in the recording industry, Motown founder and a very prosperous man. But back then, Berry didn't have substantial funding or a record company, just a lot of ambition to manage artists and to get his own record label. Berry had seen me on television on Ed McKenzie's show, Detroit's equivalent to *American Bandstand*. The show had teenagers dancing to top records, and also guests who would perform a couple of songs—Sammy Davis Jr., Della Reese, the Four Freshman, people

The "Band of Gold" recording session benefitted from the presence of backup singers and musicians such as Motown's Funk Brothers, Ray Parker Jr. (who would hit #1 with "Ghostbusters" in 1984) on lead guitar, Dennis Coffey (#6 with "Scorpio" in 1971) on electric sitar, backup vocals by Joyce Wilson and Telma Hopkins (both of whom would be the "Dawn" in Tony Orlando and Dawn) and Payne's sister Scherrie (who would be in a later version of the Supremes).

like that. I'd also been singing with the Jimmy Wilkins Orchestra, and I'd been singing on the radio on Don Large's *Make Way for Youth* show. So Berry heard about me, and that drew his attention to me."

Gordy wrote some songs for Payne and took her to a studio called United Sound to record them. "Then he, my mother and I all drove to New York. He wanted to get a deal on Roulette records, and because he got a positive response, he wanted to sign me to a managerial contract. My mother, who was not a pushover, was not receptive, they couldn't agree on terms. I think had he been more modest in his demands, she would have said okay." Ultimately, Payne didn't sign with Gordy; she instead continued to perform locally until she graduated from high school. She signed with Pearl Bailey and sang with Duke Ellington's band. She moved to New York in 1963, appeared on *The Tonight Show* and *The Merv Griffin Show*, toured with the Four Tops, and was even an understudy for Leslie Uggams on Broadway.

Despite the fact that she was singing and appearing in some of the best venues alongside some of the biggest entertainers in the business, her recording career had been somewhat underwhelming compared to her other successes. She signed a record deal with ABC-Paramount and in 1964 released a jazz album, *When the Lights Go Down*, on the ABC subsidiary label Impulse. Two years later, MGM released her album *How Do You Say I Don't Love You Anymore*. Neither of these efforts sold enough to make the national charts. By the late '60s, said Payne, "my contract was up with ABC, and so was my management contract, so I was literally free of any contractual obligations."

Though this might have been a low point for some artists, it was actually the turning point of her career. "In 1968, a friend called me and said, 'An old friend of yours from Detroit, Brian Holland, is sitting here with me and he wants you to come over.' I had gone to high school with Brian, but by that time they had become Holland-Dozier-Holland and were famous." Holland-Dozier-Holland were the former Motown songwriter-producers Lamont Dozier and Brian and Eddie Holland, who had written the #1 hits "Baby Love," "Where Did Our Love Go?" and "Stop in the Name of Love" for the Supremes, "I Can't Help Myself" and "Reach Out" for the Four Tops, and many others. In 1968, they left Motown after a dispute over royalties and decided to form their own label; now they were looking for promising young artists. "When I got there, Brian asked me if I was under contract or anything, and I told him I was not under contract. So he said, 'Would you like to come with us? We just left Motown and formed our own label called Invictus.' I flew to Detroit and that was it."

Her first single for Invictus, "The Unhooked Generation," made no

#2. "Band of Gold" (1970)

impact on the *Billboard Hot 100, Cashbox*, British or Adult Contemporary charts, but did rise to #43 on the R&B charts. But her next single, "Band of Gold," was a smash. I told her I had read somewhere that she didn't want to do the song because she didn't like it, and she clarified how she felt about it:

> I thought the lyrics were a little strange. I just told them, "This is for a 15-year-old or something—it's so immature." [*Laughs*]. I mean, why would a young girl on her wedding night want to stay in another room? The lyrics say, "That night on our honeymoon/we stayed in a separate room." What's up with that?
>
> It wasn't that I didn't want to do the song—I was going to do it whether I liked it or not. But, you know, I think those lyrics actually drew more interest to the song. And it really turned my career around.

The song benefited not only from Payne's dynamic vocals and the writing of Holland-Dozier-Holland but also from the presence of Motown's famous Funk Brothers on back-up, the then relatively unknown Ray Parker Jr. on lead guitar and Dennis Coffey on electric sitar. Back-up vocalists Joyce Wilson and Telma Hopkins became the "Dawn" in Tony Orlando and Dawn less than a year later. Also, Payne's sister Scherrie and several members of the Originals were there, so it was a veritable Who's Who of talent in the studio. It all paid off, as "Band of Gold" climbed to #3 on the *Billboard* Pop charts, #2 on *Cashbox* and #1 in the U.K. for six weeks. Surprisingly, it only hit #20 on the R&B charts. Ultimately the record sold about two million copies worldwide.

That success brought some major changes in her life. "My career took off," Payne said. "I started getting requests for interviews, getting booked on TV shows, my salary went up, everything was suddenly better." "Band of Gold" was followed by a number of Invictus singles, the highest-charting being "Bring the Boys Home," which reached #12 on the pop charts in 1971 and earned her another gold record.

Ironically, it was a disagreement over her low royalty payments—much as Holland-Dozier-Holland had had with Motown—that caused her to leave Invictus in 1973. She re-signed with ABC, but none of her subsequent recordings made the Top 40 on any chart. But with her wide range of abilities and talent in so many entertainment fields, she was able to negotiate the downturn in her recording output with ease. She branched out into television, movies and Broadway. Over the years she has hosted her own TV show, *Today's Black Woman*, acted in a number of movies and appeared on *American Idol*. She was inducted into the Rhythm and Blues Hall of Fame in 2017.

Although Payne has done so much, and even though her time at Invictus ended acrimoniously, she knows that "Band of Gold" was her turning point. "Regardless of what else I've done, I was educated on a musical basis by singing standards and jazz and show tunes, so what sustained me after the hit records faded out was the fact that I could still work and do other things like Broadway and theater. I've reinvented myself. But 'Band of Gold' started all that."

I interviewed Payne in 2011. As of this writing, she is living in California.

#3
(*Billboard* Pop Charts)
"A Hundred Pounds of Clay" (1961)

Gene McDaniels

R&B: #11; *Cashbox*: #3; Adult Contemporary, British Charts: Did not chart

---

Considering that many artists spend their careers either looking for that next hit record or performing those big charting songs from the past over and over again, Gene McDaniels was an anomaly. Between 1961 and 1963, he had eight records make the pop charts, and three made the Top Ten, including his classic "A Hundred Pounds of Clay." When his recordings stopped charting, he was hardly done in the music business: As a songwriter, music publisher and producer, he had unparalleled success. He told me that "A Hundred Pounds of Clay" taught him one of the most important lessons he learned in life.

The son of a minister, he was born Eugene Booker McDaniels in Kansas City, Kansas, and grew up in Omaha, Nebraska. As a child, he sang in the church choir and also formed his own gospel group, the Echoes of Joy, when he was 11. When he discovered jazz, he was influenced by the music of Charlie Parker and Miles Davis. He played saxophone and trumpet in high school, and later studied at the University of Omaha Conservatory of Music. He became a member of the Mississippi Piney Woods Singers, and the group toured the West Coast. He was performing with Les McCann when he came to the attention of Liberty Records, with whom he signed in 1959. "I did an album conducted and produced by Johnny Mann of the Johnny Mann singers, called 'In Times Like These'—which was also my first single, actually."

When McDaniels signed with Liberty Records, it was owned by Sy Waronker. Waronker initially had McDaniels working with producer Felix Slatkin, but a couple of singles flopped. After Waronker's death, Liberty was taken over by Al Bennet, whom McDaniels describes as "a 'bean counter' for the company who was from Lubbock, Texas." For McDaniels, that's when the troubles began. "There was also a guy in the mailroom from Lubbock, Snuff Garrett. He was a friend of Al's, and Al called him up from the mailroom to be the producer to the artists at Liberty Records. That's a helluva jump, from mailroom to head producer at Liberty!" (Actually, Garrett, who had been a deejay in Lubbock, was first employed in Liberty's promotions department. He had worked with some other artists prior to working with McDaniels.)

McDaniels continued,

> I was stunned by the fact that they had elevated this young guy to this position, and I didn't know that he had any musical background. Well, he had this song for me, "A Hundred Pounds of Clay," and he put this song together with the arrangers, and he was producing it, and he didn't like the way I was singing the song. So he asked me to clip the lyrics. Being a singer, and being very young, I was incensed by some guy from the mailroom telling me how to sing. I didn't understand; nobody explained to me that there's a specific sound out there that the audience wants to hear. He told me, "You're singing

Neither Gene McDaniels nor producer Snuff Garrett were happy about the finished recording of "A Hundred Pounds of Clay," but Liberty Records president Al Bennett said, "We're putting it out anyway."

#3. "A Hundred Pounds of Clay" (1961)

too much, clip the lyrics." I clipped them, and he thought I was responding angrily to his request. And I was! Well, he went to Al Bennet, who asked him, "How'd he do?" and Snuff said, "He blew it." Al said, "We're putting it out anyway. I'm not gonna spend $1500 and not put this thing out."

A somewhat unusual song, "A Hundred Pounds of Clay" told the story of God creating the human race. With backing vocals by the Johnny Mann Singers and McDaniels' strong lead, the song shot up the charts and earned a gold record. "After 'A Hundred Pounds of Clay' was out and went all the way to #3, it was egg on Snuff's face because he thought it was poorly done, and it's egg on my face because I wasn't performing to my ultimate ability. But it taught me a lesson, and that lesson is that you can always learn something. Snuff had a golden ear and produced Top Ten hits for a lot of Liberty artists."

The song didn't chart in England because the BBC banned it. Censors apparently objected to it on the grounds that it suggested that women were created simply to be sexual beings, and the BBC felt this was blasphemous. British pop singer Craig Douglas, who had already had a #1 hit with a cover of Sam Cooke's "Only Sixteen," saw the banned version as an opportunity for another winning cover. He decided to rewrite the lyrics the BBC found offensive; for example, McDaniels' "He created a woman and-a lots of lovin' for a man" became "He created old Adam, then He made a woman for the man." Likewise, "For every kiss you're givin'" was changed to "For all the joy He's given," "For the arms that are holdin' me tight" became "For my world full of beauty and life." "Doin' just what he should do" was changed to "Makin' land and sky and sea," and "To make a livin' dream like you" became "And doin' it all for you and me." In essence, the changes dispelled the idea that God would have created a being simply for man to love. Douglas was given BBC approval to release the song and saw it soar to #9 on the British charts.

In America, McDaniels' next single, "A Tear," went to #31 before he finished 1961 with a third straight Top 40 song, "Tower of Strength," which went to #5. Also produced by Garrett and co-written by Burt Bacharach and Bob Hilliard, it earned McDaniels his second gold record. Oddly enough, a cover of this song was also released in England by Frankie Vaughn and it peaked at #1. As well as covers of his material were doing in England, however, don't look for McDaniels' name on the British charts: He never had a recording of his own hit the Top 40 there.

In 1962, he followed the same successful pattern: After "Chip Chip" (#10), four of his next five singles made the Top 100. In just 20 months, he had recorded and released eight Top 100 hits. Between 1963 and 1967, he released seven more singles and none of them made the popular charts.

McDaniels told me that he was ready to move on when his recordings stopped selling like they had, as he had found new avenues to explore as a songwriter and producer. He composed Les McCann's 1969 #1 jazz hit "Compared to What" and wrote 1974's "'Feel Like Making Love," which was recorded by Roberta Flack; the latter went to #1 and earned platinum status and a Grammy. McDaniels later won a BMI award for the song, which had more than five million airplays by the 1980s. Flack recorded more than a dozen songs written by McDaniels. He also wrote and produced for George Benson, Johnny Mathis, Gladys Knight and the Pips, Lou Rawls and others.

Despite the fact that McDaniels questioned the producer of "A Hundred Pounds of Clay" at every turn, in the long run he realized the label's suggestions were good. He said,

> Life is different every day, and sometimes your enemy is your best friend. I was a kid—I didn't know what I was doing. Snuff Garrett got hit records from all of the Liberty artists, and it was amazing. I'm now probably one of his biggest fans. He doesn't know that, but he set me up in a way that everybody was paying attention, and then he got me two more Top Ten songs. That really helped because when I started writing people took me seriously.

I interviewed him in November 2010. He passed away in July 2011.

#4
(*Billboard* Pop Charts)

"Bad Time" (1975)

GRAND FUNK

Cashbox: #5; R&B, Adult Contemporary,
British Charts: Did not chart

For about a decade at the height of their popularity, Grand Funk Railroad was a band with very little change in personnel. Their sound and the origins of their music was another matter, as it varied a great deal. Their early music was album-oriented concert rock played on FM stations when that was the only place to go to hear hard rock album cuts; most of that music was written and sung by frontman Mark Farner. Then came a period of about three years when the group made more radio-friendly music and scored a lot of Top 40 hits (including two #1 records). During this period, songwriting chores were shared by several group members. But perhaps the song that best represents Grand Funk Railroad showcases Farner's lead singing, songwriting skills, and their success on popular radio, is 1975's "Bad Time."

The band that would become Grand Funk Railroad got their start in the blue-collar city of Flint, Michigan. A local deejay, Terry Knight, joined the Jazz Masters, a group consisting of Don Brewer, Herm Jackson, Curt Johnson and Bobby Caldwell. Knight took over as their lead singer and the group was renamed The Pack—and eventually Terry Knight and the Pack. When Jackson was drafted, he was replaced by local boy Mark Farner, who had started playing guitar when he was 15. However, even before he began playing an instrument he was heavily influenced by music, to the point that many of the moves he makes on stage to this day were developed at that time. He said:

> I knew early on, when my sister and I would go to the National Guard Armory in Flint and enter the dance contests, that music would play a part in my life. At the dance contests, I knew that I had something going because my mother got me beyond that reluctancy to dance in public when she said,

"You gotta just do this to try it out. You'll feel it." And I finally did start to feel it when my sister and I danced in public. It started paying off later when I took that to the stage.

Terry Knight and the Pack's "I Who Have Nothing" hit #46 on the *Billboard* Pop chart in 1966, just before Knight left the group. In 1968, Farner and Brewer decided to form their own band, and they enlisted bass player Mel Schacher, who was then working with Question Mark and the Mysterians. They named themselves Grand Funk Railroad after Michigan's Grand *Trunk* Railroad, and made Knight their manager. As they played the usual round of bars and VFWs where many groups cut their teeth, it was clear that the trio had something different, not the least of which was the charismatic stage presence of Farner. He said,

> I want to embody the character of a song. Even in the studio recording, I close my eyes and I take on the character of a song in order to get the emotion to the right level, to where people can really get it. I learned early on to exaggerate my movements, so the people in the seats far at the back could

"Bad Time" was the last in a three-year string of seven straight Top 40 pop hits for Grand Funk. Four of those songs made the Top 10, and two went to #1.

#4. "Bad Time" (1975)

see it. I became more theatrical in the presentation than just standing there and singing and playing. And a lot of bands, that's all they do. A lot of guys don't want to dance around. But I love to dance, so on stage I pranced around danced and jumped and everything.

For all the problems the group would ultimately have with Knight, he was a master promoter and marketing genius. In 1969, he got the new group on the program at the Atlanta International Pop Festival where they appeared with Creedence Clearwater Revival, Tommy James and the Shondells, Janis Joplin and Led Zeppelin. Grand Funk Railroad was apparently one of the most popular acts that day, and their performance got them invited to the second Atlanta International Pop Festival in 1970. They were signed by Capitol Records, which led to two singles on the *Billboard Hot 100* in 1969. The group's first album, *On Time*, did extremely well, reaching #27 on the album charts in 1969 and eventually selling over a million copies and going gold. Their next album, 1970's *Grand Funk*, hit #11 on the album charts and went gold as well. Over the next few years Grand Funk Railroad came to be known as the quintessential "album" band, as album after album charted and went gold while their singles only performed moderately well.

Their third album, 1970's *Closer to Home*, became the group's third gold album in less than a year, and they actually got a Top 40 single out of it, "I'm Your Captain (Closer to Home)." "That whole album was a great album. [It] came from a place speaking to the fans, speaking to the world, just to provoke people to think about things." A deeply religious man, Farner said of the featured single,

> When I wrote "I'm Your Captain," that was a song I prayed for, and I believe God gave me that song and that's the way I received it. I prayed and got up in the middle of the night and wrote down the words. I'm always doing that—some is poetry, sometimes just words. But that night I got up and then in the morning I started playing. The wind was blowing, it was a beautiful day, and that whole opening lick ... it all just came to me. I thought, "Maybe this is the music to those words in the other room I wrote down last night." I went and got 'em, sang the song and wrote the chords and didn't change 'em at all ... sang 'em the way I wrote them down in the middle of the night.

When Farner took it to his bandmates, "Don and Mel were just kind of blown away and said, 'That song's a hit.'" Farner said it is probably his favorite song of all that he wrote, even though it only peaked at #22 and he later had much bigger hits.

Then two things happened that sealed the band's legacy as one of the world's best-known rock bands. First, Knight had a brilliant idea for marketing the album, resulting in a flood of mostly free publicity. Farner said that Knight told them about putting the group's image and name on a Times Square billboard, and said, "We can get that billboard for one month for $50,000 and I think we should do it." Farner said that after it was up, "the billboard workers went on strike and so that billboard stayed up four extra months for free. That's like $250,000 worth of advertising!" Farner said it's no coincidence that the billboard idea came before an even more noteworthy event, because "he already had in mind about doing the Shea Stadium gig." Knight booked the group to play at Shea on July 9, 1971, and the group sold out all 55,000 seats. "We sold that out in 72 hours, faster than the Beatles [in August 1965]. And this was before Ticketron. [Buyers] had to go get the tickets. We were pretty proud of that." Humble Pie opened for them, and this is noteworthy because it led to the now apocryphal story that they asked Humble Pie guitarist Peter Frampton to join Grand Funk. Farner said that isn't exactly what happened. "No, we did talk about it between ourselves, in the band, but we never approached him. We got him to jam with us a few times later—like when we did the Bosnia tour and album, and in Detroit at the Pine Nob concert—and it was great. He's a good friend and a great guitar player, but we never asked him to join the group, no."

Grand Funk Railroad's next three albums all charted and went gold: 1971's *Survival*(#6) and *E Pluribus Funk* (#5) and 1972's *Phoenix* (#7)—despite the fact that only "Footstompin' Music" (#29) and "Rock'n Roll Soul" (#29) made the Top 40 singles charts. By now Farner was writing almost all the band's music, having written most of the songs on *Survival* and all of the songs on *E Pluribus Funk* and *Phoenix*. They were selling a lot of records, but like many groups before and after, they didn't seem to be seeing all the money. The group fired Knight, resulting in several years of lawsuits and the loss of certain rights to some of their music. At this time, the group members shortened their name to Grand Funk and also underwent a major change in their sound. They moved away from the power-trio album rock they were known for, and became more—for lack of a better word—mainstream; more Top 40–friendly. In the short term, it paid off with previously unknown levels of success with some big Top 40 hits—"We're an American Band" (#1), "Walk Like a Man" (#19), "The Loco-Motion" (#1), "Shinin' On" (#11), "Some Kind of Wonderful" (#3)—but some fans felt a bit betrayed by the change that they saw as a sellout to commercialism. Given Farner's success as a songwriter and frontman and the group's astronomical album sales, people wondered why they changed at all. Farner told me,

#4. "Bad Time" (1975)

I was outvoted, that's why, brother! I didn't want to change, but Don, because he wanted to write more music—I believe this was his motivation—and I wasn't giving him enough jams that I didn't already have an idea for lyrics for him. I think that's why he and Mel voted to have a keyboard player join the band [Craig Frost in 1973] and I was outvoted.

Perhaps one good thing that came out of the group's more AM radio-friendly approach was that Farner also wrote a song that vaulted into the Top Ten, 1975's "Bad Time." It was on the 1974 album *All the Girls in the World Beware*, produced by Jimmy Ienner, who had worked with Three Dog Night and the Raspberries. The album's first single release was 1974's "Some Kind of Wonderful," a cover of a 1967 low-charter by the Soul Brothers Six. The Grand Funk version peaked at #3, and in March 1975 the group released "Bad Time" as the follow-up. There were two cover songs on the album, and three songs written or co-written by other band members; perhaps in light of the perceived efforts to have less of Farner's material on the albums, it was ironic that it was his composition that was their sole original hit on *All the Girls in the World Beware*. The song, about a man who meets a girl at the wrong time in life due to personal complications (perhaps in the form of an existing relationship), fits a pattern established by most of the other Farner compositions on the album. "Responsibility" is about meeting the perfect girl, in "Memories" the girl is now gone, and in "Wild" he talks about how he wants to be wild and free. "Bad Time" follows a similar trajectory, and fits in with the idea that the singer is unhappy. Farner admits that the song was written when he was divorcing his first wife and he was swept up in the emotion of the moment as he wrote the song because she was in the next room and they were both very unhappy. Despite the personal nature of the song, Farner didn't mind sharing his troubles with the world. As he told me, his credo has always been that his lyrics are designed to "make you think. Anything we can do as musicians to provoke people to think without pissing 'em off is good. That was what that was all about." The song was a monster hit, peaking at #4 on the *Billboard* pop charts.

Although no one knew it at the time, it would be the group's last Top 40 hit. They changed their name back to Grand Funk Railroad and released three songs that made the *Billboard Hot 100* in 1976. Perhaps the biggest shock was that the group split up that year. Farner said:

Don Brewer walked into the studio—we were rehearsing—and he was late. He was never late, but that day he was, and he walked in and said, "Well, I'm over it. I'm going to find something more stable to do with my life." And I sat up in my chair and asked, "What did you just say?" He said, "I'm over it, man, it's over. We're through." And I went, "Okay, if that's the way you really feel. Do you really feel that way?" And he got pissed off and said, "Yeah."

Just like that, Grand Funk Railroad was no more. The group did a reunion in 1981, "then in '82 our manager died and that was the end of that reunion tour," Farner said. "Then we didn't get together again until about '96, just Mel and Don and myself, the three original founding members." Things started to get acrimonious, and once again lawsuits plagued the band. In earlier lawsuits, it had been "us" against "them"—when it came to Terry Knight, for example. Farner revealed, "When Terry was our manager, he took 100 percent of the publishing rights to our music," meaning that even though Farner wrote a song, and the band recorded it, Knight got half of the money. Farner continued:

> The way royalties are split up, publishing gets 50 percent, the writer gets 50 percent. So I got my writer's share, but not my publishing share. If you are promoting your own music the way I did in Grand Funk, you should also own your own publishing. The way the publisher comes into the picture is that if they are out shopping those tunes and the individual or performer doesn't want to perform them live, then the publisher gets people to cover them then they earn money for that.

The group had dealt with that by firing Knight, and so later Farner-written songs, such as "Bad Time," were 100 percent his. But the legal problems that beset the band in the 1990s, and created the rifts that exist to this day, were internal. Farner:

> Don Brewer came to my hotel room in '98 and said we needed to all sign our individual ownership of the trademark into the corporation, where it would have a protective umbrella. I didn't finish high school—I don't know anything about the law—and he had gone to law school. So I figured he's looking out for the band, he's my friend, so I'm gonna go with his recommendation. [Subsequently] I got a notice I was no longer in the corporation and I was no longer the president of the corporation and I was no longer eligible to be an officer in the corporation. Man, that's when I kind of woke up to what I did and kind of slapped myself. Those are the mistakes you pay for.
>
> Now Don and Mel go out and perform and call it Grand Funk and they don't tell the fans that the guy who wrote 90-some-odd percent of that music ain't gonna be there. So it's very dishonest, but it's legal. They also took me to Federal court and made it so I can only use "*formerly* of Grand Funk Railroad" in my advertisements, and it even has to be printed a certain way. They can be dishonest by deception. They deceive the audience by saying that they're Grand Funk. I've tried to get them to put the band back together, because I've told them that apart neither one of us is giving the fans what they want—they want us together. Let's bury the hatchet and get back together for the fans' sake. But they won't have no part of it. When money is the god, people become assholes.

Despite the way things ended, Farner chooses to focus on the great music the band made and the success they had. "I'm not a vindictive or hateful person. I pray for them. The Bible says, 'Pray for those who spitefully use you.' I do I pray for them and hope they get saved. Right now they're serving the god of money."

―――――――

I interviewed Farner in 2015. As of this writing, he is still performing quite successfully.

#5
(R&B Charts)
"Grazing in the Grass" (1969)
FRIENDS OF DISTINCTION
Billboard Pop: #3; *Cashbox*: #6;
Adult Contemporary, British Charts: Did not chart

Harry Elston, lead singer and founder of the Friends of Distinction, told me that he thought timing was everything, and that as far as he was concerned, his group came along at just the right time. While this is true to some extent, the Friends' first chart record came about two years after another similar-sounding black pop group kicked off a string of 30 Top 100 pop hits. That group—who were, ironically, very good friends of Elston's—was the 5th Dimension. It is hard not to compare the two groups that were alike in so many ways, with one significant difference: The 5th Dimension charted ten times between 1969 and 1971, a run which included two #1 hits and was but a small part of their 30 chart records. During the same span, the Friends of Distinction came together, recorded and split up, and only had three songs make the Top 40 pop charts. But Elston was never jealous of his friends, and in fact he says he was blessed to enjoy the success that he did.

Harry Elston was born in Dallas, Texas; the family moved to San Diego, California, when he was almost three years old. His family was very musical and both parents played the piano. His father often had friends over and they would sing and play. Although Harry was a gifted sports star, by the time he was in high school he had also taken an interest in singing and joined a group named Cell Foster and the Audios. Just about then, Johnny Otis was in San Diego, looking for new talent for the Johnny Otis Rhythm & Blues Caravan. Otis, who discovered R&B legends Etta James, Hank Ballard, Big Mama Thornton, Jackie Wilson and others, sponsored a talent show which the Audios won. Otis took the group on tour with some of his other stars, and also had them record songs such as "I Prayed for You" on his Ultra label and "Millie's Chili" on his Dig label. None charted.

#5. "Grazing in the Grass" (1969)

Hugh Masekela's instrumental "Grazing in the Grass" hit #1 in 1968; in 1969, the Friends of Distinction added lyrics for their version.

Elston finished high school and served in the Air Force. After his discharge, he tried to decide between a career in sports or music. He tried out for the California Angels professional baseball team but didn't make the final cut, so he gave music a try. While at a house party in Los Angeles, he met Lamont McLemore, and soon they were together in a group called the Hi Fi's, singing jazz with Marilyn McCoo, Fritz Baskett, Rex Middleton and Lawrence Summers. Middleton, who was older than the others, had had a group called the Hi Fi's once before, but this new one was far more successful on the club circuit and soon came to the attention of Ray Charles. Charles took them on as a back-up group of sorts and gave them the opportunity to record on their own. The group's first effort, "Lonesome Mood," was produced by Charles and recorded on his Tangerine label, but not before the group had changed their name to the Vocals and added Floyd Butler. "Lonesome Mood" and its follow-ups had no success on the national charts.

After the Vocals separated, members Lamont McLemore and Marilyn McCoo formed the 5th Dimension and, in 1968, Elston and Floyd Butler became the Friends of Distinction. Barbara Love and Jessica

Cleaves completed their group. Cleaves was just 17 when Butler met her: He worked for the Urban League and Cleaves was looking for a job. Love made an impact almost immediately: The group's first name was the Distinctive Friends, and Love suggested they change it to the Friends of Distinction. It stuck.

After the group practiced for a few months, they went about getting themselves a manager. According to Elston,

> I had a roommate named Booker Griffin, and he knew Jim Brown from back in Cleveland. When Jim came out to California for a Pro Bowl, we met and became friends. When Jim started acting and getting involved in other aspects of the entertainment industry and embarked upon a show biz career, I told him about our group and asked him to manage us, and he agreed. From there, we did a showcase, and a lot of record companies came around. Then the next day, I had to go around to the different companies and pick one—you were selecting them, not the other way around. I didn't realize the enormous power I had right then, and I think about it now and laugh. I ended up choosing RCA because of a producer named John Florez and his friend Ray Cork Jr., and so we signed, selected some songs and that's how we got started.

For their first recording, they needed a song; Elston said he found inspiration in a strange place. "We'd be on the road, touring, and that meant riding the bus for hours at a time. We'd drive past pastures, cotton fields, cornfields. I'd always see these cows, just grazing, so peaceful, and I'd think to myself, 'You know, they have it made. They just graze and shit!'" Elston's observation of those moments of serenity led to the Friends of Distinction's first hit record. Hugh Masekela had recorded a #1 instrumental called "Grazing in the Grass" in 1968, and though the music was right for Elston's purposes, a vocal group needed lyrics, so Elston wrote those himself. "I first called it 'Flaking in the Grass' because I didn't know I could use the same title as the instrumental since I was changing the song and adding lyrics," he said. In fact, they recorded the demo as "Flaking in the Grass," but when Elston told the others why he changed the name, "everybody was like, 'Get out of here!' So I came back with the same music and original title and they loved it."

Elston sang lead, and their first single was a smash. "We recorded it at RCA for our first album, and from then, things happened very quickly. We weren't teenagers, but we were pretty young, and not knowing how things worked, we just rode the wave. We didn't know until later how big the song was." The song spent 16 weeks on the pop charts, peaking at #3, and 17 weeks on the R&B charts, peaking at #5. It was a million-selling RIAA-certified gold record, and the group was on its way. Elston said that, despite the fact that the song was recorded in 1969, it had nothing to do with smoking marijuana, even though many thought it was.

The group performed their song on TV's *The Ed Sullivan Show*. Before they had time to become accustomed to the success of "Grazing in the Grass," they charted again with "Going in Circles," which went to #15 on the pop charts and also became a million-seller. "Things were happening so fast, and we were on the road all the time, so we really didn't grasp it all until years later," Elston said. "Fortunately, our egos were intact, which is something I've always loved about our group."

Egos and success couldn't fracture the group, but one joyous event did: Barbara Love was pregnant and had to take maternity leave. The group was too hot and too popular to go on an extended hiatus and needed to record and tour in order to stay in the public eye. Fortunately, Elston said, "Our bass player, Stan Gilbert, said he knew a girl in Milwaukee who would be great to fill in. So, we auditioned Charlene Gibson and brought her in."

The timing was good: "We had a song, 'Love or Let Me Be Lonely,' that had been written by Skip Scarborough, Jerry Peters and Anita Poree." Though none of the songwriters were well established at that point, Scarborough later wrote hits for Earth, Wind and Fire and Bill Withers and even won a Grammy for Anita Baker's "Giving You the Best That I Got." Peters worked with Aretha Franklin, Marvin Gaye and Diana Ross and won a Grammy for co-writing "It's What I Do." Poree co-wrote songs such as "Boogie Down" and "Keep on Truckin" for Eddie Kendricks. These songwriters were obviously top-drawer.

"They gave us time off from touring to do an album, and we went to RCA's studio in New York and recorded 'Love or Let Me Be Lonely' there." Any doubts they may have had about Gibson's abilities were quickly dispelled, as she took lead on the song "and she flat-out tore it up," Elston said. Knowing that Love's absence could have spelled disaster for the group, Gibson's success meant they didn't miss a beat. "Charlene was a godsend," he said. "She did lead on several songs, such as 'Crazy Mary,' and she was great on them all." And never better than on "Love or Let Me Be Lonely"; it went to #6 on the pop charts, #13 on the R&B charts, and was yet another smash.

Then things started to change within the group. "By then we had not revolving chairs, but revolving girls," Elston said. "Barbara came back, and then Jessica split and went with Earth, Wind and Fire and later Parliament Funkadelic. Charlene stayed on, then she split after a couple of years too. [Also,] being on the road was tiring, and when record sales started slipping, we felt like it was time to hang it up." Elston noted that RCA may not have really understood how to market

The Friends of Distinction: from left to right, Floyd Butler, Barbara Love, Harry Elston and Jessica Cleaves (courtesy Harry Elston).

the group, a sentiment that Cuba Gooding of the Main Ingredient noted of his group's time at RCA as well (see their entry in this book). According to Elston,

> When you are putting out maybe three or four records a year, it has to be planned. RCA didn't have many black artists, and they didn't seem to know what to do with them. You had the R&B department fighting with the pop department, because there was crossover. So we kind of got caught in the middle of that stuff, and it was political. We were lucky Jim Brown was

on the scene, and so it wasn't as bad as it could have been, but it caused confusion.

The group called it quits in 1975, not having had a Top 40 hit since "Love or Let Me Be Lonely" in 1970. Since then, their songs have been covered by a number of artists, resulting in chart hits for the Gap Band, Luther Vandross and Paul Davis. In 1990, Elston and Butler decided to try and get the group back together, but Butler unexpectedly died of a heart attack. Still, Elston said that he is grateful for the success they had: "We weren't out there that much and for all that long before we broke up, so for our music to last this long is really a gift from God."

I interviewed Harry Elston in 2012. As of this writing, he still performs occasionally with a new group called the Friends of Distinction. Floyd Butler passed away in 1990, Jessica Cleaves in May 2014.

#6
(R&B Charts)
"Girl Watcher" (1968)
THE O'KAYSIONS
Billboard Pop: #5; *Cashbox*: #5;
Adult Contemporary, British Charts: Did not chart

Very few songs can define the feel of a generation, but the O'Kaysions' "Girl Watcher" is one such song—or at least it would seem so. Hearing it today, one can visualize happy, male teenagers with crewcuts at the beach or on the town checking out the opposite sex and thinking about making a move and meeting that special girl. In many ways the innocence of that type of American teen doesn't seem to exist any more, but the irony is when the song hit the charts in 1968 those very same teenagers were giving way to long-haired youth who were often using drugs and into a very different way of life. Singer-songwriter Wayne Pittman said even then, "'Girl Watcher' was an anomaly and as a group we weren't like most of the popular acts on the radio." Ultimately that would lead to the group's dissolution. But "Girl Watcher" still stands out as a throwback to different times.

The O'Kaysions started as a quartet known as the K's around 1959 in Kenly, North Carolina, when Jimmy Hinnant and Wayne Pittman were middle school and high school students. For their very first performance, they were booked to play a prom and the local newspaper erroneously advertised the group as the "Kays" instead of the "K's"; they decided to stick with that name. The group played parties and other social functions until they booked a steady gig at the Silver Lake Club in Wilson, North Carolina. Their popularity grew, and before long they were filling the club with several hundred people every weekend. Between playing at the club and still doing the occasional wedding or fraternity party, the Kays were soon regarded as one of North Carolina's most popular bands. Like many bands of that era, they figured if they pressed some records, maybe they could make some extra money, so in 1964 they decided to record a single. For their first record, they chose "Hey Girl," a song (written by Gerry Goffin and Carole King) which Freddy Scott took to the Top Ten the year before. Backed with the ever-popular "Shout," the songs were recorded on the JCP label. It was not a hit.

By 1968, the group consisted of Pittman, Hinnant, Steve Watson, Gerald Toler, Eddie Dement and Donnie Weaver. Two things happened at about that time that changed the group's fortunes. One was that, as the group became more successful, they were playing more up north. "In order to play in the clubs up north, you had to become a union member," Pittman said. "You had to register your band's name, and there was a deejay in New York named Murray the K, and we couldn't register our name because it was too similar to his. We coined the name 'O'Kaysions'

After ABC Records bought the distribution rights to "Girl Watcher" from the NorthState label, the story went around that the master tape had gotten lost. Wayne Pittman said that wasn't true: "The ABC people flew down from New York, met the owners of NorthState and took the tapes back. They had and still have the master tapes."

so we could try to maintain our identity in North and South Carolina, Georgia and Virginia where we played, so people would still know who we were."

The second, perhaps most important reason things changed for the group was a song Pittman had written called "Girl Watcher." Pittman said the idea came to him from several comments people made: "We used to play down at Atlantic Beach a lot, and when we got back home people would say, 'Did you meet any girls this weekend?' I'd say, 'I didn't meet any, but I sure do like to watch them.'" According to Pittman, after he made that comment, one of the band members said, "Wayne, you're the writer, why don't you write a song called 'I'm a Girl Watcher'?"

> What was funny was that about a month before, I had written a tune and I hadn't even thought about putting any words to it yet. But when he made that comment, it was like a lightbulb went off in my head. I said, "Okay, I will, I'll go back and write it, and I'll be back next week," and that's exactly what I did. I wrote it in two nights that week. I'd go home in the afternoon and sit at the kitchen table, drink some iced tea and relax. Well, there was this great-looking girl that jogged by my house every afternoon after work around 5:30, and she'd go by when I was writing. That helped a lot too!

After he took the lyrics and guitar parts he'd written and added the music for the horns, he told Hinnant that the song that the group had practically dared him to write was ready. His bandmates really liked it, and as the group started playing "Girl Watcher" it was apparent pretty quickly that they had a hit on their hands. They took it to Pitt Sound Studios in Goldsboro, North Carolina, and with Weaver singing lead they recorded the song as well as a song for the B side, "Deal Me In." They released the record on the tiny North State label in 1968.

The catchy tune, which seemed to precisely mirror the thoughts and pastimes of many a young man, was played regionally almost non-stop and it sold very well. ABC Records liked the song and decided to release it exactly as it had been recorded. The story circulated that someone at North State had lost the master tapes and so the ABC single had to be dubbed from the original 45, but Pittman said that isn't true. "The ABC people flew down from New York, met the owners of North State and took the tapes back. They had and still have the master tapes." (Since this interview, ABC was purchased by MCA, who is now a part of EMI, and EMI now owns the masters.)

The song rose to #5 on the charts, and eventually reached gold record status with one million sales by December 1968. Unfortunately, the group didn't know what steps to take to capitalize on the success of their first record, and clearly their management didn't either. Pittman believes this may have been partly due to Atlanta promoter Bill Lowery:

The original regional release of "Girl Watcher" on the NorthState label before ABC picked it up for national distribution.

> The North State people thought they had the right to sign us to any booking agency they wanted to. They signed us with Bill Lowery without our knowledge, and he was supposed to book us, and this was even before "Girl Watcher" charted. But Lowery just wasn't booking us enough, and we cancelled our agreement with him. We then signed with Associated Booking in New York City. Well, Lowery had a lot of power and contacts in the industry, and the word we got was that he put the kiss of death on us. So we promoted the record and made it a hit, but ABC wouldn't put a lot of money behind us after that.

Around this time, Watson, Toler and Dement decided the grind of the music business was not for them. Playing at clubs and parties every weekend in North Carolina was one thing, but the tedium of traveling around the country and playing several gigs a night up to six nights a week was quite different. Weaver, Pittman and Hinnant stayed on and rounded out the group by adding Ron Watson on trumpet, Jim Spiedel on sax and Bruce Joyner on drums. ABC insisted the group record an album—and forced them to do it in just a few days. "ABC wanted

The O'Kaysions: front row, left to right: Donnie Weaver, Steve Watson. Back row: Gerald Toler, Wayne Pittman, Eddie Dement, Jimmy Hinnant (courtesy Wayne Pittman).

something quick and something fast.... We flew into Chicago to do the album at RCA Studios but we really weren't prepared." Pittman said songs that were still in the rough stages had to be recorded to fill out the album, and no one was happy with the end result.

"Honestly, it just wasn't a good product," he said of the album, "but ABC never tried to promote it either." Perhaps not surprisingly, the album was not a big success, peaking at #49 on the R&B chart and #153 on the pop albums chart. While it features some decent tracks besides "Girl Watcher" ("Deal Me In," "Little Miss Flirt" and "Love Machine" are all solid songs), perhaps the most memorable thing about the album other than the title track is its iconic cover, showing bikini-clad girls on a beach reflected in a young man's sunglasses.

The follow-up to "Girl Watcher," "Love Machine," charted at #76 on the *Billboard* pop charts and #47 on the *Cashbox* pop charts in late

#6. "Girl Watcher" (1968)

1968, but nothing else the group recorded registered. By this point, the remaining original members were starting to run low on enthusiasm. "That period was the beginning of the psychedelic and acid rock scene, and 'Girl Watcher' had been an anomaly. Everywhere we played, the acid rock groups would go on, with all the noise and distortion, and there were the drugs all around, and I just didn't want to go in that direction. I knew I'd burn myself out if I stayed in it, so I just stopped performing." Pittman left, while Donny Trexler and Gary Pugh joined the group. Trexler had been a member of Bob Collins and the Fabulous Five; he told me that in 1968, he decided it was time to move on from that group. He then joined a group called Ted Carrol and the Music Era, which had a one-off with Atlantic Records in 1968 ("What the World Needs Now Is Love"). "[But] that group didn't last long, then I joined the O'Kaysions," Trexler said. He and Pugh were immediately enlisted to sing back-up to Donnie Weaver's lead on the O'Kaysions' next single, a 1969 cover of Burt Bacharach and Hal David's "24 Hours from Tulsa." It failed to chart, and they were done at ABC. This was when Weaver decided it was time for him to leave. "Donnie quit the group in late August of '69, and I had joined the group in January of '69 as the guitar player," Trexler said. "I took over the lead singing at that point."

By now, the group's appearance had changed so much that they looked exactly like the type of band Wayne Pittman had left to avoid; gone were the clean-cut-looking guys who had done "Girl Watcher." They were also playing a lot more rock'n'roll, and a lot more covers. They had one last, brief shot at stardom: They recorded a few new songs and signed with Cotillion, a subsidiary of Atlantic. Cotillion put out "Watch Out Girl" in 1970, and there was buzz about its potential. Based on expectations, they were booked to play *American Bandstand*, and Trexler lip-synced "Watch Out Girl" as well as "Girl Watcher." But neither "Watch Out Girl" nor 1971's Cotillion release "Travelin' Life" were successful. Songs were also recorded for a Cotillion album, but perhaps based on the group's failure to follow up "Girl Watcher" with even a single Top 40 hit in the ensuing three years, the label apparently decided to cut their losses and cancelled the album even though all 12 tracks had been recorded and a $15,000 advance had been paid. Trexler left not long after that, with no regrets. "The O'Kaysions was a wonderful trip," he told me. "I learned a lot."

In 1972, what was left of the group disbanded. "Girl Watcher" lead singer Donnie Weaver stayed in the music business throughout the '70s both as a single artist and as a member of a couple of groups, but eventually got into the computer industry. Pittman's disgust with the music business and especially the drug use had driven him away from music, but he said the music business changed for the better during the decade after he left. "Disco kind of cleaned the music up," he said. Some of the harder rock gave way to more vocals and lighter, more danceable music. With renewed vigor, he re-formed the group. Though they never had another chart hit, the O'Kaysions are active to this day with Pittman as their manager, and they perform throughout the South playing their music, especially "Girl Watcher" of course. "I knew 'Girl Watcher' would be big on a long-term basis, because of the nature of the song. It was a happy song," he said.

I interviewed Wayne Pittman in November 2010. He passed away in 2021. I interviewed Donny Trexler in March 2012. As of this date he is still performing regularly.

#7
(*Cashbox* Charts)
"More Today Than Yesterday" (1969)
The Spiral Starecase
Billboard Pop: #12; R&B, Adult Contemporary, British Charts: Did not chart

---

Having a big hit or multiple hits often leads to problems that cause bands to break up. For some of the bands featured in this book, success created internal problems, but in every case it came after the group had achieved the success of having one or multiple hit records. The Spiral Starecase had problems before they had a hit; in fact, the group had actually disbanded before "More Today Than Yesterday" made the charts. In this case, it wasn't internal dissension, but problems caused by bad managers who were misappropriating their money and not paying the bills. This led to the somewhat unique situation where the band recorded a song, had had enough and broke up, then the song became a hit and they re-formed to enjoy their success. But it didn't last; the damage had been done. Other than one pop Top 40 and two other Hot 100 hits, all within a 12-month period, the band was never able to shake the feeling they were jinxed. A year after their biggest hit, they went their separate ways.

Pat Upton was the second of five children born to Elva and Ernest Upton in Geraldine, Alabama. He and his siblings grew up singing in the Methodist church; in high school, Pat and his brother Don sang with the Geraldine High School Future Farmers of America Quartet. The group was pretty successful and won a few talent contests. But once Pat heard a Duane Eddy single playing on a jukebox at a diner, he was hooked. He went out and bought a guitar, figuring to make a career in rock'n'roll. But next came a stint in the Air Force; he was stationed in Sacramento, California. During his four years in the military, he honed his guitar-playing skills and put together a band for an Air Force talent show.

Sacramento-born Dick Lopes was a member of a band named the Fydallions, based in Eureka and founded by Steve Baptiste. Tired of life on the road, the band called it quits in 1963 but Lopes decided to carry on. He'd met Upton and he liked his voice and guitar-playing, so he invited him to be a member. Upton joined the band on weekends when he had leave time from the Air Force, and when he was discharged in 1964, he joined the group full-time. By 1966 the group consisted of Harvey Kaye (born Harvey Kaplan), Bobby Raymond, Vinnie Parello, Lopes and Upton, who handled the lead vocals. They played clubs from Los Angeles to Las Vegas, and also recorded a few sides on the regional Crusader label owned by Fred Darian. None of those records were released. The group also did a demo for the Columbia label but it, too, failed to get them a contract or a single release.

That all changed when they were playing a club in El Monte, California, and Gary Usher, a producer and A&R man for the Columbia

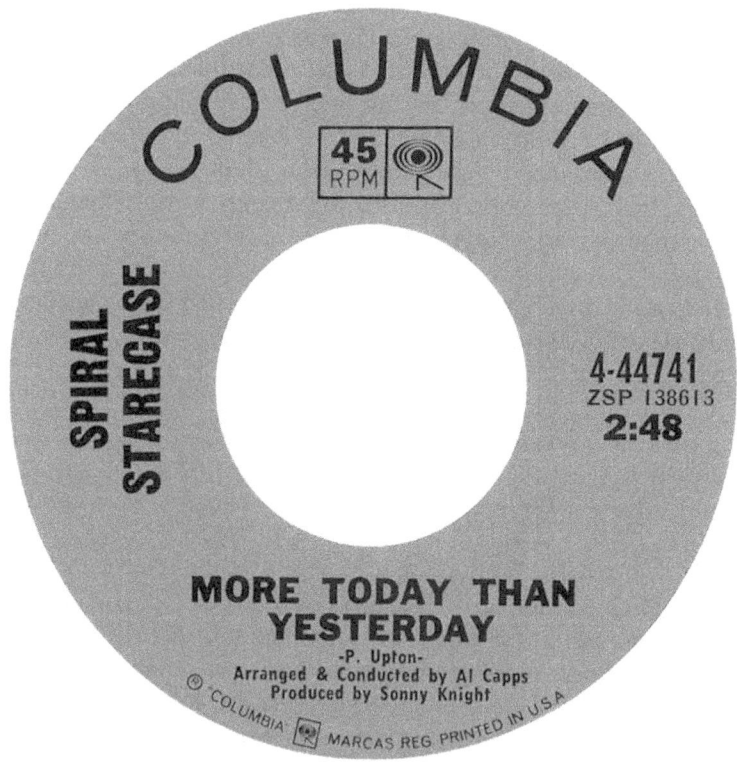

By the time "More Today Than Yesterday" broke into the Top 40, the Spiral Starecase had broken up. When the record started climbing the charts, the group re-formed.

label, heard them. Usher had worked as a producer and songwriter with the Beach Boys, Dick Dale and the Del-Tones, the Byrds, the Surfaris and Chad and Jeremy, so he clearly had an eye and ear for talent. He signed the group in 1967. The music scene was changing so Usher decided the group would have to change too. "The label didn't like our conservative clothes and hairstyles, or the name of the group, so we changed everything," Upton told me. He said they got the group name from a movie: "Dick Lopes saw a movie called *The Spiral Staircase* and we changed the name to the Spiral Starecase, deliberately misspelling it."

The Spiral Starecase: from left to right, Harvey Kaye, Pat Upton, Vinnie Parello, Bobby Raymond. Bottom: Dick Lopes (courtesy Candy Kaye).

Their first record "Baby What I Mean" was produced by Usher but was not written by Usher or the band. It flopped. About this time, Upton started writing "More Today Than Yesterday." He had conceived the song long before that: It originated when a girl told him about "L'éternelle chanson" ("The Eternal Song"), a poem that Rosemonde Gérard wrote for her novelist husband Edmond Rostand and published in 1890. The lines "Car, vois-tu, chaque jour je t'aime davantage, /Aujourd'hui plus qu'hier et bien moins que demain" (translated as "For, you see, each day I love you more, /Today more than yesterday and less than tomorrow") intrigued him.

> I'd had the title "More Today Than Yesterday" for a couple of years before I ever wrote the song. When I was jamming with a friend, he showed me a passing chord that I loved. I knew I would never use that chord with the stuff we were doing and decided the only way was to write a song and use it, and I did. When the chorus came around, those words "I love you more today than yesterday" just fell right into place." Upton thought it would be the type of song that Bobby Goldsboro might sing. He played the two verses he had written for Usher, who liked it but told Upton it needed at least one more verse.

At about that time, Usher left the Columbia label and the group was matched with producer Sonny Knight. After the failure of their first record, the label suggested the group come up with some of their own material. "When we were in Las Vegas in '68, Columbia suggested that someone in the group should write our songs, so I was the one," Upton told me. He offered up the now-finished "More Today Than Yesterday," but before committing to the song, the group tried it out in the clubs first. Candy Kaye, widow of band member Harvey Kaye, told me that her husband liked to tell people how they soon knew the song had potential. As he related it, "We were staying at the Bali Hai Motel in Las Vegas where we were performing as the house band in the Flamingo Sky Room. To test it out, we would play the song just to see if people would dance to it. Every time we played it, people would ask who originally did the song and where could they get it, so we knew we had a hit on our hands."

Even though the group felt they had found the hit they needed at long last, they were allowed only so much input. First, to record the song, Knight and arranger Al Capps brought in some ringers to play on the single and give it a little more of a polished, brassy sound. Backing up Upton's vocals were "Wrecking Crew" luminaries Hal Blaine, John Guerin, Al Casey and even Glen Campbell. The song was recorded, and although the group didn't have any say on which recordings were released as singles (Columbia Records and producer Sonny Knight made those decisions), the label decided to release it as the group's second single.

The group had a contract and a recording that the label believed in. But their manager had been misappropriating funds, people weren't getting paid and it was directly affecting the group's ability to perform. Upton recalled,

> Once we were flying out to do a performance, and we got to LAX and all of our gear was out on the street because our manager bought our tickets with a stolen credit card. Another time, we were working at the Flamingo Hotel and we bought a PA system, and then we found out that the money we were giving our manager every week to pay for the PA was not being paid and so they came to repossess it. It was one thing after another. But the incident with the PA system was the final straw, and a couple of members said, "I'm done," and we were dead in the water, so to speak.

But when "More Today Than Yesterday" started climbing the charts, everybody jumped back aboard. It rose to #12 on the pop charts and #7 on the *Cashbox* charts, and eventually sold more than a million copies and earned the group a gold record. On the heels of a hit, touring followed, and the Spiral Starecase shared the bill with Three Dog Night, Creedence Clearwater Revival, Sly and the Family Stone and the Beach Boys. They appeared on *American Bandstand, The Tonight Show, The Joey Bishop Show, The Mike Douglas Show* and others. Thanks to Upton's song, for a moment in time they were one of the hottest groups in America. As a testament to the song's popularity and longevity, it was later covered by artists Andy Williams, Sonny and Cher, Chicago and Lena Horne. Diana Ross often performs the song in her act, and it has become a wedding staple as well.

Hit records call for albums and follow-ups, and the label had them quickly cut an album to capitalize on "More Today Than Yesterday"'s success. Upton said the album was recorded mainly using session musicians except for his vocals and some cuts using Kaye on keyboards and Lopes on saxophone. They followed up with their next single, 1969's "No One for Me to Turn To." It didn't fare as well as its predecessor but did crack the Top 100 and stalled at #52.

Next came a song that should have been a big hit, "She's Ready," a cover of a song the Poppies had released on Epic in 1966. "A lot of times, we might just be driving around and hear a song that would come on the radio, and somebody would say, 'Maybe we should record that,'" Upton said. "If we heard a little-known song and thought, 'That's gonna be a hit,' we'd jump on it, and that's what we did there." "She's Ready," written by future country music songwriting and producing greats Billy Sherrill and Glenn Sutton, had been recorded by the girl-group The Poppies as "He's Ready" in 1966. It had stalled at #106, and so it was still relatively unknown. It was a good choice for a cover. The Poppies had released a vocal-heavy version with very little backing instrumentation; the added horns and lush orchestration combined with Upton's always vibrant vocals made the Starecase version a superb track. "She's Ready" reached #72 on the charts.

The group's problems with management and internal disagreements were non-stop and so "She's Ready" was their last charting single, "because that's when the group split up for good," Upton said. Just 18 months after climbing the charts and earning a gold record, the Spiral Starecase called it quits in 1970. Eventually Kaye put together a new lineup and kept the band's name alive by touring for many years. Upton played with them a while, became a session musician and "stayed around L.A. and did songs for commercials, sang demos for people, and worked in a trio called Old Friends for a few years. I released one single on RCA, and it didn't do anything." He even played with Elvis Presley in 1975, and through that connection met Rick Nelson. Nelson asked him to sing back-up on an album that became *Playing to Win*. After that album came out in January 1981, Nelson asked Upton to tour with him. For about four years, he played rhythm guitar and sang background for Nelson. The two became close friends, but eventually Upton decided to go home. In 1983, he opened his own club, P.J.'s Alley, in Guntersville, Alabama. It featured up-and-coming musicians as well as established acts. After a December 1985 performance by Rick Nelson, Upton saw his friend for the last time. Nelson was headed to Texas for a gig and asked Upton to come along. Upton declined because he had club business to take care of, but he did see his friend off at the airport and they even had a picture taken together. Nelson's plane crashed and all of the passengers were killed.

Eventually Upton sold the club and returned to performing. Fortunately for him, in the late '70s he had been able to get the copyright back on his music, including "More Today Than Yesterday," and the royalties from that song enabled him to lead a comfortable life.

Upton regretted that things went down like they did; "The band would have probably stayed together if [the manager] would have taken care of things." Yet despite recording only a few singles, they managed to produce the noteworthy "More Today Than Yesterday," still today a mainstay of stations that play '60s rock and pop.

I interviewed Pat Upton in June and October 2010, and he passed away in 2016. Harvey Kaye and Bobby Raymond have also passed away. Kaye's daughter, singer Brenda K. Starr, had several Top 40 hits in the late 1980s.

#8
(*Cashbox* Charts)

"Just Don't Want to Be Lonely" (1974)

The Main Ingredient

Billboard Pop: #10; R&B: #8;
Adult Contemporary: #42; British Charts: #27

There is a distinct separation between the Main Ingredient group that could never attain the *Cashbox* or *Billboard* Top 40 pop charts, and the group that recorded smashes such as "Everybody Plays the Fool" and "Just Don't Want to Be Lonely," songs that went Top Ten across the board. The difference was that the latter group added lead singer Cuba Gooding in 1971, and with Gooding at the helm almost overnight the group realized previously unknown levels of success. For a brief moment in time, the Main Ingredient was one of the most popular singing groups in the world.

In the early 1960s, Harlem residents Tony Silvester, Luther Simmons Jr. and Donald McPherson formed a singing group called the Poets, and they were signed to the short-lived Red Bird label owned by Jerry Lieber and Mike Stoller. This group—not to be confused with the Poets who had the #2 R&B hit "She Blew a Good Thing" on Symbol Records—recorded one single, "Merry Christmas Baby," backed with "I'm Stuck on You," in 1965. In 1966, they changed their name to the Insiders and released another single on Red Bird, this time with "I'm Stuck on You" as the A-side. In 1967, they signed with RCA and released two more singles, "I'm Better Off Without You" and "If You Had a Heart." Silvester, Simmons and McPherson wrote most of these songs, but none of them was successful.

In 1968, they changed their name yet again, this time to the Main Ingredient, a phrase which they apparently saw on a bottle of Coca-Cola. They were still signed to RCA, and with their new name they released three singles in 1969 and 1970 before their fourth, "You've Been

My Inspiration," finally earned them a glimmer of success, peaking at #25 on the R&B charts. Four more singles followed in 1970 and 1971, and though several did well on the R&B charts ("Spinning Around" moved into the Top Ten), none of them broke into the Top 40 on the *Cashbox* or *Billboard* pop charts. But before they had released the latter two of these records, lead singer Donald McPherson became sick with leukemia. The group moved childhood friend Cuba Gooding, an occasionally back-up singer, to the front mic to take McPherson's place during live performances.

Cuba Gooding came into his unusual name when his father—originally from Barbados—moved to Cuba and then moved to New York, where he drove a taxi. The Goodings named their son Cuba. "If you were a kid growing up in Harlem, and you didn't want to be a pimp or a bum or a gangster, and you weren't well-educated, you sang or hoped to be in the music business," Gooding said. "I grew up eight blocks from the Apollo

The Main Ingredient's "Just Don't Want to Be Lonely" was a hit, going to #8 on the R&B chart and #10 on the pop chart, and selling over a million copies.

Theater, and at that time I could walk down 125th Street and run into Sammy Davis Jr., Ella Fitzgerald, Sam Cooke, Jackie Wilson and that ilk. We believed it was the entertainment capital of the world." The other guys in the group came from similar backgrounds.

Gooding had been singing between working as a door-to-door salesman selling encyclopedias and magazines. Neither career was full-time and he was struggling to find direction. When he performed with the group,

> it was never promoted as four Main Ingredients. The group had a theory as to how to do music. Three singers in front, and if a fourth or fifth note was necessary to fill up the harmony, use the musicians, use instruments to do the fourth or fifth note—"stacked harmony"—with only three actual voices but two or three people in the background singing harmony at the same time.

Gooding said he would have liked to have been one of the three principals from the start, but he understood why Silvester, Simmons and McPherson handled it the way they did: "Financially it was more comfortable to spread the payroll between three people rather than five people with five families to feed...." Given that the group had not had a really big hit at that point, it made a lot of sense.

However, Gooding's role was about to change, and those big hits were just around the corner. McPherson succumbed to leukemia and passed away in July 1971. The last single release recorded with McPherson on lead was "Black Seeds Keep on Growing," released about a month after his passing; it peaked at #15 on the R&B charts, #74 on the *Cashbox* pop charts, and #97 on the *Billboard Hot 100*. Gooding became a regular member of the Main Ingredient for good, as he was elevated to the role of lead singer. "I would have never been able to join the group if Donald had lived," Gooding said. But for the group, Gooding's distinctive voice meant a new sound—and the kind of success the likes of which they had not seen.

In 1972, RCA had a song called "Everybody Plays the Fool" written by Rudy Clark, J.R. Bailey and Ken Williams, which Gooding said was actually written for Charlie Pride. Gooding heard it, liked it, and was interested to see how Pride felt about it. "I took it to him, he listened to it and decided it wasn't country enough for him to sing. He told me, 'I'll never be able to sell this as a country song. It's more like a pop song.' So we gave it to our arranger, put an orchestra behind it and recorded it ourselves." It was Gooding's first recording as the lead singer, but surprisingly, given the song's now iconic status, "Everybody Plays the Fool" wasn't a song the group was thrilled about. According to Gooding, "We never liked it—we never believed [it] was going to be a hit record. We wanted to be more like the Temptations or the Four Tops, and that's what the rest of our album was about." The group members felt the song was a bit too mellow, and it was actually so unlike the rest of the album that Gooding said they didn't really give a lot of thought to its potential as a single release. Then RCA "sent us on a European tour for two weeks" to promote that album (*Bittersweet*), and released the single. "When we came back, 'Everybody Plays the Fool' was the hottest record on pop radio."

Oddly enough, the group, who until that time had been firmly entrenched as an R&B group and had never been able to break into Top 40 pop radio, now found that they couldn't get *soul* stations to play their record. According to Gooding, "At first the black stations wouldn't even play it. They said it wasn't R&B. RCA signed me to a three-year contract as the lead singer for the group, everybody was rolling in dough because of the song, but the black stations wouldn't play it." That changed as the song got more popular, and it peaked at #2 on the R&B charts, #3 on the *Billboard* pop charts, and went all the way to #1 on *Cashbox*. The song sold more than a million copies, was certified as a gold record and was nominated for a Grammy as best R&B song of the year. It pushed *Bittersweet* up the charts as well: *Bittersweet* became their first album to break into Top Ten on the R&B album charts.

The group released three more moderately charting singles: "You've Got to Take It," "You Can Call Me Rover" and "Girl Blue" from the 1973 album *Afrodisiac*. They were only moderately successful. The album came nowhere close to the success of *Bittersweet*, despite the presence of a half-dozen songs written by Stevie Wonder as well as songs penned by George Clinton and the Isley Brothers.

It seemed clear that the group needed big singles to sell albums, and they found their next hit in an unexpected way. Gooding: "We were on the road as usual going to a gig on what used to be called the chitlin circuit, and we turned on the radio and someone was singing 'Just Don't Want to Be Lonely'—either Blue Magic or Ronnie Dyson, I'm not sure. And we said, 'Let's put that on the next album.'" The song had in fact been released in 1973 by Dyson, who "almost had a hit record with it," according to Gooding; it went to #60 on the pop charts and #29 on the R&B charts. Then Blue Magic released a version in early 1974 as the B-side of their #8 pop hit "Sideshow"; it did not chart. But the group knew they needed to put a new spin on it to make it their own. "The song had been recorded by [several] artists before we did it," Gooding said. But the group wasn't content to merely imitate the other groups—and wasn't sure that would work anyway. "'Just Don't Want to Be Lonely' was always done as a slow ballad," Gooding said,

#8. "Just Don't Want to Be Lonely" (1974)

"and it always crashed and burned. When we put the grooves on it, like at the beginning—'dum-dum, dah dah dumm dum…'—it just took off." It went to #8 on the R&B chart and #10 on the pop chart, sold over a million copies and even charted in England, becoming their only song to chart in that country where it went to #27. The single was on their album *Euphrates River*, which became their highest charting album: It went to #8 on the R&B album charts and #52 on the pop album charts.

Unfortunately, they weren't able to follow up with another big hit. Their next few singles did moderately well but lacked the special sound of "Everybody Plays the Fool" and "Just Don't Want to Be Lonely." The follow-up to "Just Don't Want to Be Lonely," "Happiness Is Just Around the Bend," did moderately well, breaking into the pop Top 40 and the R&B Top Ten. "Rolling Down a Mountainside" (1975) was "another one we adapted," Gooding said, and it did go Top Ten on the R&B charts. "It was done by Isaac Hayes as a ballad, but we put a 'dah daha daha' groove to it and it did well." Despite its success on the R&B charts, the song didn't do well on the pop charts (#92). The group members didn't know it at the time, but "Rolling Down a Mountainside" would be their last record to make the pop charts.

By 1977, the hits had stopped coming and the group was ready to split up. A solo artist with Motown, Gooding released two albums and he had a single, 1978's "Mind Pleaser," that just barely broke the Top 100 on the R&B charts. Tony Silvester released a solo album, but found his greatest post–Main Ingredient success as co-producer on Ben E. King's Top Five pop hit "Supernatural Thing" in 1975. In 1979, the group reunited and worked together for the next decade. They charted four times during the '80s, and "I Just Wanna Love You" broke the Top 20 on the R&B charts in 1989. In 1983, Gooding also had some moderate single success with his solo remake of 1974's "Happiness Is Just Around the Bend."

Over the years, the group separated and came back together several times. Gooding continued to perform those classic hits all over the country until his death at the age of 72.

#9
(*Billboard* Pop Charts)
"Tracy" (1969)
THE CUFF LINKS
R&B: Did not chart; *Cashbox*: #5;
Adult Contemporary: #5; British Charts: #4

Before 1980, very few artists had charted with more than one record in the Top Ten at the same time. Predictably, the Beatles did; in fact, they once held down the top five slots simultaneously. Elvis Presley held down the first two positions in 1956, and the Bee Gees had the top two spots in 1977. But Ron Dante did something that these rock'n'roll Hall of Famers did not: He held down two spots as lead singer on two singles in the Top Ten for three weeks in 1969, but not under his own name. In fact, the two singles weren't even attributed to the same group or Dante, as "Sugar, Sugar" was by the Archies and "Tracy" was by the Cuff Links. But the common element was Dante, who basically *was* both the Cuff Links and the Archies, and so consequently he pulled off a feat unparalleled in music history.

Dante was born Carmine John Granito in Staten Island, New York. During his childhood, there was always music around his home, and of course vocal groups on the radio were influential as well. Although he liked groups such as the Platters, he said, "I discovered Elvis when I was ten and that changed my life completely." When he was 14, he started his first band, the Persuaders, and he was hooked.

When Dante was 17, he landed a job as a staff singer and demo-maker with Don Kirshner. He worked in New York with artists such as Carole King, Tony Orlando and Neil Sedaka. In his role doing demos and writing, he worked with two other young men, Danny Jordan and Tommy Wynn. Jordan's uncle was songwriter-producer Paul Vance, who often worked with songwriter Lee Pockriss; the two co-wrote hits such as Perry Como's "Catch a Falling Star" in 1957 and "Itsy Bitsy Teenie Weenie Yellow Polka Dot Bikini" in 1960. Vance and Pockriss had

In 1969, Ron Dante sang lead on "Sugar, Sugar" by the Archies and "Tracy" by the Cuff Links; they were in the Top 10 together for three weeks.

written a parody of the Shangri-Las' #1 1964 hit "Leader of the Pack" called "Leader of the Laundromat," and were looking for someone to record it. Jordan, Wynn and Dante recorded the novelty song as the Detergents, and when released in 1965 the record peaked at #19 on the pop Hot 100. "As the Detergents song peaked we went on the road with the Dick Clark Caravan of Stars and toured for about a year then came back home and set up an office, where I was gonna be a songwriter and producer" Dante said. He recorded a number of demos and several singles and did some work on Broadway, but by the late '60s he was mainly singing as the voice of a number of faceless studio groups, often making as many as half a dozen recordings a day. It was in one such instance that he did the lead vocals on the Archies' hit "Sugar, Sugar" (see that chapter later in this book), which became his first #1 hit. Oddly enough, just as that song peaked at #1 (it stayed on top of the pop charts for four weeks), another song featuring Dante's voice soared into the Top Ten.

Vance and Pockriss had once again come to Dante in 1969 with a song they had written, "Tracy." Dante said that, as he understood it, "the name came from the fact that the lyricist who wrote the song was a big fan of Spencer Tracy, the actor, and thought it would be a cute name to put in a song!" Even if the name did come from an actor best known for tough guy roles, "Tracy" went on to become a massive hit. Dante recalled:

> I recorded "Tracy" right after I recorded "Sugar, Sugar." [Pockriss and Vance], who were very fine writers, ... told me they wanted me to do the song. I heard "Tracy" and thought it was a beautiful song. It has three key changes in it; it's a very sophisticated song for a pop song. I told them I'd do the lead and the background on it and make it sound like a group. Because it was such a well-crafted song, I knew it would be easy to put my voice and backgrounds on it.

Unlike "Sugar, Sugar," on which Dante had a fair amount of vocal support from Toni Wine, "Tracy" was Dante and Dante alone:

> The "Tracy" session was great all around. Lee did the musical arrangement, and it only took him just a few hours to get the track recorded and then I went to work on the vocal arrangement. I did the lead first, which took maybe a half an hour, and after that I did the background parts. There were at least three different parts I wanted to do to create the effect of many singers, and it turned out really well.

Like "Sugar, Sugar," "Tracy" was not released under Dante's name; instead it was credited to a non-existent group, the Cuff Links. The song quickly raced up the charts, peaking at #9 the week of October 25, 1969. "Sugar, Sugar" was #3 that week, having just ended a four-week run at the top on October 11.

"Since I did it right after 'Sugar, Sugar,' 'Tracy' was getting played every hour on the hour at one of the biggest stations in New York City, with the result that both records were being played constantly." But as had been the case with "Sugar, Sugar" when he recorded as the "Archies," once again he was the anonymous voice behind a big hit song. "I wasn't getting any credit because they weren't in my name, but I knew my voice was on the airwaves and that could only mean good things." Dante said he was fine with the anonymity:

> I was a studio singer at the time recording a lot of commercials, mainly for Madison Avenue, doing products like Pepsi, Coke and Dr. Pepper. I did thousands of commercials, so I was used to being anonymous. It was a very good living, and when I signed on for the Archies and Cuff Links records, it was with the understanding that I would be anonymous. With the Archies, Don Kirshner did guarantee I'd be able to release a solo album a few years later. Don came through on that and I did one on RCA International and it got a big push.

#9. "Tracy" (1969)

He does admit that, in hindsight, he wishes he *had* put his name on those records. "People know who I am and when they think of the groups, they research it and my name comes up immediately, but still...."

Despite the fact that he had no interest in being part of a real group, Dante had promised Vance and Pockriss he'd do a Cuff Links album if "Tracy" was successful. When the single sold more than a million copies and was awarded a gold record, Vance and Pockriss came up with some more songs for Dante to record. Working with the then-unknown Rupert Holmes, who later had his own hit with "Escape (The Pina Colada Song)," Dante churned out an album: "We did it very quickly—background vocals, leads, everything in like a day and a half." The album, fittingly titled *Tracy*, produced a second hit, *When Julie Comes Around*, which went to #41 on the U.S. pop charts.

But still, there was no group, only Dante. The album's liner notes talked about the Cuff Links as if there was actually a group by that name, but did not name them, and there were no pictures. With two Top Ten records, Dante was less inclined than ever to be a part of a real touring group. The label needed to capitalize on the Cuff Links' name, and to make money someone needed to tour as the group. Pat Rizzo, Rick Dimino, Bob Gill, Dave Lavender, Andrew Denno, Joe Cord and Danny Valentine filled in on tour as the Cuff Links, because Dante simply wasn't interested. By that time, he had entered into a deal with Don Kirshner to record under his own name at long last, and so he wasn't available in any event. Vance, Pockriss and Holmes worked together to release one more charting single, "Run, Sally, Run" (#76), under the Cuff Links name in 1970, and one more album, *The Cuff Links*, as they were still trying to capitalize on "Tracy"'s Top Ten success. One final single, 1970's "Robin's World," scratched the surface of the Easy Listening Top 40 charts, but that was it. Dante had nothing to do with any of these later efforts.

Among Dante's later accomplishments, he produced Barry Manilow and in fact sang back-up on "Mandy" ("I was lucky with girls' names!"). Dante said,

> We had 18 hit singles in a row, for five or six years we never left the charts. [My label] asked me to go down to this club called Catch a Rising Star and see this girl singer that they were going to sign. They said, "She sings a big ballad in her show and we'd like you to produce her." But she also did a few rock'n'roll songs and one was "You Better Run," and I decided that was the direction to go with her. Make her a rock'n'roll queen, not a middle of the road balladeer like other people.

That singer, who Dante basically discovered, was Pat Benatar. "She was very, very talented and you could tell she had 'it.' She was a dynamo in the studio." He also did more work on Broadway.

Dante talked about one of the reasons people still love "Tracy": "I think it having a girl's name has helped it last. Girls' name songs endure." Dante said one unexpected outgrowth of its popularity was that there were a lot of little girls named Tracy after the record charted. "I meet them at concerts and signings and things. It's nice to see that. There weren't that many Tracy girls before the song, but a lot after."

―――――――

I interviewed Ron Dante in 2016. As of this writing, he is still performing.

#10
(R&B Charts)
"Swing Your Daddy" (1975)
Jimmy Gilstrap

Billboard Pop: #55; *Cashbox*: #57; Adult Contemporary: Did not chart; British Charts: #4

Jim Gilstrap's name is probably one of the least recognizable names in this book. That's because he had only one really successful chart single, 1975's "Swing Your Daddy." But it is almost certain that you've heard his vocals more than any other singer covered in these pages. From the theme to TV's *Good Times*, to the Peter Pan Peanut Butter jingle, to his work with Stevie Wonder, Michael Jackson, Dolly Parton, Ringo Starr, Lionel Ritchie and others, Gilstrap's career as a session vocalist and back-up singer is unparalleled. He is often asked about his recordings with other music luminaries as opposed to being asked about his own music, but he's still pleased that even today, people remember "Swing Your Daddy."

James Earl Gilstrap was born in Daingerfield, an East Texas town of a few thousand people. He grew up listening to Bobby "Blue" Bland, Sam Cooke and Nat King Cole. In 1963, after his junior year of high school, his parents moved to Los Angeles. His musical talent was obvious early on, and in 1964 he started a singing group called the Duprells. He told me, "Although I was in high school, when I first started singing, I had a manager named Bumps Blackwell, and Bumps was working with Sam Cooke." Blackwell was already well-known, having jump-started Little Richard's career and produced Cooke's #1 smash "You Send Me." Blackwell liked the Duprells' sound, and they were signed to sing back-up for Cooke on tour in Japan. For the young singer, it sounded like the opportunity of a lifetime. Unfortunately, it was not to be:

> The night before we were supposed to leave, I was walking home from a party and I saw police and the coroner's people rolling a body on a gurney out of the Hacienda Motel on 92nd and Figueroa. The next morning,

When Kenny Nolan wrote "Swing Your Daddy," he was coming off a string of hits (as a writer or co-writer) that included "Lady Marmalade" for LaBelle and "My Eyes Adored You" for Frankie Valli. As a singer, Nolan released his own song "I Like Dreamin'," which peaked at #3 in 1977.

> I'd packed my bags and walked 15 blocks to another singer's house, waiting to be picked up to go on tour. Bumps called us and said, "We're not going anywhere, Sam got killed last night," and I flashed back and thought, "Oh, no, that was his body I saw." Sure enough, it was. We'd only been with Sam about a month before he passed.

There were a few other singing opportunities under Blackwell's mentorship, but Gilstrap soon decided to attend L.A.'s City College to continue his musical training. He left in 1966 to join the Navy in the midst of the Vietnam War, and was stationed on the U.S.S. *Enterprise* in the Gulf of Tonkin. He was discharged in 1968.

Once back in the States, Gilstrap auditioned for and joined the Doodletown Pipers. "We used to do *The Ed Sullivan Show*, we did the Frontier Hotel in Vegas six months a year and we opened for acts like Harry James and the Supremes." The Doodletown Pipers—as the sound of their name might suggest—was a squeaky-clean, wholesome group of young people who sang on a number of variety shows from the mid–1960s to the mid–1970s. While the Doodletown Pipers did work with groups such as the Supremes, more often than not it was with more adult, contemporary-type musical acts such as Perry Como, Eddie Fisher and the Carpenters.

After he left the Doodletown Pipers, Gilstrap had his biggest break yet—a break he has called "career-making"—when Stevie Wonder heard him and Lani Groves singing in a group recording for Jerry Butler's short-lived Memphis Records. Around the end of 1971, Wonder asked Gilstrap and Groves to come to New York and work on an album he was recording. Gilstrap and Groves made the move: "When I started working with Stevie Wonder, we were actually roommates for a couple of years in Queens."

While working with Wonder on the album *Talking Book*, Gilstrap made one of his most famous vocal contributions, one that put him in a position where listeners everywhere heard his work—even if they weren't aware it was him. "We were at Jimi Hendrix's Electric Lady Studios in the Village, and it was about three o'clock in the morning when we recorded 'You Are the Sunshine of My Life.' Stevie asked me to sing the opening lines, and my girlfriend at the time, Lani Groves, sang the next few lines." Gilstrap and Groves then sang all the backgrounds. That opening sequence may well be the most famous lines Gilstrap ever sang. The song went all the way to #1 and netted Wonder a Grammy. In gratitude, he gave Gilstrap a gold record for his efforts.

Gilstrap moved back to L.A. and soon he was working with luminaries Henry Mancini and Quincy Jones. He was also with a group known as the Cultures, who became Side Effect.

Gilstrap was ready to go out on his own by the mid–1970s. His first solo contract was with Bell Records, and in 1974 he released an unheralded single, "When You Come Back Down." He was working on an album when Arista took over the label and dropped him from their roster of performers. But as had happened so many times before, opportunity came knocking.

"A friend of mine named Carolyn Willis was in the group Honey Cone," he said. "She called me one day and said they were looking for a singer over at Chelsea Records. The guy who ran the company was Wes Farrell, who was married to Tina Sinatra, and the company was doing really well." Farrell, a well-known songwriter, had written the #1 hit "Hang on Sloopy" for the McCoys and "Come a Little Bit Closer" for Jay and the Americans, and he also co-wrote the songs "Doesn't Somebody Want to Be Wanted" and "I'll Meet You Halfway" for the Partridge

Family. He also produced the Partridge Family, the Cowsills and Lulu, among others. He started Chelsea Records in 1972, and the label quickly scored hits with "Daddy Don't You Walk So Fast" by Wayne Newton, "Get Dancin'" by Disco Tex and the Sex-O-Lettes, and "I'm Doin' Fine Now" by New York City. "So I went over and they signed me, and then they brought me 'Swing Your Daddy' to record."

"Swing Your Daddy" was written by Kenny Nolan, who'd written the #1 songs "My Eyes Adored You" for Frankie Valli and "Lady Marmalade" for LaBelle already that year; he later wrote and recorded his own song, "I Like Dreamin'," which went to #3 in 1977. Gilstrap knew "Swing Your Daddy" was a good opportunity for him, and the label thought it had the potential to be a hit as well. "They brought the song in and told me they wanted an Eddie Kendricks–Smokey Robinson kind of sound. So I did it, but I honestly did not expect it to do what it did." Released on Chelsea's Roxbury subsidiary label, "it was big all over Europe—I even went to England and did *Top of the Pops*." It didn't do badly in America, either: "It was in the Top Ten on the R&B charts here in the States. But the record did what it did due to Kenny Nolan, because he also produced it and even sang background on it too." Although the record peaked at #55 on the pop charts in 1975, in England it went to #4, and it also reached #10 on the R&B charts (called the U.S. *Billboard* Black Singles chart at the time). Two more singles from the album were released that year, but neither "House of Strangers" (#93 on the pop charts) nor "I'm on Fire" (#78) were successful. (The latter peaked at #20 on the R&B charts.)

But a miscalculation may have caused his career to lose momentum. On the strength of the success of the three singles, "we did a [second] album called *Love Talk*," he said. While he felt some of the tracks were solid, the album's artwork may have hurt sales. "I really had no input as far as what they put on the album cover, and unfortunately they put a nude couple, back to back, on the front of the album." Looking at the album today, it's hard to imagine why anyone thought the album cover was an asset, and it's easy to imagine that some people might have actually been embarrassed to buy it, *if* they could find it. "Back in those days, they wouldn't even put the album in stores in some parts of the country, and so it didn't sell," he said. Apparently the record company realized the cover was a liability, and they pulled it from shelves. Gilstrap recalled, "By the time they revamped the album and put a picture of me on the cover, the album had played itself out." Two singles from the album, "Move Me" and "Love Talk," were released in 1976, but both stalled on the upper reaches of the R&B charts.

By that point, Gilstrap was getting tired of some aspects of being

#10. "Swing Your Daddy" (1975)

a headline act. "After *Love Talk*, I got away from solo recording. It had been a lot of fun, and I got to know a lot of the artists at Chelsea, and 'Swing Your Daddy' had been a real blessing. But I started to do some other things." Indeed, Gilstrap built one of the most impressive résumés of anyone in the recording industry. During his years as an artist in a supporting role, he has worked with the Temptations, Boz Scaggs, the Four Tops, Aretha Franklin, Barbra Streisand, Rod Stewart, Whitney Houston and Dolly Parton. He worked with Michael Jackson on the *Thriller* and *Off The Wall* albums, he did movie vocals on *Grease*, *The Matrix* and *Rocky* and TV work on *Cheers*, *The Simpsons* and *Good Times*. During the theme song, it's Gilstrap we hear singing, "Temporary layoffs.... Ain't we lucky we got 'em—Good Times!" "The royalties for that alone have paid very, very well," he told me.

For decades now, Gilstrap has done session and back-up work, and as such has become one of the most successful and well-known people in the music industry. Far from being disappointed that he never had a standout solo career, he realizes he's been extremely fortunate. "I have had fun working throughout the industry—it's been a wonderful career. And I feel blessed that even today, people remember 'Swing Your Daddy.'"

I interviewed Gilstrap in September 2011. As of this writing, he is still involved in the music industry in a variety of ways.

#11
(*Billboard* Pop Charts)
"Susan" (1967)

THE BUCKINGHAMS

Cashbox: #7; R&B, Adult Contemporary,
British Charts: Did not chart

In 1967, *Billboard* declared the Buckinghams "the most listened to band in America." But despite appearances, everything wasn't exactly great for the band. Yes, their song "Kind of a Drag" had hit #1 on the last day of 1966; with that carry-over into 1967, they would have five Top 40 chart records that year. Their *lowest* charting song peaked at #12.

But while the Buckinghams were a group of undeniable talent with exceptional songwriters feeding them hit after hit, there were problems with the business aspects of their careers. First, their label dropped them even as "Kind of a Drag" hit the top of the charts. Their manager quit. People left the group. Even though they'd had all of those hits in 1967, the group eventually realized that everyone was making money off of their records except *them*. To top it all off, their last hit of that year, the delightful "Susan," was be altered in the studio without their consent: An additional 29 seconds of Beatles-esque psychedelia was added to a solid pop song, an alteration which probably affected its success. It was the group's last Top 40 hit, bringing to an end a tumultuous year and leading to the group's disenchantment with their label, their management ... and in some ways, the music business as a whole.

Chicago natives Dennis Tufano and George LeGros were in a group called the Darcells when John Poulos heard them and got them to join his group. That band became the Pulsations, so named, Tufano told me, "because we played at dragstrips and car shows and we needed a name that really moved." Over time, the group added Carl Giammarese, Curtis Bachman and Nick Fortuna of the Centuries. They got their big break in 1965 after they won a Chicago radio station's "Battle of the Bands" competition. Next they became the house band on a local TV show, *All*

#11. "Susan" (1967)

Although the "Susan" label gives songwriting credit to Holvay, Biesber and producer Jim Guercio, Guerico's only contribution was "this backwards tape thing."

Time Hits. The station asked them to change their name to something more British-sounding. Tufano said the group agreed because "the British invasion was in full swing at the time, and because other than locally, nobody really knew who the Pulsations were anyway." Tufano said a security guard heard the request and gave them a list of eight or ten suggestions, from which they chose the Buckinghams, because it "sounded British but also because there's a beautiful fountain in Chicago called Buckingham Fountain. This way we didn't feel like we were selling out Chicago to take a British-sounding name."

Around this time LeGros got drafted and Bachman and Fortuna left; as a result, Tufano was suddenly lead singer by default. During some of their shows, the group noticed people crowding around the stage instead of just dancing. A local deejay encouraged them to cut a record even though "we were just happy to play music on the weekends." They had taken on a manager, Carl Bonafede, who asked Chicago songwriter-musician Jim Holvay to listen to the band and see if he had any material that might work for them. Holvay said he did have a song that he didn't feel was right for his band The MOB, but that might be good for the Buckinghams. Tufano said Bonafede "dragged him upstairs to the hotel room and pulled out a little reel-to-reel and told him to play his song. Holvay played a song called 'Kind of a Drag' with an acoustic guitar, and we listened to the tape and really liked it."

Holvay let the group have "Kind of a Drag," and as soon as they signed with USA Records they performed it at one of their earliest recording sessions. Tufano said,

> We recorded something like 11 or 12 sides for USA Records. We'd record a few at a time, but "Kind of a Drag" was in the first session. It was really popular live, and because we liked it a lot we told the record company they needed to release the song. But they didn't seem to like it and they released just about everything we recorded except that one.

Releases such as "I'll Go Crazy," "I Call Your Name" and "I've Been Wrong" really didn't do anything while "Kind of a Drag" languished unreleased. Tufano:

> USA made all these excuses like that it was too slow, so finally at the end of 1966 our contract was up, and there were no more recordings left except "Kind of a Drag," so they released it, dropped us, and said, "We're done."
>
> Well, that was November 1966, and soon "Kind of a Drag" was #1 with a bullet. So much for the wisdom of record companies. But what was really strange was that we were very upset they had dropped us because we thought we'd made some decent records and had some regional single hits. Our keyboard player left the group because he thought it was over, and we didn't even have a manager any more. When USA dropped us, Bonafede said, "I don't know what else I can do. I'm a local guy and I can't take you any further." So there we were, no label, no keyboard player, no manager. We're sitting in Nick Fortuna's basement and John Pullos comes down and has *Billboard* magazine and plops it on the table and says, "Open it up. Open it up!" And we open it to the *Hot 100* and "Kind of a Drag" is #1.

Tufano said they realized then that they needed to continue. They added Marty Grebbs for keyboard and sax and started looking for a label and a manager.

John Pullos had a friend whose cousin Jim Guercio worked for Chad and Jeremy. In California, the band met with Guercio and, according to Tufano, told him, "Look we have this #1 record and no management." Tufano continued, "He seemed to know what he was doing so we signed with him. Guercio took 'Kind of a Drag' to Columbia and said, 'I have a band with a #1 record. Do you want them?' Clive Davis did and so we were back in business."

The band began touring to capitalize on the success of the record, and went back to the studio to record more. Guercio got in touch with Holvay, hoping maybe he had some more songs as good as that #1 smash.

#11. "Susan" (1967)

In fact, Holvay and his MOB bandmate Gary Beisber had written quite a few songs they were willing to let the Buckinghams record. First up was "Don't You Care?" which Tufano said was still his favorite: "It was a great follow-up to our first hit and it was a nice cool song." Gary Beisber, who was also in the MOB, added a few things to the songs, but Holvay really wrote 80 percent of each and Gary would add a bridge or melody line. After the record climbed to #6, they released a song Holvay and Beisber didn't write, "Mercy, Mercy, Mercy," which went to #5. The Holvay-Beisber composition "Hey Baby (They're Playing Our Song)" went to #12.

"All of our songs were about 'You broke my heart but I still love you,'" Tufano said. "Every one of them, and that's the universal theme of life. It was so well put for use with the music and the lyrics and it was the right time for us to do that." Indeed, the formula was working to perfection, which is why the decision to release the Holvay-Beisber composition "Susan" next made sense in terms of the way it was written. What made *no* sense was what Jim Guercio did to it without talking to the band or the songwriters.

Tufano said, "Jim Holvay had been working on 'Susan' for a while and I think he was stuck. [But] when Gary added the bridge, it tied it all together." Holvay had apparently written the song about a go-go dancer at Chicago's Whiskey a Go Go who he had a crush on; she and her name, Susan, were the inspiration for the song. The band recorded it as written and they went out on the road again. But unbeknownst to them, their manager had other ideas. "Jim Guercio had this crazy idea to insert this backwards tape thing in it, this [element of] the Beatles' 'Day in the Life.' We didn't hear it until we were out on the road." The band really didn't like it. "Most radio stations cut it out," Tufano continued. "We'd be doing an interview and they'd say, 'We cut that part because we didn't like it because when it's playing, people change the station.' We'd tell them we agreed and 'Thank you very much.'" Guercio's 29-second addition to the song more or less brings "Susan" to a screeching halt. You can't sing along with that part, can't dance to it, and considering the fact that "Susan" is a pop song and not a concept song like "Day in the Life," it was an inexplicably bad addition.

Despite that—or perhaps because so many radio stations deleted the interlude—the song did well, peaking at #11. "Usually Guercio was a great producer and had a great ear," Tufano said. "But putting that in there was a mistake." Tufano added that when they play the song today, "We now have this Miles Davis type interlude that we put in there and it works so much better."

At the end of 1967, *Billboard* called the Buckinghams "the most listened to band in America." Based on the group's chart success that year, that would be a hard claim to dispute. But "Susan" was their last Top 40 record. "In 1968, music took another big jump and was going in so many different directions. You had Hendrix and people like that and we saw all these great acts coming out and changing the face of music. Unfortunately, legal matters took the shine off the business for us." The group soon learned that while their recordings had sold well, they had little to no money to show for it. "We kept things going the best we could, but the last year and a half we were just paying legal fees, and problems with management changed our relationship with the label. Instead of having the band get fragmented, we figured we should just bring it to a close and we disbanded in 1970 because we couldn't put it back together."

The Buckinghams as a group ceased to exist. Giammarese and Tufano worked as a duo called Dennis and Carl (later changed to Tufano and Giammarese) before they parted ways. Most members of the group joined other bands or went into the recording and entertainment business, Tufano working in TV, film and music. Giammarese, Fortuna and Tufano reunited briefly in 1980, and occasionally played together subsequently. Today Tufano performs under his own name while Giammarese and Fortuna, owners of the rights to the group's name, perform as the Buckinghams.

I interviewed Dennis Tufano in October 2014.

#12
(*Billboard* Pop Charts)

"The Cheater" (1965)

BOB KUBAN AND THE IN-MEN

R&B, *Cashbox*, Adult Contemporary,
British Charts: Did not chart

The story behind "The Cheater" is one of the most compelling, and at the same time disturbing, episodes in rock'n'roll history. The song is about a guy you need to look out for, a guy who'll cheat with your girl and there will be dire consequences. In a twist of fate that could have been foreseen by no one, charismatic lead singer Walter Scott's wife cheated with a man and the consequences were indeed dire. Scott disappeared in 1983, and four years later his decomposed body was found hogtied and shot in the back. He had been killed by his wife's lover. The man and Scott's wife were charged with murder. Sometimes life truly is stranger than fiction.

Robert "Bob" Kuban was born in St. Louis, Missouri. After graduating from the St. Louis Institute of Music, he became a high school music teacher. He had started his first band during his senior year of high school, but after college he decided to start a band with more ambitious goals in mind. Kuban, a drummer, joined up with organist and budding songwriter Greg Hoeltzel, a student at Washington University in St. Louis. They recruited more members: John Michael Krenski on bass, Skip Weisser on trombone, Harry Simon on saxophone, Pat Hixon on trumpet and Ken Smith as lead guitarist (Smith was replaced by Ray Schulte). But Kuban knew the real key was the frontman, and when he heard St. Louis native Walter Scott (born Walter Simon Notheis Jr.), lead singer for a group called the Pacemakers, he knew he'd found his guy. "Wally was a very good lead singer, he was like a Fabian or Frankie Avalon," Kuban told me. "He was a good showman, and a good-looking guy." Scott, who was working a day job as a crane operator, accepted Kuban's offer to front Kuban's new band, now known as the Rhythm Masters.

The group started practicing and landed some gigs at Club Imperial in St. Louis, a venue where Chuck Berry and also the Ike and Tina Turner Revue often performed. Due to the club's reputation, Miles Davis and the Rolling Stones had visited the club as well. It was a good venue for the band, and it offered them prime exposure. They were soon going by the name The Bob Kuban Band, and in 1965 they released their first single, "Jerkin' Time," on the Norman label. A few months later they released another single on Norman, "I Don't Want to Know." While neither made the national charts, the songs were very popular in the St. Louis area and got a lot of airplay.

In January 1965, Dobie Gray had a Top 20 hit with "The 'In' Crowd," in which Gray sang about his "crowd," who exuded the coolness that set them apart from others and that others emulated. The song was so popular that the Ramsey Lewis Trio had a #5 *Billboard* hit with a jazz version that summer. Being "in" was suddenly the hot new word, and the group decided to change their name once again, this time to Bob

Only a few dozen records were released on the St. Louis–based Musicland label between the mid–60s and early '70s. "The Cheater" was the label's only big national hit.

Kuban and the In-Men. This change came right before their big break: a Krenski-written song called "The Cheater."

Kuban told me, "Originally the song was written in the first person: 'Look out for me, I'm a Cheater.' But I wanted to do a song that had excitement to it, had some energy and had a good driving tempo. So we added a bridge, and put it in the third person." These alterations made the song a winner. After "The Cheater" was recorded in St. Louis on the Musicland label, it was a hit in the St. Louis area (#1 in December 1965). Then it took off nationally, and was in the Top Ten in local markets across the U.S., Canada and Australia. Nationally it peaked at #12 on the *Billboard* Pop Charts at the end of January 1966 and earned a gold record in the process. Finally the group had the success they had wanted, and bookings across the nation followed. The group played with the Turtles in San Francisco and with Otis Redding at Whiskey a Go Go. They appeared on the TV programs *Where the Action Is* and *American Bandstand*. Internationally, the song did well too; it went all the way to #1 in Australia. They were so big in Australia, in fact, that they were scheduled to do a nine-week tour there. With a Top 40 hit and international appeal, it appeared as though the group's ship had finally come in.

But suddenly they were confronted with an unexpected problem. As it turned out, just being in a popular band wasn't enough to keep you out of the draft. To qualify for draft deferments, most of the band members were also college students or teachers. Hoeltzel was a student at Washington University, Krenski was a student at St. Louis University, and Hixon, Simon and Weisser all went to the St. Louis Institute of Music. As for Scott, being married gave him deferred draft status. What this meant was, if the students quit school or the teachers quit their jobs, they could be drafted and sent to Vietnam. Kuban attempted to reason with the draft board, but was told in no uncertain terms that if they went to Australia, they would immediately be classified 1-A and be drafted. This meant no nine-week tour in Australia, and effectively put an end to any plans the group had for traveling abroad.

Without the distractions of spending time on the road, the group was at least able to get back in the studio and capitalize on "The Cheater"'s success with a new single. "The Teaser," a song by Hoeltzel and Krenski, was a counterpart of sorts to "The Cheater," as "The Teaser" was about a girl who guys would do well to avoid because she was just a tease, as opposed to a guy that girls would do well to avoid, as in "The Cheater." It seems as though it would have been a good follow-up, but there was no denying that the song was far inferior to its predecessor. Kuban said, "I hated the song, and even today I have never played it live.

I fought with our manager about releasing it after 'The Cheater' because I knew a hit record needed a strong follow-up, and 'The Teaser' wasn't it. I knew that it wasn't a good song." Over Kuban's objections, their manager, Mel Friedman, released the song anyway. "The Teaser" actually climbed to #70 on the charts. That same year, they released a third single, a cover of the Beatles' "Drive My Car" which went to #93. Even though it broke into the Top 100, there's nothing very original about it. Still, three chart records in a row in roughly 12 months did seem to promise great things ahead for the band.

Their greatest challenge yet came from a source close to them: Their manager Mel Friedman tried to break up the group. According to Kuban, "At first, things were going very well with him, but it got so he had an agenda, which unfortunately didn't involve me." Apparently, Friedman saw Scott as the real talent in the band and decided that,

"Sir" Walter Scott (front) and Bob Kuban (back) of Bob Kuban and the In-Men (courtesy Bob Kuban).

rather than continue to butt heads with Kuban about the direction the band should take, he'd be better off stealing Scott and a few of the others and running things the way he wanted. Kuban:

> Mel obviously wanted to pull Wally away from the band. He started causing a lot of problems because he saw the advantage of Wally breaking away for his own purposes.
>
> Despite the fact that we had a hit record, all of a sudden, the band was breaking up, and guys were leaving. At the time, I was completely blown away, I was in shock, really, because I didn't know why this was happening. It was only years later that Wally told me what had happened, because by then he realized what an opportunity we had and that Friedman had blown it for all of us. He got hold of good talent and screwed it up.

Scott, Hoetzel and Krenski formed a new band, The Guise. Between 1967 and 1969, they released several Friedman-produced songs on the Musicland and Atco labels, but nothing charted other than locally. Lead singer Walter Scott also released several solo efforts during that period, but again, nothing charted nationally. Singles released by what was left of the original In-Men suffered a similar fate. It was clear that together the group had something record buyers wanted to hear, but not as separate entities. Kuban tried to get a few other groups together, Scott kept plugging away as a solo act, and most of the others got regular jobs (Krenski became an engineer, Hoeltzel a dentist). "I look back and I wonder," Kuban said. "We could have been as big as a lot of bands at the time. We had everything going, we had good writers, we were playing good music, everything was coming together, and then this bastard [Friedman] came along and screwed it all up."

Despite the acrimony of the group's split, the band prepared for a big reunion concert in 1984. After just one rehearsal in late 1983, Scott's wife Jo Ann reported that he'd gone to an auto parts store and never came home. His car turned up at the airport later that month, but there was no trace of Scott.

In a twist worthy of a Hollywood film noir, in 1986 Scott's now ex-wife married a widower named Jim Williams, whose late wife had supposedly died in a car wreck shortly before Scott's disappearance. In 1987, police learned that Williams' late wife had been having an affair with Scott before he disappeared; this was enough for them to reopen the cold case. Shockingly, in 1987, Scott's decomposed body was found floating face down in a cistern on property owned by Williams. Scott had been hogtied and shot in the back. The authorities then exhumed the body of Williams' first wife, and a new autopsy showed that she had died from blunt force trauma and injuries not consistent with a car crash. Williams and Jo Ann were charged with murder, but the latter was offered a plea bargain to help convict Williams. She served less than two years. Williams received a life sentence and died in prison.

Kuban always regretted that the band never had their reunion, but he has another band, Bob Kuban and the Bob Kuban Brass. Highly regarded, they play a variety of venues across the Midwest. Kuban has also recorded some solo efforts. But one can't blame him for thinking as he does, that "if Mel Friedman had stayed out of everything, we probably would have been a very successful group for many years." Fortunately, their brief moment in the spotlight did produce "The Cheater."

I interviewed Bob Kuban in August 2010.

#13
(*Billboard* Pop Charts)
"Everlasting Love" (1967)

ROBERT KNIGHT

R&B #14; *Cashbox* #11; Adult Contemporary:
Did not chart; British Charts #40

Of the 40 songs in this book, no song has been remade, or "covered," as often as "Everlasting Love," and no song has been a hit so many times when covered again—and again, and again. In fact, "Everlasting Love" is a piece of musical history. It has made the pop charts four times by four different artists in four different decades in the U.S., and it has made the U.K. charts eight times in five decades, with the English group Love Affair's 1967 cover going all the way to #1. As such, it is one of only two songs in U.S. chart history to make the Top 40 in the 1960s, '70s, '80s and '90s (the Temptations' "The Way You Do the Things You Do" is the other). It is the *only* song to make the Top 40 in England in the '60s, '70s, '80s, '90s *and* 2000s.

But with the popularity of all those later versions, some people forget that it all started way back in 1967 when a songwriter working in Nashville heard a man named Robert Knight fronting a band at a fraternity party. Impressed by his vocals, it wasn't long before the songwriter—with some help from some friends—convinced Knight to sing some songs for them. One of them, "Everlasting Love," they wrote just for Knight. It's quite possible that you know a version of the song by Carl Carlton or Gloria Estefan or Sandra or any one of a number of people better than you know Knight's original; but whichever version you prefer, there's no doubting the power of this excellent song and the version that briefly catapulted Knight to fame. Oddly enough, despite his success, his ultimate goal was to become a scientist, not a singer.

Robert Knight was born Robert Peebles in Franklin, Tennessee. When he was in his teens, he joined schoolmates Clarence Holland, Richard Sammonds, Neil Hooper and Kenneth Buttrick to form

Robert Knight's "Everlasting Love" was the tiny Rising Sons label's biggest hit before they folded circa 1970. Rising Sons artists Billy Swan ("I Can Help") and Bobby Russell ("Saturday Morning Confusion") went on to have big pop hits with other labels.

the Paramounts. They signed a contract with Dot Records and in 1961 released two singles, "Why Do You Have to Go" and "When You Dance." Neither of them charted nationally but, as Knight told me, "we made a little noise" with them and he felt they were off to a good start. However, their producer, Noel Ball, thought that a couple of changes were in order. Ball asked for a name change, from Robert Peebles to Robert Knight because, Knight said, "disc jockeys were always pronouncing my name wrong, saying 'Pebbles' and things like that." The other change Ball wanted was for Knight to go out as a solo act, and convinced him to do so. Ball felt that without the Paramounts, Knight would probably be more successful. Though technically still a member of the Paramounts, Knight recorded some solo sides on Dot. First up was 1961's "Dance Only with Me." Next was 1962's "Free Me," a cover of a Johnny Preston tune that had barely broken into the Hot 100 at #97. Neither one of Knight's records charted nationally, but they did get a fair amount of local airplay.

At this point, the group broke up and Knight stopped recording. Various sources have reported that because they voided their contract

#13. "Everlasting Love" (1967)

Robert Knight interacts with fans (courtesy Robert Knight).

with Dot, the group was banned from recording for the next four years. This struck me as an unprecedented move for a record company, one which would generate a lot of ill will. I asked Knight if this was true, and he said, "No, that's *not* true. I left the group, but I never stopped my career. I was enrolled at Tennessee State University, and just singing when I could. It wasn't like I was out looking for a recording contract during that period. I was focused on school." The itch to occasionally sing was still strong, so along with Danny Boone, Lehman Keith, Jack Jackson, Tommy Smith and Jim Tate, he formed the Fairlanes—not with the intention of recording, but simply "because I met these guys and we started singing. Everybody was singing on street corners then." The idea was to find a few local gigs, make a little extra money, and have some fun while getting his degree. As Knight and the band played dances and parties, Knight was "discovered" for the second time.

Mac Gayden told *Songwriter* magazine that he heard the Fairlanes at a fraternity house and asked Knight if they could do some recording together. He said Knight was not receptive to the idea, and didn't even want to talk to him. Having received his degree he started taking chemistry classes at Vanderbilt, and Knight didn't want to let his education take a back seat to the entertainment business. But Gayden convinced Knight to work with him through a connection with Noel Ball. "Buzz Cason had worked for Noel Ball, and Buzz was working with Mac Gayden. Cason was starting his new Rising Sons label and working on some material with Mac." Cason and Bobby Russell had started the Rising Sons label in 1967 by leveraging a distribution deal with Monument Records, but their first five singles had done nothing. They approached Knight about signing with them and put together a few tunes for him to record, one of which was "Everlasting Love." In his autobiography, Cason said the idea behind "Everlasting Love" (its name taken from Jeremiah 31.3: "Yea, I have loved you with an everlasting love") was to do a Motown-type song, and Cason and Gayden cobbled together some material they already had to complete it. It didn't get a lot of thought because it was going to be used as the flip side of a track called "The Weeper." (Ultimately, "The Weeper" was never released.) Knight didn't have access to the completed version of "Everlasting Love" until the actual recording session. He recalled:

> Buzz and Mac were country artists, and I was R&B, and so I had to make it more of an R&B song. It was a hard song to sing because at the time it was hard to sing a fast song slow. I didn't sing it the way they had written it. I made some changes to fit my voice, and I didn't do it note for note. They had the melody going too fast, and it was jamming, it wasn't doing right, it wasn't sounding right. So I started what you call a steady step. I start singing

a beat and a half: "hearts-go-a-stray," like that. It wasn't like that in the beginning, and I think that's what got "Everlasting Love" off the ground.

The song was recorded at Fred Foster Sound Studio in Nashville, with Gayden and Charlie McCoy on guitar, Kenny Buttrey on drums and Norbert Putnam on bass, with background vocals by Cason and Carol Montgomery. Knight wasn't convinced it was a great song, nor was anyone else. He thought it was supposed to be the B-side and he also thought the song that was eventually released as the record's B-side, "Somebody's Baby," was better: "[It] was a good R&B song, and I think I did a better job on it. [But] 'somebody turned the record over and started playing "Everlasting Love," and that's what we went with.'" As a result, the record that was twice destined to be a B-side became a classic.

For a struggling new label in need of a hit, "Everlasting Love" was a godsend. It went to #13 on the *Billboard* pop charts during its 12-week run and reached #14 on the R&B charts and #11 on the *Cashbox* charts. In a you-can't-make-this-stuff-up–type twist, the English group Love Affair, who had never had a chart record at that point, were given Knight's version by their managers in late 1967. They hurried to release it before Knight's recording was released in the U.K., and they saw their version go to #1 on the U.K. charts. When Knight's recording was finally released in England, it died at #40. I asked Knight: Given the many recordings of "Everlasting Love" done over the years, I asked Knight if there was one version he liked better than the others. "I liked the way I did it," he said.

Knight's U.S. follow-up on Rising Sons, "Blessed Are the Lonely," barely cracked the charts at #97, and two more Rising Sons releases did not chart at all. Knight jumped from Rising Sons to Elf, another label that Cason and Russell had founded in 1967 intending to make it more R&B–oriented. Elf's "Isn't It Lonely Together" charted nationally in the Hot 100, though it simply duplicated the marginal success of its predecessor on Rising Sons (#97). It was Knight's last chart record in this country. Rising Sons folded in 1970 after just 20 single releases, and Elf followed suit not long afterward.

In England in the late 1960s, Northern Soul began, a new movement which valued American soul music that had largely been overlooked. Though "Everlasting Love" had been a big hit in America, Knight's other songs had not, and his soulful R&B sound was exactly what English audiences were looking for. When re-released in 1973, his 1968 effort "Love on a Mountain Top" (which had done nothing in the U.S.) was a major U.K. hit, going into the Top Ten. That prompted a re-release of "Everlasting Love" in England. It had barely broken the Top 40 there in 1968; in 1974, it went to #19. As a result of the renewed interest in his music, Knight ended up with more Top 40 hits in the U.K. than in America.

By the mid–1970s, Knight had moved away from recording, but unlike many artists, he had a career and a college education to fall back on. He worked at Vanderbilt University as a chemical lab technician until he retired. He performed on and off afterwards and said he was "working on an album with Cason and Gayden now" when we talked, but he passed away at age 77 and apparently never finished the album.

I interviewed Robert Knight in 2012. He passed away in 2017.

#14
(*Billboard* Pop Charts)
"Mama Didn't Lie" (1963)
JAN BRADLEY
R&B: #8; *Cashbox*: #14; Adult Contemporary,
British Charts: Did not chart

I asked Jan Bradley if she missed the music business. She replied, Sometimes I do, sometimes I don't. It's always there, and because that's your first love, you start thinking about how much you enjoyed it. But overall, if I had to say one way or the other, I don't miss it. Music is moving, it's soothing, it means a lot to most people. So it still has a big place in my life—but I don't miss the business.

Bradley knew how to prioritize what was important in her life, so she simply walked away from the music industry when she felt it was the right time to do so. Before she did, she recorded some high-quality songs, including "Mama Didn't Lie," an R&B classic.

She was born Addie Bradley in Byhalia, Mississippi, and moved to the Chicago suburbs when she was about four years old. As a child, she sang in church. Her parents recognized her talent and saw to it that she had formal voice lessons. She sang at events such as weddings, and in high school she joined a group called the Passions. When they performed at a talent show, they attracted the attention of producer Don Talty. He liked the group, but felt that Bradley had more potential as a solo act than as a part of the group. He wanted to try and get her into the music business as soon as possible, but because she was a minor, her parents insisted she finish school before attempting to embark on a career in music.

Once Bradley she finished high school in 1961, Talty finally had the opportunity to work with her. Talty was friends with Phil Upchurch, who knew singer-songwriter Curtis Mayfield. Mayfield had recently written "Gypsy Woman" for his group the Impressions, and their recording reached #2 on the R&B charts. He had also written "He Will

Break Your Heart" for Jerry Butler and it hit #1 on the pop charts. Talty took Bradley to meet Mayfield. Mayfield later told Goldmine's Bob Pruter, "Sometimes as a singer it's not how well you sing, it's just that innocence or that certain something about an artist that makes the song appealing. Jan had that innocence in her voice." I mentioned this to Bradley and she said, "I really appreciate that, and that's where I was at that time. I was sincerely seeking to break into this business, and of course, being so young, I didn't know a lot about what was going on out there. I guess that's where that kind of came from—my demeanor at that time."

Impressed with the young Jan Bradley, Mayfield gave her a few songs to try out. The first Curtis Mayfield song she did was "We Girls," which was released on Talty's Formal records in 1962. Bradley said, "It got me started, got my name out there and got a lot of crossover airplay at that time." She added that Talty tried to get both United Artists and Columbia Records to release it nationally, but neither label believed in it enough to take a chance. The record did sell well regionally. Neither of her next two ("Whole Lot of Soul" and "Behind the Curtains") did

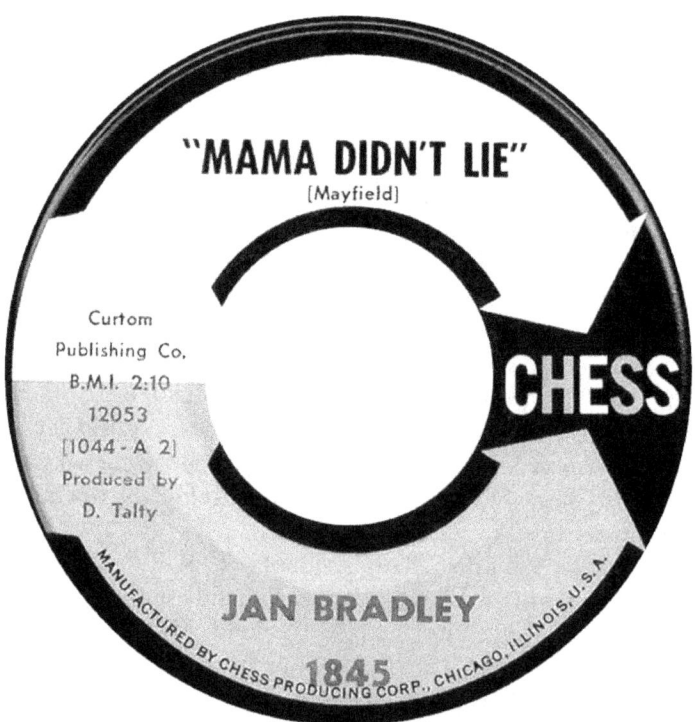

"Mama Didn't Lie" was Jan Bradley's only pop Top 40 hit.

much at all in limited release, even though the latter was also written by Mayfield.

"Next we recorded 'Mama Didn't Lie' in an effort to continue launching my career," Bradley said. This time, everything clicked. "Mama Didn't Lie" was written by Mayfield with her in mind. She recalled that he told her, "Okay, this is what I've got that I think will work for you. Take a listen."

Bradley continued, "I heard 'Mama Didn't Lie' and I thought, 'I love his style, I can do this, I really like this!'" Bradley noted that by design the electric bass guitar work by Freddy Young was featured to move the song along, yet not overpower her vocals. Bradley recorded her own back-up vocals by overdubbing, and she recalled that the song just "flowed." She said that that day in the studio they knew they had something special.

The record was first released on the Formal label in November 1962. "When [it] started getting airplay, it got a lot of interest from major record companies, and Chess pursued us too," she said. "We had tried to get them interested in 'We Girls' because they were a big label in Chicago, and they specialized in R&B. Like everybody else, they had passed on 'We Girls,' but they wanted 'Mama Didn't Lie' and took it." Owned by brothers Phil and Leonard Chess, Chess Records was the home label to artists such as Chuck Berry, Lee Andrews and the Hearts, the Moonglows and Howlin' Wolf. Chess knew how to promote an artist, and it led to Bradley's big break. "The national promotion they were able to provide made it a really big hit," she said. "Mama Didn't Lie" went all the way to #14 on the *Billboard* charts and #8 on the R&B charts in 1963. It seemed that with a big label behind them, Mayfield's writing and Bradley's voice were the magic combination for her success, and the future looked bright.

But sometimes talent alone isn't enough to overcome every obstacle, and in this case, bringing Chess to the table also meant bringing in their big-label mindset. "Curtis had his goals in mind for his songwriting and publishing career, and Chess wanted something he wasn't willing to part with: the rights to his music," Bradley said. Mayfield, very protective of the rights to his music, took a stand to protect his artistic output. As many artists would discover too late, the real way to make money in the business is by owning the rights to the songs you write. Mayfield would not give in, and with Bradley now under contract with Chess, "the label said, 'Jan can't do any more of your songs unless you're willing to give us publishing rights,' and he refused. That's what changed things for me, because his material was perfect for me. I loved working with him. He was a very kind person, very easy to work with, and I would have been able to do as many songs as Curtis would give me." But as a result of Chess' ultimatum, Bradley and Mayfield never worked together again.

For a long time after that, Bradley's releases just didn't catch on. "I was very sad and disillusioned when I could no longer record Curtis' material. Other writers tried to come up with songs for me, and they just didn't work out too well." Her next three singles did nothing, and Bradley said, "It was only when I decided that I would write a song for myself that I felt good about what I was doing again. I wrote 'I'm Over You,' and that gave me the momentum that I needed to keep going for a while. If you didn't have a record out there that people heard, they'd soon forget about you." "I'm Over You" went to #24 on the *Billboard* R&B charts and #93 on the Top 100 in 1965, and Bradley was on the charts again—just not on the lofty perch she'd attained with "Mama Didn't Lie."

Between 1964 and 1968, Bradley recorded eight singles for Chess, but other than the aforementioned "I'm Over You" nothing registered on the national charts. "Just a Summer Memory" (1966) and "It's Just Your Way" (1967) made the regional charts. Frustrated by the music business, and unhappy that no writer other than Mayfield seemed to understand the kind of music that was appropriate for her voice, Bradley was ready to call it quits—and did, in fact. "I had started college right after high school, but my musical career interests just took over. Then later on, after my musical career was at a point where disenchantment was setting in, I decided to finish college." She completed her undergraduate degree and earned her master's degree, then did social work. She got married and had two children. She was now a happy, successful woman who never looked back. Apparently that happiness and upbeat attitude have always been something identifiable in Jan Bradley, and perhaps that was what Mayfield saw when he first met the innocent 18-year-old just starting out in the music business.

I interviewed Jan Bradley in June 2010. As of this writing, she lives in Chicago.

#15
(*Cashbox* Charts)
"It's a Shame" (1970)
The Spinners (G.C. Cameron on lead)
Billboard Pop: #14; R&B: #4; Adult Contemporary: Did not chart; British Charts: #20

Today when most people think of the Spinners, they think of the Atlantic recording artists who had more than 25 pop and R&B hits: "The Rubberband Man," "Could It Be I'm Falling in Love," "I'll Be Around," "Then Came You" and many others. But before that group, there was a Spinners group in the 60s who were nowhere near as successful, that in almost a decade of recording didn't have a single record make the Top 20 of the pop charts—until 1970's "It's a Shame." The members of that group had day jobs, and often worked as chauffeurs for other recording artists. That group had their only chart hit with a lead singer who would not be with them on those Atlantic recordings, although some of the members of the early group would still be around and be fortunate enough to enjoy the success they found a few years later. For that reason, the Spinners are the only group who appear in this book twice: This is the story of that first pre–Atlantic group who had their one and only real hit on the Motown subsidiary label VIP Records in 1970.

The Spinners got their start in Ferndale, Michigan (near Detroit), in 1954 as the Domingoes. The group originally consisted of schoolmates Billy Henderson, Henry Fambrough, C.P. Spenser, Pervis Jackson and James Edwards. They all lived in the same neighborhood and they got their start like many R&B groups in the 1950s, metaphorically singing on street corners (in this case, it was actually on a basketball court). They decided to form a group with Spenser singing lead most of the time. After a few weeks, Edwards dropped out and in 1956 Bobbie Smith joined the group. A few years later, Smith suggested the group change their name to the Spinners, which was the name for the popular spinning hubcaps on the hot rods that teenagers drove at the time.

"It's a Shame" was the Spinners' only big hit in the ten years they were signed to Motown or one of its subsidiary labels. It was also the only Spinners hit with G.C. Cameron singing lead.

At this point, C.P. Spenser also decided to leave the group. The guys asked old bandmate James Edwards' brother, Chico Edwards, to join them. He did, briefly, but he had a steady job and because the band was still struggling to get bookings, he decided to keep his day job. The Spinners then added George Dixon.

By 1961, the group—now Billy Henderson, Henry Fambrough, Pervis Jackson, Bobbie Smith and George Dixon—at long last landed a recording contract, with Tri-Phi Records. Tri-Phi was a Chicago label formed that year by Gwen Gordy (songwriter sister of Motown founder Berry Gordy) and her husband Harvey Fuqua, former lead singer for the Moonglows of "Sincerely" and "The Ten Commandments of Love" fame. In 1961 and 1962, the Spinners released six singles on Tri-Phi, and one, "That's What Girls Are Made For," made the pop Top 40 (#27). It was their first real success, but once again it wasn't enough to keep the lineup stable. Dixon left to go into the ministry and Chico Edwards returned.

Other than one more low-charting single, further success eluded them on Tri-Phi. When the label was bought out by Berry Gordy's Motown Records, the group began a new phase of their career. "We went to Motown in 1964," Bobbie Smith told me. "We did some real good stuff at Motown but it just wasn't promoted. We were kind of an afterthought there." In the dozen Motown singles released before the Spinners' first release (1964's "Sweet Thing"), there were two #1 records (Mary Wells' "My Guy" and the Supremes' "Where Did Our Love Go") as well as the Four Tops' #11 debut, "Baby I Need Your Lovin'." Clearly, this was not Tri-Phi—this was the big leagues.

Right after the Supremes released their second of five straight #1 records (1964's "Baby Love"), the Spinners released "Sweet Thing," which did not chart. The group released their next single, 1965's "I'll Always Love You," which went to #35. It wasn't bad for a second release, but of the ten records Motown issued between the two Spinners releases, the Supremes hit with "Come See About Me" (#1), "Stop! In the Name of Love" (#1) and "Back in My Arms Again" (#1), and the Four Tops scored with "I Can't Help Myself" (#1). The bar was extremely high during this period at Motown, and a record that barely inched into the Top 40 wasn't going to put a group in the label's front ranks.

It would be a year before the group had another Motown single, which was "Truly Yours." It "bubbled under" the charts at #111 in 1966. It's a high-quality song, and it's hard to blame Smith for thinking they were getting a raw deal at Motown:

> We had songs like "Truly Yours." In Detroit, we knew a lot of the deejays, and we'd take our records out ourselves and do the promotion and interviews at the radio stations. They played "Truly Yours," and then all of a sudden they weren't playing it any more. We called and asked why and they said, "Marvin Gaye has a new song, and we got orders from Motown to take yours off and put his on." So they'd play Marvin's or whoever else's Motown was pushing and take ours off. I thought we did some great songs at Motown, as good as a lot that was being recorded there, but we seemed to get lost in the shuffle.

Other groups recording at the same time were facing similar problems. Label contemporaries Carolyn Crawford, Tony Martin, Choker Campbell & Band, Connie Haines and Bobby Breen were also having little success at the label, and it says a lot that the Spinners' "I'll Always Love You" at #35 was the highest charter of the bunch. It didn't seem that Motown had anything against the Spinners; it was just that you had a few releases to prove your worth, and if they weren't hits, you served out your contract and that was that.

Smith said another reason they may have had trouble gaining ground at Motown was due to his lead vocals. "I always did the leads, but I had a soft, smooth voice, and at Motown they seemed to go for a raspier voice, like David Ruffin of the Temptations on 'Ain't Too Proud to Beg' or Levi Stubbs on the Four Tops' 'Bernadette.' My voice was soft and smooth, and I started to feel like I wasn't strong enough as we kept getting overlooked." The lack of success began to wear on the group. Chico Edwards had a family and decided to leave the group again (and for the last time) in 1967 to work in the roofing business.

"That's when we brought G.C. Cameron in," Smith said. "He had the ability to sing Motown style." Vietnam veteran George Curtis Cameron could not only sing "Motown style," but it's often been said he had six different voices that covered a very wide range. When Cameron joined, he did indeed bring a different sound to the Spinners, but he was now part of a group where things were at an all-time low in terms of morale. They were largely underutilized at Motown and frequently even served as chaperones and chauffeurs for other Motown acts. Cameron told me, "Yes, a lot of the guys were working, doing odd jobs for different acts at Motown. I was fortunate that I never had to do it, but some of the other guys in the group would sometimes go and cart other artists back and forth and drive the limo. But you know, it was making a living ... it was surviving." The failure of singles released on Motown in 1968 and 1969 didn't help matters, and eventually the Spinners were relegated to the Motown subsidiary label VIP. It must have felt like the group was being sent down to the minors to play out the remainder of their contract.

But in 1970, the group's fortunes changed at long last. Cameron told me,

> After I signed with Motown and joined the group, Stevie Wonder and I became very good friends. We'd hang out together, and he knew that because I'd been thrown in the midst of all these great Motown singers like Marvin Gaye, David Ruffin, Levi Stubbs and Diana Ross, I needed to catch up. So one night we were out and he told me, "I wrote a song for you." I asked him what it was, and he had me take him to his house and he started playing this song on his electric piano. The song was "It's a Shame."

After Wonder played the song for Cameron, "the next day Stevie went in and recorded the instrumental track and three or four days later I went into the studio with the rest of the Spinners to record the vocal track." Cameron sang both leads on the song: He explained, "That means that I not only sang the part when it says 'It's a shame, the way you mess around with your man,' but the higher chorus when it says 'Why do you use me, try to confuse me?' and so on. We did the song in one take, and Stevie and everyone else was really excited." But even Cameron was unprepared for the song's success. "I didn't think much of anything

The Spinners in the mid–1960s: from left to right, Henry Fambrough, Bobbie Smith, Chico Edwards, Pervis Jackson and Billy Henderson (courtesy Bobbie Smith).

about 'It's a Shame' being special when it came out. There was too much music, too many hits. I felt like anything coming out of Motown had the chance to be a hit, but I wasn't paying any particular attention to it. I just hoped at the time that we would have the opportunity to have a hit record like so many of the great acts at Motown."

"It's a Shame" was that hit. It raced to #14 on the *Billboard* pop charts, #15 on *Cashbox* and #4 on the R&B charts, indicating the Spinners' potential. And as the first song Wonder produced for another group, it was also an indication of his marketability as more than just a singer. But more than anything else, "It's a Shame" was the first portent of the mainstream popularity that the group would soon enjoy.

But that popularity didn't come via Motown, VIP or any other Motown subsidiary label. Their contract at Motown was up, and after one final single ("We'll Have It Made") was released and did nothing, the Spinners left Motown. For his part, Cameron had been hired by Motown and so he chose to stay with the label while the others in the group left. (Their story continues in Chapter 32 of this book.)

The Spinners signed with Atlantic, where they notched 27 subsequent Top 100 hits. Cameron stayed at Motown for a while and had a solid career there and as an independent artist. He got back with the Spinners in the early 2000s, was with the Temptations a while, and he's still performing as a solo artist today. Over time, he has come to see that "It's a Shame" is a really special song. "Today they won't let me perform anywhere unless I sing that song, and I feel blessed to have it. It never gets old, it never sounds tired. It always sounds like the day we recorded it. Whenever you hear it on the radio it sounds like it's a new record. It's one of a kind."

I interviewed Bobbie Smith and G.C. Cameron in 2011. Smith passed away in 2013.

#16
(R&B Charts)
"Oh How Happy" (1966)

SHADES OF BLUE

Billboard Pop: #12; *Cashbox*: #13; Adult Contemporary, British Charts: Did not chart

---

The story behind Shades of Blue's biggest hit seems like a script for a Hollywood movie.

Some high school guys get together and form a singing group, then some members leave while replacements join. They sign with a record label, have a big hit, tour behind the record, but that second smash hit never follows. The record company uses them for a while but never invests much in them, and when it's clear the second big hit isn't coming, the record company moves on. The group, frustrated and angry, falls apart, to some degree thinking about what might have been if things had played out just a little differently. It does sound a lot like a movie, and in fact a film such as 1996's *That Thing You Do!* has a nearly identical plot. But the Shades of Blue story begins in 1966, not 1996, and while it involves names as familiar as Edwin Starr and Motown, it sadly ends in a way similar to that movie.

Hailing from the Detroit area, Shades of Blue (Dan Guise, Bob Kerr, Ernie Dernai and Nick Marinelli) got their start in high school as the Domingos. They played mainly local gigs, singing doo-wop and R&B songs and hoping to land a recording contract. Soon after high school, Guise left the group, but a replacement was at hand. Nick Marinelli said, "We played a lot of clubs back then like the Rooster Tail, the Twenty Grand and the Grande Room. We'd play at various clubs while we were out there banging around, and Linda [Allen] showed some interest in singing. She started dating Bobby, and one thing led to another. She was singing in the choir at church, had a good voice, knew music, so it just kind of fell into place."

With this new member, the Domingos continued to search for

that elusive recording contract. They were friends with some members of the Reflections, who had gone to #6 on the charts with 1964's "Just Like Romeo and Juliet" on the Golden World label. "They lived just a few blocks from us and led us over to Golden World to do a few demos," Marinelli revealed. The Reflections recommended them to Golden World owner Ed Wingate; he liked their sound but didn't sign them because, he said, he didn't want to sign another white vocal group. Then, according to Marinelli, their recordings caught the ear of John Rhys, "an independent producer working out of Golden World who'd been a producer in New York and was working at Motown some, and who had also worked with the Newbeats" (of "Bread and Butter" fame).

Rhys took an interest in the group, but "he said the name of the group wasn't going to cut it, that it sounded too much like Dominoes. So we all hashed out possible names, and being that we were a blue-eyed soul group, we wanted 'blues' in our name. So we settled on Shades of Blue."

With a new name, they needed a song to kick start a recording career. Fate smiled on them again when they crossed paths with

Although the label gave full writing credit for "Oh How Happy" to Edwin Starr, the members of Shades of Blue helped write the song.

a songwriter-performer Edwin Starr. "While we were working doing back-up vocals and demos at Golden World, Edwin Starr was there," Marinelli said. "He heard us sing and liked our sound. Well, he had an idea for a song he hadn't finished called 'Oh How Happy.' We all sat down together and finished it, and we even contributed some of the wording and the chorus."

But the Shades of Blue made a critical mistake at this point: They assumed that the musicians and writers were one big happy family and they'd get their due as co-writers of the song. "But we never got co-writing credit because at the time we were young and stupid and didn't know that we could have and should have," Marinelli said. Maybe it wouldn't have made a difference in one case out of 100, but if the one case results in a hit, it can come back to haunt you. That was the case with "Oh How Happy."

Despite the fact that they didn't secure a writing co-credit, they did get the sound down just right in the studio when they recorded the song in the late fall of 1965. Rhys took the record to Harry Balk at Impact Records, who signed the group. But the record's release, and success, took the group by surprise. Marinelli:

> We had a lot of songs we had recorded already in the can. You never know what the record company is going to release at a certain time, so we kind of went on about our business—we were still in college at the time. We were out one evening with some girls, and "Oh How Happy" came on the radio on a local station. We're in the car, and we said, "That's our song!" We were surprised, so we called the record company, who said they had released it and were starting to push on it. Everything just took off.

The record was released in March 1966 and almost immediately shot to #1 in several local markets. Eventually it ascended the national charts as well, going to #12 on the pop charts and #16 on the R&B charts. Predictably, the group's fortunes changed overnight. "We wanted to at least finish that year of college, but as soon as we were out of school we hit the road. We were out on the road for about a year; we hardly had a chance to take a breath." The group went on a national tour and appeared on *Where the Action Is* and several other TV series. Expectations were high for their follow-up single.

That's when things started to go wrong, said Marinelli. "We had a battle as to what we wanted to release as our second song, and the biggest problem was that 'Lonely Summer' was released late in August, but it should have been released in June right as 'Oh How Happy' was staring to move back down the charts. I think it was a bad decision to release it so late, but like a lot of groups, we didn't have much input back then." "Lonely Summer," also written by Starr, lacked the cohesive sound of

"Oh How Happy" and peaked at #72. Another release, 1966's "Happiness," peaked at #78. These songs didn't do as well as "Oh How Happy" but they all charted, and considering that they released an album in September 1966, it had been a very successful year.

Impact pushed the group to tour behind the record, and they traveled with Dick Clark's Caravan of Stars. Their "tourmates" included B.J. Thomas, the Rascals, Steve Alaimo, the Critters and the Knickerbockers. According to Marinelli, "We got along really well with the Rascals because were both into the R&B sound."

But touring wasn't exactly a luxury, as they often only booked hotel rooms every other night, and spent most of their time traveling. Most performers—including the Shades of Blue members—did not enjoy touring like that, singing two or three songs and averaging a show a day for a month. (Marinelli actually kind of enjoyed it, and liked watching other groups perform.) But success wasn't quite the tangible form it should have. Marinelli said,

> At Impact, we were the big moneymaker in the company at the time, and of course they started seeing residuals coming in. But we were out on the Dick Clark tour, and we were hearing the other artists talking about the royalty checks they were getting, and we're going, "Wait a second, we haven't gotten any royalty checks." Though we were making money on the road, the company was sucking up our royalties and using them to promote other Impact artists like Mitch Ryder and the Detroit Wheels and the Volumes. They were using our income to produce *them*.

That didn't make for a good marriage between Shades of Blue and the label, and after a couple more singles that weren't well-promoted, the group sensed that their careers were at a standstill. They felt that Harry Balk was lining his own pockets. They later learned that Del Shannon and Johnny and the Hurricanes had had a similar experience with Balk, but by then it was too late.

Then Motown came along, and the group hoped that maybe they'd finally get their due. Marinelli revealed, "Motown was like any other big corporation, and they'd buy up record companies, take the stable and get rid of the competition." After Motown bought out Impact, "they kept booking us in shows, [but] they weren't really interested in developing anything new for us or promoting us as a group. After Motown took over in late '67, we saw the handwriting on the wall."

But it wasn't just Motown; music was changing too. By the late '60s, the great harmonizing and vocals that had been a mainstay of the group's repertoire were not as fashionable as they once had been, "and that's when we decided to hang it up." They called it quits as performers about 1970. They reunited for a while in the mid–'70s and recorded

Shades of Blue: from left to right, Nick Marinelli, Ernie Dernai, Linda Allen and Bob Kerr (courtesy Nick Marinelli).

some new songs that have never been released. "We cut a few things, but the others, their hearts weren't in it," Marinelli said. "It wasn't meant to be." The group broke up again, and the other original members got out of show business.

Marinelli did television production work, and eventually went back into the music by hooking up with a group called the Valadiers, whose record "Greetings (This Is Uncle Sam)" had reached #89 on the pop charts in 1961. (It was later recorded by the Isley Brothers and the Monitors.) Marinelli recalled:

> They'd lost their lead singer to the Reflections and were looking for another. They already had some shows booked, so I decided to join them. They brought me in, and we did a show in Wilmington, Delaware, and I sang "Oh How Happy." Five thousand people stood up on their feet. Afterwards, the guys said, "You know what? You've obviously got a lot bigger hit than we do. How about if we work with you as the Shades of Blue?" We did. I worked with them for six years before deciding to go out on my own.

Some of the Valadiers who sang as Shades of Blue after Marinelli joined the group, continued to sing under that name (and still do) even after Marinelli left to pursue other opportunities. Marinelli still does other things; when I interviewed him, he was working on a new record and writing some new songs. As for "Oh How Happy," he said he "really appreciates" that people still like the record. He knows that he helped create a timeless hit, even if everything didn't go as planned in terms of the group's longevity.

I interviewed Nick Marinelli in February 2012. As of this writing he is still active but performs only occasionally.

#17
(R&B Charts)

"Private Number" (1968)
Judy Clay and William Bell

Billboard Pop: #75; *Cashbox*: #84; Adult Contemporary: Did not chart; British Charts: #8

Judy Clay and William Bell were born in the adjoining states of North Carolina and Tennessee, and in many ways their early lives followed a somewhat similar trajectory. Career-wise, however, as a solo artist Clay really never had much success, and never had a Top 40 hit on any chart. Bell, on the other hand, was immensely successful on his own, with almost a dozen R&B solo chart hits, led by his #1 R&B and Top Ten pop hit "Tryin' to Love Two" (1977). The circumstances that brought these two together in the '60s, and how they created a smash hit with "Private Number," is a tale as odd as the fact that their "duet" was recorded while the pair was separated by more than a thousand miles.

William Yarborough was born in Memphis, Tennessee; he later took the stage name William Bell to honor his grandmother, whose first name was Belle. He grew up listening to blues and early R&B; his favorite singers were solo artists Nat King Cole and Sam Cooke. The church was important in his life, and when he was about seven, he started singing in the choir. In just a few years he was doing solos in church, and by the time he was ten he had written his first song, "Alone on a Rainy Night." A friend entered him into the Mid–South Talent Contest and he won first prize: $500 and a trip to Chicago to sing with the Red Saunders Band. Saunders recommended Bell to a man named Phineas Newborn, who had a band in Memphis. For the next few years, Bell sang with Newborn's band on weekends. He also started his own group, the Del-Rios, and when he was 14 they recorded "Alone on a Rainy Night" on Meteor Records. Though that song was not a hit, Bell and the Del-Rios got work at Satellite Records (which would soon become Stax), singing back-up

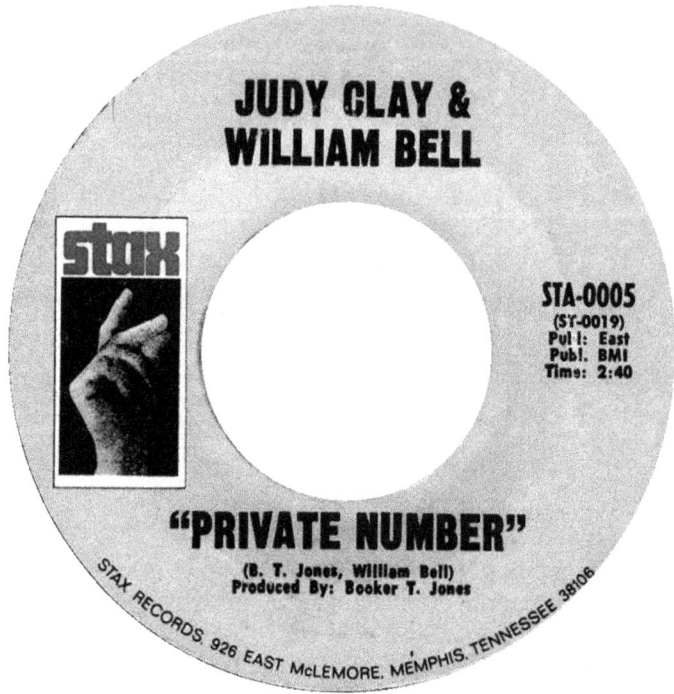

The Judy Clay–William Bell duet "Private Number" was a big R&B hit for Stax in 1968. The artists were not in the studio together for the recording.

on Carla Thomas' "Gee Whiz," which eventually went Top Ten on the Atlantic label in 1961.

Bell first went to Stax as a songwriter, but by the early '60s he had signed with Stax as singer as well, becoming the first male solo artist to sign with the label. He scored a minor hit with a song he had written, "You Don't Miss Your Water," which reached #95 on the *Billboard Hot 100*. It was the beginning of a long, productive relationship: Bell was soon regarded as one of the label's top draws and he produced a number of hits.

Just as it seemed as though Bell was about to make it big, Uncle Sam came calling: He was drafted to serve in the Army from 1962 to 1966. Stax had Bell record a number of sides while he was home on leave, but none of the six singles the label released between 1963 and 1965 charted. As soon as he was out of the Army, a couple of singles made the Top 40 on the R&B charts. Then he released "Everybody Loves a Winner," which crossed over to the pop charts in 1967. It was also included in his 1967 album *The Soul of a Bell*. Additionally, Bell wrote material for other artists, including "Born Under a Bad Sign" for Albert

#17. "Private Number" (1968)

King, which made the R&B charts in 1967. But as 1967 drew to a close, Bell's good friend Otis Redding died in a plane crash, on a flight that Bell himself likely would have been on had his own Chicago concert not been cancelled. He wrote "A Tribute to a King" with Booker T. Jones. In April 1968, his homage to Redding became his highest charting record to that point.

Judy Clay's career had a trajectory that paralleled Bell's. Born Judy Guions, she was raised by her grandmother in Fayetteville, North Carolina, before she moved to New York in the early 1950s. Like Bell, she did most of her early singing in the church. Through singing, she met the gospel group the Drinkard Singers. She started singing with the group when she was about 14. At various times, the group included Emily "Cissy" Drinkard (aka Cissy Houston—Whitney Houston's mother) and Dionne and Delia Warrick (later known as Dionne Warwick and Dee Dee Warwick). Though the group was successful, Clay left the Drinkard Singers in 1960 and moved from label to label (including stints at Ember, Scepter and one recording with Stax) without ever having any real chart success. But once she teamed with Billy Vera, her music at last started to sell. "Storybook Children" (1967) went to #54 on the pop charts and #20 on the R&B charts, and the duo's 1968 release "Country Girl, City Man" went to #36 on the pop charts and #41 on the R&B charts. It was when Clay went to Memphis to work on a new album that everything came together at last.

As Bell and Clay rolled into 1968, both were coming off some success but it might also be said that both needed a big hit. Bell told me,

> "Private Number" was a song that had been kicking around in my head for a while, and I happened to be in the studio when Judy was doing a session and she didn't have enough material. Her producer asked me if I had anything that she could record. Well, this song came to mind, but I only had one verse and a chorus written. I told him I'd finish it and have it ready the next day, and Judy could record it then.

Clay was signed to Atlantic Records at the time, but because Stax and Atlantic were in the middle of a contract under which Atlantic artists were able to record at the Stax studios with Stax's far superior musicians, writers and producers, Clay was recording in Memphis that week. Bell said,

> As luck would have it, she had to leave the next morning and go back to New York for some business. So Booker [T. Jones, of Booker T. & the MG's] and I finished up the song that night and went back into the studio and did a demo of it. On that, I sang the entire song. We sent the tapes to New York for Judy to hear so she could learn the song and then put her voice on the tapes.

When the tapes arrived at Atlantic Studios in New York, "somebody—it might have been Jerry Wexler—had the bright idea that this would be a great duet," Bell said. "They kept my verse and chorus and they put Judy on the second verse and on the choruses singing harmony with me." The end result was a polished hit with two mature voices, and it sounded as if Clay and Bell were singing the heartfelt vocals to one another. Bell was impressed. "It turned out great and was a monumental hit for us, and it was one of the first Stax crossover pop hits." "Private Number" was a modest hit on the pop charts, peaking at #75, but it was bigger on the R&B charts, rising to #17. It was even more successful overseas, going all the way to #8 in the U.K. Bell thinks it's funny that the song was so big because the two of them were never together in the studio singing, even though it sounds like they were. "We did eventually get a chance to perform it together three or four times live on stage but never in the studio," Bell said.

As is often the case with duets by artists who don't normally record together, the chances of lightning striking twice were slim. That was the case with Clay and Bell. They went on to do one more duet for Stax, 1968's "My Baby Specializes," but it was much less successful and only made the R&B charts. Clay returned to Atlantic for another duet with Billy Vera and had a few solo efforts during the next decade. After 1970's "Greatest Love," which reached #45 on the R&B charts, she was dropped by Atlantic. She went on to a career largely as a back-up singer, working with Ray Charles, Wilson Pickett, Booker T. & the MG's, Donny Hathaway, Patti LaBelle and others. After surgery for a brain tumor in 1979, she moved back to North Carolina, where she remained until she passed away in 2001.

For Bell, the rest of 1968 brought even more success. A song he wrote for himself and recorded in 1968, "I Forgot to Be Your Lover," broke into the Top Ten on the R&B charts. (It was recorded by Billy Idol in 1986 as "To Be a Lover" and went to the #6 position on the pop charts.) At that point, Bell was riding a string of four consecutive Top 20 R&B hits.

But Stax was in trouble. After the death of Redding, their biggest star, the label lost its distribution deal with Atlantic Records in 1968 and started to overextend itself and make some poor financial decisions. "The downfall of Stax was kind of systematic deflation of the label by the powers that be," Bell told me.

> There was money borrowed, and when you say you'll release 50,000 records for a new William Bell single, and then once you get into that borrowed money you only release 5000 records instead, automatically your earning potential has diminished. A lot of people don't realize it, but we had two

or three hit records on the charts when Stax folded. But the thing about it was that we weren't selling as many records. [The public] loved the artists and loved the production and everything, but we weren't competitive in the market. We were forced out of the business because we had to make monthly payments on these huge loans, and with the diminishing numbers of pressed products, if it wasn't pressed, we couldn't sell it, so we were forced to file bankruptcy.

Bell left Stax in 1974. "I'd gone to Stax as a young kid and never thought that would end. But when that was over, I decided I wasn't going to record any more and I was going to do something else." But he was soon contacted by his old friend Charles Fach, who was now with Mercury. "Mercury wasn't known for a lot of R&B products, but Charlie had his finger on the pulse of R&B and he talked me into going back into recording." Bell's first release for his new label, a song he'd co-written, was the biggest of his career. "Tryin' to Love Two" peaked at #10 on the pop charts and #1 on the R&B charts and sold a million copies. He followed this with "Coming Back for More" which, while not a huge hit, did make the R&B charts. Up next was what would be his third—and final— Mercury release, "Easy Comin' Out (Hard Goin' In)."

"After the two previous singles, Mercury was pressing me for a new record, and I sat down over a period of about three months and wrote a lot of songs, and this was the first of those." "Easy Comin' Out" made the Top 40 on the R&B charts. It might have done better, but some corporate upheaval at Mercury hurt the record's promotion. Charles Fach left, and Bell said that he would be leaving as well. After that, it was obvious to him that Mercury quit pushing "Easy Comin' Out," even as it was moving up the charts. "It probably could have been bigger, and I was disappointed by its performance—it never got promoted the way 'Tryin to Love Two' did. I understood their position, though.

William Bell (courtesy William Bell)

They knew I wasn't going to stay on as one of their artists, so why should they promote the record?" Mercury did hold him to a contractual agreement that said he owed them one more album, which he recorded. It was never released. In any event, Bell was done with Mercury: "I got my release after delivering the album."

Bell continued to record, and his songs occasionally charted right up until the mid–1990s. He founded his own record company, Wilbe, in 1985. He eventually received the Rhythm & Blues Foundation's R&B Pioneer Award. Today he considers "Private Number" one of the highlights of his career.

I interviewed William Bell in 2011. As of this writing, he is still performing.

#18
(Cashbox Charts)

"Double Shot (of My Baby's Love)" (1966)

The Swingin' Medallions

Billboard Pop: #17; R&B, Adult Contemporary, British Charts: Did not chart

---

In a 1993 column, writer Lewis Grizzard referred to "Double Shot (of My Baby's Love)" as a one-of-a-kind song, noting, "Even today, when I hear [it], it makes me want to stand outside in the hot sun with a milkshake cup full of beer in one hand and a slightly drenched 19-year-old coed in the other." Grizzard had attended the University of Georgia and was in a fraternity, and amongst the Southern college party crowd, there's no question that "Double Shot (of My Baby's Love)" was somewhat of an anthem. Anyone who was fortunate enough to have lived at a time when they might have actually played the song on the radio, in clubs and at parties, knows the full impact of Grizzard's words, but even today the song is still fairly well known as it epitomizes the pleasures of simpler times. As Grizzard noted, absolutely nothing says good music and good times like the Swingin' Medallions singing "Double Shot (of My Baby's Love)."

The group known as the Medallions got together in 1962 at Lander College in Greenwood, South Carolina. Group founder John McElrath and his friends formed the band to make a little extra money to help pay for school. Their act was based in rhythm and blues, and like many local bands during the '60s, they made their money lining up gigs in the area. Though the membership fluctuated their first few years, they stayed based in Greenwood. When school wasn't in session they went where the gigs took them. "We spent two or three summers in Panama Beach, Florida, early in our career," McElrath told me. "That was before 'Double Shot.' Panama Beach was sort of our base of operations during the summer, even though most of the guys were all in college at Lander

The version of "Double Shot (of My Baby's Love)" released by the Mercury subsidiary Smash Records. Smash's stable of artists at the time included Roger Miller, James Brown, the Walker Brothers and the Left Banke.

or the University of South Carolina." John Townsend, who was part of a band called the Magnificent Seven, recalled, "There was a club called Old Hickory where the Medallions were the house band, and it was a hive of activity every night, especially during the summer."

After a few years in the clubs and on the campus party circuit, McElrath and his group decided they wanted to record "Double Shot," a huge regional hit that had been originally recorded by Dick Holler and the Holidays. "I had heard it played in Columbia at USC," McElrath recalled. "It was a local hit on the stations there and when we put our band together, we started to play it." But the song the Medallions played and made famous was not exactly the same song that Dick Holler and the Holidays played.

Holler had started a band while a student at LSU in the 1950s, and eventually that band—first called the Dixie Cats, then Dick Holler and the Carousel Rockets, then just the Rockets, before becoming the Holidays—based themselves in Columbia, South Carolina. In a sense, they were the Swingin' Medallions before there was a Swingin' Medallions, a

#18. "Double Shot (of My Baby's Love)" (1966)

party band playing the college circuit. Though Holler himself was quite a songwriter, he did not write "Double Shot (of My Baby's Love)." Holidays band members Don Smith and Cyril Vetter wrote it; at first, it was a slower-paced, piano-driven song. The Holidays had already released singles on the Ace, Herald and Comet labels, and as their fourth release and second on Comet in 1963, "Double Shot (of My Baby's Love)" got some regional play but didn't make an imprint on the national charts. The Swingin' Medallions (they added the "Swingin'" moniker to the Medallions name around 1965) saw the potential, however, and decided to make it their own. They turned it into more of a party tune. Before they ever recorded it, they played it at their gigs. The Swingin' Medallions' version soon became a favorite in the clubs and at college parties across the South.

"We were with Bill Lowery talent agency," McElrath said. "They had a producer and studio and everything in Atlanta, and they kept trying to have us record it there." In a classic case of micromanagement where none was needed, they tried to get the group to record it "with different arrangements and in different ways with horns and so forth that didn't fit the song. We told them we just wanted to play it live like we did at shows." McElrath said he and the group—now consisting of McElrath, Carroll Bledsoe, Steve Caldwell, Jim Doares, Brent Forston, Charlie Webber, Jimmy Perkins and Joe Morris—"decided to just take off and do it on our own, and we went to Arthur Smith Studios in Charlotte. North Carolina. We recorded 'Double Shot' the way we wanted to do it." McElrath apparently came up with the idea of the organ intro, and so they "did it with keyboards. We had horns in the band too but we didn't want to use horns on it." For background, "we

Dick Holler and the Holidays released several singles, including 1964's "Double Shot (of My Baby's Love)." Holler also wrote "Snoopy vs. the Red Baron" (the Royal Guardsmen, #2 in 1966) and "Abraham, Martin and John" (Dion, #4 in 1968).

actually pulled in people off the street and had a big crowd in the studio to make background noise, party noise, and that party atmosphere gave us the sound we were looking for. That's how and why it became a hit."

When the group had it down the way they wanted it, they released it on their own 4 Sale label to sell at their gigs. When they quickly sold out, another run was issued. Some copies found their way into the hands of deejays and soon the record really started to take off. As Southern radio stations played the song, demand for copies of the record rose.

The song came to the attention of the Mercury subsidiary Smash Records, whose stable of artists around that time included Roger Miller, James Brown, the Walker Brothers and the Left Banke. The Smash people liked what they heard, but before distributing the record nationally they wanted the song altered a bit because they were worried about offending people who might not like the references to alcohol. McElrath told me, "They didn't like some lines, like 'Woke up this morning, my head hurt so bad/ The worst hangover that I ever had.' They made us redo that line in order to clear the record to be played in certain areas. They made us change it to 'worst morning after that I ever had'—which was stupid, I thought. Just the word 'hangover' came out, really." The record became a million-seller, going all the way to #17 on the *Billboard* pop charts and #18 on *Cashbox*. McElrath thought that it might have done even better if hadn't already been on the air and available regionally for so long in the South before Smash picked it up. "It had already started down the local charts in the South before it even got played up North and out West and became a hit." While that ultimately may have hurt sales, "it did help us as far as our touring went because we got to tour in different cities when the song was popular and being played on the air."

Success was good to the group, and they traveled the country playing their big hit. In the Los Angeles market, where the

The 45 version of "Double Shot" pressed by the 4 Sale label.

record hit #1, they were asked to play at Frank Sinatra's daughter Tina's Sweet 16 party, and there they met such luminaries as Sammy Davis Jr., Joey Bishop, Dean Martin and Sinatra himself. Touring was great and they played to packed venues everywhere. Soon the label wanted another release and the song chosen was "She Drives Me Out of My Mind." McElrath told me, "Freddie Weller, a friend of ours who was on the staff at Bill Lowery talent, wrote the song." Weller co-wrote Tommy Roe's "Dizzy," "Jam Up and Jelly Tight" and "Jack and Jill," and later played with Paul Revere and the Raiders and recorded as a solo country act. He wrote "She Drives Me Out of My Mind" like the label wanted, and what the label wanted was a song "as close to 'Double Shot' as we could make it. We used a lot of the same sounds that we had in 'Double Shot,' the party atmosphere and everything." Just as Jay and the Techniques learned after the success of "Apples, Peaches, Pumpkin Pie" and "Keep the Ball Rollin'," Smash had a tendency to make artists repeatedly record songs similar to their big hits. In this case, the soundalike song "did pretty good but it wasn't as big a hit as 'Double Shot' by any means" said McElrath. The record stalled at #71 on the *Billboard* pop charts.

The group released an album that year. In addition to "Double Shot" and "She Drives Me Out of My Mind," it contained mainly

The Swingin' Medallions: from left to right, Joe Morris, Brent Fortsen, Fred Pugh, John McElrath, Carroll Bledsoe, Steve Caldwell, Perrin Gleaton and Rick Godwin (courtesy John McElrath).

party-time cover tunes such as "Louie, Louie," "Wooly Bully," "Barefootin'" and "Hang on Sloopy." They had several more releases on Smash in 1966 and 1967 but before long the group members decided they needed to finish college, and they did so. McElrath and his sons kept various incarnations of the group playing for almost 50 years, and over time he made sure the band maintained a clean-cut image and had a reputation as a good-time party band.

Though McElrath has passed away, the Swingin' Medallions continue to wow crowds today, often joined onstage by former members. McElrath summed up the group's experience by saying, "We had a lot of fun, but I think we just lucked into it." Certainly there was a lot more than luck involved; perhaps Lewis Grizzard put it best when he wrote: "I have asked often what, if anything, endures? Well, the Swingin' Medallions and their kind of music—my generation's music—has." When it comes to the Swingin' Medallions' "Double Shot (of My Baby's Love)," it's hard to disagree.

I interviewed John McElrath in 2010; he passed away in 2018.

#19
(R&B Charts)
"The Oogum Boogum Song" (1967)

BRENTON WOOD

Billboard Pop: #34; *Cashbox*: #43;
Adult Contemporary, British Charts: Did not chart

What does a singer-songwriter do when he doesn't like the song his label gives him to record? Maybe a big recording star digs in his heels and refuses to do it, and if he's lucky, maybe the label will change its mind. But what if you have never had a chart record, and in fact were lucky to sign a contract with an up-and-coming company after a patchwork of failed recordings on a string of fly-by-night labels? Common sense says you don't buck the system. But Brenton Wood had a unique way of dealing with the problem of the song he didn't like. He rewrote the lyrics, changed the feel of the song, and even gave it a new name. By the time he was finished with 1967's "The Oogum Boogum Song," he had a song he really liked, and better yet, a song the label and audiences really liked too.

Alfred Jesse Smith was born in 1941 in Shreveport, Louisiana; when he was a child, the family moved to San Pedro, California. As a child, his interest in music started to develop, and he started playing piano when he was around seven years old. He said he watched people play and then tried it himself, sounding out the melodies because he couldn't read music. Yet even when he was young, he wanted to play Top 40–type pop and R&B, rather than strictly the blues. His earliest influence was Nat King Cole, then Jesse Belvin, and as a teenager, Sam Cooke. He started writing songs by the time he was 10 or 11, but he admitted that it wasn't until he had a girlfriend that his songwriting really started to improve.

His family moved to Compton and he finished high school there, and then attended Compton Junior College. By this point he was interested in a music career. His singing had developed to the point that he was performing as a member of the Dootones under his real name. He soon changed his name to Brenton Wood (he liked the sound of the name Brentwood, an area of California) and sang under that name for the first time as a member of his group the Quotations and next as a member of Little Freddy & the Rockets; they recorded "All My Love" on the Chief label in 1958. Over the next few years, he cut a number of singles on different labels: "The Kangaroo" (1960) on the First President label, "Mr. Schemer" (1963) on the Wand label, and "Good Lovin'" (1966) on the Brent label. Perhaps as a sign of how his career was going, his name was misspelled as "Breton Wood" on some of the Brent pressings.

But none of this was really paying the bills. After considering working as an auto mechanic, he took a job as a crane operator at an aluminum factory. He was still writing songs, although after a while he really began having doubts about continuing to pursue music because he hadn't had a hit and the aluminum factory was good-paying, steady work. In somewhat of a last-ditch effort, he signed with the Hollywood-based Double Shot Records in 1967.

That last-ditch effort paid off big-time. One of the songs the label suggested he record was "The Oogum Boogum Song," although it took

"The Oogum Boogum Song" was one of the first dozen releases for the Double Shot label. It was the label's second Top 40 pop hit; the Count Five's "Psychotic Reaction" had hit #5 eight months earlier.

#19. "The Oogum Boogum Song" (1967)

some work to get it where it ended up. Wood said that initially the song had a very different sound and feel—and didn't have the "Oogum Boogum" hook: "The record company gave me a song one day called 'Casting My Spell on You.' I didn't like it very much, so I took the song and rewrote it and added the hook 'oogum boogum,' which is another word for abracadabra. I listened to it and basically made it more cheerful than it was, and added the things about fashion. It was a song that I really enjoyed writing." He wrote it during his lunch breaks at the factory. "It took me six weeks, but I laughed all through it. It was a joy."

The song is notable for a couple of reasons. It often references '60s fashion, which Wood did by design. He said wanted to write a song about the things you saw on the street every day, things that young people could relate to, and as a result, the lyrics reference high-heeled boots, a hip-hugger suit, "that cute miniskirt," "your brother's sloppy shirt," "big earrings" and that "cute trench coat." "Miniskirts and bell-bottom pants were all the new fashions of the '60s," he told me. "'The Oogum Boogum Song' was a sign of the times." Those references no doubt helped the song become popular, and in 1967 it went to #19 on the R&B charts, #34 on the pop charts, and #43 on *Cashbox*.

Perhaps counterproductive to the song's chart success was the presence of one of the best-known mondegreens in '60s music. For the uninitiated, a mondegreen is a misunderstood or misinterpreted word or phrase in song lyrics. In the closing refrain, Wood *seems* to sing "Stick out your poo-say" or "check out the poo-say," which is a different way to pronounce a vulgar term for a part of the female anatomy. "No," Wood told me. "It's, 'Check out the boots, hey!' in keeping with the topic of '60s style." In *The Heart of Rock and Soul*, critic Dave Marsh agreed, but sees how the mondegreen came to be. "Brenton chortles 'check out the boots, eh?' so many times and so fluently that it becomes 'check out the poossah, check out the poossah,'" he writes, "which is probably exactly what kept the record out of the Top Ten but it is certainly what allows it to live on in the hearts of all mortals similarly affected by such views." Marsh certainly thought highly of the record, ranking it #577 of the 1001 greatest singles ever recorded.

But while Wood was adamant that he did not say "Stick out your poo-say," he has not been as consistent as to what he *did* say. He told me and other interviewers it was "check out the boots, hey," and told *other* interviewers that he was saying "ooga-ga-oosay," which he said was simply another made-up word like "oogum boogum." During his 1967 interview with *American Bandstand*'s Dick Clark, he said he uses nonsensical phrases because he was at a loss for words; he does not call attention to the final lines, just that he says things such as "ooga-ga-oosay." So what did he really say? We may never know, and it's certainly possible that he was just having fun with both listeners and interviewers.

As memorable as "The Oogum Boogum Song" was, Wood's follow-up, "Gimme Little Sign," was far more successful. Wood often mentioned the importance of his relationships and how they affected his songwriting, noting that he asked the advice of female friends when composing. In a similar way, even when they weren't trying to help, that affected his music too. He told me, "'Gimme Little Sign' came to me after a few breakups with my girlfriend," and was his plaintive plea for his girl to give him some sign that things weren't as they could be.

Though "Gimme Little Sign" lacked the nonsensical words, the catchy tune has its own little lyrical oddity. Despite the title, at no point in its lyrics do you ever hear "gimme little sign"; instead he said, "gimme some kind of sign." With its theme of heartbreak and a failed relationship, the song greatly appealed to listeners, and it raced to #9 on the *Billboard* charts and #19 on the R&B charts. It was Wood's only song to make the British charts, where it peaked higher than any of his songs on any chart: all the way to #8. Wood said that over the years, the song was covered by more artists than anything else he wrote, having versions released by at least a dozen artists, including a version which went to #3 on the Australian charts by Peter Andre in 1993, a version by Danielle Brisebois which peaked at #75 in England and #23 in Sweden in 1994, and a non-charting 1977 version by Ricky Nelson.

After two substantial hits, it looked like Wood was well on his way. His next 1967 release, "Baby You Got It," peaked at a respectable #34 on

Brenton Wood's second Double Shot hit, "Gimme Little Sign," went to #9 on the pop charts. His next release also hit the Top 40, making Wood, with just three Top 40 singles, the label's most successful artist. Double Shot folded in 1972.

#19. "The Oogum Boogum Song" (1967)

the pop charts and #30 on the R&B charts in November. It was Wood's last Top 40 record on any chart. His next single, "Lovey Dovey Kinda Lovin'," barely made the Top 100 on the pop charts, peaking at #99 in March 1968. That same year, "Some Got It, Some Don't" made only the R&B charts, reaching #42. He released five more Double Shot singles up through 1971, but other than "Me and You" (1968), which bubbled near the Hot 100 at #121, and "A Change Is Gonna Come" (1969), which reached #131, none of his subsequent Double Shot efforts charted anywhere. Releases throughout the '70s on a variety of labels (Mr. Wood, Prophesy, Midget, Warner Brothers) all failed to register. His 1977 disco cover of the Fleetwoods' 1959 hit "Come Softly to Me" barely entered the bottom of the R&B charts at #92.

Brenton Wood (courtesy Brenton Wood)

Wood's success can be measured by the numerous covers of "Gimme Little Sign" as well as the frequent use of "The Oogum Boogum Song" in movies and in commercials from businesses as diverse as Apple in 2015, Macy's in 2018 and Kinder Joy and Zillow in 2019. Consequently, Wood's memorable "The Oogum Boogum Song" remains a snapshot of popular '60s fashion. It has been a media staple for 50 years.

I interviewed Brenton Wood in 2010. As of 2021, he is still performing occasionally.

#20
(Adult Contemporary Charts)

"Love Grows (Where My Rosemary Goes)" (1970)

Edison Lighthouse

Billboard Pop: #5, R&B: Did not chart;
Cashbox: #4, British Charts: #1

Most stories about hit songs start with a group, their origins, their struggles to find their sound, and ultimately the moment in time when one song really "clicks"—*more* than one song, if they are lucky. Rarely does the story start with the song, *then* the group comes along after the fact, after the song has been sung and recorded; and so that moment in time for the group doesn't click because they are one and done. Though during the late 1960s and early 1970s there were a number of one-hit wonders and contrived studio groups, few groups had an origin as bizarre—and as confusing—as Edison Lighthouse. In the beginning, there was no group, no singer, no name, just a song. And although it wouldn't be the first time that a group toured behind a song essentially sung by studio musicians, never has the story been as convoluted as the story of Edison Lighthouse.

It wasn't all that complicated initially. Tony Macaulay, who by 1970 had produced and written "Baby, Now That I've Found You" and "Build Me Up, Buttercup" for the Foundations, and had written hits for many other groups, finally freed himself from his contract with Pye Records. Back then, Macaulay said, "To become a record producer was not the easiest thing in the world. A label used to give you a year's tryout and if you didn't have a hit, they let you go. If you did have a hit, they kept you for ten years on no percentage just on a low salary." After his success with the Foundations (see the entry for "Baby, Now That I've Found You"), he had been locked in with Pye Records. Macaulay: "But I finally got out of my deal with Pye, and signed this deal with Bell Records."

He said his first task was to find a song—a big song—to make a

#20. "Love Grows (Where My Rosemary Goes)" (1970)

splash with his new label. "I don't usually work with lyricists, but in this case I was working with Barry Mason, a friend of mine, who wrote a lot of Tom Jones– and Engelbert Humperdinck–type ballads. He wrote this ballad, and I said, 'That's all very well, but I just signed this big deal and they're going to want something with a dance feel to it.'" Macaulay was aware that he had no artists to work with, because everyone he had written for and produced was still at Pye. He said,

> I had this thing in my head that was one of those big debates: If you start a song with a verse by an unknown act, are they even going to wait until they get to the chorus? So I had this idea that maybe you could compress the whole verse chorus, "She ain't got no money, her clothes are kind of funny, her hair is kind of wild and free," then do the chorus "Oh my love grows, where my Rosemary goes…" that fast, and turn the whole thing over so you get the entire experience of the song in about 20 seconds. That was my idea, so we wrote this thing very quickly.

Even without a proven artist, he felt that if the song was good enough and catchy enough, maybe it could work. The song title includes the name Rosemary, and a 1969 hit he had written for the Flying Machine, "Smile a Little Smile for Me," includes the very similar name Rose Marie, but according to Macaulay, "There's no significance whatever in the Rosemary–Rose Marie names. I guess my need for 'Love Grows' to have a nursery rhyme simplicity may have resulted in me subconsciously channeling 'Mary, Mary, quite contrary' or something like that, but I'm not sure. It was just a name that had not been used in songs to that point, that happened to fit both melodies."

He also realized that the song needed a quick musical hook.

I was influenced, like the Beatles and others were influenced, by "Pretty Woman" and that kind of rolling guitar intro—like

Songwriter Tony Macaulay of "Love Grows (Where My Rosemary Goes)" fame also wrote or co-wrote "Baby, Now That I've Found You" and "Build Me Up Buttercup" by the Foundations, "(Last Night) I Didn't Get to Sleep at All" by the 5th Dimension and "Don't Give Up on Us" by David Soul.

you hear on "Day Tripper" too. So for "Love Grows," the first half of the melody was like a verse with this rolling guitar playing and then vocals backing. The morning of the session, I came up with that idea and just played it, then had everyone in the studio, the strings, the brass, everyone play in unison. I had a big orchestra and was laying backing tracks. Basically, we made this elaborate demo, and that's why we had about 20 minutes left at the end of the session. We had done the thing in only about three takes and it sounded good.

That's when Tony Burrows came in to record a demo. Burrows had, arguably, one of the best-known voices in the world. He had started his career with a vocal group called the Kestrels, and they were successful enough that in 1963 or '64, they did two tours in Britain with the Beatles. He left the group around 1965 and, Burrows said, "joined the Ivy League. And a couple of years later, the Flower Pot Men. We did 'Let's Go to San Francisco,' which hit #4 in the U.K."

By 1970, Burrows had been touring for ten years and was tired of it: "living in hotel rooms, out of a suitcase. I had a family. I decided that was enough of that." But he decided that he would still record. That's when he became the voice of a number of "studio" groups, and was in the middle of a run of Top 40 hits with the Brotherhood of Man ("United We Stand," *Billboard* pop #13), White Plains ("My Baby Loves Lovin'," #13) and the Pipkins ("Gimme Dat Ding," #9). Macaulay said,

> Tony Burrows came in and he was booked in for the next session after mine. For [musical director] Lou Warburton, he played a track of him singing "You've Got Your Troubles," singing it with this kind of Frankie Valli sound. So I asked him, "Can you sing three of those? ... Like sing 'She ain't got no money,' three of those, with like a Bronx accent?' I meant a very nasal sound, that's what I got in my head. So he did it and I said, "That's pretty good."

Burrows told me,

> I was actually going to be doing a session that day, and at the time, Tony Macaulay had stockpiled four or five songs that he wanted to do, but he didn't have any artists. I was doing a lot of back-up vocals, and the musical director that day was Lou Warburton. We had worked together before, and I had recorded a demo of the old Fortunes hit "You've Got Your Troubles" I wanted Lou to hear. We were still on Tony's time, and I asked Tony if he would mind if I played a tape of the track for Lou. Halfway through the song, Tony turned to me and said, "Do you want to do the lead on 'Love Grows'?" I said, "Yeah, okay," and that's really how it happened.

Macaulay said, "And so he came back a few days later and we put the vocal on, and we used two girls on back-up, Sue and Sunny, who had backed Joe Cocker on 'With a Little Help from My Friends.'" Sue and Sunny were sisters, born Yvonne and Heather Wheatman; their

#20. "Love Grows (Where My Rosemary Goes)" (1970)

professional names were Sue Glover and Sunny Leslie, or most commonly, Sue and Sunny; they also sang with Burrows in Brotherhood of Man. "I met them on *Top of the Pops* and asked them if they'd do sessions for me," Macaulay said. "They were on so many of my records, and on 'Love Grows' they did the 'Hey, Hey's' and vocal backing and all that."

Despite the talent assembled in the studio, "I didn't think the song was going to be a hit as it was first recorded," Macaulay said. "I thought the *sound* was a hit, so I mixed the vocal backing down, so the vocals were audible but further back in the track. But I thought those guitars, with that stomping bass, that where the hit was. We waited 'til after Christmas to put it out, because everybody thought it was a hit, but we didn't want it to get lost in the Christmas rush. So it came out second week after Christmas."

Burrows said, "It was released, and then in two weeks it was a #1 hit." Macaulay added, "[I]t was the fastest moving record by an unknown artist ever, at that point."

It wasn't the first hit recorded by a non-existent group, but usually there's a process where, as the record climbs the charts, a group can be found, can rehearse, and can figure out how to pass as the group who actually did the song. But when a song goes to #1 in two weeks, it doesn't leave much time for planning. "When the song became a hit [so fast], it caused a lot of problems. We needed a group, and Tony didn't want to go on the road. So we got a group to tour and record as Edison Lighthouse."

The first group to became Edison Lighthouse was actually a pre-existing group called Greenfield Hammer, consisting of Stuart Edwards, George Weyman, Dave Taylor and Ray Dorey. Macaulay notes that despite the fact that Greenfield Hammer had nothing whatever to do with the recording of "Love Grows," they were tutored on the song and went out to front the hit. However, when it came to them actually recording songs on their own as Edison Lighthouse in order to maintain the momentum of "Love Grows," that was another problem. According to McCauley:

> I came up with a good song for a follow-up called "Blame It on the Pony Express," but the new group couldn't do it. It required a more gutsy voice than any of them had, so I gave it to Johnny Johnson instead. The song was a big hit in England [going to #7], and it would have been the next Edison Lighthouse single but they couldn't cut it. If you think about it, though, those songs were more productions than anything else. They were just a moment in time. I didn't particularly want to go on doing Edison Lighthouse tracks. "Love Grows" was good, it was a moment in time, it made a lot

of money, and it did very well. Next! No one was going to buy an album of Edison Lighthouse in my mind.

If you look at clips from Edison Lighthouse's TV appearances and promotional photographs from 1970 and '71, you'll notice that the band members seemed to change from picture to picture. The list of musicians and singers who performed and recorded with Edison Lighthouse is extensive. After "Love Grows," they managed just one feeble low charter, "It's Up to You, Petula," that didn't make anybody's Top 40. Burrows was not singing with the group and Macaulay was not writing for them, and so the band existed for a short while simply to milk the popularity of "Love Grows."

Yet for all that, one does well to remember that "Love Grows (Where My Rosemary Goes)," #1 for five weeks in the U.K., was a massive hit. In America, it sold a million copies and earned a gold record while going to #5 on the pop charts, #4 on *Cashbox* and #20 on the Adult Contemporary charts. As for Macaulay, some of his biggest hits were still ahead. Macaulay won the British Academy of Songwriters, Composers and Authors award for Songwriter of the Year that year and again in 1977, and was a nine-time Ivor Novello Award–winning songwriter.

Burrows had more success ahead as well. Not only did he sing lead on "Beach Baby" by the First Class in 1974 (see the story behind that song elsewhere in this book), he was in the Coca-Cola "I'd Like to Teach the World to Sing" commercial. He sang backing vocals on Elton John's "Levon" and "Tiny Dancer" and he worked with Rod Stewart, Tom Jones and others. That's a pretty successful résumé for a singer-songwriter-producer who put together a group that didn't really exist and that was, as Burrows said, "just a moment in time."

For more information, see the entries for "Beach Baby" by the First Class and for "Baby, Now That I've Found You."

I interviewed Tony Burrows in 2016, Tony Macaulay in 2018.

#21
(British Charts)
"So Much in Love" (1963)
THE TYMES
Billboard Pop: #1; R&B: #4; *Cashbox*: #2;
Adult Contemporary: Did not chart

In many ways, the success of the Tymes' "So Much in Love" never should have happened. They got a recording contract based on a contest sponsored by a bread company—a contest they did not win. Then they auditioned for the Cameo-Parkway record company, and the label lost their phone number and never called them. Once *they* contacted the label, they were signed and their antiquated name was dropped and replaced with a new name—although no one seems to know why it was given to them. Their label was at a loss as to what to do with their first song, and had them rename it and record it multiple ways, once even as a calypso number! Then when the label finally found the sound they wanted, they had the group record a spoken intro to the song. After it was released, the intro was seen as such an impediment that the record was pulled, edited, renamed (for the second time) and reissued. Finally, when it did race up the charts, the group was so inexperienced that they didn't have a stage routine down to perform the song. This was painfully obvious to anyone watching them.

The Tymes' "So Much in Love" overcame all of these obstacles, and led to a string of hits for the group in America and abroad.

In Philadelphia in 1956, Norm Burnett and George Hilliard met at summer camp, formed a little group and started competing in Saturday night talent shows. After winning a few competitions, they decided to put together a more permanent group. After Albert "Caesar" Berry and Hilliard's cousin Donald Banks were added, "we called ourselves the Latineers," Burnett told me. "We thought the name sounded good, like we had a Latin sound, and there were also a lot of groups with that -eers sound at the end of their names." All of the guys had odd jobs trying to make ends meet; Burnett worked at a hospital with a young man named George Williams. When Burnett heard Williams singing one day at work, he asked him if he wanted to join the Latineers. Up to this point, Banks, Berry, Hilliard and Burnett had been taking turns singing lead but things really hadn't fallen into place. Williams agreed to join the group, and by 1960 they had the lineup that would enjoy a great deal of recording success.

First, however, they had to get themselves in the public eye, and so they did what had brought them success in the past: They entered a talent contest. "About that time, there was a WDAS radio station contest for Tip Top bread, the Tip Top Talent Hunt," Burnett said. "The deal was that you'd do your song, they'd play it on the radio and people would send them the end wrappers of the bread telling them who they liked in the contest. Well, we were nervous, and we didn't sing our best." Burnett and the others thought they'd blown their big chance, but apparently there were people listening who disagreed. "Believe it or not, a promoter

The first recording of the Tymes' "So Much in Love" was for a contest sponsored by a bread company—and they did not win. When released as a single, it was a #1 hit.

heard our audition when we were doing our tape for the radio program, and he told us to go to Cameo-Parkway records. He gave us the number and we called and set up an audition with Billy Jackson, the A&R man."

Cameo Records started in Philadelphia in 1956, Parkway was created as a subsidiary in 1958, and the label became Cameo-Parkway, created by Bernie Lowe and Kal Mann, in 1962. One of the first moves Lowe and Mann made was to sign the up-and-coming Billy Jackson to be their A&R man, producer and talent coordinator. Even though the merger of Cameo and Parkway was relatively recent in 1963, Cameo had been home to acts such as the Rays, Dee Dee Sharp, the Orlons and Bobby Rydell, while Parkway had the Dovells, the Turbans, Bobby Freeman and Chubby Checker.

For their audition, the group sang a song Williams had written and that they all had contributed to, called "As We Strolled." They sang it for Cameo-Parkway. According to Burnett, "A few weeks went by, and nobody called us, and nothing happened." Feeling they had nothing to lose, "we called *them*. They were happy we called because they said they had lost the phone number!"

When Cameo-Parkway signed them, the first order of business was to change their name. "Bernie Lowe, the owner of Cameo-Parkway, didn't like our name, so he named us the Tymes. I don't know where he got it." When the Tymes signed with the label, George Williams and Billy Jackson went to work on "As We Strolled" and retitled it "So Much in Love." The label decided that the song would be perfect for the group's first recording, but weren't sure what kind of arrangement the song should have. After it was arranged by Roy Straigis, the group apparently recorded the song several different ways—with a jazz beat, orchestrated, and as a calypso number—before Lowe suggested they basically do it as an *a cappella* number backed by Berry's finger-snapping and accompanied by Marlena Davis of the Orlons. At Jackson's urging, the sound of seagulls and waves breaking on the shore were added because he thought it would be good for the record's summer release. Burnett said, "The surf and water sounds were added to the intro for something different. The O'Jays had 'Lonely Drifter' at about the same time; it was just a novelty thing." In fact, "So in Love" (the title of the song at that point), "Lonely Drifter" *and* Robin Ward's "Wonderful Summer" all used a similar sound in 1963. Also added was a roughly ten-second spoken intro by Jackson. Under the title "So in Love," the record hit stores in 1963.

It didn't sell at first. In an unusual move, the label pulled the 45s from stores, cut the spoken intro and re-released it as "So Much in Love." With a newly titled and redesigned song, the group was hoping to get a little more airplay this time, but they were in no way prepared for what was about to happen. "So Much in Love" went all the way to #1 on the *Billboard* pop charts, #4 on the R&B charts, #2 on *Cashbox* and #21 on the British charts. "We were young kids, just trying to make it, and money and stuff didn't interest us at that time," Burnett said. "But the song was bigger than us—we were really unprepared. We were on the label with Chubby Checker, Dee Dee Sharp, Bobby Rydell, the Orlons, the Dovells, and all of a sudden, 'So Much in Love' is a #1 record." In addition to not really having the mindset of a top-notch act on a label filled with hitmakers, the group was unprepared to go on the road: They had no "act" in the way that headliners featured on tours were expected to perform. "We did a tour with Dick Clark, but our inexperience showed," Burnett said. "Len Barry was with the Dovells at the time, and he came up and said, 'You guys perform like you just met right here on stage!' We really had to grow into the song."

With their success came a whirlwind of touring and new releases. They released an album, *So Much in Love: The Story of a Summer Love*, to capitalize on their #1 single. It has often been called one of the earliest "concept" albums, as it had spoken introductions to the songs linking them together. The cover had a picture of the group and an illustration of two people in silhouette strolling along a path under a full moon. Not shy about changing things they felt were not working, Cameo-Parkway pulled the first album and reissued it with a picture of the group looking at their watches. Whether or not this helped sales is open for debate, but the album climbed into the Top 20. It also didn't hurt album sales that the record also featured their next release, a cover of a 1957 hit for Johnny Mathis called "Wonderful! Wonderful!" The original idea was to play up the ocean-seaside theme again and release "Come with Me to the Sea" as the A side, but Billy Jackson decided their cover of Mathis' #14 1957 pop hit fit the group's harmonies better. It was a good decision: The Tymes' version peaked at #7 on the pop charts in August 1963.

After two straight Top Ten hits, the group followed with a third release for 1963, "Somewhere," which peaked at #19 in early 1964. An album of the same name followed, but it did not do as well as its predecessor, and failed to break into the Top 100 of the album charts. One factor that may have affected the group's sales was that they were doing a lot of cover tunes on their albums; *Somewhere* only had a couple of original songs. A second single from the album, "Isle of Love," failed to chart at all. In 1964, "To Each His Own," "The Magic of Our Summer Love" and "Here She Comes" broke into the pop charts' Top 100 but not the Top 40, while a fourth release, "The Twelfth of Never," didn't chart at all.

Like many groups in those days, the Tymes also sang back-up for other artists, and they provided background vocals for old label mate Len Barry on his #2 smash "1-2-3." But by the mid–60s, Cameo-Parkway was in trouble. Declining sales weren't helped by Billy Jackson's departure. The label folded in 1967.

The Tymes got out just in time, following Jackson to MGM. In 1966, they released two singles for MGM, but neither "Street Talk" nor "What Would I Do" did anything. Next the group recorded a song on the fledgling Winchester label, co-founded by the Tymes and partially financed by others, including their old friend Jackson. The Tymes' "These Foolish Things" was the label's second release in 1967, but it failed to find an audience. It appears that this was the second and last single the label released. Jackson then went to Columbia Records, and perhaps predictably the Tymes followed. They returned to the charts with the Top 40 hit "People" in 1968. (In England, "People" did better than "So Much in Love," going to #16.) Four more Columbia singles did nothing. After being released by Columbia, they tried for several years to get signed by another label to no avail.

Finally, in 1974, they signed with RCA and once again worked with their old friend Jackson. They recorded some new songs; and the first released was "You Little Trustmaker." Oddly enough, it wasn't one of the members of the group doing the lead, but Jackson: He was producing, and felt that Williams needed to change the way he was singing the song, so he did the vocals and demonstrated what he wanted. Everyone liked the way it sounded, and they ended up cutting the track with Jackson singing lead and the group on background vocals. When released, it shot up to #12 on the *Billboard* pop charts. The Tymes were in the Top 40 for the first time in six years. They followed that in 1974 with the release of the Jackson-produced "Ms. Grace," written by husband-and-wife team John and Johanna Hall. (John later became a member of the group Orleans, which charted with the hits "Still the One" and "Love Takes Time.") While "Ms. Grace" only reached #91 on the *Billboard* pop charts and #75 on the R&B charts, in England it soared all the way to #1. Burnett:

> It's a nice song, a different type of song, a really beautiful song. It was just one of those records that took off. Even though it didn't chart as well here, we weren't disappointed. Sure, we would have liked for it to have been a big record here, but we were just happy it went to #1 there—it made us a really big act overseas. We did a show with Stevie Wonder, and *we* were the featured act!

Surprisingly, the Tymes' newfound success was short-lived. They charted once more in America in 1976 with "It's Cool" (#3 R&B, #68 pop), and then there were no more chart records. After more than a

The Tymes: sitting, Albert "Caesar" Berry. Standing, left to right: George Williams, Norm Burnett, George Hilliard and Donald Banks (courtesy Norm Burnett).

decade and a half the group had started to splinter in 1974, when George Hilliard left, and multiple personnel changes followed. In 1976, they had one last chart record in England: "God's Gonna Punish You" peaked at #41. The group had no chart records after 1976.

    Considering all of the group's ups and downs, with everything from label changes to reissues and hit records followed by disappointing subsequent releases, their personnel stayed consistent for most of their recording run. They also did what few other groups have done: recorded multiple #1 records, in different decades and in different countries.

I interviewed Norm Burnett in December 2010. As of this writing, he performs as part of the Tymes.

#22
(Adult Contemporary Charts)
"Sugar, Sugar" (1969)
THE ARCHIES
Billboard Pop: #1; R&B: Did not chart;
Cashbox: #1; British Charts: #1

Don't let the #22 ranking on the Adult Contemporary charts fool you: The Archies' "Sugar, Sugar" was one of the biggest hits of the '60s, going to #1 on the Pop, *Cashbox* and British Charts, and it hit #1 in markets around the world as well. The man who sang the song, Ron Dante, may have one of the most famous voices in this book, but you will be excused if you don't know his name as soon as you hear it. That's because Dante, despite a long and impressive career in music, often operated in near-anonymity and rarely under his own name.

As a member of the Detergents, he first made the Top 40 when his group recorded "Leader of the Laundromat" when he was just 20 years old. He worked with Don Kirshner, and sang and worked as a songwriter with Carole King, Tony Orlando and Neil Sedaka before most of them became household names. He produced several Broadway musicals, including the Tony-winning *Ain't Misbehavin'*. He produced Barry Manilow's hit albums, sang back-up on Manilow's "Mandy," and basically discovered Pat Benatar. But as a singer, Dante's most famous work is as the voice of the two studio groups, the Archies and the Cuff Links. Because of this, he has the distinction of being one of only two artists in this book to appear twice. While his other appearance (as the lead singer for the Cuff Links on their mega-hit "Tracy") can be found elsewhere in this book, his biggest hit was his recording of "Sugar, Sugar."

Ron Dante was born Carmine John Granito in Staten Island, New York. He said that music was a part of his everyday life:

> My dad wasn't a professional singer but he loved to sing, as did his six brothers. When we'd go to a wedding, everybody would get up and sing, everybody was a ham. I heard music very early in my life. My dad loved his

records and had a big stack of 78s on the record player. He'd run a string to the couch so he could change the records and listen to six or seven records in a row. I listened to the Platters, Patti Page, and then I discovered Elvis when I was ten and that changed my life completely. A few years later, I fell from a tree and injured my arm, and the doctor said I needed to exercise it, to do something to work the arm. I decided I'd play the guitar so Dad bought me one. Then when I was about 14, I put my first band together, the Persuaders. One New Year's Eve I made $75 playing, so I said, "Well, this is the profession I want to be in!" I mean, I'm 14 and made $75 for one gig, and my dad worked all week for $50. I said, "This is something I can do."

When he was 17, Dante landed a job as a staff singer and demo-maker with Don Kirshner. He recalled:

I was signed to a publishing contract, and told to write songs. I was in the New York office writing with artists like Carole King and Tony Orlando and Neil Sedaka. It was amazing. This publishing company was one of the hottest in the world. I had the opportunity to be a staff demo-maker, and Don Kirshner gave me my start in the business. I'll forever be grateful to him for that opportunity. I got to see all these writers, the way they produced their demos, and I got to see the singers, I actually got to sing background on

Ron Dante and Toni Wine did vocals on the #1 hit "Sugar, Sugar." The session also included songwriter Andy Kim playing guitar and Ray Stevens clapping.

some of Neil Sedaka's early hits. As a teenager out of Staten Island, I had the opportunity of a lifetime.

Dante worked with Danny Jordan and Tommy Wynn. Jordan's uncle was songwriter-producer Paul Vance who, along with Lee Pockriss, had written a parody of the Shangri-Las' #1 hit "Leader of the Pack" called "Leader of the Laundromat." Jordan, Wynn and Dante recorded the song as the Detergents. When released in 1965, it peaked at #19 on the pop Hot 100. According to Dante,

> As the Detergents song peaked, we went on the road with the Dick Clark Caravan of Stars and toured for about a year, then came back home and set up an office, where I was gonna be a songwriter and producer. I started doing commercials and any odd job I could just to stay in the music business. I actually wrote a Broadway show. Jeff Barry, a producer and friend of mine who I had done backgrounds for, was writing the score for a Broadway show. He said, "You should be the voice of this rock band that's in the show." I did it but the show closed after a couple of weeks.

Meeting Barry proved to be important a little later:

> A friend of mine was playing keyboard in the band doing the tracks for the new Archies show that Jeff Barry and Don Kirshner were putting together. They didn't have any singers, but they had musicians, and one of the musicians was the best man at my wedding. Well, he said, "You know Don Kirshner. You should call him and come over and be the voice." So I told him I would, and I called and went in for an audition, sang one of the songs, and got the job of being the voice of Archie on the songs. It was great working with people I knew; it was like a homecoming. They knew what I could do and that I'd be there and do my vocals and make it sound magical.

Barry and Kirshner knew that they needed a big breakout hit for the show. Barry called singer-songwriter Andy Kim, who had recorded a cover of the Ronettes' "Baby, I Love You," a song that Barry had co-written. According to Dante, "The word I got from Andy, who co-wrote 'Sugar, Sugar' and wrote the hook, is that Jeff called Andy and said, 'We need a single for the show, we need a hit. What do you think we should do?' Over the phone, Andy said, 'Why don't you do something like this...' and he sang, 'Sugar, dah da dah dah da dah, awww, honey honey...' And that was the beginning of that song."

I asked Dante how he thought Kim felt about not being lead on a hit as big as "Sugar, Sugar," and if it bothered him:

> No. I think Andy—and we're close friends—I think he appreciates and knows I was the right voice for that song. That was the right platform—the television show—to deliver the song. He's done well financially from the show and does it in his own show when he performs. I think his songs were more elevated, an older market, than ours. We were shooting for teenagers

and pre-teenagers, kids who chewed bubblegum—that's how the term 'bubblegum music' came about. The songs were aimed at a very young audience. He's fine with it.

Because the Archies was a studio group, there has been a lot of confusion about who actually sang on the record in addition to Dante. One was Toni Wine, whose voice can be clearly heard singing the lyrics in the middle section. Dante:

> Toni was signed to Don Kirshner as a teenager. We were the two teenagers in the office, and she was singing and writing and doing demos. So we were there all those years. Don loved her voice, and she was a very successful songwriter. She wrote a big hit with Carole Bayer Sager, "Groovy Kind of Love," and later another one for Tony Orlando, "Candida." She was a good friend and also a big-time studio singer and so it was a natural thing for Toni to come in and do the song. We needed a high voice to sing the middle section of "Sugar, Sugar," where you hear "I'm gonna make your life so sweet." She sang it low first, and then sang the answer high. People come up to me and say, "Oh yeah, you had those two girls singing with you." And they've said they wanted to know who the black girl was singing on the record. It's interesting because Toni's a nice Jewish girl from Brooklyn! But she's got a great street voice, the kind of voice that can do any song.

Some sources have credited Andy Kim and Ellie Greenwich as back-up vocalists. Ray Stevens, who went on to fame with "Everything Is Beautiful" and "The Streak," has also been listed as a participant. So who, besides Dante and Wine, *was* there? According to Dante,

> Ellie and Andy never sang on any Archies sessions, but yes, Andy did play his guitar on "Sugar, Sugar." The band couldn't get the right feel on the track so Andy came out and decided to show them what he wanted on guitar. He didn't have a guitar pick, so he used a matchbook—several as it turned out—to play his guitar. They recorded it and that made it onto the track. It was the perfect sound for the record.... As for Ray Stevens, that is true. He was a friend of Toni Wine's and he did clap on "Sugar, Sugar" the night we did vocals.

Ron Dante doing lead vocals, Toni Wine doing back-up, Andy Kim playing guitar and Ray Stevens clapping is an all-star lineup, and certainly that superstar vibe carried over onto the song's success. "Sugar, Sugar" was #1 for four weeks on the *Billboard Hot 100* and hit #1 in Canada, England, Belgium, Germany, Ireland, Austria, Norway, Spain and elsewhere. Oddly, it would not make the R&B charts, and only went to #22 on the Adult Contemporary charts—perhaps because it was a little *too* bubblegummy. Nevertheless, it was the #1 song for 1969 in the U.S., and went on to become legendary. There's no question it's a great song, but Dante thinks it's more than just that: "I think it's due to the simplicity of it. It went to #1 around the world. I think it's the accessibility of that song in any language. You don't have to understand English to know it's a fun sound and a happy song. It's also very danceable, and it just has a certain kind of magic that delivers when sung by a voice that's meant to sing it. It brings smiles to people's faces."

"Sugar, Sugar" is one of the most famous and recognizable American songs of the 20th century. Amazingly, as a member of the studio group the Cuff Links, Dante sang lead on another song in this book, "Tracy," which is featured in the #9 position. His story is continued there.

I interviewed Dante in 2016. As of this writing, he was still performing.

#23
(*Billboard* Pop Charts)
"What Kind of Fool" (1969)
Bill Deal and the Rhondels
Cashbox: #22; R&B, Adult Contemporary,
British Charts: Did not chart

Very few artists can sustain a successful recording career and enjoy continued chart success doing "cover versions" or "covers," those being recordings of songs previously done by other artists. Many groups record covers, of course; in the early days, even the Beatles recorded cover versions until John Lennon and Paul McCartney grew as songwriters and no longer needed to re-record music performed by earlier artists. It is even rarer for a group to be successful on the charts over and over doing covers, and again the Beatles come to mind with a couple of covers charting early in their careers. However, those covers account for only a few early recordings out of nearly 75 chart records, so the caveat about "sustaining continued chart success doing cover versions" clearly applies here. Perhaps one thing that makes Bill Deal and the Rhondels unique in rock'n'roll annals is that *every one* of their Top 40 chart hits was a cover version, culminating in their highest charter of all, 1969's "What Kind of Fool."

When they met as teenagers, Virginia Beach resident William "Bill" Deal was a student at Wilson High School and Ammon Tharp a student at nearby Princess Anne High School. Deal was with a group called the Blazers, Tharp with the Saints, and they encountered each other a few times playing gigs. Their friendship developed through their shared love of rhythm and blues and soul music, and they decided to form their own band in 1960. They added Mike Ash, Mike Stillman and Bryan Bennet and called themselves Bill Deal and the Rhondels after a rondel, which was a form of poetry that originated in France in the 14th century and which used repeated lines. According to Tharp, Deal often joked, "That's because we only know a few songs, and repeat them over and over!"

#23. "What Kind of Fool" (1969)

"What Kind of Fool" was Bill Deal and the Rhondels' third straight cover record that made the Top 40 charts, their highest charting.

In those early years, they played as much for the love of music as anything else, and frequently took home $25 a night each for their gigs (not bad money at the time). At that point, however, they were willing to trade off any more ambitious aspirations in favor of playing clubs in Virginia and the Carolinas, where audiences accepted old-style R&B. South Carolina native Maurice Williams was very popular in the Southeast, and with his group the Zodiacs had hit it big nationally with the record "Stay" in 1960. In 1965, he recorded another song, "May I," and although nationally it didn't make any chart, it was extremely popular in the South and audiences clamored for the song when the Rhondels played clubs and parties. Tharp said,

> We played down in the Carolinas every summer, and during the summer of 1968 people kept requesting "May I." Deal didn't like the song at all, and he didn't like the version, and so we changed it up by him putting in a polka-type back beat, like a double time keyboard on it. We did it live on stage, and they went crazy down there. We were there the rest of the week, and we'd get requests to do it two or three times a night. We came back home to Virginia Beach and said, "Wow—we really gotta record this damn thing. It was really working the way we were doing it." Bill was the one responsible for putting that whole thing together musically. Then he told

me how to sing it. My voice was unique, but not a good voice. I understand that, but he knew what I could do, and he was the only one who could figure out, "You can go this high, or you can go this low. This is what you need to do and how you need to do it." He was involved with the vocals, the instrumentation, everything. He loved recording, and that's good because I wasn't really that fond of recording in the first place.

Deal apparently had a gift for it, because almost overnight the group sold 3,000 copies of "May I" locally. This brought them to the attention of Jerry Ross at Heritage Records, who released the record nationally; "May I" entered the Hot 100, and then the Top 40, before it stalled at #39. It ultimately sold more than 400,000 copies.

Having that much success, they decided not to mess with the formula: For their next record, they chose another regional hit by the Georgia-based group The Tams. Tharp said, "Then we did 'I've Been Hurt.' We were doing Tams songs in our set and liked the songs, but thought, 'Let's change it up for a national audience.'" "I've Been Hurt," while popular in the Southeast, hadn't charted anywhere when released in 1965, so the Rhondels' 1969 version obviously surpassed it, going to #35 on the *Billboard* pop charts. The record sold more than a million copies worldwide and was voted song of the year in Mexico.

For their next release, they not only did another cover, but a song that was another cover of a Tams song: "What Kind of Fool." "I don't really know why we chose it next, but Deal just had an insight on how to do those songs in our style. Audiences requested those Tams songs a lot, and I'm guessing Bill thought doing 'What Kind of Fool' in that Rhondels style was a really safe bet considering that unlike 'May I' and 'I've Been Hurt,' this time we were recording a song that was originally a pretty big chart success."

"What Kind of Fool" had been released by the Tams in 1964, but unlike the Rhondels' previous two releases, it was not an unknown cut. Written by Ray Whitley, the songwriter who wrote almost every one of the Tams' biggest hits, the song had been the Tams' most successful chart release in America, peaking at #9 on the *Billboard* pop, R&B and *Cashbox* pop charts. It was to become the Rhondels' biggest hit as well, peaking at #23 on the *Billboard* pop charts and #22 on the *Cashbox* charts.

As Tharp, Deal and the others learned, the way to make money was through touring. But that had its drawbacks, however, on a lot of levels. "We were going to New York every week promoting and doing TV and radio, and traveling and playing," Tharp said. But these were no longer those Virginia and Carolina crowds who were steeped in classic R&B, and very soon, that became obvious. "We played Madison Square

Garden with Neil Young, Deep Purple and Crazy Elephant, and we realized, 'We're in the wrong place here.' We're a bunch of short-haired, Ivy League–looking guys doing Motown and old-style R&B and having to play with these rock bands. We really weren't into the rock thing, which was coming on really strong. Every time we played up there, we'd go against a rock band, and while they loved our records, they'd come on and blow our ass away with their rock'n'roll." Add to that the fact that living out of a suitcase just wasn't fun. The band decided they'd had enough. "We were making decent money, but we weren't getting rich, and we thought, 'You know, we could do this at home and just play the Southeast.' We were kind of homebodies—we loved Virginia

Bill Deal and the Rhondels. Bottom, left to right: Bob Fisher, Ken Dawson, Ronny Rosenbaum. Center, left to right: Ammon Tharp, Bill Deal. Top, left to right: Mike Kerwin, Don Queinsenbury, Jeff Pollard (courtesy Ammon Tharp).

Beach—and we figured financially we could do just as well and not be gone all the time. So we said bye-bye. We thought success was fine, but … nah.'"

Although the group had a couple more moderately popular single releases in 1969 ("Swinging Tight," #85) and '70 ("Nothing Succeeds Like Success," #62), they were content to become a bar and club band once again. By removing themselves from the national spotlight and focusing on regional venues, they were able to maintain some semblance of normality in their lives. Working out of Virginia Beach, they mainly played at Rogue's Gallery, a club Deal co-owned. They played as the house band there until he sold the bar in the late 1970s. They remained popular for many years in the Carolinas and Virginia, and after the group stopped playing together regularly, Tharp started Fat Ammon's Band, which performed from the late '70s until the 1990s. Over the years, many band members got "real jobs" for a while, but the band reformed on occasion. Deal passed away in 2003, and Tharp in 2017.

Even as Tharp played those songs during the last years of his life, he told me, "I don't get tired of it, and if I don't do those songs every night, I'm upsetting people. But I don't mind doing those songs at all. I'm still having fun 40 years later."

I interviewed Tharp in November 2010.

#24
(*Cashbox* Charts)

"Hey, Western Union Man" (1968)

JERRY BUTLER

Billboard Pop: #16; R&B: #1; Adult Contemporary, British Charts: Did not chart

---

Trying to nail down just one Jerry Butler hit as his most important or most representative song is difficult, because he had more than five dozen very recognizable records on the pop and R&B charts. Trying to nail down his "sound" can be difficult as well, because his songs with the Impressions aren't exactly like his solo efforts on Vee Jay, his duets, his Mercury hits or his later releases with Motown or Philadelphia International. Then there are cases where the sound might be somewhat passé today, and songs such as "Moon River" or "Let It Be Me" certainly sound like throwbacks now. Even the wording may date the song. For example, Butler told me that he didn't perform "I Dig You Baby" for a long time because "I was performing it, and a boy said, 'That's so square!' ... I think I was intimidated, and for a long time I didn't want to sing it any more."

So how does one define the classic Jerry Butler song, the song that showcases his soulful voice, skillful songwriting and top-notch production values, the likes of which resulted from his collaborations with Kenny Gamble and Leon Huff? Despite its anachronistic title, "Hey, Western Union Man" was one of his finest efforts and representative of Butler at the height of his powers.

Butler was born in Sunflower, Mississippi; the family moved to Chicago when he was three. He credits his earliest musical influences to his mother, "who used to sing to me all the time." He and three friends formed his first singing group, the Quails, when he was a teen. His father died when he was 15 so he had to drop out of the group in order to work and help his family. But like many future R&B artists, he found time to sing in the church choir. Around this time, he met Curtis

Mayfield, and they became part of a gospel group called the Northern Jubilee Gospel Singers. When Butler was 17, he met three Tennesseans who had recently moved to Chicago, Arthur and Richard Brooks and Sam Gooden. Along with Mayfield, he joined their group, the Roosters.

The group landed a contract with Chicago's Vee-Jay Records. At the insistence of their manager, who thought "The Roosters" sounded too much like a country act, they had renamed themselves the Impressions, which the label changed to Jerry Butler and the Impressions. For their first release, they settled on a song whose lyrics Butler had written when he was 16, "For Your Precious Love." It climbed to #11 on the pop charts and #3 on the R&B charts in 1958, and became the group's first hit and their first gold record. Their next, "Come Back My Love," also made the R&B charts. By this time, Butler was attracting a lot of attention as the group's frontman, and in fact had been singled out with the name the "Iceman" by a Philadelphia deejay for his "cool" delivery. He decided to become a solo act, leaving Mayfield and the Impressions to carry on without him—which they did, quite successfully.

From 1960 to 1966, Butler recorded a number of solo pop hits for Vee-Jay, including "He Will Break Your Heart" (#7, 1960), "Moon River" (#11, 1962), "Make It Easy on Yourself" (#20, 1962), and several duets, including "Let It Be Me" (#5, 1964) with Betty Everett. When Vee-Jay went bankrupt in 1966, Butler signed with Mercury for what some might say was the third and most consistently productive phase of his career. His first chart release for Mercury was the aforementioned "I Dig You Baby" (1966), a smooth, soulful song that peaked at #60. "The original version was done by Lorraine Ellison and produced by Jerry Ross, and

"Hey, Western Union Man" was one of a series of six straight *Billboard* Pop Top 40 hits for Jerry Butler, starting with "Never Give You Up" in 1968 and ending with "What's the Use of Breaking Up" in 1969. On the R&B charts, "Hey, Western Union Man" went to #1.

#24. "Hey, Western Union Man" (1968)

he produced mine too," Butler told me. Butler enjoyed moderate success at first with songs such as "I Dig You Baby" and "Mr. Dream Merchant"; when he started working with Kenny Gamble and Leon Huff, his records really started to take off.

> I met Kenny through Jerry Ross after I recorded "You Don't Know What You Got," a Kenny Gamble composition. I told Jerry, "This guy has a way of putting things, and I think he's very creative and unique." Later, I was in Philadelphia and I met Gamble and Huff and I was complimenting Kenny on his song. He said, "We sure would like to do some work with you." So he, Leon and I went to a show lounge across the street from their office and came up with some songs. After I went back to Mercury, I told them I wanted to try something with the two of them, and out of that came the *Ice Man Cometh* album.

According to Butler, one of the songs they wrote that first day was "Never Give You Up." "That's a very interesting song from the first session after we decided we were going to work together. We recorded it at the Sound of Philadelphia Studios, but the unique thing about it was that we were locked into—by chance or by divine guidance—using my musicians instead of their studio musicians." Butler said that meant the musicians knew him and his style, and things just clicked. "Joe Tarsia, the engineer at the session, always talks about how we came in, my band set up their five pieces and we went in and did it in one take. Joe says, 'I remember you were on your way someplace for a gig, and you stopped in, and we did it in one take and you were gone.' We did, but one take makes you always suspect that you didn't do it well enough!" Clearly, Butler did do it well enough, as it went to #20 on the pop charts and #4 on the R&B charts. The Butler-Gamble-Huff hit-making machine was on its way.

Up to this point, Butler's Mercury recordings had done well on the R&B charts: The first five had all gone R&B Top 40, with two in the Top Ten. But his next single, off the same album, was a Gamble-Huff-Butler composition called "Hey, Western Union Man," and it was truly groundbreaking. "Kenny, Leon and I were not only the writers, but they produced, did the background vocals and just about everything that was needed," he said. "A lot of times, Leon would play music, we'd hum along, I'd add the words—it was a very collaborative process." Butler said the song seemed pretty special when they recorded it:

> I tell people all the time that 90 percent of the arrangement was in the way Leon Huff plays piano. A lot of arrangers and orchestrators would take a word or phrase that Leon sang or played on the piano and put it in the string or horn section and end up building most of what they were doing around the way he plays the piano. I really believe he's one of the great unsung

musicians of our time. And because of Kenny's aura, I guess, he often gets overlooked in terms of his contribution to the sound of Philadelphia, but his spirit is enormous. Both Gamble and Huff cast a big shadow.

The song went to #16 on the pop charts, but perhaps more importantly it went all the way to #1 on the R&B charts in the fall of 1968. It was Butler's first #1 on Mercury, and his second #1 (of three) overall.

By this point, Butler was no longer coming across as a crooner singing just adult contemporary tunes, which he had come close to being pigeonholed as during the Vee-Jay years. Gamble and Huff were up-and-comers and had their fingers on the pulse (or ears) of young America, and suddenly Butler was a very hot commodity. His next release, "Are You Happy," did moderately well (#39 pop, #9 R&B). The biggest hit of his career was his final release off of the "Ice Man Cometh" album, "Only the Strong Survive":

> That was a song that everybody seemed to derive their own personal meaning from; everybody heard whatever message they wanted to put into it. I went to perform at Prairie View College in Texas and this guy asked if I was going to sing it, but I really hadn't planned on it because it was a newly released song that we really hadn't worked into the act yet. He said, "But you gotta do it." I asked him why, and he said, "That's the school's theme song." So we picked our way through it to begin with, but once we started to play it, the kids just picked it up and ran with it. It was one of those things where they were singing along as opposed to listening to me sing. But it was quite complementary and was very wonderful.

With its anthem-like nature, it was a song that many people felt strongly about. It went to #4 on the pop charts and #1 on the R&B charts. Butler's first record to go platinum, it was later recorded by Elvis Presley, Billy Paul and others.

The Ice Man Cometh spawned four Top 40 singles on the pop charts and five on the R&B charts. It was time for a follow-up album. Working once again with Gamble and Huff, Butler produced *Ice on Ice*. It generated four charting singles in 1969 and '70, only two made the pop Top 40: "Moody Woman" at #24 ("a play off of being married," Butler said) and "What's the Use of Breaking Up" at #20. According to Butler, the latter "dealt with people who are always going through some conflict or another, and then after getting the steam out, they go back to being what they were before the pot got hot!" Butler said the album largely centered around "the concept of people falling in and out of love." Despite the solid writing and producing, single sales were not as impressive as those of the previous album. Butler told me,

> After we did the first two albums, Kenny and Leon decided that they weren't going to produce any outside artists any more and they were going to

concentrate on building their own label. I was under contract with Mercury and couldn't leave, so when they decided to opt out of recording outside artists, I was one of the opt-outs. I had to figure out what to do. [I started] a songwriters' workshop in Chicago and started trying to come up with writers who could fill that void. We had a lot of success, but it wasn't necessarily for me. As a matter of fact, Natalie Cole's first two or three hits came out of guys who were involved in the workshop.

While Butler had 18 R&B chart singles for Mercury between 1971 and 1974, none of them made the pop Top 40. He then signed with Motown, though with basically the same result. His career seemed to have slowed down. Butler:

> By this time, Kenny and Leon had made Philadelphia International a *big* label. They had Teddy Pendergrass, Lou Rawls and on and on. What do they need with a Jerry Butler at this point in time? But because of our relationship as friends, they said, "Let's go back into the studio, and see if we can recapture what we did at the very beginning." So we did. We went up to this resort up in the Pennsylvania mountains and sat down, and just started talking about just cooling out, getting away, taking a break from the routine. The idea is, you need to just slow down because you're moving too fast. And that's how the song's title came about. So the song was about what it's like to 'cool out.' I jokingly told one reporter that were shooting for disco and missed!

"Cooling Out" did not make the pop charts, but did hit the R&B charts at #14. It was the last time Butler had a Top 40 record on any chart.

He continued to record until the early 1980s, then became a successful businessman while embarking on a long political career (he was a Cook County, Illinois, commissioner from 1985 until he retired in 2018). As the Impressions' original lead singer, he was inducted into the Rock and Roll Hall of Fame in 1991, and as a solo artist he was inducted into the National Rhythm & Blues Hall of Fame in 2015. The "Ice Man" has left a legacy as one of America's "coolest" soul voices.

I interviewed Butler in October 2012. As of this writing, he still performs occasionally.

#25
(*Cashbox* Charts)
"Searching for My Love" (1966)
BOBBY MOORE AND THE RHYTHM ACES

Billboard Pop: #27; R&B: #7; Adult Contemporary, British Charts: Did not chart

---

It's a safe bet that very few groups who had a Top 40 record started out as an Army marching band. It might not be surprising for an Army band to become a back-up band, however. Bobby Moore and the Rhythm Aces morphed into a back-up band playing behind the likes of Ray Charles, Sam and Dave, Etta James, Wilson Pickett, Sam Cooke and Otis Redding. When they decided to cut a demo of a song they had written for themselves, Chess Records heard it, had them re-record it, and a hit was born. Although their time on the charts was brief, their one and only pop Top 40 record was one of the finest mid-'60s recordings to come out of the FAME studios in Muscle Shoals, Alabama.

Robert "Bobby" Moore was born in 1931 in New Orleans. As a teenager, he joined the Army and was stationed at Fort Benning near Columbus, Georgia. He learned to play the tenor saxophone, and while in the Army he decided to put together his first band with members of the Fort Benning marching band. They went by the name The Rhythm Aces and by 1952 they were playing jazz and R&B, scheduling performances when they could get leave and book gigs relatively close to the base. After Moore's discharge, the band broke up and Moore moved to Montgomery, Alabama.

By this point, Moore had decided that he needed to make music his profession because, as he told a newspaper reporter, he wanted to "have a few kicks." He met a group of Montgomery guys who asked him to join a group they were putting together, and the second group known as the Rhythm Aces was born in 1961. There were some personnel changes along the way but, according to Bobby Moore Jr., when the group's lineup solidified, "there were six of us: Dad, me (on alto sax), Chico

#25. "Searching for My Love" (1966)

Bobby Moore Jr. said that he and the Rhythm Aces played "Searching for My Love" in clubs for a long time before they recorded it.

Jenkins (vocals and guitar), Joe Frank (bass), Clifford Laws (organ) and John Baldwin (drums)." The Rhythm Aces quickly gained a reputation as a first-class ensemble. They had a driving rhythm and blues sound. Headlining R&B performers on the "chitlin' circuit" who needed accompaniment while performing in the Deep South—mainly vocalists who didn't travel with a regular back-up band—could call on the Rhythm Aces to provide first-rate instrumentation. Soon the group was in great demand. They backed up singers Ray Charles, Sam and Dave, Etta James, Kim Weston, Wilson Pickett, Sam Cooke and Otis Redding.

With the accolades and success came a desire by the group to do more than play back-up; they also felt they were ready to record music of their own. For a couple of years, they had been working on a song written by Moore, "Searching for My Love." "We were playing the song in clubs for a long time before we ever recorded it," Moore Jr. said. "Dad and Chico decided it would be a good one to record because people liked it when we were playing it in clubs—I think the response there had a lot to do with it." "Searching for My Love" was a classic rhythm and blues tune of the "begging and pleading" type. In this, the group's first attempt at creating their own hit, Chico Jenkins' plaintive vocals conveyed a sense of loss far better than the singers of similar songs.

In 1965, the group packed up their equipment and drove upstate to the FAME (Florence Alabama Music Enterprises) studios in Muscle Shoals, Alabama. Though a few Top 40 hits had already emerged from the studios (Tommy Roe's "Everybody," the Tams' "What Kind of Fool," Arthur Alexander's "You Better Move On"), the string of smashes by Etta James, Aretha Franklin, Wilson Pickett, Otis Redding *et al.* were still a year or two away. "We went to Muscle Shoals and cut the record" Bobby Moore Jr. said.

Chess Records in Chicago heard a demo of the tune, responded positively, and decided to sign them. After acquiring the rights to the song, Leonard Chess released it on his Checker subsidiary label in 1966. "We were one of the first Chess groups to record there at Muscle Shoals," Moore said. In fact, they were the *very first* Chess group to record there; label mates Etta James and the Dells followed them later with great success as well. With a good song and a good sound, and the kind of promotion only a company like Chess could provide, the group released the song and watched it race up the charts. In some parts of the country, it sold only moderately well, but in markets such as Los Angeles it was a #1 hit on all four of the biggest radio stations. The group watched the song soar into the *Billboard* Top 40 nationally before finally settling in at #27 and #25 on *Cashbox*. It reportedly sold more than a million copies. The benefits of having a hit record were immediately obvious, Moore said: "Before the record came out, we had been making like $25 to $30 a night, and after the record, we were making $300 a night." They toured behind the song, and they performed on TV's *Where the Action Is* as a follow-up to the single. Checker also released an album to capitalize on the hit, appropriately titled *Searching for My Love*.

It was a great debut for the group, and they hoped their next release would sustain that momentum. That release, again on Checker, was 1966's impressive "Try My Love Again," though it had not been on the group's first album. The group had introduced a few changes, starting with the wording on the single's label, where the artist was listed as Bobby Moore's Rhythm Aces "featuring Chico." The song had a somewhat different sound as well, and some listeners have noted an almost ska-like sound, which is interesting because other than Millie Small's cover of "My Boy Lollipop," the ska sound really hadn't worked its way onto American Top 40 radio. Moore Jr. told me that the song "didn't do that much." It peaked at #97 on the *Billboard Hot 100* and only spent two weeks on the charts before dropping off. On the R&B charts for three weeks, it squeaked in at #40.

#25. "Searching for My Love" (1966)

Bobby Moore and the Rhythm Aces: from left to right, Moore, Chico Jenkins, John Baldwin, Clifford Laws, Ted Ford, Joe Frank and Bobby Moore Jr. (courtesy Bobby Moore, Jr.).

The group's third—and as it would turn out, final—Checker release was 1967's "Chained to Your Heart," backed with "Reaching Out." The former was different for the group in many ways. First, Bobby Moore didn't write it; the label says it was arranged and produced by Rick Hall. Hall was the owner of FAME studios, so perhaps the group was hoping lightning would strike again. The label also says it is by Bobby Moore, but no mention is made of the Rhythm Aces. The song has more of a Chicago sound with its brassy horn sections. But even with the changes. the song did not make the Top 100, though it did make the R&B charts, peaking at #49. "Reaching Out" performed well in some western states.

Despite the promise shown by their first three singles, Checker didn't seem to have much faith in the group's ability to produce long term, and even though they released a few more songs that had previously been recorded and were on the *Searching for My Love* album, the Chess brass seemed unwilling to invest any more time or money on the group. After being dropped by the label, the group underwent a number of changes. They released their second (and final) album, *Dedication of Love*, as Bobby Moore and the Rhythm Aces on the obscure Phinall

Sound label in 1976. The album was only a limited pressing, and today is highly collectible.

For years afterwards, Bobby Moore and his band toured on the strength of those few hits. After Moore died of kidney failure in 2006, Moore Jr. took over and they are still playing today. "Dad kept the band going even after [Chess] released us, and we have been playing for four decades now," Moore said. "Dad was a class act, and today I'm still trying to carry on the legacy." The group's legacy has indeed endured on the strength of the great "Searching for My Love."

I interviewed Bobby Moore Jr. in 2010. As of this writing, he continues to perform as frontman for the Rhythm Aces.

#26
(R&B Charts)
"Be Young, Be Foolish, Be Happy" (1968)
THE TAMS

Billboard Pop: #61; *Cashbox*: #63; Adult Contemporary: Did not chart; British Charts: #32

The Tams are something of an anomaly in American music: While their music is still fairly well-known, chart success was largely elusive despite a prodigious recording output. Of their seven songs to make the *Billboard* Top 100, only one, 1963's "What Kind of Fool," made the *Billboard* pop Top 40. None of their records made the adult contemporary charts, but six made the *Cashbox* Top 100, seven made the R&B Top 100, and three of their songs made the British charts, including one that went to #1. During a recording career that spanned three decades and multiple labels, 1968's "Be Young, Be Foolish, Be Happy" stands as perhaps their most memorable recording, having made the *Billboard* and *Cashbox* pop Hot 100 charts and the R&B and British Top 40 charts.

The Tams got their start around 1952 as students at David T. Howard High School in Atlanta, Georgia. As the Four Dots, brothers Joe and Charles Pope, Robert Lee Smith and Willie James "Frog" Rutherford played in Atlanta area clubs in the 1950s. After Floyd "Little Floyd" Ashton joined to make the group a quintet, they needed a new name. When they saved a little money, Rutherford purchased red sweaters and blue tam o' shanter hats for the group; Charles Pope told me, "[That was] because we really couldn't afford anything else." Taking their cue from their stage wear, they became the Tams.

After Rutherford ran into to some legal trouble, he was replaced by Horace "Sonny" Key; the group's 1960 lineup (the Popes, Smith, Ashton and Key) remained the same for the next four years. The Tams came to the attention of Atlanta song publisher–entrepreneur Bill Lowery, who arranged for them to record a song named "Untie Me."

Originally intended to be a one-off demo, the song was written by future Grammy winner Joe South. (South recorded several Top 40 hits of his own, and later worked as a sideman with Aretha Franklin, Simon and Garfunkel, and Bob Dylan. He also wrote "Down in the Boondocks" for Billy Joe Royal, "Hush" for Royal and Deep Purple, "Rose Garden" for Lynn Anderson and many others.) South was one of several on-the-cusp-of-fame studio musicians Lowery employed, including Jerry Reed and Ray Stevens. (The latter was in the studio to play piano on "Untie Me.") Lowery sold the recording to Philadelphia's Arlen Records, who released it in 1962. A surprise hit, "Untie Me" climbed to #62 on the Hot 100 and #12 on the R&B charts. The group followed with "Deep Inside Me," "You'll Never Know" and "Find Another Love" on Arlen in 1962 and 1963, but none made the charts.

At this point, the Tams started working with a protégé of Lowery's, 20-year-old songwriter Ray Whitley. (The Columbus, Georgia, native went on to write for Brian Hyland, Tommy Roe, the Swingin' Medallions and others.) His first song for the Tams, "What Kind of

Tams lead singer Joe Pope heard the song "Be Young, Be Foolish, Be Happy" performed by the Sensational Epics, a South Carolina group who played mainly college fraternity and sorority functions. The Epics' version didn't chart while the Tams' version went to #26 on the R&B charts and sold more than a million copies.

Fool," was recorded at Rick Hall's FAME Studios in Muscle Shoals, Alabama. One of that studio's first recordings had been Arthur Alexander's hit "You Better Move On," and the studio magic that worked for Alexander worked for the Tams as well. ABC-Paramount picked up the song and it went to #9 on the *Billboard* Pop, *Cashbox* and *Billboard* R&B charts, and all the way to #1 on the *Cashbox* R&B chart. Charles Pope was surprised by its success: "I didn't want that song to be our second release. I just didn't think it was that good." Nevertheless, the combination of Whitley's songwriting and the Tams' vocals seemed to be a recipe for success. Whitley continued to work with the group on song after song.

Sales of subsequent records were fair but not as impressive. Their next, 1964's "You Lied to Your Daddy," came in at #70 on the pop charts and the flip, "It's All Right (You're Just in Love)," charted at #79. Both sides made the R&B and *Cashbox* charts as well. Then "Hey Girl, Don't Bother Me," stalled just outside the Top 40 at #41. "Silly Little Girl" charted at #87. Charles Pope recalled that "Silly Little Girl" was his brother Joe's favorite song: "He especially liked to perform it live and would ad-lib a lot of lines that weren't in the song originally. He'd add, 'I'll even beg you, girl' and things like that." "Silly Little Girl" was the first single release written for the group by Joe South since "Untie Me"; its flip side "Weep Little Girl" was by up-and-coming songwriter Mac Davis. While the Tams' records weren't always charting high, the records were selling and the group was developing a following. They played a number of venues, including the world-famous Apollo Theater.

By this time, Floyd Ashton was reportedly having problems with alcohol and it was affecting his performances, so in 1964 he was replaced by Albert Cottle. This was the point at which the group entered their longest sustained period of success. After several more singles, they released "I've Been Hurt" (1965); according to Pope, it was "a favorite with the college kids." It became a monster regional hit and was reportedly the best-selling and most often played Tams song of all time—despite the fact that it never made the Top 100 on any chart.

The success of "I've Been Hurt" and other songs from this period ("Laugh It Off," "Hey Girl, Don't Bother Me," more) could essentially be chalked up to the songwriting abilities of Whitley and the producing of Joe South. According to Charles Pope, however, what songs the group recorded were still chosen for them by management, and not the group. "Bill Lowery chose all the songs for us," Pope said, and considering the group's success it would be hard to argue with the formula.

But Charles' brother Joe had heard a song that Whitley and J.R.

Cobb had co-written, "Be Young, Be Foolish, Be Happy," and wanted to record it. Whitley and Cobb—who later co-wrote "Spooky" and "Stormy"—had given the song to the Sensational Epics, a South Carolina group that played mainly college fraternity and sorority functions. In 1967, the Epics recorded "Be Young, Be Foolish, Be Happy" on Warner Brothers, and though produced by Whitley it failed to find an audience. According to Charles Pope, his brother Joe "really wanted to do the song, so Bill let us do it."

The Tams' version was released on ABC Records in April 1968. It was produced by Joe South, who was just a few months from his own first Top 20 pop hit, "Games People Play." While "Be Young" only hit #61 on the *Billboard* pop charts, it went to #26 on the R&B charts and eventually sold more than a million copies; it was the group's only RIAA-Certified Gold Record. The song became the anthem for college crowds across the Southeast in particular. Not surprisingly, given England's love for American R&B that emerged with the Northern Soul boom in the late '60s and early '70s, the song was a hit there as well, going to #32 on the British charts in 1970.

After a few more non-charting ABC releases, the Tams and the label parted ways. They next released "The Tams Medley" (1971), a Capitol Records compilation of Whitley-penned hits by the group, including "Hey Girl, Don't Bother Me," "What Kind of Fool," "You Lied to Your Daddy," "I've Been Hurt," "Laugh It Off" and "Be Young, Be Foolish, Be Happy." "We had all wanted to do a medley of our songs, so we talked to Bill and he had the writers put together 'The Tams Medley'—and we loved it," Pope said. It failed to chart nationally but became yet another popular regional hit in the South.

Meanwhile, 1964's "Hey Girl, Don't Bother Me" suddenly found a new audience: Upon re-release in England in 1971, it went to #1, stayed there for three weeks, and was song of the year in the U.K. Pope noted that this was a pleasant surprise and that, as a side benefit of the song's popularity in England, "we went over and performed at Top of the Pops with Rod Stewart in 1971." Hoping to capitalize on this success in the States, ABC Dunhill re-released the song in a sleeve that said "It's Number ONE in England and the Biggest Selling Record in the U.K. This Year." This U.S. re-release failed to chart.

Things were not going well in the relationship between the group and their manager Bill Lowery at this time. Pope said that, though the group was selling a lot of records, very little money was trickling down to them, and their relationship with Lowery reached a breaking point. "Lowery just seemed to get all of the money; he always did," Pope said. "I have paperwork about all kinds of money we were supposed to get for

#26. "Be Young, Be Foolish, Be Happy" (1968)

The Tams: from left to right, Charles Pope, Robert Smith, Joe Pope, Al Cottle and Horace "Sonny" Key (courtesy Charles and Diane Pope).

record sales, but we never saw it." After the Tams split with Lowery, they remained popular on the club circuit—but no more records made the American charts.

The Tams had more chart success in England, with "There Ain't Nothing Like Shaggin'" going to #21 on the British charts in 1987 and "My Baby Sure Can Shag" going to #91 in 1988. Lead singer Joe Pope died in March 1996. Today, despite the deaths of Joe and Charles Pope, the Tams continue to perform with Charles' son "Little Redd" singing those classic hits. "He started with me and my brother Joe when he was seven years old and he'll be taking over the Tams [when I'm gone]," Pope told me in our last interview. "That's why I say the Tams will never die."

I interviewed Charles and Diane Pope in June, July and August 2010. Charles Pope passed away in 2013.

#27
(R&B Charts)
"This Time It's Real" (1973)
TOWER OF POWER
Billboard Pop: #63; *Cashbox*: #62; Adult Contemporary: #46; British Charts: Did not chart

---

Tower of Power founder Emilio Castillo broke into music as the result of an ultimatum from his father. It was not because his father wanted him to be more cultured, or because his father didn't want his talent to go to waste, or even because Emilio, like many artists in this book, had spent years singing in the church choir. Instead, it was because his father wanted to keep him off the streets and out of trouble. As a result, Emilio became the founder and leader of one of the greatest horn bands in music.

Emilio Castillo's entrance into the music world came in 1964 when he got into some trouble. He told me, "My brother Jack, a friend and I were going to the pool one day to scope chicks ... and back then, these pastel-colored, muscleman-type t-shirts were really popular. Well, we went to a store, put two or three of these shirts on under these baggy shirts we had for the pool, and decided we'd walk out and steal the shirts." They didn't get far before they were caught, and their father was called to come to the store. "I had a really short criminal career: It lasted one day because we got caught first time out! After my dad picked us up and we apologized to the store manager and all of that, he got us home and said, 'You and your brother need to think of something that's gonna keep you occupied and off the streets and out of trouble. And if you don't come up with something you can just stay in your room the rest of your lives.' Well, the Beatles had just hit America, and a friend of ours had bought a guitar, and so we said, 'We want to play music.'"

Their father took his sons to a music store where Emilio picked out a sax for himself and his brother got a drum set. According to Castillo,

#27. "This Time It's Real" (1973)

Dad was the bar manager at the Cabana motel, and they always had show bands. He had taken us there a few times, and I'd noticed that the guy who always seemed to get all the attention was the guy who played the sax. So when he took us to the store and told us we could have any instrument we wanted, I pointed to the sax. We started the band that day, and I've had a band ever since. But it's not like we practiced for years and joined a band; we started the band, *then* learned to play the instruments.

The high schoolers—first known as the Roadrunners—weren't all that ambitious, and initially they were happy to play parties and dances, hoping to gravitate towards playing the bar scene in Sacramento. They next became the Extension Five and then, inspired by the success of the *Batman* TV series, Batman and Robin. Turns out they couldn't use the latter name for reasons of copyright infringement, so they switched to the Gotham City Crime Fighters. They dressed in Batman costumes and mainly played covers of R&B hits. They also recorded one single on the Batwing label in 1966, "Who Stole the Batmobile." As time went on and the *Batman* TV series' popularity waned, the novelty of the name and costumes was played out.

It seemed that another change was needed, and this time Emilio and his bandmates decided to embrace their roots: R&B and the Motown sound. "We always sort of leaned towards more soulful stuff," he said. "My parents always had real soulful music playing, like Dinah Washington, Nat King Cole and Bill Doggett, so I was all about soul music. I patterned myself and my band after those artists." Initially they named their repurposed band Black Orpheus, "but we didn't like that name. My mother told me that since my brother and I were originally from Detroit and were going to play soul music, we should call the band The Motowns. So we did."

In 1968, when Stephen "Doc" Kupka came into the band,

The 1973 album *Tower of Power* earned a gold record. The album included the classic "This Time It's Real" (pictured).

things started to fall into place. Kupka was a hippie with long hair, so Castillo and his bandmates "grew our hair long and changed our name to Tower of Power." Kupka also had a good ear for music, and while he appreciated the band's sound, he believed they could do more than cover tunes. Castillo: "He said, 'What you're doing with these soul tunes is amazing, and I like how you make them your own. But you need to write your own songs.' I don't think that ever would have occurred to me, but I thought we could give it a try."

At the time, the pinnacle of success in the Bay area was to play the Fillmore East, and that became the band's primary goal. "We had an audition at the Fillmore, where everyone was trying to get signed by Bill Graham, who had two labels. He decided to sign us, and that's where it all started." They released an album, *East Bay Grease*, on Graham's San Francisco label in 1970 and recorded the singles "Back on the Streets Again" and "Sparkling in the Sand" in 1971. While neither the album nor the singles did anything nationally, it was enough to interest Warner Brothers, who signed the group in 1972.

Their debut album for Warner Brothers was *Bump City* (1972) and their first single from the album, "You're Still a Young Man," went to #29 on the pop charts in and #24 on the R&B charts. The album's second single, "Down to the Nightclub," hit #66 on the *Billboard Hot 100*, and the album itself hit #85 on the *Billboard* album charts and #16 on the R&B Albums chart. The group had found tangible national success at last.

In 1973, they released their third album, the eponymous *Tower of Power*, and from it came their biggest hit, "So Very Hard to Go" (#17). By then Lenny Williams was lead vocalist, and his contributions made not only "So Very Hard to Go" a big hit but also the album as a whole. *Tower of Power* went to #15 on the album charts. Its sales were also helped by another chart record, the now-classic "This Time It's Real."

According to Castillo, "David Bartlett was the main guy who wrote the song. He was a drummer and joined the band later. David had an amazing aptitude for writing, but when he brought it to us, he had less than half of the tune written. He had the chorus, the chords and the first verse. He brought it to us, and we sat down and wrote that tune quick." Bartlett, Castillo and Kupka added a few things they felt made it more listener-friendly: Castillo said, "We added the modulation—the way it goes [*singing*] 'And I know, I can feel it, this time it's real. And I know, I can feel it...' You know the way it goes up, and it goes down, and it goes up? And so we finished it that way."

"This Time It's Real" was released on the Warner Brothers label in September 1973, as the follow-up to "So Very Hard to Go." Perhaps it didn't climb as high as the group hoped when it stalled at #65 on the pop charts. It fared better on the R&B charts, going to #27, and it hit #62 on *Cashbox* and #46 on the Adult Contemporary charts. Despite its failure to climb high on the national charts, Castillo said they were very happy with it. Certainly having three chart records on the *Tower of Power* album was something to be happy about (a third single, "What Is Hip?," peaked at #39 on the R&B charts), and sales of the album earned the group a gold record, their first. The album peaked at #15 on the *Billboard* album sales chart.

Lenny Williams stuck around for two more albums, *Back to Oakland* and *Urban Renewal*. After his departure, he was replaced by Hubert Tubbs. The group left Warner Brothers and signed with Columbia, and their first album for the label was 1976's *Ain't Nothin' Stoppin' Us Now*. That album spawned another big single, the party anthem "You Ought to Be Havin' Fun." Castillo: "It was mainly written by Hubert Tubbs. He came to us, started clapping his hands and singing, 'You ought to be havin' fun,' but that was really about all he had other than the line 'Put your troubles on the run' and the chant, 'You ought to be, you ought to be! You ought to be, you ought to be!'" Sensing that there was a good song hidden in these fragments of lyrics, Castillo and Kupka went to work. According to Castillo, "I wrote the tune, was really excited about it, gave it to the band. The intro, that bass line, was directly inspired by the bass line intro on 'Bad Luck' by Harold Melvin and the Blue Notes. I mean, we didn't steal their line, we made up our own, but it was the inspiration."

Like "This Time It's Real," "You Ought to Be Havin' Fun" didn't chart very high, going only to #68, and #62 on the R&B charts. Castillo said,

> That song was one of my heartbreaks. As a record producer, I felt like I missed the mark on that song. I'm usually good at getting to that place. I have the picture, and I get it there. But in that case, I felt like it fell short. It was good, but not the way I pictured. Then later in my career, I did something that I never do: I redid the song, but it still missed the mark. I'd love to see another artist do that song. I just had a higher ideal for that tune.

"You Ought to Be Havin' Fun" was the group's last single on the pop charts, although they'd have several more make the R&B charts. At around this time, in addition to recording and touring, they were in high demand to add their sound to other artists' releases; they'd play with Huey Lewis and the News, Aerosmith, Bonnie Raitt, Santana, Heart and others. Two of their most noteworthy contributions were adding horns to 1974's "The Bitch Is Back" by Elton John (peaked at #4

Tower of Power in 1973: top row, left to right: Greg Adams, Chester Thompson, Bruce Conte, Emilio Castillo and Mic Gillette. Middle row: Doc Kupka, Lenny Pickett and Rocco Prestia. Bottom row: David Garibaldi, Lenny Williams and Brent Byars (courtesy Emilio Castillo).

on the *Billboard* Top 40) and 1979's "Jane" by Jefferson Starship (#14 on the *Billboard* Top 40); there were many others. "We realize our horn section is well known, even more so because we've recorded and played with a lot of artists." In the end, he said, they've always loved the music, and remained true to themselves and their R&B roots. After 19 albums and more than 60 members over 50-plus years, there is little doubt that the group has made their mark on American music.

I interviewed Emilio Castillo in August 2011. As of this writing, he is still performing.

#28
(British Charts)
"I Got Rhythm" (1967)
The Happenings
Billboard Pop: #3; *Cashbox*: #1;
R&B, Adult Contemporary: Did not chart

It's not unusual for musical acts to redo or "cover" songs other artists have done previously, and in fact a half dozen of the chart records discussed in this book were cover versions. Usually, though, the songs covered are songs that were released not long before the redone version; in fact, of the other five cover versions in this book, four were redone within a year of the original's release, and one was done five years later. In that sense, the Happenings' release of "I Got Rhythm" is an anomaly. Not only did the group cover it nearly four decades after its composition, it was a George Gershwin–composed tune from a musical, and not a pop song. Add to that that every one of the group's nine chart records was a cover of a song done by another artist, and you have a set of unique circumstances surrounding the group and their 1967 release of "I Got Rhythm."

Paterson, New Jersey, natives Bob Miranda, Harry Arthur, Ralph DiVito and Thomas Giuliano formed the singing group the Four Graduates after finishing high school. Although some sources say the four of them met while in the Army at Fort Dix, Miranda said that they in fact met at "a St. Leo's Church dance in East Paterson." They mainly worked the tri-state area (New York, New Jersey, Connecticut) and especially the Catskills. Miranda said they also spent some time working as session singers, most notably for Bob Crewe, who was associated with the Four Seasons at the time. "We were just doing background vocals to tracks mostly," Miranda said. "I don't think we ever did any Four Seasons tracks that I know of, because most of the time there were no lead vocals on the tracks yet so we didn't always know who or what group it was for. I know we did some vocals for Mitch Ryder, but don't know who else."

The group's first break as a featured act came when they signed with the Laurie label's Rust subsidiary. They released an updated cover version of the Ink Spots' 1944 recording "A Lovely Way to Spend an Evening" in 1963 and "Candy Queen" in 1964. Neither record made the national charts, but while at Rust they came to the attention of the Tokens, who had hit #1 with "The Lion Sleeps Tonight" in 1961. By this point, the Tokens were producing for some other acts on Laurie and Rust, and although they did not produce anything for the Four Graduates at the time, Miranda had been writing music and they did ask him to pass along any songs he might have for their Bright Tunes Music company. One song he wrote, "Girl on a Swing," went on to be a Top 40 hit for Gerry and the Pacemakers in 1966; Miranda later recorded it himself.

When the Tokens formed their own label, Miranda asked them if they'd sign the Four Graduates. They auditioned, and while the Tokens liked their sound, they felt they should change their name because it seemed dated. From a number of possibilities that included the Corduroys and the Bitter Lemons, they chose the Happenings because "What's happening?" was a popular phrase at the time. Harry Arthur decided to leave the group; his replacement David Libert "was our piano player at first and was not one of the Grads until Harry decided to leave." He then became a member of the regular lineup. The newly constituted and renamed Happenings signed with B.T. Puppy Records.

Their first release, "Girls on the Go," did not chart, but their second, "See You in September," was a smash. A Sid Wayne–Sherman Edwards composition, it was originally recorded by the Tempos in 1959 and went to #23 on the national pop charts. The Happenings had been performing the song for a while, and while they had always felt it was a good song, they also thought the Tempos' version was a bit lackluster. Putting their own twist on it and turning it into an up-tempo number, they recorded it that spring. By July 1966, their Bob Crewe–produced version was on the national pop charts, reaching a peak of #3 in, appropriately enough, September. By the end of the year, they'd sold more than a million units and received a gold record. They followed with "Go Away Little Girl" (Pop #12) and "Goodnight My Love" (Pop #51) before releasing another updated cover version, "I Got Rhythm."

"I Got Rhythm" was a 1930 George Gershwin tune from the musical *Girl Crazy*, and had been featured in movies and recorded many times since. Miranda said,

> Most of the selections for songs came from within the group, but I think I brought "I Got Rhythm" to the table. I came up with a lot of those old songs because I was a fanatic for old movies, even as a kid, and they were old then. I spent my whole youth glued to a Philco radio so I had a vast

#28. "I Got Rhythm" (1967)

awareness of the great songs that stirred me. Songs like "I'm Always Chasing Rainbows," which we did, and "If You Loved Me Really Loved Me," which we also did. When I started considering "I Got Rhythm" lyrically I thought, "Well, if we stay with those lyrics like 'I got my girl, who could ask for anything more,' they could be contemporary even now." So what I did first was strip the song down. It was a pretty simple melody; if I could get the Ethel Merman out of my head and start kind of fresh with it. I'd be okay!"

One thing Miranda he felt he needed to do to improve the song was to write an introduction and change some lyrics, but announcing that you're going to improve a Gershwin song is akin to claiming one can improve on Shakespeare. "I felt like I was gonna get sued and castrated and everything else for changing Gershwin lyrics. I changed the second verse from 'I've got daisies and green pastures' because I didn't think kids in 1967 would relate to daisies and green pastures." Miranda instead opted for "'I've got good times, no more bad times,' and that kind of stuff. We spent about two weeks, and I mean every day, working on the vocals, and probably several days of that was just experimenting with the sound of 'dip.' It sounds silly as hell, but after trying 'do' and 'wah' and everything else, we felt like the 'dip' had to be a big part of this song, part of the rhythm part of the song." It was the right word, because "when people saw us, the first thing they'd do is sing that 'dip, dip, dip,' and that still happens today. It seems so silly and simple, but it really works."

Miranda said that given the formula that the group had settled into, "taking a proven hit song and stripping it down and making it our own by changing the tempo, 'I Got Rhythm' just felt right. Taking an old song and making it sound like the Happenings, adding a

Despite having hits with "I Got Rhythm" and "See You in September," the Happenings tired of doing covers of other people's recordings. But the label wouldn't let them do their own material.

falsetto—it became our pattern of success. Not every time, but a lot of the time." But more than any other song the group ever did, they knew from the first playback that "I Got Rhythm" was going to be a hit. "I can remember after we did it and were in the studio and sound room when the playback on the final mix came in. I was there with Jay Siegel and I think Hank Medress and we all had a jaw-dropping experience because we all said the same thing. We all said, "If that isn't a hit record, then I don't know what is." And I know that the Tokens had had other groups that they produced, and either Hank or Jay said there'd only been a couple of records that they produced that had had this effect on them: 'He's So Fine' by the Chiffons and 'I Got Rhythm.' We just knew it was a hit."

"See You in September" was big; "I Got Rhythm" was bigger. Both went to #3 on the *Billboard* pop charts, but "I Got Rhythm" broke into the Top 40 in England whereas "See You in September" had not. Either way, both were huge hits and each of them had sold more than a million units and received gold records within a year of release. According to Miranda, the difference was that they didn't know "See You in September" was going to be as good as it was when we heard it. "We did with 'I Got Rhythm'; it was one of my favorites."

To maintain their momentum, the group needed a follow-up hit, but by this point the group was beginning to tire of doing covers. "Honestly, I thought some of the things that I wrote and Dave Weigert wrote could have worked just as well or better with that Happenings sound, the falsetto lead, but we just never got to do it. The Tokens were hellbent on not changing the formula because it worked for a while." While that makes sense to some degree, Miranda pointed out, "Times were changing. My God, there were so many types of music—Motown, acid rock, bubblegum—it was just a crazy time musically. The fact that we survived as long as we did as a sweet-sounding vocal group is amazing." But while their producers weren't on board with having them change anything, they weren't coming up with original material that would work for them either. "Honestly, we basically produced ourselves except for the technical end of going into the studio. We'd come up with the song and the arrangement and then embellish it around vocals and then go to the Tokens and say, 'Here, what do you think of this?' and most of the time they loved it and would carry it on to the studio. So that was the formula that we were following, and that they wanted us to keep following."

In other words, like many groups, they simply had to do what the record company said. But with the label's next suggestion Miranda felt they were pushed too far.

Mitch Margo of the Tokens came up with the idea of doing "My Mammy," the old song Al Jolson had made famous while singing in blackface, and I was so against doing it. I thought with the racial turmoil that was going on in 1967 and '68, I just wasn't a good idea to go back to a blackface artist singing a song that portrayed "the help." It just didn't sit right with me and I refused to record the song.

We got together with Herb Bernstein and the song was adapted to what was supposed to be a Happenings sound and ultimately it was, but still I said, "I can't do this. I think it's the wrong move career-wise. I think we should be doing original material, whether it's ours, or somebody else's, but we've got to get on the original material train here. We've milked this formula to the point where now were going back to the '30s and in blackface."

But contractually the group did have to do a follow-up. "If we didn't come in and do the songs, there would have been breach of contract, a lawsuit—who knows what would have happened? So meanwhile, the clock was ticking and the Happenings needed a follow-up to that huge Top Ten record. So finally I conceded and we did it." Miranda has never been happy about the situation. "It sounded like the Happenings, it was a good track, but honestly, I get black people that walk out when they hear that song. I mean, it's not like I'm doing it in blackface, but understandably they just can't get past the Al Jolson history with the song." Surprisingly, even with its baggage, it hit #13. Miranda continued:

> God only knows I would take a #13 hit now, but it's one of my least favorite things that we have done because of that. I don't get asked about that song much, and I don't volunteer to talk about it usually, but in a way, it's part of the "I Got Rhythm" thing since it was the follow-up.
>
> After the thing with "My Mammy," our relationship with the Tokens really got sticky, and it wasn't the same. Frankly, it wasn't that great before that. It's difficult to have four guys in the group, and four opinions from the producers, and it caused a lot of confusion. They made some not-so-great decisions with our career. Also, by that point, Jubilee, the parent company, was falling apart, they were losing their executives left and right. It was just a small label and for a while there, they were killing it. But when that started falling apart and we weren't having any hits, we weren't sure if it was us, or them, or what. We could have gone on, I thought, for quite a while longer. Nobody was doing drugs, we were all there and present, and it worked so many times, but jeez, we were still writing and performing and doing it.

Although four more of their records charted between 1967 and 1969, "My Mammy" was their last Top 40 hit. They did one more album for the label, but by that time it was all over.

By then, group members had started to leave. Libert went on to be a well-known music executive and worked with George Clinton, Alice

Cooper, Sheila E and others. Miranda toured with a new group of Happenings and still performs today. Despite the brevity of their career as a headline act, the Happenings clearly put their mark on popular music in the late 1960s, even if their sound and song selection was a bit anachronistic.

I interviewed Bob Miranda in 2018.

#29
(British Charts)
"Mother-in-Law" (1961)
Ernie K-Doe

Billboard Pop: #1; R&B: #1; *Cashbox*: #1;
Adult Contemporary: Did not chart

The story of Ernie K-Doe's "Mother-in-Law" is actually the story of two recordings, with essentially the same singers on both, with the same songwriter, and with distinctly similar sounds. Both songs made the pop charts, although "Mother-in-Law" is by far the most famous of the two today, having gone to #1. But Ernie K-Doe's story is about more than just one song. According to New Orleans musician Deacon John Moore, who played with K-Doe on his biggest hits, "K-Doe had a pretty big ego. He always thought he was the best there was in show business and later in life called himself the 'Emperor of the Universe.' The only performers he felt were up to his standards were James Brown and Sammy Davis Jr.!" Still, Moore said, "Despite his braggadocious nature, he was a really good showman on stage. Everybody can attest to that." Perhaps that's part of what makes K-Doe's career special: It's a story of his rise to fame, a descent to homelessness and singing on the streets for change, and renewed fame and success at the end of his life.

The artist who would eventually be known as Ernie K-Doe was born Ernest Kador Jr. in New Orleans, one of nine children of a Baptist minister. Like many R&B artists, his first experience singing was in the church; he later sang in the New Orleans–based Golden Choir Jubilee. As he got older, he became more interested in a future as a performer of rhythm and blues. After living in Chicago for a while, he returned to New Orleans to front a group named the Blue Diamonds. The group played most of New Orleans' R&B hotspots, including the renowned Dew Drop Inn. The Blue Diamonds released one single on the Savoy label, "Honey Baby," but it was not successful.

Even in those early days with the Blue Diamonds, Ernie Kador was developing a reputation as the consummate showman. That showmanship certainly got him noticed, and he was offered a record deal as a solo act. He first recorded "Eternity" on the Specialty label as Ernest Kador in 1955. His next recording came four years later: as Ernie Kador on Ember's "My Love for You." Neither of these records made an impression on the national charts. K-Doe's biggest opportunity came after he signed with the fledgling New Orleans–based Minit label owned by Joe Banashak. One thing Banashak insisted on was that Kador change his name because people were unsure how to pronounce "Kador." After signing with Minit in 1959, he changed his name to Ernie K-Doe, the name he would use for the rest of his career.

At Minit, he had the chance to work with New Orleans native Allen Toussaint. In the late 1950s, Toussaint had played and recorded with several famous New Orleans musicians, including Fats Domino; Banashak hired him as a writer, producer and arranger for Minit. Toussaint, who often registered his writing credits under the name C. Toussaint or Naomi Neville as well as under his own name, wrote K-Doe's second release, 1960's "Hello My Lover." The record generated enough regional

Ernie K-Doe claimed he decided that he wanted to perform "Mother-in-Law" after finding it in the trash can where songwriter Allen Toussaint had dropped it. Toussaint tells a different tale. Either way, it became a #1 hit.

#29. "Mother-in-Law" (1961)

interest that it reportedly sold 100,000 copies. But it was with the 1961 Toussaint composition "Mother-in-Law" that Ernie K-Doe finally had that elusive hit. Toussaint—who was single—had written the song after hearing so many mother-in-law jokes on television. Toussaint apparently envisioned it as more of a novelty song like Larry Verne's "Mr. Custer," the Hollywood Argyles' "Alley Oop" and Brian Hyland's "Itsy Bitsy Teenie Weenie Yellow Polka Dot Bikini," all three of which hit #1 the year before. As such, when K-Doe wasn't really connecting with the song during his first attempt to record it, Toussaint gave up on it and literally threw it in the trash can.

What happened next depends on which of the principals involved was asked. Toussaint said he left the room to take a break and a back-up singer named Willie Harper fished the song out of the trash and talked K-Doe into trying the song again when Toussaint came back. On the other hand, K-Doe later claimed (though Toussaint disputed it) that *he* found the song in a trash can where *Toussaint* threw it, and decided that he wanted to perform it. K-Doe told the *Chicago Tribune*'s Dave Hoekstra that the song resonated with him because "my mother-in-law was staying in my house. I was married 19 years, and it was 19 years of pure sorrow. When I sang 'Satan should be her name,' I meant that."

In the early days at Minit, the label's resources, talent and money were scarce, and so artists who were billed as solo acts would often put in studio time and earn extra money by singing back-up vocals on other artists' efforts. On "Mother-in-Law," the saxophone player was Robert Parker, who had the 1966 hit "Barefootin'. Another contributor was Benny Spellman, another struggling Minit artist. Spellman agreed to help out on "Mother-in-Law," and his bass voice can be heard echoing K-Doe by singing the words "mother-in-law" throughout the record. Between K-Doe's playful lyrics and Spellman's resonating bass, this recording of the song was just what was needed. It hit #1 on the *Billboard* Pop, R&B and *Cashbox* charts, and #28 on the British charts.

But the song's success had some unexpected negative consequences. Deacon John Moore noted that the more success "Mother-in-Law" brought K-Doe, the more it irritated Benny Spellman. "K-Doe went out on a national tour when 'Mother-in-Law' was hot, and Benny was a little peeved at K-Doe because K-Doe didn't take him out on the road with him. Benny was upset because, he said, 'Mother-in-Law' wouldn't have sold if they didn't have my bass voice in there—that's really what Benny thought sold the record." Born in Pensacola, Florida, Spellman was a good athlete as a youth, and ultimately a football scholarship took him to Southern University in Baton Rouge. After college and a stint in the military, he joined Huey "Piano" Smith and his group the Clowns in

1959. Singing at the Dew Drop Inn, Spellman came to the attention of Banashak and Toussaint, who signed him to Minit as a solo artist. His first records, "Life Is Too Short" and "Darling No Matter Where" (both 1960), failed to generate any substantial sales. Like every other Minit artist, he sang back-up on other artists' records for extra money, and that put him in the studio that day to do vocals on "Mother-in-Law."

When "Mother-in-Law" hit #1, Spellman was still without a hit, and he was angry because he felt his contributions were being overlooked. Moore was present in the studio one day when anger erupted. He recalled,

> K-Doe had just come back off his successful road tour, and they went back to the studio to do a follow-up to "Mother-in-Law" with the same kind of line called "Get Out of My House." Benny was there, and K-Doe and Benny were in the booth for the singers and you could just see the tension between the two of them. All of a sudden, K-Doe and Benny came tumbling out of the booth with their hands at each other's throats. They were rolling on the ground, fighting, and Allen Toussaint called off the session! We assumed they were arguing about who made the record sell, over whether or not it was Benny's bass voice. Later on, I also heard it might have been over a woman!

After "Mother-in-Law" made K-Doe a star, his next song, 1961's "Te-Ta-Te-Ta-Ta," wasn't a big hit. "That was written because Ernie had his trademark style of singing where he'd go 'ah-ah-ah,'" Moore said, "and so Allen wrote 'Te-Ta-Te-Ta-Ta' to rhyme with that." Recorded at that same follow-up session with "Get Out of My House," "Te-Ta-Te-Ta-Ta" went to #53 on the Top 100 and #21 on the R&B charts. K-Doe had a few more low-charting records before 1962's "Popeye Joe" (#99) was his last chart record.

But "Mother-in-Law"'s success was also responsible for another chart record—for Spellman. Moore said, "Because Benny believed his bass voice was so instrumental in making 'Mother-in-Law' a hit, he worried Allen Toussaint to death to write him a song that sounded similar to it. Benny kept hounding Allen and hounding him. 'Please write me a song,' Benny would say. He wanted a song that would work with his bass vocals." Spellman felt that given the chance, he could do as well as K-Doe, and he wanted a hit song all his own. "So, Allen did write him his own song, 'Lipstick Traces.'" He continued:

> The story behind the song is that if you listen, "Lipstick Traces" is almost identical to "Mother-in-Law," with the same chord changes but a different storyline. If you listen to the melodic line, "Don't leave me no more," it's the same as "Mother-in-law." He used that little hook to construct "Lipstick Traces" because Allen said Benny bugged him so much, he finally

gave in and just sat down and wrote a song much like "Mother-in-Law." Allen was able to write around people's personalities and vocal styles, and he successfully did it with Benny and K-Doe. And though the songs, construction-wise, were similar, they had their own identity because of the personalities of the different singers. Benny was a baritone bass, and K-Doe was a tenor. So Allen knew how to write for both of them and yet give them individuality at the same time.

There's no denying the similarities between the songs, including having Willie Harper on back-up again as well as the great Irma Thomas and even K-Doe himself. "Lipstick Traces" wasn't as big a hit as "Mother-in-Law," going only to #80 on *Billboard* and #89 on *Cashbox*. It fared much better on the R&B charts, peaking at #28 in June 1962. Spellman's singles never seemed to really take off. He never got over his grudge against Minit because he felt that the label had exploited him; he left Minit a couple of years later and recorded a number of unsuccessful singles for small labels such as Alon and Sansu. Failing to find any more chart success, Spellman retired from the music business in 1968 and went to work for a beer distributor.

As for K-Doe, by 1964 he had left Minit, but stints at the Instant, Metric and Duke labels brought no further success. Perhaps his biggest success story post–"Mother-in-Law" came in 1971 when he released "'Here Come the Girls," the first song Toussaint had written for him since they were both at Minit. It failed to find an audience, but in 2007, a British pharmacy chain used it in a commercial; K-Doe's version, re-released, went to #43 on the British charts. In 2008, the British girl group Sugarbabes released a cover version of the song called "Girls," which went to #3 in England. Nearly four decades after its initial release, K-Doe's music was in the Top Ten again.

K-Doe didn't live to see the resurgence of his popularity. After "Here Come the Girls," he recorded only three more songs between 1973 and 1976, and none of them charted. He struggled with alcoholism and homelessness and by the late 1970s he was reportedly singing in the streets of New Orleans for change. In 1982, he broke into radio and had a successful career in the New Orleans market. In the 1990s, he married Antoinette Dorsey Fox, and she helped him rebrand and market himself. In 1994, they opened the successful Mother-in-Law Lounge in New Orleans, where he frequently performed, often in a cape and a crown in his "Emperor of the Universe" persona. A flamboyant performer until the end, he died from liver and kidney failure in 2001. Deacon John Moore said K-Doe was an impressive performer right up until the end: "Ernie used to say, 'At the end of the world, there's only gonna be two records playing: 'The Star Spangled Banner' and 'Mother-in-Law.' He was quite a character." Though Ernie K-Doe had just one big chart hit, there was a lot more to the man and his music than that solitary hit record.

I interviewed Deacon John Moore in November 2010; he is still involved in the New Orleans music scene. In 2008, he was inducted into the Louisiana Music Hall of Fame. This was a year before Ernie K-Doe was inducted.

#30
(Adult Contemporary Charts)
"Can't Find the Time" (1971)
Rose Colored Glass
Billboard Pop: #54; *Cashbox*: #53;
R&B, British Charts: Did not chart

When you think about '60s and '70s rock bands from Texas, the first group that comes to mind is probably ZZ Top. If you really know your music, you might recall the psychedelic sounds of Bubble Puppy, garage rockers Mouse and the Traps, or the cross-cultural music of the Sir Douglas Quintet. One thing all these groups had in common was that their sound was synonymous with the "rock" in rock'n'roll. Some of these groups are more guitar-heavy than others, but they all have that edge, that rock sound. As a result, if you are making a list of Texas rock bands, you might have to be reminded that Rose Colored Glass was a Texas band as well, although their biggest hit, 1971's "Can't Find the Time," is one of the most laid-back, easygoing, heartfelt songs of that era.

Larry Meletio, Roe Cree, Mary Owens and Bobby Caldwell comprised Rose Colored Glass, but they didn't start out as members of the same band and they were influenced by music that was a bit harder-edged than the song they eventually came to be known for. Meletio said he met Cree in high school when Cree was in the Sensations, a group who "set the standard for what was going on in the Dallas music scene. At the time, I don't think he was all that interested in anything I was doing because I was more of a hard rock drummer." Cree agreed, saying, "When the Sensations started, we idolized the Beach Boys and had the same equipment in the mid–60s until the Beatles invaded. We changed over to Gibson guitars and Vox amps immediately and did covers of their music for years. Then during my freshman year of college, our drummer enlisted in the Navy and the group disbanded. I was not a happy camper but continued college at Texas Tech University."

Caldwell and Owens were in a different band, a folk group named

Rose Colored Glass. "Mary Owens and I had formed a trio as a folk group in 1969," Caldwell said. "It was the two of us and Bob Penhall, and we played a lot of coffee houses and places like that." The name of the band came from a local record producer named Erroll Sober, who listened to them play and said, "I've got a perfect name for this band. This band should be called Rose Colored Glass." The group adopted the name.

When Penhall left the group, they started searching for a replacement. Caldwell knew Cree, and told him that he and Owens wanted to add more guitar and vocals to their little group. Cree happened to mention that he knew Meletio, who could also sing. Meletio said:

> We decided to get together one evening at Mary's house. We sat around and started playing with some harmony pieces—Crosby, Stills and Nash, the Byrds. Bobby has such a big, deep voice and tremendous range, and Roe is more of a mid-range but has a very definable voice. We played around and we knew it sounded good. It's funny how things work out. You sit around and wait long enough and finally the right people get together, and the chemistry was just phenomenal. We could play just about anything and we could harmonize.

The group had been working together for a few months, playing clubs and developing their harmonies, when their manager Norm Miller booked them some time in an old 8-track studio. Miller brought them to the attention of Jim Long, who was using a studio for producing jingles. Long was impressed by what he heard, and ultimately Miller and Long had the group record some songs. Long got hold of a song called "Make It with You" by an unknown writer, David Gates, who had published the song but hadn't yet recorded it. Long believed the song was perfect for the group. According to Meletio,

> David Gates got wind that we were thinking about

"Can't Find the Time," written and recorded by the group Orpheus, peaked at #80 in 1969. When Rose Colored Glass was given the song, they were not enthusiastic and had to be convinced to record it.

#30. "Can't Find the Time" (1971)

making it our first single and we got a call from him and he said, "Don't pursue that song any more because Bread is going to release it." So Jim told us we were off that project, but he said, "Here's a song a guy has written and his group recorded, but it just didn't go anywhere. It needs something else."

The song was "Can't Find the Time" by the Massachusetts-based group Orpheus, who had released it on the MGM label in 1969. Although the Orpheus version had cracked the *Billboard Hot 100* (peaking at #80), Rose Colored Glass heard it and they were underwhelmed. "We'd never heard of the song" Meletio said, "and we thought it kind of just droned along." Despite the group's lack of enthusiasm, they were persuaded to record it. Meletio:

> One night about 2:30 in the morning, we'd just finished playing at one of the local clubs, and we were asked if we wanted the recording time in the studio. We got in there and started working on "Can't Find the Time." Mary was instrumental in a lot of the vocal arrangement—she and Bobby both were—and she came up with some really dynamic ideas. Roe was good with the instrumental tracks and with the guitar, and then Bobby with that robust voice of his. It's funny because Roe had always said, "Larry we need to slow you down," because I was a rock drummer, but I said the song needed a jump tempo. When it was done, Miller said he wanted Long to hear the track and the band went back to playing in the clubs and thought that was the end of that.

But Miller and Long were enthused about the song. Caldwell said, "[Management] shopped the record around in September or October 1970, and Bang Records decided to release it." Cree said he didn't even know the record was out until he was driving around Dallas one day and heard it on the radio; "I almost ran off the road!" Caldwell said his sister heard the song on the radio and told him.

The song took off and, like many rising stars, their dreams came true when they were asked to appear on *American Bandstand*. Meletio:

> We got the call to go to L.A. to be on *American Bandstand*, and we were told Dick Clark had requested us because "Can't Find the Time" had really taken off. It had been in the Top Ten in Chicago for like six weeks or something and people just loved it. We get out there and they met us at the airport in a limo. They took us to the studio and the Jackson Five and Paul Revere and the Raiders were there too, because they'd shoot like three shows on the same day. Dick Clark was really, really wonderful.

Cree agreed:

> Dick had us in his office for lunch and more conversation. He treated us like we were big stars. One of the nicest men I ever met in the music business. He took us to Rodeo Drive for sightseeing and shopping. He took us into a very nice store, and the first thing I see is Ricky Nelson looking at chamois suede pants and a top! I met one of my childhood idols.

Meletio said that Clark told the band, "I want you to know I have a special place in my heart for musicians from Texas and for that Texas sound. When I heard this song, it was very refreshing—it wasn't a California sound or an East Coast sound and so I really wanted to have this interview with you and have you on the show." Meletio added, "Well, at that point, we were on top of the world."

Even though they were living the dream, the song didn't perform exceptionally well on the *Billboard Hot 100*, peaking at #54. It did considerably better on the Adult Contemporary charts, rising to #30. But like many bands before and since, the quick success and the group's inexperience meant additional problems. "We had a tiger by the tail at this point because we were young and really weren't sure how to handle it," Meletio said. Bang insisted the group get new management, "and that was the beginning of the end. Norm always had a big picture of where he wanted Rose Colored Glass to go, and things were going well and we didn't want to lose him, but other people were very interested by then. By that time, we'd also gone into the studio and recorded 'If It's All Right with You.'" The result was a second chart record; it peaked at #95 on the *Billboard* pop chart in October 1971.

Meletio said, "We left Dallas on a couple of charter planes, and we were flying over Kansas City and the motor quit. The prop was dead steady and you could hear wind." Caldwell said, "The pilot hit the reserve fuel tank and the engine coughs and restarts. We were on a glide path going down, but we were still going down." They landed safely.

The other members of the group were in another plane, and their experience wasn't a whole lot better. According to Meletio, Cree, Owens and guitar player John Govroe "landed at an abandoned airport where there'd been a lot of drug-running and a lot of suspicious activity. Back then, all of us were long-hairs and had mustaches, and Mary was dressed for the times. Everybody was detained three hours and finally released, but we were all pretty shaken by that point. Eventually, we got to our concert an hour and a half late; the crew that was supposed to load and unload our equipment wasn't there, and someone had left all of the equipment we shipped ahead of time out in the rain."

The group's equipment "was on the tarmac covered in ice," according to Caldwell. "At the college where we had to play later, none of the microphones worked so we had to borrow four from the drama department. It was ridiculous."

"This is when our eyes really opened to what was going on," Meletio said. "We later learned that the airplane's pilot never got checked out. All of this was due to our new management, and it kind of made us start looking at the fact that we were pretty vulnerable. The way we were being handled showed us how quickly things can change."

The group realized that being handled by a national label means that when you aren't the primary act, you can get lost in the shuffle. Travel plans were botched, and details weren't being attended to.

They also started to doubt that the label was making the right decisions about their music. "The flip side of 'If It's All Right' really should have been our second single release. It was a Mac Davis song called 'You're Good for Me.' I think it was a better song." Despite the group's wishes, the label went with "If It's All Right." The group also wanted to do an album, and the label was at least in agreement about that. Caldwell said,

> We all wrote songs and started recording them, and it was good stuff, and it was fun. But we never got to finish it, and it was never released. By that point, I don't think Bang had the money to promote an album. They didn't even have any singles left. They didn't have the right financing. Believe it or not, we never saw one dime in royalties from "Can't Find the Time," and they wouldn't even let us listen to the tracks we'd recorded for our album.

The label was struggling financially, and by 1971 they had lost Neil Diamond and Van Morrison, their two biggest acts. CBS Records eventually purchased the label.

Despite the fact that they weren't paying the group, the label was nevertheless insisting on changes in the group's operation and make-up. Meletio:

> Management wanted there to be a person who was a focus of the group, a frontman. There really never was a focus of the group, and while we called Roe our group leader, it was because he was organized, but there was not one leader. And they wanted Bobby to do more single-artist things. They started getting involved in our careers, and there started to be some backbiting. They also brought in another guy named Bill Tillman, a big guy, and he had charisma, and the new management thought he'd be a good fit. Bill was really more of a Vegas-type entertainer, but the problem was that all that charisma was only on stage, and it was never off stage. He kept to himself a lot.

According to Caldwell, the group realized that the label "didn't think Larry and Roe were talented enough to take it to the next level, so they were trying to surround Mary and me with more talented musicians. Bill was talented, but he had a strong personality, and the others didn't get along with him."

Interference by management and the forced addition of another member meant the chemistry was off. Meletio and Cree had had enough, and they quit the group.

Rose Colored Glass: top, left to right, Roe Cree and Bobby Caldwell. Bottom: Larry Meletio and Mary Owens (courtesy Bobby Caldwell).

"I was the first to leave the group, and then Roe left as well," Meletio said. Cree recalled, "Our time together as Rose Colored Glass was priceless, but there came a point when I had to move on. I sold my two Les Pauls and a stacked Marshall, got a haircut and a real job." Caldwell called the day Larry and Roe left "one of the worst days of my life. Mary and I kept the band together a little while, but neither one of us really enjoyed playing after that and we ended it." Just as quickly as it had started, Rose Colored Glass was done.

Cree stayed in the music industry a while, then went into sales, and finally retired in Mexico. He still plays occasionally. Meletio was in several bands over the years, meeting and working with some of the biggest names in the business: Alice Cooper, Don Henley, Glenn Frey, Willie Nelson, Charley Pride and others. After Meletio opened his own recording studio, his friend Eric Clapton did his first rendition of "Lay Down Sally" there. Bobby and Mary had a band called Texas Rose; Caldwell eventually moved back to Texas. "Maybe 15, 20 years ago, I told Larry we should play again and he agreed," Caldwell said. "That's when we started the Texas Rock Association. We only play four or five times a year but its rock'n'roll from the beginning to the end. And of course we play 'Can't Find the Time' every time we get together."

Meletio said he learned one very valuable life lesson from the Rose Colored Glass experience: "Whenever you have a recipe to anything that is successful, you don't change even one ingredient. Because if you do, the chances of you capturing that magic may be lost."

I interviewed Larry Meletio, Bobby Caldwell, and Roe Cree in 2014.

#31
(British Charts)

"Keep It Comin' Love" (1977)
KC and the Sunshine Band
Billboard Pop: #2; R&B: #1;
Cashbox: #2; Adult Contemporary: #36

There are very few artists in popular culture that have become so synonymous with a certain style of music that without them, one wonders if that type of music would have existed at all. Elvis and the Beatles made their mark in very recognizable ways, and the Supremes, the Four Tops, the Temptations and Marvin Gaye collectivity represent the Motown sound. There's also Led Zeppelin, Bob Dylan and the Beach Boys, each so firmly entrenched in our collective psyche that it seems obvious that '70s rock, folk music and surf music could not have existed without them.

The same can be said of KC and the Sunshine Band, because when it comes to disco, it's impossible to think it would have been as popular and important as it was without the band's music.

Harry Wayne Casey, aka "KC," was born in Opa-locka, Florida, one of two children to Jane Ann and Harry L. Casey. "I grew up in the '60s so my influences were the Motown sound, Stax Records, the great Atlantic stuff like Aretha Franklin and the Drifters," KC told me. "I loved Otis Redding and James Brown and those great R&B performers. I always liked more R&B than anything else, and I was lucky to grow up in a time of so many great songs." He said he knew early on that he wanted to be an entertainer. After graduation from Hialeah High School, he took piano at Miami-Dade College North while working at a record store. He went to work for Tone Record Distributors "just to be close to the recording industry," he said. He swept floors, unpacked boxes, anything. "I started in retail and ended up in wholesale and was doing everything that I could to work with promotions and that sort of thing. The place I ended up happened to have a recording studio in the back of

#31. "Keep It Comin' Love" (1977)

the building. I had access to that studio. I was there five years before I had any major success."

Tone Distributors and T.K. Recording Studios were owned by Henry Stone and Steve Alaimo, and they had several subsidiary labels. One subsidiary, Glades, had a hit in 1972 with Timmy Thomas' "Why Can't We Live Together" (#1 R&B, #3 *Billboard* Pop), while another, Allston, had a hit with Betty Wright's 1971 release "Clean Up Woman" (#2 R&B, #6 *Billboard* Pop). But Tone was still searching for a really big song across the charts and a big act with staying power.

It was reportedly at a party at Betty Wright's house that KC figured out what kind of sound his band should use. There was a "Junkanoo" band playing the party, and KC was intrigued by their multi-ethnic sound that incorporated horns, whistles, drums and keyboards as opposed to the guitar-driven music so prevalent at the time. In 1973, he formed KC and the Sunshine Junkanoo Band using studio musicians, local Junkanoo musicians and friends from an earlier group called Casey and the Oceanliners. Just prior to this, he had met bass player Richard Finch, an aspiring songwriter who also worked at T.K. All the pieces were in place.

Oddly enough, KC's first big success came with someone other than his own group. "I wrote a song called 'Rock Your Baby,' but at the time I wrote it, I was working on songs for KC and the Sunshine Band and that song just didn't feel like it was in the direction I wanted us to go in. It didn't fit our group." He took the song to George McCrae, who recorded it (KC played keyboard) and released it in 1974. "Rock Your Baby" went to #1 on the R&B chart, #1 on the British Charts, and was #1 for two weeks on the *Billboard* Pop Charts. Perhaps most significantly, it's often called one of the very first disco songs.

To date, "Rock Your Baby" has sold more than 11 million copies,

In the two years prior to the release of "Keep It Comin' Love," KC and the Sunshine Band had four #1 records on the pop charts.

meaning that if that's the only song KC had ever written, he would probably be wealthy from that song alone. But it didn't bother him that his first #1 was recorded by someone else:

> It was fine because I was part of a company and I co-wrote songs with people and performed on other people's records, I produced some for other artists before KC and the Sunshine Band, so I was just doing whatever I needed to do. It didn't matter where I was going to land there. Whether it was songwriter, producer, artist or whatever, I was doing what I loved and enjoyed and having a lot of fun doing it. It didn't matter if I had sung the song or George sang the song, just as long as it was successful.

Before McCrae's record topped the charts, KC and the Junkanoo Sunshine band had released "Blow Your Whistle," which hit #27 on the R&B charts. Next, as KC and the Sunshine Band, they released "Sound Your Funky Horn," which went to #21 on the R&B charts. Their next release came right after McCrae's release in 1974, but "Queen of Clubs" didn't make the American charts at all—though it went Top Ten in England.

Although these were respectable showings, they still had not had a song make the pop charts in America. "I got to T.K. in 1969 or '70, but it wasn't 'til '74 or '75 till I had a major hit record," KC said.

That 1975 hit was a song he and Finch co-wrote, "Get Down Tonight," which rose to #1 on the *Billboard* pop and R&B charts, and was a monster smash around the world. When I asked him what his favorite song was out of all his recordings, he waffled a bit ("I can't narrow it down to one because they all mean something special to me") but eventually he said, "If I had to pick one, it'd probably be 'Get Down Tonight' because it was my first major hit and my first #1 record in America."

KC and the Sunshine Band were just getting started. After "Get Down Tonight," there was 1975's "That's the Way I Like It" (#1 on the *Billboard* Pop and R&B charts), 1976's "Shake Your Booty" (#1 on the *Billboard* pop and R&B charts) and 1977's "I'm Your Boogie Man" (#1 on the *Billboard* Pop charts, #3 on R&B charts). Their second album, *KC & the Sunshine Band*, went triple platinum, and KC won the American Music Award for Best R&B Artist. At that point, they were perhaps the hottest band in the world.

Their next release was 1977's "Keep It Comin' Love." Like "Get Down Tonight," "That's the Way I Like It," "Shake Your Booty" and "I'm Your Boogie Man," it was written, produced, and arranged by KC and Finch. The band seemed to have figured out that music fueled by double entendres did exceptionally well in the ultra-liberal and permissive 1970s, especially among the disco crowd. A song that says to make a little love and "get down tonight," or chants "That's the way I like it," leaves a lot of room for the listener to fill in the blanks, so to speak. Without a doubt "Keep It Comin' Love" is the pinnacle of the double entendre, and the "it" to keep "comin'" is really open to interpretation. According to KC, "I think any song can be interpreted in different ways, and I leave it up to the individual to decide what he or she thinks it means." Ultimately though, although songs such as "Keep It Comin' Love" might be somewhat suggestive,

> they were really love songs and songs about being in love and all the things that go with being in love. There was nothing really to hide, you could take them any way you wanted to take them. I want each and every [listener] to interpret those songs the way they want to interpret them. We all do that anyway.
> Songs are the backbone of our lives, the music is the soundtrack of our lives. I know sometimes I hear a song and could swear it had been written about me or my life. So I just think whatever my interpretation was what I thought it meant. You know what I mean.

Listeners also loved interpreting the songs the way they liked, as "Keep It Comin' Love" went to #1 on the R&B charts, making it the group's fifth song in just two years to make it to #1 on the pop chart, R&B chart or, as three of them had, #1 on both charts. It only went to #2 on the pop charts, peaking there for the weeks of October 1 and 8, 1977, behind the #1 record, Meco's "The *Star Wars* Theme," then was still in the #2 position when Debby Boone's "You Light Up My Life" leapfrogged it the week of October 15. Boone's record was #1 for 10 weeks (her only Top 40 hit), while Meco had three more Top 40 hits (all movie themes) but no more #1s. "Keep It Comin' Love" came along at the wrong time to make the top spot on the pop charts. It did hit #1 in Canada (but only went to #31 in England). The album it was on, *Part 3*, went triple platinum.

In 1978, things started to change. There was success. "Boogie Shoes," a former flip side, was re-released after it was included on the *Saturday Night Fever* soundtrack, and KC won two more Grammys as a performer and producer on the album. But as a single, "Boogie Shoes" topped out at #35 on the pop charts and #29 on the R&B charts, and that was the highest position any of the band's records reached on their next five singles released in 1978 through May 1979. Disco was dying, and the group that embodied the soul of disco was struggling.

KC could see that change was in the air, and he was determined to stay in front of it:

> I was always trying to change because my peers were able to change. But people wouldn't let me change. They wanted what I'd always done. Then you

have those people who say, "Well, that just sounds like KC and the Sunshine Band." How the hell ... what do you want me to sound like? You know what I mean? Diana Ross sounds like Diana Ross. You hear one song she sings, it sounds like her. But for some reason, it seems like I was not allowed to change for whatever reason. But I wanted to, I wanted to experiment and try different things. Sometimes it worked and I guess sometimes it didn't work.

One that did work was his second release of 1979, the ballad "Please Don't Go," which was his sixth #1 and fifth #1 on the pop charts. It was a complete departure from the disco sound of just a year before, but audiences ate it up. Next was another departure from the disco sound, a song with singer Teri De Sario, "Yes, I'm Ready." A remake of a Barbara Mason standard, it peaked at #2, though it hit #1 on the Adult Contemporary charts. It was his first hit without the Sunshine Band; he was billed simply as KC.

Disco was dead and it seemed that KC would move on. But for whatever reason, it was at this point that the hits stopped coming. He left T.K. Records and signed with Epic, and in 1983 he released the catchy "Give It Up."

> That was a great record. There was some other stuff on that album that would've done well, I think, too, but we didn't put it out. I was on Epic Records and it was a huge hit in Europe; it was #1 in England and Ireland. But they didn't want to release it in the U.S. So I said, "Let me release it" and they gave me $100,000 and gave me the rights to the song and I released it. Then I left the label. It wasn't so smart on their part, I think.

The song hit #18 on the U.S. pop charts in early 1984, but would be KC's last chart record.

By the '80s, KC was tired of the music business. So tired, in fact, that he took a sabbatical for a decade, and started performing again in the 1990s. Among his many career achievements are a star on the Hollywood Walk of Fame, Grammys, People's Choice Awards, American Music Awards—and, above all, from 1974 to 1979, KC and the Sunshine Band sold 75 million records. And he is proud of the body of work he has produced. "I love all of [the songs] and they all have some special meanings. Of course, some I like are really obscure and I probably liked them while nobody else did." But all in all, KC acknowledges it has been a long and successful career, and one he plans on continuing for many years to come.

I interviewed KC in February 2015. As of this writing, he is still performing.

#32
(British Charts)
"Could It Be I'm Falling in Love" (1973)
THE SPINNERS (BOBBIE SMITH ON LEAD)
Billboard Pop: #4; R&B: #1; *Cashbox*: #1;
Adult Contemporary: Did not chart

There is such a difference between the Spinners who worked for Motown in the 1960s and the Spinners who recorded on Atlantic in the 1970s that they are the only group who appear in this book twice. Whether it was the different lead singers or the different writers and producers or the obvious fact that at Motown they were an afterthought whereas at Atlantic they were a highly valued group, the results were tangible. In ten years on Atlantic, they had more than 25 pop and R&B hits, whereas in ten years on Motown, 1970's "It's a Shame" was just about the only thing that anyone paid attention to. The Spinners' Atlantic years show how a label dedicated to a group can make a substantial difference. Gifted individuals reached their full potential—and made the label a lot of money.

The Spinners got their start in Ferndale, Michigan (near Detroit), in 1954 as the Domingoes and originally consisted of members Billy Henderson, Henry Fambrough, C.P. Spenser, Pervis Jackson and James Edwards. Over the years, they lost and added members. By 1970, the group recording for the Motown subsidiary label VIP consisted of Henderson, Fambrough, Jackson, Bobbie Smith and G.C. Cameron. With Cameron singing lead, they had finally broken into the Top 20 on the pop charts with "It's a Shame" (see Chapter 15). "It's a Shame" finally showcased the Spinners' abilities, and they were ready to leave Motown. According to Smith,

> We left because they had a lot of groups of the same caliber as the Spinners. They had a staff of writers, and naturally the writers had a choice about who

to work with. If you were an artist with a hit, like Marvin Gaye or the Temptations, that's who the producers wanted to work with. When you had a hit, you needed to follow a hit with another record, but at Motown, even if we had a hit, it might be another year before we had another record. It was like starting all over. So when our contract was up, we decided to leave.

While leaving a great label like Motown right after your first hit may not seem to make sense, after a decade at the label, averaging just one single release a year, they knew it was time to go. Most of the guys worked a second job to make ends meet, and even with a Top 20 hit most of them were barely hanging on. Smith said that as they pondered the move, they were helped by a music legend. "Aretha Franklin was a good friend of ours, and she thought [her label] Atlantic would be a good place for us because they didn't have a lot of groups playing the kind of music we were." Considering that some of Atlantic's biggest acts around that time were Franklin, Led Zeppelin, Yes, Roberta Flack, the J Geils Band, Stephen Stills and Bette Midler, it was good advice. The group changed labels in 1971, but minus Cameron, who stayed at Motown to pursue a solo career. His cousin Philippé Wynne took his place in the group. Smith recalled,

After the Spinners had some lean years at Motown, their first two Atlantic releases, "I'll Be Around" and "Could It Be I'm Falling in Love," made the Top Five in 1972.

#32. "Could It Be I'm Falling in Love" (1973)

So all of a sudden we didn't have all the competition we'd had at Motown, because there really wasn't another group exactly like us at Atlantic. They promoted us like we should have been promoted at Motown, and things took off from there. [Once signed,] we recorded four songs right away. One of them, "Oh Lord I Wish I Could Sleep," was just about to be released. But at the last minute, they called us and said, "Do you guys want to go with your song, or do you want to do another session?" We asked why, and they said it was because we had a chance to have Thom Bell produce us.

Bell was then one of the hottest names in the music industry, having worked with the Delfonics, Jerry Butler, the O'Jays and the Stylistics. "They gave Thom a choice to work with anyone there, and he chose us," Smith said. "He said he used to be the piano player at the Uptown Theatre, and he remembered hearing us do 'That's What Girls Are Made For,' and the song stuck in his mind because he liked the harmony. So when he saw our name on the Atlantic roster, he said, 'I'll take them.' It was a great marriage that brought us our great success."

Bell joined the group in Detroit, and they went into the studio and recorded four new songs. Smith told me that at the end of the session, Bell said, "Well, I'm going back to Philadelphia, and when I come back, you'll be #1." Smith added, "Of course, we'd heard that before! But to make a long story short, those records were million-sellers."

Smith went on to say that they almost misfired on their first effort for Atlantic. "'I'll Be Around' was actually the B-side of the first record. 'How Could I Let You Get Away' was the A-side, but it was moving up the charts slowly, and I said, 'We've got to turn this record over.' We did, and it shot right to the top." "How Could I Let You Get Away" was a slow, sad song, not the up-tempo type song the group would come to be known for. Consequently, while "How Could I Let You Get Away" did go to #77 on the pop charts and #14 on the R&B charts, "I'll Be Around" went to #3 on the pop charts and #1 on the R&B charts. That made "I'll Be Around" their first Top Ten hit, their first million-selling single, and their first #1 on any chart. It was awarded a gold disc by the RIAA.

For their next release, "Could It Be I'm Falling in Love" was the designated A-side and "Just You and Me Baby" the B-side. The former was written by Melvin and Mervin Steals, twin songwriter brothers who sometimes went by the names Mystro and Lyric. Over the years, they also wrote songs for Gloria Gaynor, O.C. Smith, the Trammps and others, but "Could It Be I'm Falling in Love" was their biggest hit. Melvin had written the song about his future wife Adrena (to whom he is still married) and it had been offered to Peaches & Herb four years earlier; they had passed on it. Bell—who had also written for Peaches &

Herb—knew of the song and offered it to the Spinners. Smith said that when Bell gave it to them, they knew it was a winner.

The group recorded the song at Philadelphia's Sigma Sound Studios. MFSB, who did most of the backing at that venue, backed them up. Smith sang lead on most of the song and Wynne finished it off. While this may seem unusual (lead singers are usually *the* lead singers),

> We were always the type of group who didn't let success go to our heads. We learned a long time ago that you can't take an ego to the bank. Philippé was the strongest voice and had a lot of charisma on stage, so sometimes he sang lead. You'll hear some smooth ballads that Henry was singing lead on, because that was the type of voice he had. Then you'll hear one I'm lead on, or G.C. when he was with us, and so on. We never looked at any one person as the lead, it was whoever the song fit, even if that meant more than one person sang lead on the same song. We didn't care who was singing lead on the song because we were all the Spinners. We didn't let those egos get in the way.

Backing vocals were by Jackson, Fambrough and Henderson, as well as Bell associate Linda Creed, and Barbara Ingram, Carla Benson and Yvette Benton—known as "Tommy's Girls" (because Bell had discovered them) and "The Sweethearts of Sigma." "Could It Be I'm Falling in Love" peaked at #1 on the R&B chart and #4 on the *Billboard* pop charts, and like its predecessor it sold over a million copies. In England it peaked at #11. (The group was known as the Detroit Spinners in that country to avoid confusion them with an English group called the Spinners.)

Despite two straight hits, Smith still was not convinced after 20 years in the business that they had made it:

> I had gotten a job because I was getting to the point where I was thinking, "It ain't gonna happen" and was thinking about giving up music. In show business, you can't hold a steady job, but you had to have one because you have one of those mediocre hits and you go out of town and work for a while with the band and then you're back to zero. So I always tried to have part-time jobs in between. I had just gotten a good job at the GM building with good benefits, so I had to make the decision after we recorded those songs with Thom. I had to decide if I wanted to keep that job or try one more time. I asked GM for a leave of absence, and they wouldn't give it to me. So I decided to take one last chance, and it was the right one.

After "One of a Kind (Love Affair)" went to #11 and became their third straight #1 record on the R&B charts, it was clear the Spinners were going to be around a while. But for the first time, the group was also involved in controversy over a song's lyrics. Philippé Wynne sang lead on the tune, and some listeners thought he sang, "One-of-a-kind love affair/Makes you want to love her/You just got to f**k her, yeah...." Atlantic felt they needed to make sure that the song was radio-worthy,

#32. "Could It Be I'm Falling in Love" (1973)

The Spinners in the 1970s: top, left to right, Bobbie Smith and Pervis Jackson. Bottom, Henry Fambrough, Philippé Wynne and Billy Henderson (courtesy Bobbie Smith).

so they sent the group back into the studio. Smith said. "Just because some deejay thought that, we had to go back into the studio and clean up that one line. When we were coming up, you did everything you could to protect your career, because one scandal could end it all. So we didn't think anything about being told to do it, we just went in and cleaned it up. If a disc jockey said he thought it said that, we wanted to clear it up for everybody."

The group went on to an unbelievable level of success with "Ghetto Child," "Mighty Love" and their #1 song with Dionne Warwick, "Then Came You." "Rubberband Man" was their last big hit working with Thom Bell before he went his own way. Also, after "Rubberband Man" Wynne had left the group after demanding his name be given lead billing, and he was replaced by John Edwards. Without Bell or Wynne, the group still had two more big hits, 1979's "Working My Way Back to You/Forgive Me Girl" (#2 *Billboard* Pop) and "Cupid/I've Loved for a Long Time" with producer Michael Zager.

The group recorded well into the '80s and nearly a dozen of their songs made the R&B charts' Top 100. But for all the hits on all the levels over a period of three decades, Smith believed it was their chemistry that led to their success. It's hard to dispute considering they had 30 hits on the pop charts and 40 on the R&B charts, and are today viewed as recording legends.

I interviewed Smith in September 2011. He passed away in 2013.

#33
(R&B Charts)
"Baby, Now That I've Found You" (1967)

The Foundations
Billboard Pop: #11; *Cashbox*: #8;
Adult Contemporary: Did not chart;
British Charts: #1

Consider the problems surrounding the recording of the Foundations' "Baby, Now That I've Found You" in 1967. The group's bass player couldn't play at all, the lead singer didn't have the vocal range to sing what was required, and Tony Macaulay, who was tasked with producing and writing for the Foundations, thought they were "absolutely terrible." The record was released, and initially it flopped. But sometimes miracles occur, and eventually it started to race up the charts, even peaking at #1 in England.

Trinidadian Clem Curtis (born Curtis Clements) moved to England as a teenager. As a young man he searched for his niche, holding a variety of jobs and even pursuing a career in professional boxing. Although he didn't play an instrument, music was in his blood, as his mother was a singer in Trinidad and his uncle used to play guitar and sing with Clem for fun. According to Curtis, the uncle, impressed with his singing, told him, "There's this guy with a band called the Ramongs who is looking for singers." Curtis decided to give it a shot, and landed his first job as a professional singer.

Singer Raymond Morrison led the Ramongs, but the group underwent several changes. Arthur Brown sang lead for a while, and the group also changed their name to the Foundations. By 1967, Brown was gone and Curtis had emerged as the group's lead, fronting Mike Elliott, Tim Harris, Pat Burke, Eric Allandale, Alan Warner, Peter Macbeth and Tony Gomez. Curtis told me that the Foundations was "a very versatile bunch of musicians," noteworthy not only for their R&B-based sound (considering that most English groups had an edgier rock sound at the time), but also because of their very diverse make-up. In addition to Trinidadian Curtis, there were two Jamaicans, a Dominican and a mix of Brits. They were also diverse age-wise, ranging from 18 to 38. While their diversity may have initially contributed to their group's success, ultimately it may have also contributed to its demise due to their disparate ideas about the work ethic and cultural differences.

In 1967, the group came to the attention of producer-songwriter Tony Macaulay. Later, in the 1970s, Macaulay became one of the music business's biggest names, writing the 5th Dimension's "(Last Night) I Didn't Get to Sleep at All," David Soul's "Don't Give Up on Us Baby," Edison Lighthouse's "Love Grows (Where My Rosemary Goes)" and others. In 1967, however, he was just starting, and his label asked him to give the Foundations a listen and see if he could do anything with them. "As with a lot of these things, it started ignominiously," Macaulay told me. He continued:

> They used to give you a year's tryout and if you didn't have a hit, they let you go. I'd been on the job about six months and was starting to look at jobs like becoming a waiter or anything else. I'd recorded some of my own songs

With Clem Curtis singing lead, the Foundations' first release "Baby, Now That I've Found You" went to #11 on the *Billboard* pop charts and #33 on the soul charts.

but was losing faith in them. I'd been out drinking one night and the next morning I got a phone call from the studio saying, "Where the hell are you? There's a group here and we've given them an audition." So I got a taxi in and I had the worst hangover in history.

The group auditioning were the Foundations, "and I thought they were absolutely terrible."

But Macaulay realized that maybe he didn't like the group because he was hung over, and agreed to work with the group. He also offered them a couple of songs he had written. According to Curtis, "At first there were two songs offered to us. One was 'Let the Heartaches Begin,' but instead we chose 'Baby, Now That I Found You' because I didn't think I could sing 'Let the Heartaches Begin' as well. 'Baby, Now That I've Found You' just seemed to be a better song for me." Macaulay said:

> We had the song "Baby, Now That I Found You," but it was unfinished. The chorus was fixed but the lyrics were a bit fluid. One indication of that is how repetitive some of the verses and lyrics are. I thought it was a good tune, and in my mind, I was influenced by Burt Bacharach and Holland-Dozier-Holland. I thought if you could put Bacharach-type lyrics against a good tune with a lilting melody against a thumping good rhythm, you might have something."

But Macaulay still did not have the highest opinion of the Foundations:

> I didn't think they were a lot better when I didn't have a hangover, actually. When we went in to make the records, the bass player couldn't play at all. The song had a complicated moving bass line and he couldn't handle that so I had to dub that over the mix. Then, Clem Curtis just couldn't sing the line "Darlin', I just can't let you..." at all, and we did a hundred passes at it. I went to the general manager of the record company and said, "I've got this track and it's quite good but there's this one line the singer can't get and I don't know whether to dump the band or what." They said, "Just get someone else to sing it," which on the face of it sounded pretty stupid. So three other guys and I sang the one line just like vocal backing. One Saturday morning we'd put the vocal backing on and took out some of the bits of vocals that were really bad and put handclaps and stuff over the top of the mix.

Despite all the problems, Macaulay admitted that, in the end, "It really did sound good." He continued:

> Everybody thought it would be a hit, but it came out and flopped completely. But what happened was they had those pirate radio stations and the government stopped the pirate stations and they hadn't been playing the record. A lot of those deejays got jobs with the brand new station called Radio One. They were told to go back through the last six months' records and find anything they thought might have been a hit so that they weren't playing the

Top Ten that the pirates had played. Tony Blackburn picked the record up and it hit the charts and that was the beginning of my career. It went to #1 [in England].

"Baby, Now That I've Found You" also raced to #11 on the *Billboard* pop charts and #33 on the soul charts in the U.S. When it went to #1 on the U.K. charts, it had the distinction of being the first #1 hit in the U.K. by a multi-racial act. Despite all of that, Curtis admitted, "I really had no idea it would be such a success." Interestingly, the song the group turned down, "Let the Heartaches Begin," recorded by Long John Baldry, also hit #1 in England.

The Foundations followed up with their next single, "Back on My Feet Again," which hit a respectable #18 in the U.K. but only hit #59 on the U.S. pop charts. Given that their first two collaborations had been hits, one would think the relationships between all the parties involved would have been harmonious. Though Macaulay stayed as the group's producer and of course wrote the songs, things didn't improve that much. "Clem Curtis never learned the material. It used to drive me crazy. He'd turn up and swear he knew it but he had to do a line at a time and I hated that. Then he wanted to quit the band, which as far as I was concerned was the best thing that could have happened." Curtis felt Macaulay was trying to push their output in a more pop-oriented direction, and Curtis didn't think they needed to change "[because] our music made people happy." Curtis wanted to stick with more R&B-influenced dance music, "like Otis Redding and Wilson Pickett and some other American artists." In addition, he felt that the group had become complacent. They'd had two Top 20 records in the U.K., and some of the group seemed to take it as an indication they didn't have to worry about showing up for rehearsals or anything else.

Curtis said that by this point he was feeling the need to go out on his own. Sammy Davis Jr. recommended that he come to the States because he, Davis, felt that Curtis would be a draw here and had the potential to be a huge solo act. In 1968, Curtis made it official and left the Foundations, although he first helped them find a new lead singer. Macaulay said the new lead, Colin Young, "was a much better singer, frankly." But better or not, the group needed a new hit. It turned out to be "Build Me Up, Buttercup." Macaulay said,

> I was with Mike d'Abo, who was the lead singer of Manfred Mann at that point. He was a friend of mine from way back, and one evening I went around to dinner with my girlfriend. Mike said, "I've got the beginnings of this song. But it has a dummy lyric, a nonsense lyric." By the time dinner was served, we had the whole melody fixed. And the general idea was that we were going to get rid of the "Buttercup" because it was stupid.

#33. "Baby, Now That I've Found You" (1967)

By the time "Build Me Up, Buttercup" was released, Colin Young was singing lead. It became the group's biggest hit, going to #2 in the U.K. and #3 in the U.S.

Macaulay said he did come up with other possibilities, but none of them really seemed to click. "I've got a lyric written down somewhere that says 'Build me up, baby, I love you' or something like that. But come the day we still hadn't come up with anything better so we just sang that. I didn't know what the hell it meant, really."

Recording the song was a trial, Macaulay recalled:

> We put the vocal on, and it was in the early hours of the morning. Back in those days, you didn't normally wear headphones and you'd put a speaker near the mike. Problem was that you got so much playback on the vocal track that it screwed up the sound. That's what happened. The engineer got too much of the backing track on the vocal track. So we had to get the guy back in at four in the morning literally in his pajamas. He did it again in a couple of takes. You can't hear how tired he was. I had one go at mixing it and that was it and they took it straight down and pressed it.

The result was that their first record with Young on lead was the group's biggest hit. It went to #2 in the U.K. and to #3 in the U.S. in 1969, and the Foundations were back on top. Curtis somewhat regretted not doing the song: "It's true I had nothing to do with the song at the time, and then I realized I really liked it."

But by then, Curtis had moved on. "Sammy Davis Jr. introduced me to a lot of nice people and I went to America. There I saw a lot of other black artists and learned more about the business." He eventually toured with the Four Tops, Stevie Wonder and the Temptations. He loved America and didn't look back with regret on his decision to leave the Foundations at the height of their success.

After "Build Me Up, Buttercup," the group's next single was another great Macaulay-penned song, "In the Bad, Bad Old Days." It became a U.K. Top Ten hit but only went to #51 in the U.S.

At this point, Macaulay left the group, apparently because things had become even more acrimonious. Some band members later claimed they were incensed that Macaulay wouldn't let them record any of their own music, and Macaulay felt they were ungrateful because he'd been writing hits for them but they weren't satisfied with that. One thing is certain: After Macaulay left, with the Foundations being produced and recording songs by other writers, the magic was gone. The group broke up in 1970.

Not long afterwards, Curtis started headlining a new version of the group. He said, "'Baby, Now That I've Found You' [was always] a crowd-pleaser, a song that [was] fun to do because everyone in my age group and young people like[d] hearing it too." He told me he had "sung these songs all over the world," and how he felt the Foundations' music was universally recognized. "Those recordings brought me a whole lot of happiness over the years."

As for Tony Macaulay, he had even greater acclaim ahead. Another one of his hits, "Love Grows (Where My Rosemary Goes)," is featured elsewhere in this book.,

---

I interviewed Clem Curtis in 2010; he passed away in 2017. Tony Macaulay holds two British Academy of Songwriters, Composers and Authors Awards as "Songwriter of the Year" (1970 and 1977) and nine Ivor Novello Awards for songwriting. I interviewed him in 2018.

#34
(Adult Contemporary Charts)
"Smoke from a Distant Fire" (1977)
THE SANFORD TOWNSEND BAND
Billboard Pop: #9; *Cashbox*: #9;
R&B, British Charts: Did not chart

The term "one-hit wonder" gets thrown around a lot, but generally it means an artist or group that has just one song enter the *Billboard* pop Top 40 and no more. There are several such artists in this book, a list that includes the Cuff Links, the Tams, Jan Bradley, Wild Cherry and Ernie K-Doe. The thing about those groups is that while they may have had only one Top 40 pop song, they all had additional songs register on the Top *100* of the *Billboard* pop charts, so to say they are one-hit wonders is slightly misleading. Many of the groups also may have had only one Top 40 *pop* hit, but did quite well on the Top 40 of other charts. For example, of the groups listed above, the Cuff Links had more than one Top 40 hit on the Adult Contemporary and British charts, the Tams had more than one Top 40 hit on the R&B charts and British charts (in fact, they had a #1 in England that didn't even make the pop Top 40 in the U.S.), and Bradley, Wild Cherry, and Ernie K-Doe did so as well. In that sense, maybe the term "one-hit wonder" is misleading. But oddly enough, there is one true "one-hit wonder" in this book, a group that had only one pop Top 40 hit, but who also never had another song break into the Top on 100 on the *Billboard* pop charts, and never had another song make the Top 40 on the *Cashbox, Billboard* R&B or Adult Contemporary charts. In fact, the group never had another single even make the "Bubbling Under" chart, that being the chart that tracked songs ranked from #101 to #115 and later to #135. The group was the Sanford Townsend Band; that 1977's "Smoke from a Distant Fire" was their only song to make any chart at any time. This earns them the distinction of being a true one-hit wonder.

Tuscaloosa, Alabama, native John Townsend grew up surrounded by music; the church was responsible for his earliest musical influences. He hoped to grow up to be a star athlete but his mother wanted him to play piano, so he took piano lessons to please her. When the dream of being a pro athlete didn't pan out, he gravitated towards the music. Townsend said he was particularly influenced by Ray Charles, Otis Redding, Marvin Gaye, Wilson Pickett, James Brown and other male R&B artists. When he was 17, he joined some other guys in a band that was soon to be named the Specters. They made $10 each for playing their first gig at a junior high prom.

Townsend and his friends entered the University of Alabama. Despite his intention to eventually go to medical school, the money and satisfaction he got from the band (now called the Nightcaps) playing frat parties and clubs prompted him to chart a different course. During his sophomore year, he was contacted by an Alabama student named Johnny Wyker. "Soon I was part of a seven-piece band, and we called ourselves the Magnificent Seven," Townsend said. "Almost overnight we became the most popular band on campus and played all the

"Smoke from a Distant Fire" was the only Sanford Townsend Band record to break into the Top 100, making them a true one-hit wonder.

fraternity parties." They eventually became a part of the Gulf Coast club scene. "Some of our first gigs were at Dauphin Island and beaches like Pensacola, Destin, places like that." They even played a few times with the Swingin' Medallions, but when "Double Shot" took off, the Medallions started touring and playing bigger venues. "There was a club called Old Hickory where the Medallions had been the house band. They needed a band because the Medallions were touring, so they hired us."

The band made some recordings at a small studio in Alabama. One standout was a song called "Let Love Come Between Us," written by Wyker and Magnificent Seven keyboard player Joe Sobotka. New York producer Charlie Calello heard them and signed them to a Columbia Records contract. Calello knew talent, and over the course of his career he worked with Barbra Streisand, Frank Sinatra, Neil Diamond, Engelbert Humperdinck, Ray Charles and many others.

The first order of business was to change the group's name, because the Magnificent Seven was the title of a famous—and copyrighted—movie. They renamed themselves the Rubber Band. Townsend said their first release, "Let Love Come Between Us," was "a turntable hit all over the country." The problem was that while Columbia sent out promotional copies in 1966 (and copies of a second single the next year), they didn't promote the records at all. Clearly "Let Love Come Between Us" had potential, evidenced by the fact, as Townsend noted, "some months later, James and Bobby Purify [did it]. When we heard their version on the radio, we knew it was us who should have had the big record." The Purifys' version went to #23 on the pop charts, and was their second biggest hit after their Top Ten recording "I'm Your Puppet."

After the Rubber Band broke up, Townsend spent time working with Paul Hornsby and Greg and Duane Allman, but eventually he decided to start another band. He got together with former Auburn student Ed Sanford, a former member of the Rockin' Gibraltars, a group that played at a club down the street in Townsend's old Gulf Coast days. Townsend, Sanford and a few others went on to found a band called Heart (no relation to the '80s band). The group had several single releases, according to Townsend, but none were successful—although Heart did open for Jimi Hendrix on tour. Heart soon fell apart. Townsend was next with a group called Feather, and their song "Friends" made the upper reaches of the *Billboard Hot 100*. Townsend then moved on from that band as well.

Not long after that, Townsend ran into Ed Sanford again. He revealed,

Ed and I became writing partners and before long had written maybe a dozen songs together. We were just taking a crack at it, realizing that was where the money was in the business, when you can write and reap the publishing rewards of your own songs. Ed and a guy named Steve Stewart were living in a duplex in Hollywood, and I'd go hang out with them every day. Ed had a little piano, and Steven was a guitar player and one of those people who would actually sit up all night with a music stand in front of him thinking that if he couldn't be Bach, then life wouldn't be worth living.

I go over one morning, and Ed had been up all night because he'd been kept awake by Steve playing in the next room. Ed says, "When are you going to knock that crap off and write something that's gonna make you some money?" Steven turns around—he was making coffee and still had his guitar around his neck—and he says, "Anybody can write that crap!" and he starts playing this great riff he'd made up. Ed and I looked at each other and said, "Hey, that's pretty cool!"

We sat down at the piano and started the song using Steven's riff, and Ed said, "I think this will fit a poem I wrote in college. Check out these lyrics and see if they work for you." This poem he'd written when he was at Auburn was actually called "Smoke from a Distant Fire." He'd had this girlfriend who was fooling around on him, and I thought it was a great image. I don't remember anything else about the poem—we just took the title from it.

Townsend did mention the use of one line that was a nod to how many a jilted guy might feel during a break-up: "The part about 'Don't let the screen door hit you on the way out' we, of course, borrowed from the idioms in our language! Well, in no time at all, a song that essentially started as a joke became 'Smoke from a Distant Fire'—and wound up making us a great deal of money."

The guys called on an old bandmate from Feather, Merel Bregante, who set them up with recording engineer Alex Kazanegras. Kazanegras, who worked with the rock-pop duo Loggins and Messina, let them cut some demos which eventually got them a deal with Warner Brothers Records. The Sanford Townsend Band—Sanford, Townsend, Otis Hale, Jerry Rightmer, Jim Varley and Roger Johnson—recorded the song at Muscle Shoals with producer Jerry Wexler. "We decided we needed a producer, and we wanted the best, so we got Jerry Wexler. We were the first group he'd produced—he'd always worked with solo artists like Ray Charles and Aretha Franklin. He made Alabama native Barry Becket co-producer, because he had a great musical mind and he could assess material and get the most out of it." During his career, Beckett worked and sometimes recorded with artists such as Bob Dylan, Etta James, Aretha Franklin, Paul Simon, Rod Stewart, Lynyrd Skynyrd and Dire Straits, and for a while he was a member of Traffic.

The combination of Wexler and Beckett was a godsend for the band

and, according to Townsend, their relationship with their producers was fantastic. "Part of our deal with Barry was that in addition to his percentage on the record, he got $5,000. Barry didn't pocket the money and he hired a promotion man instead. He got 'Smoke' on 25 to 30 stations in Alabama, Mississippi and Georgia, and that was the springboard for us and for the song going national." Townsend said that in the music business, that type of acumen paid dividends very quickly. "The next week, one of the Warner Brothers guys walked in and said, 'Hey, this record's just picked up 30 stations in the Southeast in a week. We need to get on this record.' Well, the minute they did, stations in L.A. and Boston went big on it."

The song shot up the charts. Townsend said, "I can remember exactly where I was when I heard 'Smoke' for the first time come out over the radio, and I tell you, it's an experience that's unparalleled. You know you've made it. I had a similar experience in Rome, walking around not far from the Vatican. I was walking by some old courtyard, and I heard the song spiraling down from some apartment through those 3000-year-old walls, and I said, 'Okay, we've really made it!'"

One of the biggest songs of 1977, the song went to #9 on the *Billboard* and *Cashbox* charts and #34 on the Adult Contemporary charts. Townsend thinks part of the song's success was that it had a sound similar to the music he grew up with: "It's clear that old R&B music influenced the sound of the song. We had started as a band playing Otis Redding, Little Anthony and the Imperials, Sam and Dave, the New Orleans music, the Muscle Shoals stuff, mostly by black artists. It was the music of the day, and when it came time to do our own songs, they came out of the music we were really in love with."

After the success of the song, the band started a rigorous touring schedule that saw them playing as many as 200 nights a year, working with groups such as Fleetwood Mac, the Marshall Tucker Band and the Charlie Daniels Band. When it was finally time to do a follow-up album, Wexler was working with other groups and the band had to cut the second album, *Duo Glide*, without him. Furthermore, this album was recorded in L.A. and not Muscle Shoals, and as a result Townsend felt something about the album just didn't work. That album peaked at #97 on the album charts; it's successor, 1979's *Nail Me to the Wall*, did not chart at all.

The band broke up and Townsend spent subsequent years working with artists Don Henley, Kenny Loggins and Gregg Allman. He did some music for commercials and movies. If not for a twist of fate, "Smoke from a Distant Fire" might have been the *second* most famous song Townsend ever recorded. He sang the original demo for "Lift

The Sanford Townsend Band: left to right, Otis Hale, Jerry Rightmer, John Townsend, Jim Varley, Roger Johnson and Ed Sanford (courtesy John Townsend).

Us Up Where We Belong," which was chosen as the title song for the 1982 movie *An Officer and a Gentleman*. After Joe Cocker missed several recording dates to sing the song with Jennifer Warnes, the studio decided that if Cocker missed once more, they would go with Townsend due to his performance on the demo. Cocker showed up this time. The Cocker-Warnes recording went to #1 on the pop charts won a Golden Globe and an Oscar for Best Original Song, as well as a Grammy for Best Pop Performance by a Duo.

Ed Sanford kept writing; he co-wrote "I Keep Forgettin'" with Michael McDonald. He and Townsend have occasionally reunite. Townsend said he still gets a thrill out of playing "Smoke from a Distant Fire": "I've never stopped playing it, and it always gets a great reaction. I remember I was in a band when we played at a club once and people came up and said, 'You sound just like that guy who sang that song,' and I'd say 'Well, that's because I *am* that guy!' Other people would say, 'I never knew you guys were white!' For someone with my musical roots, that's one of the greatest compliments I could ever have."

I interviewed Townsend in August 2011. He is still performing.

#35
(*Cashbox* Charts)
"I Love You 1000 Times" (1966)
THE PLATTERS
Billboard Pop: #31; R&B: #6;
Adult Contemporary, British charts: Did not chart

In the early 1960s, before Motown became the R&B music industry's driving force, there weren't a lot of R&B groups who had built up a long, sustained record of success. A few black solo artists hit it big (James Brown, Nat King Cole, Fats Domino and Sam Cooke come to mind), but only a few black *groups* had amassed much of a catalogue of hits. The Drifters had done well, and the Clovers, Coasters and Impressions to a lesser extent. But without a doubt, the biggest pre–Motown black group would have to be the Platters. In the 1950s alone, they released 26 chart records, including four #1s. But as the 1960s began the group started to splinter as many successful acts do, and they were on the verge of becoming an oldies act. Fortunately, a change of lineup and a change of label allowed them to resurrect their careers. With Sonny Turner singing lead in the mid–1960s, they were on the charts once again. They got their second wind as few groups in rock'n'roll history have done.

Like many successful groups, the Platters had fluctuating lineups over the years and thus recorded different-sounding hits in very distinct periods. Unlike the Drifters, however, the Platters really only had two lead singers during the years they were charting. In the 1950s, the Platters consisted of lead singer Tony Williams, backed by David Lynch, Herb Reed, Alex Robi and Zola Taylor. This lineup cut a number of early singles; none of them did much on the charts, but "Only You" made some noise regionally. After the Mercury label picked up the single and released the record nationally, it soared to #5, and their next single, "The Great Pretender," became their first #1 hit. With Williams on lead, between 1955 and 1960 the group churned out some of the greatest hits of the early rock'n'roll era, including "My Prayer" (#1, 1956), "Twilight Time" (#1, 1958) and "Smoke Gets in Your Eyes" (#1, 1958). But the continued success as a group wasn't enough to keep all the members happy, and by 1959, Williams decided it was time to go out on his own. He thought he could be even more successful as a solo act, perhaps emboldened by the success of contemporary frontmen Clyde McPhatter, who had left the Drifters (and whose "A Lover's Question" would peak at #1 on the R&B charts that year), and Jackie Wilson, who had left the Dominoes (and whose "Lonely Teardrops" would also peak at #1 on the R&B charts that year).

The man who filled the void left by Williams was West Virginia–born Sonny Turner. Turner began his musical career in Cleveland, where his family moved when he was ten. Strongly influenced by his mother, a gospel singer, Turner first performed with a group called the Skylarks. His first real renown came as the lead singer for an R&B group, the Metrotones. Like many local groups, they made their living playing dances and clubs, and were successful enough that on occasion they opened for groups such as the Moonglows and the Flamingos. In 1957 and 1958, they cut a couple of singles on the Duke and Reserve labels.

"I Love You 1000 Times" was the Platters' first Top 40 pop record in five years.

When the group broke up after several members were drafted, Turner continued as a solo act. Deejay Bill Crane happened to be in the audience one night when Turner opened for comedian Redd Foxx. This was after Williams had announced his intention to leave the Platters; since Crane scouted talent for the music industry, he asked Turner if he would be interested in auditioning as the Platters new lead singer. Turner of course said yes, and made an audition tape. Crane sent it to Platters manager Buck Ram. He was interested.

In late 1959, Turner went to Milwaukee to audition for Ram and group members Lynch, Reed, Robi and Taylor. Also there was Tony Williams, and he heard Turner's rendition of "Smoke Gets in Your Eyes." Ram, Williams and the other Platters agreed that Turner was the right person, and he was chosen over more than 100 singers who also auditioned for the lead.

Turner was eased into the background slowly, while Williams remained a while, and then other members took lead on different songs. Williams finally left in 1961, but unlike McPhatter and Wilson he was not to find success as a solo act.

Unfortunately, the group was experiencing other problems. Members were getting in trouble and facing personal demons, and Zola Taylor quit in 1964; Alex Robi was fired in 1965 after being arrested with narcotics. During this tumultuous period, the group's records stopped charting. Their last #1 hit had been "Smoke Gets in Your Eyes" in 1958-59; of their next 13 releases, only "Harbor Lights" broke the Top Ten (it was #8 in 1960). With the exception of just one of these records, 1962's "It's Magic," their last chart record for Mercury (#91), all of the records had Williams on lead. In most cases they were songs he recorded before leaving and Mercury dribbled them out between 1960 and 1962. After "It's Magic," however, the group had no records on the pop charts for the next four years and none on the R&B charts for five years.

Part of this was due to Mercury's resistance to change. Mercury didn't seem interested in releasing anything that Williams didn't sing lead on, and they also didn't seem to want the group to do anything unless it was the same type of material that had worked for them in the '50s. By the mid–'60s, between defections and dissatisfaction and Williams' departure, it looked like the Platters were destined to become just another oldies act.

Throughout this period, Sonny Turner worked as the loyal and capable replacement and, as he told me, he had even learned to sing like Williams so he could fill his shoes. And while Turner had the voice and charisma to make it all work again as a Williams stand-in, he was also smart enough to see that to be successful, the group's output would have to adapt to the new musical styles. "We felt the change coming," Turner told me. "The Beatles hit and then they had Motown, and we felt the whole format of the rhythm-and-blues era was changing. The soul mixed with the R&B and pop music—the writers were beginning to combine the sounds." Turner and the other group members realized what Mercury didn't: The old '50s ballads and slow burners just weren't what audiences in the 1960s wanted. Turner, Lynch and Reed, along with new members Nate Nelson and Sandra Dawn, knew they would have to adapt to the changing music scene. After several legal squabbles, they left Mercury in 1965 and went to Musicor, where they knew they were going to have to reinvent themselves.

While their first big chart success with their new label wasn't like their doo-wop, adult-oriented music of the 1950s, it wasn't all that far *from* it. Certainly 1966's smooth and soulful "I Love You 1000 Times," their very first single release for Musicor, had a different sound, more like the Burt Bacharach–Hal David compositions that had been racing up the charts for artists such as Dionne Warwick and Chuck Jackson. "Inez Foxx and Luther Dixon came up with 'I Love You 1000 Times,'" Turner said. "They felt we needed another hit, and they asked Buck to give the song to me." Foxx, who had her own Top Ten hit in 1963 with "Mockingbird," had just signed with Musicor; she was married to Luther Dixon, the former Scepter Records A&R man who had produced and written for the Shirelles and for Chuck Jackson.

The group worked on the song, though initially not everyone agreed on how it should be sung. Dixon told Turner, "Just sing it like you feel it." Turner responded, "Buck wanted me to sing it a different way." Dixon told Buck, "Buck, you're thinking old school, old-fashioned. The music's changing. Sonny has a feel for it. Let him sing it the way he feels it."

"So I sang it my way and from the heart," Turner told me. "Afterward, Luther told me, 'That's it—you nailed it.' And sure enough—bam!—hit record." The single version reached #31 on the *Billboard* pop charts, #6 on R&B–Soul charts, and #35 on the *Cashbox* charts. While it may seem that Turner overstated its success by calling it a "hit record," it was the group's first Top 40 hit on any chart since 1961. After ending a lengthy chart absence, any Top 40 chart record had to be considered a hit.

Interestingly enough, the version of the song most music fans now know is the version later reissued on oldies 45s and albums. The original single version was shorter at 2:30; later versions were not that 45 version. The versions released later run about 18 seconds longer because, according to Turner, they included a verse and chorus not on the

#35. "I Love You 1000 Times" (1966)

The Platters: left to right, Herb Reid, Paul Robi, Sonny Turner, David Lynch and Zola Taylor (courtesy Sonny Turner).

original: "The lines about 'Love notes I treasured/Loving you was not a sin/Punishment was pleasure/Oh I'd do it all over again' were not on the original single release." Otherwise, the versions are basically identical.

For the first time in years, the Platters' music was relevant and, Turner said, the group knew they had what it took to be hit-makers again. Next they were given another song with a more up-to-date sound, 1967's "With This Ring." "Richard 'Popcorn' Wylie came up with 'With This Ring,'" Turner said, "and this was yet another move toward that new sound." Wylie, who had worked at Motown with the Supremes, Marvin Gaye, Mary Wells, and Smokey Robinson and the Miracles, gave them a song that at last completely separated them from the more conservative sounds of the Tony Williams era. "On that song, I came into my own—I didn't have to mimic or try to sound like Tony Williams any more. We wanted a brassy song and sound and—bam!—another hit record." Charting at #14, it was their first Top 20 tune since 1960. The Platters were a hot national act once again.

Turner said that their next release, "Washed Ashore," also came from Wylie's pen. "We were in Chicago performing at the Lamplighter, and Popcorn said, 'I got another hit for you.' He was thinking in terms of summertime and the beach, and we took the song into the studio and we nailed it. I said, 'Hell, yeah! I like this. Another hit.'" "Washed Ashore" didn't make a huge impact on the pop charts, stalling at #56, but on the *Billboard* R&B charts it did considerably better, peaking at #29.

The group would have one more chart record in 1967, "Sweet, Sweet Lovin'," which went to #32 on the R&B charts (though only #70 on the pop charts). David Lynch finally left that year, joining Paul Robi and Zola Taylor in a Platters splinter group; Herb Reed left two years later to form his own group. But perhaps unknown to them all, 1967 was the end of the Platters' resurgence as once more they faded into the background. Turner thought it was due to their management. "Buck Ram had a few hits under his belt, and he thought he was

The Platters: left to right, Paul Robi, Herb Reid, Zola Taylor, David Lynch and Sonny Turner (courtesy Sonny Turner).

Svengali. I always feel like had Buck stayed out of the way, we might have had four or five more hits, but as it was, that was it." Turner himself left in 1970.

Turner said that although the Platters are known for many hits, crowds expect to hear the Musicor songs as well as the older Mercury hits. Though the sound of the Musicor releases is much different from the sound of the Williams-led Platters of the 1950s, there are a number of listeners who consider those Musicor tunes such as "I Love You 1000 Times" great tunes in their own right.

I interviewed Sonny Turner in 2010. He passed away in 2022.

#36
British Charts

"There's Gonna Be a Showdown" (1968)

Archie Bell and the Drells

Billboard Pop: #21; R&B: #6; *Cashbox*: #20;
Adult Contemporary: Did not chart

During the 1950s and '60s, songs about specific dances became very popular, and none more so than Chubby Checker's "The Twist." It had the distinction of hitting #1 on the pop charts in 1960, and then again in 1961. There were many other songs about dances, before and after Checker's hit, including Bob and Earl's "The Harlem Shuffle," the Diamonds' "The Stroll," Dee Dee Sharp's "The Mashed Potato," Little Eva's "The Loco-Motion" and many others. At the same time, there have been hundreds—if not thousands—of songs about dancing in general, and there are probably as many songs about dancing as there are about love. But dance *contests*? Probably not so many. But after charting with three consecutive dancing songs—"Tighten Up," "I Can't Stop Dancing," and "Do the Choo Choo"—Archie Bell and the Drells had Kenny Gamble and Leon Huff come to Houston and experience a "showdown"—a type of dance contest. This song about a specifically named dance contest may have been the first of its kind.

Archie Bell was born in Henderson, Texas, one of seven brothers to Langston and Ruthie Bell. (One younger brother was Southern California and NFL running back Ricky Bell.) Like many young men in the South, Archie was raised singing gospel in the church, but in his teens, he decided to turn his attention to R&B. He particularly liked Sam Cooke and Jackie Wilson, and wanted to make music that made people feel good like Cooke and Wilson did. "I've always been a guy who wanted to do music to uplift people," Archie told me. "And I want my music to make them get up and move." With this in mind, he formed his first group with some friends in 1966.

We started out as just "The Drells." L.C. Watts, who left the group before we became famous, loved the Dells and added the r to come up with Drells. We always said that a Drell is an excellent entertainer and a perfect gentleman. It was only later when I came to be seen as the frontman that we went to Archie Bell and the Drells, and my name just happened to rhyme.

Bell and the Drells performed at talent shows and dances. At one such performance, they were noticed by Skipper Lee Frazier, a disk jockey starting his own label, Ovide. For the label's debut single in 1967, he released Archie Bell and the Drells' "She's My Woman, She's My Girl."

They recorded some other sides for the Ovide label, including a song called "Tighten Up." Drell member Billy Butler had shown Bell a dance he called the Tighten Up, and Bell and Butler built a song around it. The group recorded the song, but just when Ovide was about to release it, Bell got his draft notice from the Army and had to leave. It seemed as if his musical career might be over almost before it started.

Frazier pushed the record to radio stations with the result that it began selling by the truckload in Texas. Audiences there couldn't get enough of the song whose lead-in proudly proclaimed they were "Archie Bell and the Drells from Houston, Texas." Bell told me, "I said that about being from Texas because after the Kennedy assassination, I heard a deejay say nothing good had ever come out of Texas. I knew that wasn't true, and that was my way of making a statement."

The record sold several hundred thousand copies regionally and came to the attention of Atlantic Records, which released it nationally and watched it sell a million records, climb all the way to #1 and earn a gold record in 1968. "We never thought 'Tighten Up' would be as big as it was. It was a real surprise to everybody." Perhaps even more so because other than Bell's lead, there was almost no

According to Archie Bell, "There's Gonna Be a Showdown" was about Texas dance competitions.

participation by the rest of the group on the record. The backbone of the song is the instrumental work of a Texas group signed to Ovide, the TSU Tornadoes. Except for some hand-clapping and whistling, the Drells don't contribute much.

Bell heard about the record's success from a hospital bed:

> "After I was drafted, I served in the Fifty-third Transportation Unit stationed in Germany. I'd been in a wreck and was in the hospital when my manager called me and told me that "Tighten Up" had just gone gold. Earlier I'd been telling the guys I served with, "Hey, that music you hear on the radio, that's me." One of them said, "You guys from Texas sure can tell some big lies! I guess that's because everything's big in Texas!" They didn't believe me. But when Skipper called me, I rolled my wheelchair down the hall and told my buddies my record had gone gold, and they realized what I'd been telling them was really true—it really *was* me! Suddenly I had an entourage! We'd be on bivouac, and there'd be 12 men trying to get in a four-man tent! Everywhere I went, people knew me. There was a paper called the *Overseas Weekly*, and about two weeks later, they had an article there about me that said I was "the richest GI in the army since Elvis"! It was [like] a dream.

But it could have been a nightmare. The group needed to follow up their big hit, but that was hard to do with their frontman away. Fortunately, the Army was pretty liberal with Bell after "Tighten Up" became a hit and frequently allowed him to go home for a few days to perform. One of those trips resulted in a meeting that was to pay big dividends. Bell said, "After 'Tighten Up' came out, we were in Lawnside, New Jersey, in a bar called Loretta's High Hat. The manager had connections with the Philadelphia music scene, and after the show, Kenny Gamble and Leon Huff came into the dressing room.... They said they liked 'Tighten Up' and told me, 'We've got a song for you.'" Atlantic was excited that Gamble and Huff wanted to work with the group, and their first collaboration was 1968's "I Can't Stop Dancing." A strong follow-up for "Tighten Up," it went to #9 on the pop charts, perhaps because it closely followed the same formula as their previous hit. "If you listen to 'Tighten Up' and 'I Can't Stop,' they have almost the same riffs, tempo and everything," Bell told me. "It turned out to be a big, big number for us." They rushed out an album produced by Gamble and Huff, *I Can't Stop Dancing*, which reached #28 on the R&B album chart. Around this time, Archie's brother Lee joined the band to replace the departing Butler, and Lee introduced more choreography into the band's stage routines. The band came to be known as much for their dancing during performances as for their songs.

Now the formula was in place: A Gamble and Huff–penned and/or –produced song featuring Bell's smooth vocals meant a hit was almost sure to result. But Gamble and Huff weren't above taking some direction from the boys from Texas, as was the case with their next hit, "There's Gonna Be a Showdown." Bell said,

> Gamble and Huff were in Houston, and we used to do a sock hop, a big dance party for this radio station. All the people would get together and have those dance competitions, and they'd have this thing called a 'showdown.' They'd form a big circle and put money in a hat, and the one who ended up winning would win the pot." Gamble and Huff were intrigued by the competition, and also incorporated some of the local customs into their lyrics. "Every time you would win, you'd put a notch on your shoe," Bell said. "That's why the words to the song say, 'I got ten notches, on my shoes'— that's where that came from."

The songwriters added a few twists of their own. "So Gamble and Huff saw us doing it," Bell said, "and they came up with, 'Hey man, they tell me you think you're pretty good. But don't you know you're in my neighborhood?'" When Gamble and Huff finished the song, the guys recorded it for their fourth Atlantic release. The finished product peaked at #21 on the *Billboard* pop charts, #20 on *Cashbox* and #6 on the R&B charts. It was their third big hit of 1968 in America. Bell also noted that it was their first big hit in England, where it went to #36. (That did happen but not until 1973, during the Northern Soul boom in England when many old R&B songs became hits.)

In 1969, Bell was mustered out of the army, and that left him free to tour with the group and record more material as the need arose. The group released two more 1969 songs that charted, "Girl You're Too Young" and "My Balloon's Going Up." "'Girl You're Too Young' was a song I wrote about a young lady I was interested in, but she was little bit too young," Bell said. "That's why it goes 'You're just a baby' in the same spirit as 'Go Away Little Girl.'" Bell told me that Elvis gave him some advice about that very subject: "Elvis said, 'Archie, 15 [years old] will get you 30 [years in jail], baby!' I said, 'Yeah Elvis, but you married a 14-year-old!' 'Yeah,' he said, 'but I got her parents' permission!'" "Girl You're Too Young" peaked at #59 on the pop charts and #13 on the R&B charts.

Bell said of "My Balloon's Going Up," "That was another Gamble and Huff number, and that was the type of song that could have been in a Broadway play or movie. It's about a guy who's losing his girlfriend. The balloon was his love, going up, getting away from him. He's saying, 'I'll find a new love.'" It peaked at #87 on the pop charts and #36 on the R&B charts. Bell said it was big with audiences because "it was danceable; it's what we called the old soft shoe." "Girl You're Too Young," "My Balloon's Going Up" and "There's Gonna Be a Showdown" were all on their 1969 album *There's Gonna Be a Showdown*.

After so much success in 1968 and 1969, including a #1 record in "Tighten Up," almost overnight the group's music stopped selling. Of their next seven Atlantic singles, three barely snuck into the *Billboard* pop Top 100: "A World Without Music" (#90), "Don't Let the Music Slip Away" (#100) and "Wrap It Up" (#93). They wouldn't fare much better on the R&B charts, where only "A World Without Music" (#46) and "Wrap It Up" (#33) charted. The poor performance was not because of any drastic changes—"A World Without Music" and "Don't Let the Music Slip Away" were written and produced by Gamble and Huff, and "Wrap It Up" was co-written by Isaac Hayes. In addition, the four releases that didn't chart at all were recorded at the famed Muscle Shoals Studios. Nevertheless, none of them were successful, and after 1971's Gamble and Huff–produced "I Can't Face You Baby" failed to chart, Atlantic released them.

The group was disappointed that Atlantic dumped them but found there were other suitors willing to step in. The fledgling Miami-based Glades label, fresh off the success of Timmy Thomas' 1972 hit "Why Can't We Live Together," was all too happy to sign a group of the Drells' caliber and pedigree. "They had come to us and said, 'Come on, Archie, record with us—we have a smash for you.' Everybody's got a smash, you know," Bell laughed. They did sign with Glades, but they were in for a shock after working with a long-established label like Atlantic. "When we signed with the label and went down there, they were supposed to have all this music prepared for us, ready to record. But when I arrived, I had to sit down with Steve Alaimo and KC [later to find fame with the Sunshine Band] and write the words with them. I told my manager, 'I thought this stuff was supposed to be ready. This is not going to work.'" But he admitted that their biggest song for the label, "Dancing to Your Music," was a great record. "We recorded it down in Muscle Shoals, Alabama. They wanted us to keep that 'Tighten Up' pattern with a dance song, and it was a great song, one of my favorites." But despite Bell's enthusiasm about "Dancing to Your Music," it only went to #61 on the pop charts and #11 on the R&B charts. It was, in fact, their *last* entry on the pop charts.

One of the two other Glades singles recorded during the same session did moderately well on the R&B charts, but Bell and his group were done with Glades. "We made the one trip down there and never went back," Bell said. "We were with the label for about a year. They didn't pay their royalties either, and they ripped a lot of people off."

Bell called Gamble and Huff and told them he would like to sign with their label, and they were very receptive. They signed with the TSOP subsidiary of Philadelphia International, a '70s soul label with

#36. "There's Gonna Be a Showdown" (1968)

Archie Bell and the Drells: clockwise from top, James Wise, Lee Bell, Archie Bell and Willie Parnell (courtesy Archie Bell).

acts such as the O'Jays and Harold Melvin and the Blue Notes. They were given another song in the dance-mode genre, 1975's "I Could Dance All Night." Bell: "It was the disco era by then, and we used to work in New York at Studio 54 and places like that. The show would kick off at ten p.m., and when you'd come out of the club, it would be daylight—and you'd have been dancing all night! In the disco era, that's exactly what happened."

"I Could Dance All Night" failed to make the pop charts, but it did rise to #25 on the R&B charts and was a good start for their time at TSOP.

Over the next four years, they had R&B chart hits twice more on TSOP and then four times on Philadelphia International. But in 1979, a lack of chart success and a general weariness led to them deciding to call it quits. Bell went solo for a while but, despite an album and a few singles, success was elusive. Nevertheless, the group left a great legacy, and their music is still popular today.

I interviewed Archie Bell in 2012. He had a stroke in 2021 and as of this writing he is not performing, though he expects to resume.

#37
(British Charts)
"Rhapsody in the Rain" (1966)
Lou Christie

Billboard Pop: #16; *Cashbox*: #20; R&B,
Adult Contemporary: Did not chart

There have been very few unique voices in rock'n'roll. Bob Dylan, Elvis Presley, Freddie Mercury, Neil Young, Janis Joplin—certainly there are more, though it is a debatable topic. Lou Christie has to be counted among that number. It's possible that the unknowing might confuse his voice with another great falsetto, Frankie Valli, but Christie's three-octave vocal range makes him truly exceptional. Once you hear him sing, you aren't likely to forget it. His voice was at or near its best in one of his biggest hits, 1966's "Rhapsody in the Rain."

The man now known as Lou Christie began life as Lugee Alfredo Giovanni Sacco:

> I grew up in Pennsylvania, and I knew that later in life I didn't want to work in a steel mill and I didn't want to live on a farm. My dad worked so hard—he was a very physical Italian—and he had a pick and shovel and hammer and could build anything and tear it down. We grew whatever we ate on the farm; it was that type of existence. I heard records my mother played and music was my escape from reality. And I sang all the time. My whole family sang; my mother sang, my dad sang, all my brothers and sisters sang, and they all have perfect pitch. I kept following that track trying to figure out "How do I get to sing?" to give me the life I envisioned for myself. I sang "Away in a Manger" in first grade at school. I played Joseph and I got applause and I thought, "Oh, what's this?" That was my first time moving forward with this idea of singing.

When he was a little older, he started his first group, the Crew Necks. But he still lived out in the country and knew that in order to eventually make it as a singer, he'd have to go somewhere else. "I kept pursuing singing and trying to get involved with rock'n'roll if I could," he said, "and the closest I could get was Pittsburgh, Pennsylvania, and that was about 35 miles from where I was raised." It was there that a life-changing event occurred: He met former classical concert pianist Twyla Herbert.

> Her daughter used to come downtown—we had a pizza place—and she used to say, "My mom can write songs too and she plays piano." We ended up meeting and together we wrote our first song, "The Gypsy Cried," in 15 minutes and that was it. All of our songs would have very interesting scenarios written into them, and they were all interesting stories. I was an observer, and so was Twyla. We'd see the world, and we saw it in another way. She was much older than me, and she opened my eyes to many, many different things in life.

He recorded "The Gypsy Cried" in a little studio and it was released on the Pittsburgh-based C and C label under the name Lou Christie. He explained:

> I'd had a group called Lugee and the Lions [they recorded "The Jury" on the Robbee label in 1961], and I thought I'd just record under the name Lugee now. I walked into the record company after "The Gypsy Cried" had been recorded and said, "I think I'm gonna use just my one name." But they said, "Nahhh, your name's Lou Christie." And I said "Oh God" because I didn't like it. But the record came out that day and I had to live with it. My dad

In 1966, some of "Rhapsody in the Rain"'s lyrics got it banned on many radio stations. *Time* **magazine said it was corrupting youth.**

said, "It'll bring you good luck because it has Christ's name in it." And it has! He had a lot of wisdom. And as it turned out, it was my first million-selling record.

Roulette picked up "The Gypsy Cried" for national distribution and it earned a gold record and peaked at #24 on the *Billboard* pop charts.

Christie's next Roulette release, "Two Faces Have I," was another song he and Herbert wrote together—and another million-seller.

> Both of my first two songs had interesting titles, because we always wanted to be innovative and interesting. Didn't want to say I love you 14 times in a song. But [Roulette] said about the title "Two Faces Have I," "We don't know what 'two faces' means." I told them to listen to the words, but their suggestion was to call it "Mr. Happy, Mr. Blue"! I said there already was a "Mr. Blue," done by the Fleetwoods. I wasn't about to copy them. I said, "No, listen to what I'm saying. Two faces have I, one to laugh, one to cry. It's much more poetic than 'Mr. Happy, Mr. Blue.'"

Christie was right again. "Two Faces" became his second million-seller and went to #6 on the charts.

Two million-sellers earned Christie a spot on the Dick Clark Caravan of Stars. "It was usually 32 shows," he said. "I was performing with Diana Ross and the Supremes, Ruby and the Romantics, Brian Hyland, Johnny Tillotson, Gene Pitney—we were all traveling around the country singing our hits."

When Christie was drafted, life as he knew it came to an abrupt end. "I had two more nights on the road when I had to leave and go to Fort Knox. I marched around there for six months in a reserve unit. I was walking around thinking, 'I gotta get out of this damn army!'"

After his term of service was up, "I went back to Twyla and said, 'Come on, let's go. We need to get on the charts again!'" Christie said that one thing that made them successful was that they had a feel for what would be successful, even if sometimes the record executives were doubtful:

> We wrote what we liked, we wrote what we felt, and we'd try to sell it that way. Sometimes they'd say, "We don't know what you're doing. The sound is a little different..." Oh, thank God. I didn't want to sound like anybody else. Most record companies, the so-called A&R people, they were supposed to have their finger on the pulse. But if someone had a #1 record that was, say, a ballad, then it's like everyone wanted to do a ballad. I'd say, "No. Why would I want to do a ballad? That was someone else's ballad. It wasn't my ballad." I just could not stand to follow the pattern of someone else, and make a Beatles-type record, or an English record. We had to do it our own way.

His philosophy was tested by "Lightning Strikes," the first song he and Herbert wrote after his enlistment was up. Record executives still hadn't learned that Christie could pick a winner. "The president of the company tossed 'Lightning Strikes' in the waste basket. 'This thing ain't going nowhere,' he said. Well, three months later, he was presenting me with a gold record. I was on the cover of *Billboard, Cashbox* and other magazines with a #1 record and selling millions." It hit #1 in the U.S. and Canada. After his stint in the Army, his career had picked up right where it left off.

His next hit was the most controversial of his career. Herbert and Christie had written a song called "Rhapsody in the Rain," and in many ways it was their masterpiece. "I was imagining if I was with my girlfriend and in the back seat of a car," he said. "And we used to say the phrase 'making out'—that was the way kids were talking in school when I was growing up, and I thought it was clever. 'We were making out in rain. And in this car our love went much too far. And the windshield wipers seemed to say, 'Together ... together ... together....' So it was making love to the rhythm of the windshield wipers." Christie said that in this song, especially the words the back-up singers were singing—in this case Denise Ferri, Arleen Lanzotti and Peggy Santiglia, also known as the Delicates—were a significant part of the song's success. "When Twyla and I were writing a song, we would say, 'Let's bring the girls in' and we'd write what we wanted them to sing before they sang it. We wanted a certain sound. I wanted this kind of whiny sound with clips—I think that was the magic of the record."

Christie said they were particular about who sang behind them:

> I'd go to the studio sometimes and the label would say, "We have some girls to sing behind you," and I'd say, "No, no. I'm not singing with girls I do not know." I could never walk into a studio and sing with girls I didn't know. They can't do the parts—it never works. So I'd bring my girls in, whether we had to fly them in or drive them in or cut it somewhere else. I worked with exactly who I needed. Before the horns, the drummer or anything else, we had the song completed with me singing, Twyla playing, and the three girls singing in the background. I looked at us as a group. It all came together. There was just a handful of people I could always count on.

But it wasn't the singing that made the song controversial, it was the above-mentioned lyrics. Innocent enough today, maybe, but not in 1966. It seemed clear to a lot of people that this meant the couple was having sex, and that was not acceptable on radio. Apparently all of the radio stations owned by ABC were ordered not to play the song, and religious groups decried its lewdness. MGM panicked, and had Christie record a tamer version. "We changed the lyrics," Christie said, "and 'We were making out in the rain' became 'we fell in love in the rain' and 'In this car our love went much too far' became 'Our love came like a falling

#37. "Rhapsody in the Rain" (1966)

star.'" Once released, the new version stalled at #16. It's hard to say how much the delays, re-recording and bad press hurt its sales.

After "Rhapsody in the Rain," Christie had only one more Top 40 hit, 1969's excellent "I'm Gonna Make You Mine," which peaked at #10 on the American pop charts and #2 in England. It's one of the few hits Christie recorded that he and Herbert didn't write, and perhaps that signaled a change in his career. By that time, he was signed to Buddah, and not long afterwards he moved to England, got married and had children. He eventually moved back to the States and he performs to this day. "I still love going out there and performing," he said, "I really enjoy it." As for the "Rhapsody in the Rain" controversy, Christie thinks the whole thing was ridiculous, especially given today's music. "Oh, our music sounds like church music compared to music today. It's so bizarre. I watched the American Music Awards and I'm sure Dick Clark rolled over in his grave. Today's music is so vulgar and unappealing. When I grew up, life was innocent and it was a wonderful way to live. I was raised to respect girls. It's unbelievable. But what happened with 'Rhapsody' just paints a picture of that period in AM radio."

I interviewed Lou Christie in November 2016. Twyla Herbert passed away in 2009.

#38
(Adult Contemporary Charts)
"Beach Baby" (1974)
THE FIRST CLASS

Billboard Pop: #4, R&B: Did not chart;
Cashbox: #3, British Charts: #13

Despite the sound of the song and its subject matter, the California homage "Beach Baby" was a song written in London by Englishman John Carter and his wife Jill Shakespeare, and sung principally by Englishman Tony Burrows. Perhaps similarly contradictory was that there was not really a group named the First Class, at least not until the song became a hit. To confuse matters more, once a group was formed to capitalize on the song's success, Burrows (the lead voice on the record) wasn't with the group when they toured behind the record. All in all, "Beach Baby" is a case study that involves studio groups and session musicians and the tale of how one catchy, well-crafted song can seize the moment when the stars align just right.

To really understand "Beach Baby," one has to first understand the life and career of Tony Burrows. He isn't a household name but his voice took a number of songs straight up the charts: "Love Grows (Where My Rosemary Goes)" (U.S. *Billboard* Pop #5), "United We Stand" (#13), "Gimme Dat Ding" (#9), "My Baby Loves Lovin'" (#13). Of course, the catch here—and the reason why you may not know him—is that none of them were recorded under his name; on those hits, he was the voice of Edison Lighthouse, the Brotherhood of Man, the Pipkins and White Plains. Throw in earlier recordings by the Kestrels and the Flower Pot Men, his work in the Coca-Cola "I'd Like to Teach the World to Sing" commercial, providing backing vocals on Elton John's "Levon" and "Tiny Dancer," and working with Rod Stewart, Tom Jones et al. and Tony Burrows was one of the most recognizable voices on pop radio in the late '60s and early '70s. It's just that you might not recognize his name. For the most part, his chart hits are classics, still known by legions almost half a century later.

#38. "Beach Baby" (1974)

"Beach Baby" by the First Class came towards the end of the progression noted above. Burrows said,

> I started my music career with a vocal group called the Kestrels when I was 16. The group and I [future songwriter-producer Roger Greenaway, Roger Maggs and Jeff Williams; in 1963, they added Roger Cook] stayed together in the Army because we all went in at the same time. When I came out of the Army, we were performing occasionally, and I left the group around 1965. I joined the Ivy League, and a couple of years later I was with the Flower Pot Men. When I was with the Flower Pot Men, we did "Let's Go to San Francisco," written and produced by John Carter and Ken Lewis, which was a success in the U.K. [#4]. There was a guy in America who had a hit with a San Francisco record, Scott Mackenzie ["San Francisco (Be Sure to Wear Flowers in Your Hair)" in 1967]. It wasn't the same record as ours, though; ours wasn't a hit in the U.S.

Burrows had plenty of exposure to the big time world of rock'n'roll early on: "When I was with the Kestrels about '63 or '64, we did the two tours in Britain with the Beatles. We were paid extra to go on before them. No one could hear anything at all, and we used to just talk amongst ourselves to be quite honest, because no one could hear. It was just one continuous scream!" Burrows soon grew tired of some aspects of the music business, tired of "living in hotel rooms and living out of a suitcase. I had a family. I decided that was enough of that."

By the late 1960s, he had established enough of a reputation that he didn't have much trouble finding work as a studio musician. It offered good steady work and, ultimately, more fame than he expected. "That's when I had the hits with White Plains, Edison Lighthouse, Brotherhood of Man and the

"Beach Baby" had a Beach Boys–esque, California-influenced sound, but it was recorded in London and the songwriters, musicians and even the studio crew were British. So was lead singer Tony Burrows, who faked an American accent.

Pipkins," he said. "They were recorded during a six- to nine-month period, but came out at about the same time. But I actually did one edition of a program called *Top of the Pops* where I did three different songs by three different groups on the same program!" Indeed, in what has become one of music's most famous legends, Burrows performed "Love Grows," "My Baby Loves Lovin'" and "United We Stand" on the same day on *Top of the Pops* in 1970. The story is that he would sing one song, go offstage and change clothes, then come back and do another, change and do another. After singing all three songs on that show, afterwards he was banned from the program because he embarrassed the network. Burrows explained how this came about: "If you had a Top 20 record, they'd ask you to do the program. I'm assuming they didn't do their homework and didn't know I was doing lead vocals for three different groups. It's insane, really, but that's what happened."

> The Flower Pot Men did "My Baby Loves Lovin'," but then I quit because I didn't want to tour any more. I had a call and the record company wanted to release some of the unreleased tracks and I said that was fine. The song was released as being by White Plains, was a hit, and the group got back together again. But not me—I'd had enough of touring. I sang on the first couple of records but that was it. I just wasn't going to do it. I was just going to concentrate on studio work.

This impacted a video of the song because the record company had someone other than Burrows featured who appeared to sing the song. "Well, because I refused to tour, the group continued to record and do television, and I wasn't around. Once the song became a hit, they wanted to do an album and book White Plains for concerts, but I wasn't going to do that. So what they'd do is find someone to lip sync the song and film it so the listeners would recognize that person as the lead singer when they were on tour."

In America, Burrows' biggest hit was 1974's "Beach Baby," credited to the First Class. The song was written by John Carter, "who had been part of the Ivy League, and had written 'Let's Go to San Francisco.' He called me and told me he had a song he wanted me to do and told me, 'I've got a feeling about this demo.' The demo was just John and a guitar, and he was singing the song, but I could tell there was something there. So we went in the studio and recorded it. There were basically about 18 different tracks, and John and I did all of the backing vocals as well as the lead." The song was apparently recorded to sound as if First Class was an American group, with Burrows making a conscious effort to Americanize his voice. Apparently, he succeeded. "I heard that when Brian Wilson first heard 'Beach Baby,' he said, 'I don't know who it is but it's definitely West Coast America.' I took that as a great, great tribute,

I really did. I grew up with American pop music. We had recorded the song as basically a tribute to the Beach Boys. Actually, I've since met him two or three times and the other guys as well, and I've heard that when people are going into the theater for one of his shows, he often plays 'Beach Baby.' That's really nice."

The song went to #4 on *Billboard*, #3 on *Cashbox* and #38 on the Adult Contemporary charts. In England, it went to #13, and in Canada all the way to #1. Nevertheless, Burrows was still adamant about not touring, so although he and the studio group did an album as First Class, a whole new group was formed to tour. Some of whom had worked with Burrows in other studio groups. Robin Shaw (once part of White Plains) and Eddie Richards (who had been in Edison Lighthouse) were joined by Spencer James, Clive Barrett and singer Del John. Signed to tour as First Class, they were even pictured on the cover of the group's first album—although none of them sang or played on the album. The album singers were Carter, Burrows and Chas Mills singing, and musicians Brian Bennett, Les Hurdle, Alan Parker, Gerry Butler and Carter again (on acoustic guitar).

Based on "Beach Baby"'s success, there was a First Class follow-up single called "Bobby Dazzler," which did not chart. Of the other follow-up singles, "Dreams Are a Ten Penny" charted highest on the *Cashbox* charts (#71) and "Funny How Love Can Be" charted highest on the *Billboard* pop charts (#74). None of their other songs charted at all, and the album failed as well. John and the record company were persistent and released yet another First Class album. More singles were attempted, but eventually all involved realized the magic of First Class was in its one-off hit.

Burrows has no regrets about doing "Beach Baby." He said that of all the songs he's recorded, his favorites include "Beach Baby" and "Love Grows." Burrows has relented a bit about traveling and has made a few trips to the U.S., where he has actually performed the song. "I go to America a couple of times a year and sing it. People still want to hear it. I've had the pleasure of performing it in California, overlooking the sea and doing it live, which was really nice. I really enjoyed that one, I must admit! I work in Nashville, New York, California. It's still fun. I enjoy just keeping my hand in. ... When I go to America, I go on my own, when I want to. I just travel and pick up the band where I am. No group scheduling to worry about."

I interviewed Burrows in 2016. As of this writing, he is still performing.

#39
(*Billboard* Pop Charts)
"Strawberry Shortcake" (1968)
Jay and the Techniques
Cashbox: #29; R&B, Adult Contemporary,
British Charts: Did not chart

"Strawberry Shortcake" may well be a case study in how you can take a concept or a style of music one step too far.

By 1968, Jay and the Techniques had already had two million-selling hits, "Apples, Peaches, Pumpkin Pie" and "Keep the Ball Rollin'," and both had earned them gold records. Their songs were light and poppy and feel-good, with a childlike simplicity in both their melody and lyrics. But "Strawberry Shortcake" didn't come close to matching the success of its predecessors when it peaked in early 1968 at #39 on the *Billboard* pop charts. The public had seemingly tired of the group's pop stylings, which came as no real surprise to the group's lead singer because he hadn't liked their music much either. Jay Proctor knew that singing the group's type of music wasn't sustainable over the course of a long career, and it wasn't what he wanted to sing in the first place. "Strawberry Shortcake" was the group's last Top 40 hit, perhaps underscoring the ephemeral nature of what audiences find pleasing and purchase-worthy and what they do not.

Allentown, Pennsylvania-born Proctor was a singer who had first recorded with a group called the Sinceres (one of *many* groups to use that name). The group convinced the owner of the local Jordan Paint Company to front the money for them to cut a record, and so "You're Too Young" was released on the appropriately named Jordan Label in 1960. It sold a few copies locally. Proctor and George "Lucky" Lloyd then formed the Floridians and recorded "I Love Marie," a doo-wop number that was released on ABC Paramount.

But the bigger label didn't change the group's fortunes much, and so by the mid–60s Proctor hadn't found a steady job in the music industry and was working in Philadelphia as a keypunch operator. He said that he and Lloyd were sitting in a bar having a beer when a friend came in, said he was starting a group and asked them to audition. Proctor and Lloyd decided to give a try.

> We tried out in groups. There was one white guy and three black guys trying out in my group and each of us took a turn singing a song. Well, when the white guy got through with his song, and it was time for our songs, he said, "It ain't right for a white guy to be in the background," so I kicked him out. It wasn't my house or my group, and I just took over. I started kicking everybody out so only the ones I wanted were there. I was kicking people out left and right! But that's how we ended with the seven guys we ended up with.

By the time Proctor was finished ejecting the people he didn't think needed to be there, he and Lloyd were left with Chuck Crowl, Karl Landis, Ronnie Goosley, Jon Walsh and Dante Dancho. They formed the Techniques.

By 1966, the group had come to the attention of Philadelphia producer Jerry Ross, who was riding a string of pop-star discoveries such as Dee Dee Warwick, Keith, Spanky and Our Gang, and Bobby Hebb. Ross had offered Hebb a song written by Maurice Irby called "Apples, Peaches, Pumpkin Pie" as a follow-up to his smash "Sunny," but Hebb refused it. Ross gave it to his new group instead. Proctor said:

> Actually, several people and groups had tried recording the song—I think even Jerry Butler. Jerry Ross didn't like the way any of them did it, and so he gave it me. I'm raw off the street, I don't know anything about music, so I just opened my mouth and whatever came out, came out. Well, whatever came out pleased him, so we got to release it. But I didn't like "Apples, Peaches, Pumpkin

"Strawberry Shortcake" was Jay and the Techniques' last Top 40 hit. Jay Proctor attributes this to the fact that after "Apple, Peaches, Pumpkin Pie," Smash Records had them record similar-sounding songs over and over.

Pie" either. I'm a very soulful singer, and there wasn't any soul in that song at all. I didn't want to sing about no damn fruit!

But as an unknown artist he wasn't in a position to argue, and so he did the song. He also wasn't in a position to disagree with Ross on another point: Proctor says he was the only group member to actually perform on the recording. "Jerry used session musicians on everything we did. The band was the road group, and they never went in the studio. I asked Jerry to use them, but he just felt they weren't good enough because they didn't read music well."

The song was arranged by Joe Renzetti, and for the back-up vocals Ross chose several artists (Melba Moore, Nick Ashford and Valerie Simpson) who went on to be extremely successful. Despite the fact that the Techniques weren't actually involved in the recording (or perhaps *because* they weren't), the record climbed to #6 on the *Billboard* pop charts and #8 on the R&B charts. It sold more than a million copies and received a gold record.

The release of the song they didn't actually sing brought another surprise for the group. When the record was released, the label said it was by Jay and the Techniques, though no one had told the band about this and they simply considered themselves the Techniques. "I think Jerry changed it because there was Smokey Robinson and the Miracles, and Martha and the Vandellas, and he just didn't like that single-name thing. It wasn't that I was the leader of the group, just the lead singer on the song. Then it didn't make sense to change it back after the song was a hit." Because the song was a hit, the group shrugged it all off. "The rest of the group wished they could have played on it, but early on it wasn't a problem—though I think it became a problem later when some of them got jealous and things like that." Besides, on television they were the faces of the group. Appearances on *The Ed Sullivan Show* (where they received their first gold record live on TV) and *American Bandstand* no doubt went a long way towards keeping the Techniques happy.

With the fame came a problem, said Proctor:

> There was a woman who was the head of the draft board in Allentown whose son went into the Army, and she was pissed because we didn't go in. She tried to have the guys drafted out of anger, and she didn't even know us. But the governor invited me to come see him, and he told me, "As long as you guys stay together, you'll never have to go into the Army."

The governor was true to his promise, and Jay and the Techniques were able to record and release their next hit soon after. "'Keep the Ball Rollin'' was written just for us," Proctor said. It was written by Sandy Linzer and Denny Randell, who had written "A Lover's Concerto" for the

Toys, "Let's Hang On!" and "Working My Way Back to You" for the Four Seasons, and it should have surprised no one that "Keep the Ball Rollin'" was a hit. It soared to #14 on the charts, sold a million copies and earned them another gold record.

Despite the fact that they had a big hit, Proctor and his bandmates had no say in what they released. "Jerry Ross picked the song. I didn't pick anything, and I didn't do anything but go in and perform what I was told or asked to. I wasn't crazy about 'Keep the Ball Rollin'' either. But of course I did it, and I'm glad I did."

It's hard to blame a label for continuing to grind out formulaic music to capitalize on a group's gold-record success. But most successful groups evolve over time, and those that don't generally aren't around long. Jay and the Techniques' first two hits were good, upbeat songs, but not exactly repetitive. The same cannot be said for "Strawberry Shortcake," another food-based, almost childlike song by Maurice "Apples, Peaches, Pumpkin Pie" Irby. It even sounded very similar to "Apples, Peaches, Pumpkin Pie." By this point, the group, especially Proctor, were tiring of the formula. "The music was all way too bubblegummy—they even called it bubblegum soul. You look back at it, and it was kind of ridiculous. It was way far from what I thought my career would be like. I never really had the chance to do anything soulful like I wanted to." Proctor said they made the label aware that they were ready to do something else, and that "Strawberry Shortcake" wasn't it. "I mean, it was by the same writers, used the same musicians, same singer. It was okay, and it had a nice beat, but those kinds of songs, you hear them once and you don't want to hear them no more. But the label insisted we do it." But it seems the public realized that they were being presented with a rewrite of an earlier hit, and it stalled at #39. The group hated "Strawberry Shortcake" to the point that "we never did it live but once because it was too close to 'Apples, Peaches, Pumpkin Pie.'"

After their first three releases had all broken the Top 40 and earned them gold records, the group should have been poised to go on to a successful chart run. It was not to be. Their next release, 1968's "Baby Make Your Own Sweet Music," peaked at #64 on the *Billboard* pop charts and was in fact their last record to make the Top 100 of the pop charts. By the time of their next release on Smash, "The Singles Game," which peaked at #116, Landis and Walsh had left the group and were replaced by Paul Coles Jr. and Danny Altieri. Also added was Jack Truett as an organ player. The lineup changes didn't change their chart fortunes, and only resulted in two more non-charting releases and a peak of #107 for "Change Your Mind." With even Proctor unhappy about the music they were offered, dissension started to set in and the group broke up. And

Jay and the Techniques: right to left, Ronnie Goosley, Dante Dancho, George *Lucky* Lloyd, Jay Proctor, Chuck Crowl, Jon Walsh and Karl Landis (courtesy Jay Proctor).

just as the governor had said, when the group fell apart, "some of the other guys in the group were drafted."

Eventually Proctor and a new group recorded one single as the Techniques for Motown's Gordy subsidiary, but it failed to chart, as did a subsequent single on the Silver Blue label and their first single on Event. Their next Event single, "Number Onederful," did make the R&B charts in 1976, peaking at #94. It was their last chart record of any kind on any chart.

To this day Proctor believes that had the label allowed the group to grow a little and do some songs that weren't formulaic, they might have lasted longer. Proctor still doesn't think much of a lot of those songs, but he is thankful for the career it gave him.

I interviewed Jay Proctor in 2012. Despite some health issues in recent years, he still occasionally performs.

#40
(*Cashbox* Charts)
"Jack and Jill" (1969)
TOMMY ROE

Billboard Pop: #53; R&B, Adult Contemporary,
British Charts: Did not chart

No matter how successful a recording artist may be, it goes without saying that not every release will be a hit. Sometimes, however, when a song doesn't hit, it seems to defy explanation, especially if the song is so familiar that you'd swear it was a really big hit. "Tequila Sunrise" by the Eagles, "Tiny Dancer" by Elton John, "Rock and Roll" by Led Zeppelin, "Changes" by David Bowie and "From Me to You" by the Beatles are among the songs that failed to break into the Top 40 on the *Billboard* pop charts. Tommy Roe's "Jack and Jill" is not as well-known as the songs listed above, but the fact that it struggled to find an audience when it was sandwiched between Roe's big hits of 1969—"Dizzy" (#1), "Heather Honey" (#29), and "Jam Up and Jelly Tight" (#9)—is mystifying. Essentially all of the songs have the same writer or writers, obviously the same performer, and usually even the same musicians. In fact, they all sound similar in one way or another. In that way, "Jack and Jill" is an oddity.

Thomas David "Tommy" Roe was born and raised in Atlanta, Georgia. As a young man, his interest in music was enhanced by the success of Buddy Holly. In the late 1950s, Roe marketed himself as a clean-cut singer of rockabilly music, and while a student at Brown High School he formed a group called Tommy Roe and the Satins. What is perhaps most amazing about this stage of Roe's life is not just the music he was able to write, but the competitors in the Atlanta music industry who set the bar high so that they all had to work hard to get gigs. Joe South, Mac Davis, Ray Stevens and Billy Joe Royal were all part of the Atlanta music scene and all had achieved fame by the end of the 1960s. "We all knew each other and hung around the neighborhood and that kind of thing," Roe

Tommy Roe's "Jack and Jill" only made one Top 40 chart in the U.S. but it went Top 10 in Canada.

told me. "Joe South was a little older and had already cut a record [*I'm Snowed*, 1958]. I was interested in the business but still very young and in high school, so I followed Joe. Then Mac and I came along after that. Mac had a band called the Zots and I had a band called the Satins, and we were both in high school but we would play fraternity parties and we'd bump into one another at parties and things."

Roe said he also worked with Ray Stevens and Jerry Reed, "because we all kind of hung out together. We didn't really go to the same high schools, but because of our interest in music, we would play off of one another. We would work together on songs. Songwriting was the key for us—we all wanted to write songs and so we'd get together for that and then do our shows on the side. The songwriting was what brought us together." Considering that assemblage of future-superstar talent, it's interesting to note that by the end of the decade, Roe had more #1 hits (two) and more *Billboard* pop Top Ten hits (six) than all the others combined.

One of Roe's earliest compositions was about "a girl I had a crush on in high school, and her name was Freda." He continued:

> I wrote this poem called "Sweet Little Freda," and it was also about that time my dad bought me this three-chord guitar. I thought, "You know, if I can put

some music to my poem, maybe I can write songs." So I put a melody to this poem, and it was "Sweet little Freda, you'll know her if you see her. Blue eyes and a ponytail." But the interesting thing was, before I could tell her how I felt and give her the poem, she moved away and I never saw her again. So Freda really started the whole thing but then like a puff of smoke—poof!—she was gone.

Actually, the first Roe song to be released was "Caveman," which came out on the Atlanta-based Mark IV label. It did nothing nationally, but when he signed with the Memphis-based Judd label, owned by Sun Records founder Sam Phillips' brother Jud, things started falling into place. For a first release, he had in mind that song he had written as a starry-eyed teen in school. "I had carried that song around through high school until I had a chance to audition for a record producer. I sang it for him and he liked it but didn't like [the name Freda], so he changed it to Sheila." The song did well regionally. Then ABC-Paramount picked it up, had Roe record a faster, more polished version, and released it nationally; it became a massive hit. The influence of Buddy Holly's music on it is unmistakable, as well as its rockabilly beat. It went all the way to #1.

> "Sheila" became a hit, and was #1 all over the world, and #1 in England. So in 1963, they called from England and wanted to know if I would book a tour over there. They also wanted Chris Montez (he'd had a hit in 1962 with "Let's Dance"), and Chris and I would headline. Chris and I went, and as it turned out, there was a little-known group on our tour called the Beatles. The Beatles were a featured act on our tour, and it ended up being a springboard for their career because there was so much attention—you know, they were like four Elvis Presleys on stage. They would perform and it would turn into chaos in the audience. Chris and I were headlining the tour, but we had to flip the billing around because you couldn't follow these guys. It was like once they got on stage, the show was over, because the audience would go berserk. Then, when they came to America, they were doing *The Ed Sullivan Show* and they called my management and asked if I would open for them in Washington, D.C., on their first concert, and I did. Touring with them in England and then here, I used to tease John [Lennon], saying, "John, you know it's because of my tour you that guys are where you are now!" Those were fun times.

The interaction with the Beatles, and especially Lennon, played a part in Roe's next chart Top Ten hit "Everybody."

> We traveled around England for three weeks doing our tour. Of course, John and Paul were writing songs on the bus and John had this Gibson guitar and he'd let me borrow it and I started writing "Everybody" on that tour. Then when I came back to the States, I took the *Queen Elizabeth*, which was a five-day trip across the Atlantic from England to New York, and I finished

the song on the trip. When I got back, I went to Muscle Shoals and recorded "Everybody" and it turned out to be a big record for me.

The England trip an effect on the song's sound. "When I toured in England, rockabilly music was very big in 1963, and I always loved rockabilly, and when I started out, I was considered a rockabilly artist. So I was influenced by the rockabilly sound, and even the Beatles were doing it early in their career. It influenced me with 'Everybody.' I loved that acoustic sound with that slapback echo so I did that on purpose." "Everybody" went to #3 on the pop charts, making Roe one of the hottest acts in the business.

Roe then had an eye-opening experience with record executives that amazes him to this day.

> When I did the tour in England, Brian Epstein and I got together and we were talking business. He asked me if I would take a promo pack back to my label and see if they'd sign the Beatles. I was kind of the golden boy at ABC Paramount at the time and I could just walk into the president's office, so I said sure. When I got back, [producer] Felton Jarvis and I went to the president's office. He said, "I heard your tour was very successful and while you were over there, you found an act you want us to hear and maybe sign." I said, "Yeah, they're called the Beatles." No response. I pulled their album out, it had their picture on it with the hair and the bangs. When they saw that album, the whole office just got quiet. Like "What the hell has this kid brought us?" Felton said, "Well, you really have to hear them." So he takes the album out and drops it on the turntable, plays a few bars and the president says, "I'll tell you what, kid: Let us be the talent scouts. That's the worst piece of crap I've ever heard in my life. You go over to the room we got you at the Waldorf and write us some more hits and don't worry about finding us new artists. We'll take care of that." Turned the Beatles down. But the record executives back then were so clueless. So many of them were just bean counters. It was a crazy business.
>
> Right after I did the show with the Beatles in D.C. in 1964, I joined the Army Reserve because I was about to get drafted, and so the whole of '64 I was out of the picture. When I was in the Army, I was thinking "When I get out of here, I have to go do a session. How am I going to survive all these British acts? They're coming in with this different sound." So I consciously made a decision to start writing what I called at the time "soft rock," which turned out to be what the deejays would call bubblegum music. So I wrote "Sweet Pea" when I was in the Army, and when I got out I went to L.A. and recorded it with that soft rock sound. I think that's how I was able to continue having hits in the '60s, because we had to maneuver my sound so it wasn't like everyone else's. The bubblegum thing was fresh and new and fit right in with everything because no one else was doing it at the time. After a while, they started calling me the King of Bubblegum.

While Roe accepts the title now, that wasn't always the case. In fact, he really didn't like being called that.

> I was in my mid-twenties and my ego was on my sleeve and a little derogatory remark about my music back then would really set me off. So in the beginning I resented it, but the interesting thing was that the Beatles were really the first bubblegum artists. If you think about it, look at their audience in Washington and so on. They're all teen and pre-teen kids bouncing up and down. We were all playing to the same audience, but my sound was so different that the deejays just had to tag it with something, and bubblegum was what they tagged me with. But today I walk on stage and sing "Sweet Pea" and see a smile on the face of the audience and I think, "What's wrong with that?" I mean, they're having a good time and they love this little song I wrote, so call it whatever you want to call it. If it makes people happy, that's what it's all about. That's part of entertaining. And it's kind of cool to know you put a spark of happiness in someone's heart with what you created.

His first post-military release, "Sweet Pea" went to #8. His next release was also considered "bubblegummy." "After 'Sweet Pea,' it was 'Hooray for Hazel.' I got the idea while watching the program *Hazel* on TV. I used to love the show and was watching it one evening and just picked up the guitar and started writing 'Hooray for Hazel.'" Roe said that "Hooray for Hazel" may have been the record that pleasantly surprised him most.

> Since "Hooray for Hazel" was the follow-up to "Sweet Pea," and usually follow-ups tend not to be as successful, it was a surprise. But "Hooray for Hazel" turned out to be a Top Ten record as well [#6]. Back then, the record companies would push the artists to follow up a hit with a song that was similar to the hit. It was the constant battle with the record company executives and me to not do that. I really felt like we were wasting a release. It would never be as big as the original. I was always fighting that battle. Right after "Sheila," I put out a song called "Piddly Pat" with the same sound and it didn't do anything. Finally I got "Everybody" released and it was so different and that's why it caught on.

Roe's next #1 was "Dizzy."

> I started writing it and couldn't finish it. We were doing a tour with Paul Revere and the Raiders, and we finished our gig one night and were traveling all night to the next city, and so I told Freddy Weller (another old friend from Atlanta), "I've got this song 'Dizzy' and I can't finish it." So we worked all night traveling on that bus and finished it. Then when I got back to L.A., I recorded it. It was one of the few records I made that when I left the studio, I knew it was a hit. I knew it would be big. With the other records, you were never sure. You didn't know if the deejays would play them but with "Dizzy," I knew. It was released and it was one of the fastest-rising records in the

history of singles. It went to 34 on the charts and from there to the Top Ten. It skyrocketed to the top of the charts.

In 1969, Roe was still going strong. He'd had two #1 records and 14 chart hits since "Sheila" in 1963. While not all his songs had been super hits, he admitted that he was surprised that his next release, "Jack and Jill," didn't do just as well as some of his more successful songs; "It just fell a little flat." He again worked with his "Dizzy" co-writer Freddy Weller, and "Jack and Jill" had a similar (but not *too* similar) sound to his other hits. The song was arranged by Steve Barri, who had also worked with him on "Dizzy." "Jack and Jill" is a song that, like Brenton Wood's "Oogum Boogum Song," mentions many late '60s cultural references including bikinis, miniskirts and health clubs. All in all, the song was topical, had good writing and producing and sounds great, but even with that pedigree, it topped out at #40 on the *Cashbox* charts, and #53 on the *Billboard* pop charts. Some might wonder if the nursery-rhyme title hurt it, but Crispian St. Peters' "The Pied Piper" hit #4 and Sam the Sham and the Pharaohs' "Little Red Riding Hood" hit #2. Then again, both of those charted in 1966, and the music scene had changed a lot since then. "I thought it was an interesting song and a well-made record, but it just didn't do as well as some of the others. I had 'Dizzy,' then 'Heather Honey,' and then 'Jack and Jill' came along. It just didn't work, for some reason. You never know why those things happen." Oddly enough, it was one of Roe's most popular songs in Canada, where it went Top Ten. "It's requested [in Canada] a lot, and since I normally don't do it in my show, I have to prepare for it," Roe told me in 2015 when he was still touring.

After his next release, "Jam Up and Jelly Tight," went Top Ten later that year, the 1970s rolled in. "Over the next few years, the music scene changed dramatically. In 1971, 'Stagger Lee' was my last Top 40

Tommy Roe (courtesy Tommy Roe)

chart record. Disco came along, FM album sales were up, it was difficult for me to be successful with those singles I'd always done." Roe had a record barely break into the Top 100 in both 1972 and 1973, but from then until 1979, none of his occasional release charted. Then between 1979 and '87, he had more than a half dozen songs make the country charts. He continued to perform for many years, and in the end, three decades of chart records is a legacy few artists can match.

I interviewed Tommy Roe in 2015. At the time, he was still performing. He retired in 2018.

Works Cited

Aswell, Tom. "Ernie K. Doe." *The Louisiana Music Hall of Fame*. https://louisianamusichalloffame.org/ernie-k-doe/.

Baker, Greg. "The Boogie Man is Back." *Miami New Times*, 19 September 1990. https://www.miaminewtimes.com/news/the-boogie-man-is-back-6365133.

Bell, Archie. Telephone interview with the author. 27 September 2012.

Bell, William. Telephone interview with the author. 11 October 2011.

Bernstein, Jonathan. "This is Where I Live: William Bell on Making the Ballads that Made Him." *Brooklyn*, June 2016. https://www.bkmag.com/2016/06/02/william-bell-this-is-where-i-live/.

"Black Bubblegum." *Bubblegum University*. www.bubblegum-music.com/blackbubblegum.

Bogdanov, Vladimir. *All Music Guide to Soul: The Definitive Guide to R&B and Soul*. Backbeat Books, 2003.

"Box in the Garage—Shades of Blue." *MOG*. http://mog.com/Dashboard DJ856/blog/2844246.

Bradley, Jan. Telephone interview with the author. 15 August 2010.

Braheny, John. "Interview with Thom Bell." 28 September 2007. http://johnbraheny.com/2007/09/28/interview-with-thom-bell/.

"Brenton Wood's Biography." www.brentonwood.com/html/biography.html.

Brewster, Bill, and Frank Broughton. *Last Night a DJ Saved My Life*. Grove Press, 2000.

Bronson, Fred. *The Billboard Book of Number One Hits*. Billboard, 1988.

Broven, John. *Rhythm and Blues in New Orleans*. Pelican, 1978.

———. *South to Louisiana: The Music of the Cajun Bayous*. Pelican, 1983.

Burnett, Norm. Telephone interview with the author. 20 December 2010.

Burrows, Tony. FaceTime interview with the author. 2 October 2016.

Butler, Jerry. Telephone interview with the author. 1 October 2012.

Caldwell, Bobby. Telephone interview with the author. 25 May 2014.

Cameron, G.C. Telephone interview with the author. 4 February 2011.

Casey, Harry Wayne (KC). Telephone interview with the author. 6 March 2015.

Cason, Buzz. *The Adventures of Buzz Cason: Living the Rock n' Roll Dream*. Hal Leonard, 2004.

Castillo, Emilio. Telephone interview with the author. 7 August 2011.

Childs, Marti, and Jeff March. *Where Have All the Pop Stars Gone?* EditPros LLC, 2011.

Christie, Lou. Telephone interview with the author. 25 November 2016.

Cooper, Francis, and Bill Friskics Warren. "Back With the Beat." *Nashville Scene*, 12 October 1995. http://www.nashvillescene.com/arts-culture/article/13000098/back-with-the-beat.

Cree, Roe. "Rose Colored Glass." Email to the author. 9 August 2014.

Dante, Ron. Telephone interview with the author. 16 September 2016.

Deffaa, Chip. *Blue Rhythms: Six Lives in Rhythm and Blues*. Da Capo Press, 1999.

Detroit Record Labels. http://www.seabear.se/detroit2.htm.

Driggs, Frank, and Chuck Haddix. *Kansas City Jazz: From Ragtime to Bebop—a History*. Oxford University Press, 2006.

Elston, Harry. Telephone interview with the author. 21 May 2012.

Farner, Mark. Telephone interview with the author. 31 May 2015.
Gayden, Mac. "How I wrote 'Everlasting Love.'" *Songwriting Magazine*, 2 November 2013. https://www.songwritingmagazine.co.uk/interviews/how-i-wrote-everlasting-love-by-mac-gayden.
Gillett, Charlie. *Making Tracks: Atlantic Records and the Growth of a Billion Dollar Industry*. Dutton, 1974.
Gilstrap, Jim. Telephone interview with the author. 27 September 2011.
Goldberg, Marv. "The Metrotones." http://www.uncamarvy.com/Metrotones/metrotones.html.
———. "The Platters." http://www.uncamarvy.com/Platters/platters.html.
Hayes, Bernie. *The Death of Black Radio: The Story of America's Black Radio Personalities*. iUniverse, 2005.
Jackson, John A. *A House on Fire: The Rise and Fall of Philadelphia Soul*. Oxford University Press, 2004.
James, Gary. "Interview with Nick Marinelli of Shades of Blue." http://www.classicbands.com/v ShadesOfBlueInterview.html.
Jancik, Wayne. *The Billboard Book of One-Hit Wonders*. Billboard Books, 1990.
"Judy Clay Biography." *The Stax Site*. http://staxrecords.free.fr/judyclay.htm.
Kaye, Candy. "The Spiral Starercase." Email to author. 14 April 2010.
Kilgour, Colin. "Gene McDaniels." *Black Cat Rockabilly*. www.rockabilly.nl/references/messages/ gene_mcdaniels.htm.
Knight, Robert. Telephone interview with the author. 6 July 2012.
Kuban, Bob. Telephone interview with the author. 23 August 2010.
Leszczak, Bob. *The Encyclopedia of Pop Music Aliases, 1950–2000*. Rowman & Littlefield, 2014.
Macaulay, Tony. Telephone interview with the author. 2 March 2018.
Marinelli, Nick. Telephone interview with the author. 1 February 2012.
Marsh, Dave. *The Heart of Rock & Soul: The 1001 Greatest Singles Every Made*. Da Capo Press, 1999.
McDaniels, Gene. Telephone interview with the author. 15 November 2010.
McElrath, John. "The Medallions.com." www.medallions.com/index5F/history.html.
———. Telephone interview with the author. July 19, 2010.
Meletio, Larry. Telephone interview with the author. 29 August 2014.
Miranda, Bob. Emails to the author. 4–5 April 2017.
Moore, Deacon John. Telephone interview with the author. 19 November 2010.
"The Northern Soul Top 500." Steve Parker Micro Site. http://www.rocklistmusic.co.uk/steveparker/northern_soul_top_500.htm.
Parissi, Rob. "Wild Cherry." Emails to the author. 8–10 August 2011.
Parker, Steve. "The Northern Soul Top 500." Steve Parker Micro Site. http://www.rocklistmusic.co.uk/steveparker/northern_soul_top_500.htm.
Payne, Freda. Telephone interview with the author. 5 February 2011.
Pittman, Wayne. Telephone interview with the author. 3 November 2010.
Pope, Charles. Emails to author. 25 June, 11 July and 23, 25, and 27–28 August 2010.
Pope, Dianne, and Charles Pope. E-mails to author. 12 December 2011 and 21 February 2012.
Proctor, Jay. Telephone interview with the author. 20 July 2012.
Pruter, Robert. *Chicago Soul*. University of Illinois Press, 1991.
Reuss, Jerry. "Ernie K. Doe: Mother-in-Law." *Jerry Reuss*. https://www.jerryreuss.com/erniek- doe- mother-in-law.html.
Rizik, Chris. "The Friends of Distinction." *Soul Tracks*. http://www.soultracks.com/friends_of_distinction.htm.
Roberts, Kev. *The Northern Soul Top 500*. Bee Cool, 2003.
Roe, Tommy. Telephone interview with the author. 3 June 2015.
Rosalsky, Mitch. *Encyclopedia of Rhythm and Blues and Doo Wop Vocal Groups*. Scarecrow Press, 2008.
"Shades of Blue History." *SOB Entertainment*. http://www.sobentertainment.com/history2.html.
Smith, Bobbie. Telephone interview with the author. 10 September 2011.
"Sonny Turner." *The History Makers*. 2 November 2007. https://www.the

historymakers.org/biography/sonny-turner-41.
"Soulful Kinda Music." http://www.soulfulkindamusic.net/discographies.htm.
"Spiral Starecase." *McLane & Wong Entertainment Law.* http://www.benmclane.com/spiral.htm.
Townsend, John. *Johnny Townsend.* http://johntown.com/index.html.
Townsend, John. Telephone interview with the author. 16 August 2011.
Tufano, Dennis. Telephone interview with the author. 4 October 2014.
Turner, Sonny. Telephone interview with the author. 10 August 2010.
Upton, Pat. "More Today." Emails to author. 10 June and 19 October 2010.
_____. Telephone interview with the author. 7 July 2011.
Warner, Jay. *American Singing Groups.* Hal Leonard, 2006.
Whitburn, Joel. *Billboard Hot 100 Charts—The Sixties.* Hal Leonard, 1995.
_____. *Bubbling Under the Hot 100, 1959–1985.* WS: Record Research, 1992.
_____. *Top Pop Singles, 1955–1986.* Record Research, 1987.
_____. *Top R&B Singles, 1942–1995.* Hal Leonard, 1996.
Whiting, Richard. "Greenwood music legend, Swingin' Medallions founder John McElrath dies." *The Index Journal,* 12 June 2018. https://www.indexjournal.com/news/greenwood-music-legend-swingin-medallions-founder-john-mcelrath-dies/article_45e196dc-eaa2- 5b73-abd6- c2633042b514.html.
Wood, Brenton. "Brenton Wood Information." E-mails to author. 5 May and 18 October 2010.

Index

ABC/ABC-Paramount/ABC Dunhill (label) 14, 15, 36–40, 146, 212, 218, 225, 226
"Abraham, Martin, and John" 103
Academy Award (Oscar) 194
Aerosmith 151
Afrodisiac (album) 50
Ain't Misbehavin' 123
"Ain't Too Proud to Beg" 86
Alaimo, Steve 92, 173, 206
Alexander, Arthur 140, 145
"All My Love" 108
All the Girls in the World Beware (album) 25
All Time Hits 62–63
"Alley Oop" 161
Allman, Duane 191
Allman, Greg 191, 193
Allston (label) 173
Alon (label) 163
"Alone on a Rainy Night" 95
American Bandstand (television show) 13, 39, 45, 69, 109, 167, 220
American Idol (television show) 15
American Music Awards 10, 174, 176, 213
Anderson, Lynn 144
Andre, Peter 111
The Apollo Theater 48–49, 145
Apple (company) 111
"Apples, Peaches, Pumpkin Pie" 218–222
Archie Bell and the Drells 202–208; *see also* Bell, Archie
The Archies 52–54, 123–127
"Are You Happy" 136
Arista (label) 59
Arlen Records (label) 144
Army (British) 215
Army (United States) 96, 153, 198, 203, 204, 205, 211, 212, 220, 226
Arthur Smith Studios 103
"As We Strolled" 119; *see also* "So Much in Love"
Ashford, Nick 220
Atco (label) 71
Atlanta, Georgia 23, 36, 103, 143, 223, 225, 227
Atlanta International Pop Festival 23
Atlantic Records (label) 39, 83, 88, 96, 97, 98, 172, 177, 178, 179, 180, 203, 204, 205, 206, 225
Auburn University 191
Australia 69, 110
Avalon, Frankie 67

"Baby, I Love You" 125
"Baby I Need Your Lovin'" 85
"Baby Love" 14, 85
"Baby Make Your Own Sweet Music" 221
"Baby, Now That I've Found You" 112, 113, 183–188
"Baby What I Mean" 44
"Baby You Got It" 110
Bacharach, Burt 19, 39, 198
"Back in My Arms Again' 85
"Back on My Feet Again" 186
"Back on the Streets" 150
Back to Oakland (album) 151
Bailey, J.R. 49
Bailey, Pearl 14
Baker, Anita 31
Bali Hai Motel 44
Balk, Harry 91, 92
Ball, Noel 74, 76
Ballard, Hank 28
Banashak, Joe 160, 162
"Band of Gold" 12–16
Bang (label) 167–169
"Barefootin'" 106, 161
Barri, Steve 228
Barry, Jeff 7, 125
Barry, Len 120, 121
Batman (television show) 149
Batwing (label) 149
The BBC 19
"Be My Baby" 7
"Be Young, Be Foolish, Be Happy" 143–147
"Beach Baby" 116, 214–217
The Beach Boys 43, 45, 165, 215, 217
The Beatles 3, 5, 6, 24, 52, 62, 65, 70, 113, 114, 128, 148, 165, 172, 198, 211, 215, 223, 225, 226, 227
Beckett, Barry 192–193
The Bee Gees 52
"Behind the Curtains" 80
Beisber, Gary 65

235

Index

Bell, Archie 202–208; *see also* Archie Bell and the Drells
Bell, Ricky 202
Bell, Thom 179–181
Bell, William 95–100
Bell Records (label) 59, 112
Belvin, Jesse 107
Benatar, Pat 55, 123
Bennet, Al 17–19
Benson, George 20
"Bernadette" 86
Bernstein, Herb 157
Berry, Chuck 68, 81
Bill Deal and the Rhondels 128–132
Billboard Magazine 62, 64, 81, 82, 87
Billboard's All Time Top 100 Songs 11
Bishop, Joey 105
"The Bitch Is Back" 151
Bittersweet (album) 50
Black Orpheus 149
"Black Seeds Keep on Growing" 49
Blackburn, Tony 186
Blackwell, Bumps 57–58
Blaine, Hal 44
"Blame It on the Pony Express" 115
Bland, Bobby "Blue" 57
The Blazers 128
"Blessed are the Lonely" 77
"Blow Your Whistle" 174
The Blue Diamonds 159
Blue Magic 50
BMI Award 20
Bob and Earl 202
Bob Collins and the Fabulous Five 39
Bob Kuban and the In-Men 67–72
"Bobby Dazzler" 217
Bobby Moore and the Rhythm Aces 138–142; *see also* Bobby Moore
Bonafede, Carl 63, 64
"Boogie Down" 31
"Boogie Shoes" 175
Booker T. and the MGs 98; *see also* Jones, Booker T.
Boone, Debby 175
"Born Under a Bad Sign" 96
Bowie, David 223
Bradley, Jan (Addie Bradley) 79–82, 189
Bread 167
"Bread and Butter" 90
Breen, Bobby 85
Brent (label) 108
Brewer, Don 21–26
Bright Tunes Music 154
The Brill Building 7
"Bring the Boys Home" 15
Brisbois, Danielle 110
British Academy of Songwriters, Composers, and Authors award 115, 188
Broadway 53, 55
The Brotherhood of Man 114, 214
Brown, Arthur 183

Brown Bag Records (label) 9
Brown, James 102, 104, 159, 172, 190, 195
Brown, Jim 30, 32
B.T. Puppy Records (label) 154
Bubble Puppy 165
The Buckinghams 62–66
Buddah (label) 213
Buckingham Fountain 63
"Build Me Up Buttercup" 112, 113, 186–188
Bump City (album) 150
Burnett, Norm 117–122
Burrows, Tony 114–116, 214–217
Butler, Floyd 29
Butler, Jerry 59, 80, 133–137, 179, 219
The Byrds 43, 166

C and C (label) 210
Cabana Motel 149
Caldwell, Bobby 165–171
The California Angels 29
Cameo/Parkway/Cameo-Parkway (label) 117–121
Cameron, G.C 83–88, 177–178
Campbell, Glen 44
Canada 69, 126, 175, 212, 217, 224, 228
"Candida" 126
"Candy Queen" 154
"Can't Find the Time" 165–171
Capitol Records (label) 23, 146
Capps, Al 44
Carlton, Carl 73
The Carpenters 59
Carter, John 214–217
Casey, Al 44
Casey and the Oceanliners 173
Castillo, Emilio 148–152
"Casting My Spell on You" 109
"Catch a Falling Star" 52
Catch a Rising Star 55
"Caveman" 225
CBS Records (label) 169
Cell Foster and the Audios 28
The Centuries 62
Chad and Jeremy 43, 64
"Chained to Your Heart" 141
"A Change Is Gonna Come" 111
"Change Your Mind" 221
"Changes" 223
"Chapel of Love" 7
Charles, Ray 29, 98, 138, 139, 190, 191
The Charlie Daniels Band 193
"The Cheater" 67–72
Checker (label) 140–141
Checker, Chubby 119, 120, 202
Cheers (television show) 61
Chelsea Records (label) 59, 60, 61
Chess, Leonard 81, 140
Chess, Phil 80
Chess Records (label) 81, 82, 138, 140–142
Chicago (group) 45
Chicago, Illinois 38, 45, 62, 63, 65, 81, 82,

Index

84, 95, 97, 133, 134, 137, 140, 144, 159, 161, 167, 200
The Chicago Tribune 160
Chief (label) 108
The Chiffons 156
"Chip Chip" 19
Chitlin' Circuit 50, 139
Choker Campbell and Band 85
Christie, Lou (Lugee Alfredo Giovanni Sacco) 209–213
Clapton, Eric 171
Clark, Dick 53, 92, 109, 120, 125, 167, 211, 213; *see also American Bandstand*; The Dick Clark Caravan of Stars
Clark, Rudy 49
Clay, Judy 95–100
"Clean Up Woman" 173
Cleaves, Jessica 29–33
Cleveland, Ohio 9, 30, 196
Clinton, George 50, 157
Closer to Home (album) 23
The Clovers 195
Club Imperial 68
The Coasters 194
Cobb, J.R. 146
Coca-Cola 47, 54, 116, 214
Cocker, Joe 114, 194
Coffey, Dennis 13, 15
Cole, Nat King 57, 95, 107, 149, 195
Cole, Natalie 137
Columbia Records (label) 42, 44, 64, 80, 121, 151, 191
"Come a Little Bit Closer" 59
"Come Back My Love" 134
"Come See About Me" 85
"Come Softly to Me" 111
"Come with Me to the Sea" 120
"Coming Back for More" 99
The Commodores 9
Como, Perry 52, 59
"Compared to What" 20
Compton Junior College 107
Cooke, Sam 19, 49, 57–58, 95, 107, 138, 139, 195, 202
"Cooling Out" 137
Cooper, Alice 157–158, 170
Cotillion (label) 39
"Could It Be I'm Falling in Love" 83, 177–182
The Count Five 108
"Country Girl, City Man" 97
The Cowsills 60
Crane, Bill 197
Crawford, Carolyn 85
Crazy Elephant 131
"Crazy Mary" 31
Cree, Roe 165–171
Creedence Clearwater Revival 23, 45
The Crew Necks 209
Crewe, Bob 153, 154
Crispian St. Peters 228

The Critters 92
Crosby, Stills, and Nash 166
The Cuff Links 52–56, 123, 127, 189
The Cuff Links (album) 55
The Culture 59
"Cupid/I've Loved You for a Long Time" 181
Curtis, Clem 183–188

D'Abo, Mike 186
"Daddy Don't You Walk So Fast" 60
"Dance Only with Me" 74
"Dancin' to Your Music" 206
Dante, Ron 52–56, 123–127
The Darcells 62
"Darling No Matter Where" 162
David, Hal 39, 198
Davis, Clive 64
Davis, Mac 145, 169, 223–224
Davis, Marlena 119
Davis, Miles 17, 65, 68
Davis, Paul 33
Davis, Sammy, Jr. 13, 49, 105, 159, 186, 188
"A Day in the Life" 65
"Day Tripper" 114
"Deal Me In" 36, 38
Dedication of Love (album) 141
"Deep Inside Me" 144
Deep Purple 131, 144
The Del-Rios 95
The Delfonics 179
The Delicates 212
The Dells 140, 203
Dennis and Carl 66
De Sario, Teri 176
The Detergents 53, 123, 125
Detroit, Michigan 12, 13, 14, 24, 83, 85, 89, 149, 177, 179, 180
The Detroit Spinners 180; *see also* The Spinners
The Dew Drop Inn 159, 162
Diamond, Neil 169, 191
The Diamonds 202
The Dick Clark Caravan of Stars 53, 92, 125, 211
Dick Dale and the Del-Tones 43
Dick Holler and the Carousel Rockets 102
Dick Holler and the Holidays 102–103
Dig (label) 28
Dion 103
Dire Straits 192
Disco Tex and the Sex-O-Lettes 60
The Dixie Cats 102
Dixon, Luther 198
"Dizzy" 105, 223, 227, 228
"Do the Choo-Choo" 202
Dr. Pepper 54
"Doesn't Somebody Want to Be Wanted" 59
Doggett, Bill 149
The Domingoes 83, 177

Index

The Domingos 89
Domino, Fats 160, 195
The Dominoes 90
"Don't Give Up on Us Baby" 184
"Don't Let the Music Slip Away" 206
"Don't You Care?" 65
The Doodletown Pipers 58–59
The Dootones 108
Dot Records (label) 74, 76
Double Shot (label) 108, 110, 111
"Double Shot of My Baby's Love" 101–106, 191
Douglas, Craig 19
The Dovells 119, 120
"Down in the Boondocks" 144
"Down to the Nightclub" 150
Dozier, Lamont 14
"Dreams Are Ten a Penny" 217
The Drifters 172, 195, 196
The Drinkard Singers 97
"Drive My Car" 70
Duke (label) 163, 196
Duo Glide (album) 193
The Duprells 57
Dylan, Bob 144, 172, 192, 209
Dyson, Ronnie 50

E Pluribus Funk (album) 24
The Eagles 223
Earth, Wind, and Fire 31
East Bay Grease 150
"Easy Coming Out (Hard Goin' In)" 99
Ed Mackenzie's Saturday Night (television show) 12, 13
The Ed Sullivan Show (television show) 31, 58, 220, 225
Eddy, Duane 41
Edison Lighthouse 112–116, 184, 214, 215, 217
Edwards, Sherman 154
Electric Lady Studios 59
Electrified Funk (album) 11
Elf (label) 77
Ellington, Duke 13, 14
Ellison, Lorraine 134
Elston, Harry 28–33
Ember (label) 97, 160
EMI (label) 36
USS *Enterprise* 58
Epic Records (label) 10, 45, 176
Epstein, Brian 226
"Escape (The Pina Colada Song)" 55
Estefan, Gloria 73
"Eternity" 160
Euphrates River (album) 51
Event (label) 222
Everett, Betty 134
"Everlasting Love" 73–78
"Everybody" 140, 225, 226
"Everybody Loves a Winner" 96
"Everybody Plays the Fool" 49

"Everything Is Beautiful" 126
The Extension Five 149

Fabian 67
Fach, Charles 99
Fairlanes 76
FAME (Florence Alabama Music Enterprises) Studios 138, 140, 141, 145; *see also* Muscle Shoals
Farner, Mark 21–27
Farrell, Wes 59
The Fat Ammons Band 132
Feather 191–192
"Feel Like Making Love" 20
The 5th Dimension 28, 29, 113, 184
The Fillmore East 150
Finch, Richard 173–174
"Find Another Love" 144
The First Class 116, 214–217
First President (label) 108
Fisher, Eddie 59
Fitzgerald, Ella 13, 49
Flack, Roberta 20, 178
Flamingo Sky Room 44
The Flamingoes 196
Fleetwood Mac 193
The Fleetwoods 111, 211
The Floridians 218
The Flower Pot Men 114, 214–216
The Flying Machine 113
Foghat 11
"Footstompin Music" 24
"For Your Precious Love" 134
Formal (label) 80–81
Fort Benning, Georgia 138
Fort Dix 153
Fort Knox 211
The Foundations 112, 113, 183–188
The Four Dots 143
The Four Freshmen 13
The Four Graduates 153, 154
4 Sale (label) 104
The Four Seasons 153, 221
The Four Tops 5, 14, 50, 61, 85, 86, 172, 188
Fox, Antoinette Dorsey 163
Foxx, Inez 198
Foxx, Redd 197
Frampton, Peter 24
Franklin, Aretha 31, 61, 140, 144, 172, 178, 192
Frazier, Skipper Lee 202, 204
Fred Foster Sound Studio 77
Free 8
Freeman, Bobby 119
Frey, Glen 170
Friedman, Mel 70, 72
The Friends of Distinction 28–33
"From Me to You" 223
The Frontier Hotel 58
Frost, Craig 25

Index

The Funk Brothers 13, 15
"Funny How Love Can Be" 217
Fuqua, Harvey 84
The Fydallions 42

Gamble, Kenny 133, 135, 136, 202, 204, 205, 206
"Games People Play" 146
The Gap Band 33
Garrett, Snuff 18–20
Gates, David 166
Gayden, Mac 76, 77, 78
Gaye, Marvin 31, 85, 86, 172, 178, 190, 199
Gaynor, Gloria 179
"Gee Whiz" 96
Gérard, Rosemonde 44
Gerry and the Pacemakers 154
Gershwin, George 153–155
"Get Dancin'" 60
"Get Down" 9
"Get Down Tonight" 174–175
"Get Out of My House" 162
"Ghetto Child" 181
"Ghostbusters" 13
Gibson, Charlene 31–33
Gilstrap, Jimmy 57–61
"Gimme Dat Ding" 114, 214, 216
"Gimme Little Sign" 110, 111
"Girl Blue" 50
Girl Crazy 154
"Girl on a Swing" 154
"Girl Watcher" 34–40
"Girl You're Too Young" 205
"Give It Up" 176
"Giving You the Best That I Got" 31
Glades (label) 173, 206
Gladys Knight and the Pips 20
GM (General Motors) 180
"Go Away Little Girl" 154, 205
"God's Gonna Punish You" 122
Goffin, Gerry 35
Golden Choir Jubilee 159
Golden Globe 194
Golden World (label) 90, 91
Goldmine 80
Goldsboro, Bobby 44
"Good Lovin'" 108
Good Times 57, 61
Gooding, Cuba 32, 47–51
"Goodnight My Love" 154
Gordy (label) 222
Gordy, Berry 13, 14, 84, 85, 222
The Gotham City Crimefighters 149
Graham, Bill 150
Grammy Award 10, 20, 31, 50, 59, 144, 175, 176, 194
Grand Funk 9
The Grande Room 89
Gray, Dobie 68
"Grazing in the Grass" (Friends of Distinction version) 28–33

"Grazing in the Grass" (Hugh Masekela version) 30
Grease 61
"The Great Pretender" 195
"Greatest Love" 98
Greenaway, Roger 215
Greenfield Hammer 115
Greenwich, Ellie 7, 11, 126
"Greetings (This Is Uncle Sam)" 93
Grizzard, Lewis 101, 106
"Groovy Kind of Love" 126
Groves, Lani 59
Guerico, Jim 64–65
Guerin, John 44
The Guise 71
"The Gypsy Cried" 210–211
"Gypsy Woman" 79

Haines, Connie 85
Hall, Joanna 121
Hall, John 121
Hall, Rick 141, 145
"Hang On Sloopy" 59, 106
"Hanky Panky" 7
The Happenings 153–158
"Happiness" 92
"Happiness Is Just Around the Bend" 51
"Harbor Lights" 197
Harlem 47
"The Harlem Shuffle" 202
Harold Melvin and the Blue Notes 207
Harper, Willie 161, 163
Hathaway, Donny 98
Hayes, Isaac 206
Hazel (television show) 227
"He Will Break Your Heart" 79–80, 134
Heart 151
Heart (Gulf Coast Band) 191
The Heart of Rock and Soul 109
"Heather Honey" 223, 228
Hebb, Bobby 219
"Hello My Lover" 160
Hendrix, Jimi 59, 66, 191
Henley, Don 170, 193
Herbert, Twyla 210–213
"Here Come the Girls" 163
"Here She Comes" 120
Heritage Records 130
"He's Ready" 45
"He's So Fine" 156
"Het, Western Union Man" 133–137
"Hey Baby, They're Playing Our Song" 65
"Hey Girl" 35
"Hey Girl, Don't Bother Me" 145–146
The Hi-Fis 29
Hilliard, Bob 19
Hinnant, Jimmy 34
Hoekstra, Dave 161
Holland, Brian 14
Holland, Eddie 14
Holland-Dozier-Holland 14, 15, 185

Holler, Dick 102–103; *see also* Dick Holler and the Holidays
Holliday, Billie 12
Holly, Buddy 223, 225
Hollywood, California 71, 89, 108, 192
The Hollywood Argyles 161
Hollywood Walk of Fame 176
Holmes, Rupert 54
Holvay, Jim 63–65
"Honey Baby" 159
Honey Cone 59
"Hooray for Hazel" 227
Hopkins, Telma 13, 15
Horne, Lena 45
"House of Strangers" 60
Houston, Cissy (Emily "Cissy" Drinkard) 97
Houston, Whitney 61, 97
Houston, Texas 202, 203, 205
"How Could I Let You Get Away" 179
How Do You Say I Don't Love You Anymore? (album) 14
Howlin' Wolf 81
Huey Lewis and the News 151
Huey "Piano" Smith and the Clowns 161
Huff, Leon 133, 135, 136, 202, 204, 205, 206
Humble Pie 8, 24
Humperdinck, Englebert 113
"A Hundred Pounds of Clay" 17–20
"Hush" 144
Hyland, Brian 144, 161, 211

"I Can Hear Music" 7
"I Can't Face You Baby" 206
"I Can't Help Myself" 14, 85
"I Can't Stop Dancin'" 202, 204
I Can't Stop Dancin' (album) 204
"I Got Rhythm" 153–158
"I Dig You Baby" 133, 134, 135
"I Don't Want to Know" 68
"I Feel Sanctified" 9
"I Forgot to Be Your Lover" 98
"I Keep Forgettin'" 194
"I Like Dreamin'" 58, 60
"I Love Marie" 218
I Love My Music (album) 11
"I Love You 1000 Times" 195–201
"I Prayed for You" 28
"I Who Have Nothing" 22
The Ice Man Cometh (album) 135, 136
Ice on Ice (album) 136
"I'd Like to Teach the World to Sing" 116, 214
Idol, Billy 98
Ienner, Jimmy 25
"If It's All Right With You" 168
"If You Had a Heart" 47
"If You Really Loved Me" 155
The Ike and Tina Turner Review 68
"I'll Always Love You" 85
"I'll Be Around" 83, 179

"I'll Meet You Halfway" 59
"I'm Always Chasing Rainbows" 155
"I'm Better Off Without You" 47
"I'm Doin' Fine Now" 60
"I'm Gonna Make You Mine" 213
"I'm on Fire" 60
"I'm Over You" 82
"I'm Stuck on You" 47
"I'm Your Boogie Man" 174
"I'm Your Puppet" 191
Impact (label) 91, 92
The Impressions 79, 133, 134, 137, 195
Impulse (label) 14
"The In-Crowd" 68
"In the Bad, Bad Old Days" 188
The Ink Spots 154
Invictus (label) 14, 15
Irby, Maurice 219, 221
"The Isle of Love" 120
The Isley Brothers 50, 94
"Isn't It Lonely Together" 77
"It's a Shame" 83–88, 177
"It's All Right, You're Just in Love" 145
"It's Cool" 121
"It's Just Your Way" 82
"It's Magic" 197
"It's Up to You, Petula" 116
"Itsy Bitsy Teeny Weenie Yellow Polka Dot Bikini" 52, 161
"I've Been Hurt" (Bill Deal and the Rhondels version) 130
"I've Been Hurt" (Tams version) 130, 145, 146
Ivor-Novello Award 116, 188
The Ivy League 114, 215–216

J Geils Band 178
"Jack and Jill" 105, 223–229
Jackson, Billy 119, 121
Jackson, Chuck 198
Jackson, Michael 57, 61
"Jam Up and Jelly Tight" 105, 223, 228
James, Etta 28, 138, 139, 140, 192
James, Harry 58
James and Bobby Purify 191
"Jane" 152
Jarvis, Feltonn 226
Jay and the Americans 59
Jay and the Techniques 105, 218–222
The Jazz Masters 21
JCP (label) 35
Jefferson Starship 152
"Jerkin' Time" 68
The Jimmy Wilkins Orchestra 14
The Joey Bishop Show (television show) 45
John, Elton 116, 151, 214, 223
Johnny and the Hurricanes 92
Johnson, Johnny 115
Jolson, Al 157
Jones, Booker T. 97, 98; *see also* Booker T. and the MGs

Jones, Quincy 59
Jones, Tom 113, 116, 214
Joplin, Janis 23, 209
Jordan Paint Company 218
"The Jury" 210
"Just a Summer Memory" 82
"Just Don't Want to Be Lonely" 47–51
"Just Like Romeo and Juliet" 90
"Just You and Me Baby" 179

Kador, Ernest *see* Ernie K-Doe
"The Kangaroo" 108
Kaye, Harvey 42, 44
Kazanegras, Alex 192
KC (Harry Wayne Casey) 172–176, 206
KC and the Sunshine Band 172–176
KC and the Sunshine Junkanoo Band 173–174
K-Doe, Ernie 159–164, 189
"Keep It Comin' Love" 172–176
"Keep On Truckin'" 31
"Keep the Ball Rollin'" 218–222
Keith 219
Kendricks, Eddie 31, 60
The Kestrels 114, 214–215
Kim, Andy 124, 125, 126
"Kind of a Drag" 62, 64
Kinder Joy 111
King, Albert 96–97
King, Ben E. 51
King, Carole 26, 35, 52, 123, 124
Kirshner, Don 52, 54, 55, 123–126
The Knickerbockers 92
Knight, Robert (Robert Peebles) 73–78
Knight, Sonny 44
Knight, Terry 9, 21–23, 26; *see also* Terry Knight and the Pack
The K's 34
Kupka, Stephen "Doc" 149–152

Labelle 58, 60
Labelle, Patti 98
"Lady Marmalade" 58, 60
The Lamplighter Club 200
Lander College 101
Las Vegas, Nevada 42, 44
"(Last Night) I Didn't Get to Sleep at All" 113, 184
The Latineers 117–118
"Laugh It Off" 145–146
Laurie (label) 154
"Lay Down Sally" 171
"Leader of the Laundromat" 53, 123, 125
"Leader of the Pack" 53, 125
Led Zeppelin 8, 23, 172, 178, 223
Lee Andrews and the Hearts 81
The Left Banke 104
Lennon, John 128, 225
"Let It Be Me" 133, 134
"Let Love Come Between Us" 191
"Let the Heartaches Begin" 185, 186

"*L'éternelle chanson*" ("The Eternal Song") 44
"Let's Dance" 225
"Let's Go to San Francisco" 114, 215–216
"Let's Hang On" 221
"Levon" 116, 214
Liberty (label) 17–19
Lieber, Jerry 47
"Life Is Too Short" 161
"Lift Us Up Where We Belong" 193–194
"Lightning Strikes" 211–212
Linzer, Sandy 220
"The Lion Sleeps Tonight" 154
"Lipstick Traces" 163
Little Anthony and the Imperials 193
Little Eva 202
Little Freddy & the Rockets 108
"Little Miss Flirt" 38
"Little Red Riding Hood" 228
Lloyd, George "Lucky" 218–219, 222
"The Loco-Motion" 24, 202
Loggins, Kenny 193
Loggins and Messina 192
"Lonely Drifter" 119
"Lonely Summer" 91
"Lonely Teardrops" 196
"Lonesome Mood" 29
Long, Jim 166
Long John Baldry 186
Loretta's High Hat 204
Los Angeles, California 42, 57, 104, 140
"Louie, Louie" 106
Louisiana State University (LSU) 102
Love Affair 73, 77
Love, Barbara 29–33
"Love Grows Where My Rosemary Goes" 112–116, 184, 188, 214, 216, 217
"Love Machine" 38
"Love on a Mountaintop" 78
"Love or Let Me Be Lonely" 31–33
"Love Takes Time" 121
Love Talk 60–61
"Love Talk" 60
"A Lovely Way to Spend an Evening" 154
"A Lover's Concerto" 220
"A Lover's Question" 196
"Lovey Dovey Kinda Lovin'" 111
Lowe, Bernie 119
Lowery, Bill 36–37, 103, 105, 143–147
Lugee and the Lions 210
Lulu 60
Lynyrd Skynyrd 192

Macaulay, Tony 112–116, 183–188
Macy's 111
Madison Square Garden 130
"The Magic of Our Summer Love" 120
The Main Ingredient 32, 47–51
"Make It Easy on Yourself" 134
"Make It with You" 166
Make Way for Youth (television show) 12, 14

Makenzie, Scott 215
The Magnificent Seven (band) 102, 190, 191
"Mama Didn't Lie" 79–82
Mancini, Henry 59
"Mandy" 55, 123
Manfred Mann 186
Manilow, Barry 55, 123
Mann, Johnny 17–18; The Johnny Mann Singers 17–19
Mann, Kal 119
Marinelli, Nick 89–94
Mark IV (label) 225
Marsh, Dave 109
The Marshall Tucker Band 193
Martha and the Vandellas 220
Martin, Dean 105
Martin, Tony 85
"The Mashed Potato" 202
Maskela, Hugh 30
Mason, Barbara 176
Mason, Barry 113
Mathis, Johnny 20, 120
The Matrix 61
"May I" (Bill Deal and the Rhondels version) 129–130
"May I" (Zodiacs version) 129
Mayfield, Curtis 79–82, 133–134
MCA (label) 36
McCann, Les 17, 20
McCartney, Paul 128
McCoo, Marilyn 29
The McCoys 59
McCrae, George 173–174
McDaniels, Gene 17–20
McDonald, Michael 194
McElrath, John 101–106
McLemore, Lamont 29
McPhatter, Clyde 196, 197
"Me and You" 111
Meco 175
The Medallions 101–103
Medress, Hank 156
Meletio, Larry 165–171
Memphis, Tennessee 59, 95, 97, 225
Memphis Records (label) 59
Mercury (label) 99, 100, 102, 104, 133, 134, 135, 136, 137, 195, 197, 198, 201
Mercury, Freddy 209
"Mercy, Mercy, Mercy" 65
"Merry Christmas Baby" 47
The Merv Griffin Show (television show) 14
Meteor Records (label) 95
Metric (label) 163
The Metrotones 196
MFSB 180
MGM (label) 14, 121, 167, 212
Miami Dade College North 172
Midget (label) 111
Midler, Bette 178
Mid-South Talent Contest 95
"Mighty Love" 181

The Mike Douglas Show (television show) 45
Miller, Norm 166, 168
Miller, Roger 102, 104
"Millie's Chili" 28
"Mind Pleaser" 51
Minit (label) 160–163
The Miracles 198, 220
Miranda, Bob 153–158
The Mississippi Piney Woods Singers 17
"Mr. Blue" 211
"Mr. Custer" 161
"Mr. Dream Merchant" 135
"Mr. Schemer" 108
Mr. Wood (label) 111
Mitch Ryder and the Detroit Wheels 92, 153
The MOB 63, 65
"Mockingbird" 198
Molly Hatchet 11
The Monitors 94
Montez, Chris 225
Monument Records (label) 76
"Moody Woman" 136
"Moon River" 133, 134
The Moonglows 81, 84, 196
Moore, Bobby 138–142; *see also* Bobby Moore and the Rhythm Aces
Moore, Bobby, Jr. 138–142; *see also* Bobby Moore and the Rhythm Aces
Moore, Deacon John 159–164
Moore, Melba 220
"More Today Than Yesterday" 41–46
Morrison, Van 169
"Mother-in-Law" 159–164
Motown (label) 13, 14, 15, 51, 76, 83, 84, 85, 86, 87, 88, 89, 90, 92, 131, 133, 137, 149, 156, 172, 177, 178, 179, 195, 198, 199, 222
The Motowns 149
Mouse and the Traps 165
"Move Me" 60
"Ms. Grace" 121
Murray the K 35
Muscle Shoals, Alabama 138, 140, 145, 192, 193, 206, 226
Musicland (label) 68, 69, 71
Musicor (label) 198–201
"My Baby Loves Lovin'" 114, 214, 216
"My Baby Sure Can Shag" 147
"My Baby Specializes" 98
"My Balloon's Goin' Up" 205
"My Boy Lollipop" 140
"My Eyes Adored You" 58, 60
"My Guy" 84
"My Love for You" 159
"My Mammy" 157
"My Prayer" 196

Nail Me to the Wall (album) 193
Nashville, Tennessee 73, 77, 217

Nelson, Rick 46, 110, 168
Nelson, Willie 170
"Never Give You Up" 134, 135
New Orleans, Louisiana 138, 159, 160, 163, 164, 193
New York City (group) 60
New York City, New York 7, 14, 31, 35, 36, 37, 48, 52, 54, 59, 60, 90, 97, 98, 124, 130, 153, 191, 207, 217, 225
The Newbeats 90
Newborn, Phineas 95
Newton, Wayne 60
The Nightcaps 190
"No One for Me to Turn To" 45
Nolan, Kenny 58, 60
Norman (label) 68
The Northern Jubilee Gospel Singers 134
Northern Soul 77, 146, 205
Northstate/North State (label) 35–39
"Nothing Succeeds Like Success" 132
"Number Onederful" 222

Off the Wall (album) 61
An Officer and a Gentleman 193
"Oh How Happy" 89–94
"Oh Lord I Wish I Could Sleep" 179
The O'Jays 119, 179, 207
The Old Friends 46
Old Hickory (club) 102, 191
On Time (album) 23
"1-2-3" 121
"Only the Strong Survive" 136
Only the Wild Survive (album) 11
"The Oogum Boogum Song" 107–111, 228
The Originals 15
Orlando, Tony 13, 15, 52, 123, 124, 126
Orleans 121
The Orlons 119, 120
Orpheus 166–167
Otis, Johnny 28
Ovide (label) 202–203
Owens, Mary 165–171

The Pacemakers 67
Page, Patti 124
The Paramounts 74
Parissi, Rob 7–11
Parker, Charlie 17
Parker, Ray, Jr. 13, 15
Parker, Robert 161
Parliament Funkadelic 31
Parton, Dolly 57, 61
The Partridge Family 59–60
The Passions 79
Paul, Billy 136
Paul Revere and the Raiders 105, 167, 227
Payne, Freda 12–16
Payne, Scherrie 12, 13, 15
Peaches and Herb 179–180
Pendergrass, Teddy 137
Penhall, Bob 166

"People" 121
People's Choice Award 176
Pepsi 54
The Persuaders 52, 124
Peters, Jerry 31
Philadelphia, Pennsylvania 117, 119, 133, 134, 135, 136, 137, 144, 179, 180, 204, 206, 207, 219
Philadelphia International (label) 133, 137, 206, 207
Phillips, Jud 225
Phillips, Sam 225
Phoenix (album) 24
Pickett, Wilson 98, 138, 139, 140, 186, 190
"Piddly Pat" 227
"The Pied Piper" 228
The Pipkins 114, 214, 216
Pitney, Gene 211
Pitt Sound Studios 36
Pittman, Wayne 34–40
P.J.'s Alley 46
The Platters 52, 124, 195–201
"Play That Funky Music" 7–11
Playing to Win (album) 46
"Please Don't Go" 176
Pockriss, Lee 52, 54, 55, 125
The Poets 47
Pope, Charles 143–147
Pope, Joe 143–147
"Popeye Joe" 162
The Poppies 45
Poree, Anita 31
Prairie View College 136
Presley, Elvis 46, 52, 124, 136, 172, 204, 205, 209, 225
Preston, Johnny 74
"Pretty Woman" 113
Pride, Charlie 49, 170
Princess Anne High School 128
"Private Number" 95–100
Proctor, Jay 218–222
Prophesy (label) 111
Pruter, Bob 80
"Psychotic Reaction" 108
The Pulsations 62, 63
Pye (label) 112, 113

The Quails 133
The Queen Elizabeth 226
"Queen of Clubs" 174
Question Mark and the Mysterians 22
The Quotations 108

Radio One 185
Raitt, Bonnie 151
Ram, Buck 197–201
The Ramongs 183
The Ramsey Lewis Trio 68
Randell, Denny 220
The Rascals 92
The Raspberries 25

Rawls, Lou 20, 137
The Rays 119
RCA (label) 30, 31, 32, 38, 46, 47, 49, 50, 54, 121
"Reach Out" 14
"Reaching Out" 141
Recording Industry Association of America (RIAA) 10, 30, 146
Red Bird (label) 47
The Red Saunders Band 95
Redding, Otis 69, 97, 98, 138, 139, 140, 172, 186, 190, 193
Reed, Jerry 144, 224
Reese, Della 13
The Reflections 90, 94
Renzetti, Joe 220
Reserve (label) 196
"Rhapsody in the Rain" 209–213
Rhys, John 90, 91
The Rhythm and Blues Foundation R&B Pioneer Award 100
The Rhythm and Blues Hall of Fame 15, 137
The Rhythm Masters 67
Richie, Lionel 57
Rising Sons (label) 74, 76, 77
The Roadrunners 149
Robbee (label) 210
"Robin's World" 55
Robinson, Smokey 60, 199; see also The Miracles
"Rock and Roll" 223
Rock and Roll Hall of Fame 137
"Rock 'n Roll Soul" 24
"Rock Your Baby" 173
The Rockets 102
The Rockin' Gibraltars 191
Rocky 61
Rodeo Drive 167
Roe, Tommy 105, 140, 144, 223–229
Rogue's Gallery 132
"Rolling Down a Mountainside" 51
The Rolling Stones 5, 6, 8, 68
The Ronettes 125
The Rooster Tail 89
The Roosters 134
Rose Colored Glass 165–171
"Rose Garden" 144
Ross, Diana 12, 31, 45, 86, 176, 211
Ross, Jerry 130, 134, 135, 219, 220, 221
Rostand, Edmund 44
Roulette Records (label) 14, 211
Roxbury (label) 60
Royal, Billy Joe 144, 223
The Royal Guardsmen 103
The Rubber Band 191
"Rubberband Man" 83, 181
Ruby and the Romantics 211
Ruffin, David 86
"Run Sally Run" 55
Russell, Bobby 74, 76

Rust (label) 154
Rydell, Bobby 119, 120

Sager, Carole Bayer 125
St. Louis, Missouri 67–69
St. Louis Institute of Music 67, 69
The Saints 128
Sam and Dave 138, 193
Sam the Sham and the Pharaohs 228
San Francisco (label) 150
"San Francisco (Be Sure to Wear Flowers in Your Hair)" 215
Sanford, Ed 189–194
The Sanford Townsend Band 189–194
Sansu (label) 163
Santana 151
Satellite Records (label) 95; see also Stax Records
Saturday Night Fever 175
Savoy (label) 159
Scaggs, Boz 61
Scarborough, Skip 31
Scepter (label) 97, 198
Schaacher, Mel 22
"Scorpio" 13
Scott, Freddy 35
Scott, "Sir" Walter (Walter Simon Notheis Jr.) 67–72
Seals, Melvin (aka "Mystro") 179
Seals, Mervin (aka "Lyric") 179
"Searching for My Love" 138–142
Searching for My Love (album) 140, 141
Sedaka, Neil 52, 123, 124, 125
"See You in September" 154–156
The Sensational Epics 144, 146
The Sensations 165
Shades of Blue 89–94
"Shake Your Booty" 174
Shakespeare, Jill 214
Shakespeare, William 155
The Shangri-Las 53, 125
Shannon, Del 92
Sharp, Dee Dee 119, 120, 202
"She Blew a Good Thing" 47
"She Drives Me Out of My Mind" 105
"Sheila" 225, 227, 228
Sheila E 158
Sherril, Billy 45
"She's My Woman, She's My Girl" 203
"She's Ready" 45–46
"Shinin' On" 24
The Shirelles 198
"Show Me Your Badge" 9
The Side Effect 59
"Sideshow" 50
Sigma Sound Studios 180
"Silly Little Girl" 145
Silver Blue (label) 222
The Silver Lake Club 34
Simon, Paul 192
Simon and Garfunkel 144

Index

Simpson, Valerie 220
The Simpsons (television show) 61
Sinatra, Frank 105, 191
Sinatra, Tina 59
"Sincerely" 84
The Sinceres 218
"The Singles Game" 221
Sir Douglas Quintet 165
The Skylarks 196
Slatkin, Felix 17
Sly and the Family Stone 45
Small, Millie 140
Smash (label) 102, 104, 105, 106, 219, 221
"Smile a Little Smile for Me" 113
Smith, Bobbie 83–88, 177–182
Smith, Don 103
Smith, O.C. 179
"Smoke from a Distant Fire" 189–194
"Smoke Gets in Your Eyes" 196–197
"Snoopy vs. The Red Baron" 103
"So Much in Love" 117–122
So Much in Love: The Story of a Summer Love (album) 120
"So Very Hard to Go" 150
Sober, Errol 166
"Some Got It, Some Don't" 111
"Some Kind of Wonderful" 24, 25
"Somebody's Baby" 77
Somewhere (album) 120
Sonny and Cher 45
Soul, David 184
Soul Brothers Six 25
The Soul of a Bell (album) 96
"Sound Your Funky Horn" 174
South, Joe 144–146, 223–224
Southern University 161
Spanky and Our Gang 219
Sparkling in the Sand 150
Specialty (label) 160
The Specters 190
Spector, Phil 7
Spellman, Benny 161–163
The Spinners 83–88, 177–182; see also The Detroit Spinners
"Spinning Around" 48
The Spiral Starecase 41–46
"Spooky" 146
"Stagger Lee" 228
"The Star Spangled Banner" 163
"Star Wars Theme" 175
Starr, Brenda K. 46
Starr, Edwin 89–91
Starr, Ringo 57
Stax Records 95–100, 172
"Stay" 129
Stevens, Ray 124, 126, 144, 223, 224
Stewart, Rod 61, 116, 146, 192, 214
Stewart, Steve 192
"Still the One" 121
Stills, Stephen 178
Stoller, Mike 47

Stone, Henry 173
"Stop in the Name of Love" 14
"Stormy" 146
"Storybook Children" 97
Straigis, Roy 119
"Strawberry Shortcake" 218–222
"The Streak" 126
"Street Talk" 121
Streisand, Barbara 61
"The Stroll" 202
Stubbs, Levi 86
Studio 54 207
The Stylistics 179
Sue and Sunny 114
"Sugar, Sugar" 52–54, 123–127
The Sugarbabes 163
Sun Records (lable) 225
"Sunny" 219
"Supernatural Thing" 51
The Supremes 12, 13, 14, 58, 59, 85, 172, 199, 211
The Surfaris 43
Survival (album) 24
"Susan" 62–66
Sutton, Glenn 45
Svengali 201
Sweet City Records (label) 9
"Sweet Pea" 226–227
"Sweet, Sweet Lovin'" 200
"Sweet Thing" 84
"Swing Your Daddy" 57–61
The Swingin' Medallions 101–106, 144, 191
"Swinging Tight" 132
Symbol Records (label) 47

Talking Book (album) 59
Talty, Don 79–80
The Tams 130, 140, 143–147, 189
"The Tams Medley" 146
Tangerine (label) 29
Tarsia, Joe 135
"Te-Ta-Te-Ta-Ta" 162
"A Tear" 19
"The Teaser" 69–70
Ted Carrol and the Music Era 39
Ted Mack Amateur Hour (television show) 12
The Tempos 154
The Temptations 50, 61, 73, 86, 88, 172, 178, 188
"The Ten Commandments of Love" 83
Tennessee State University 76
"Tequilla Sunrise" 223
Terry Knight and The Pack 21, 22
Texas Rock Association 171
Texas Tech University 165
That Thing You Do! 89
"That's the Way I like It" 174–175
"That's What Girls are Made For" 84, 179
"Then Came You" 83, 181
"There Ain't Nothing Like Shaggin'" 147

Index

"These Foolish Things" 121
"There's Gonna Be a Showdown" 202–208
There's Gonna Be a Showdown (album) 205
"This Time It's Real" 148–152
Thomas, B.J. 92
Thomas, Carla 96
Thomas, Irma 162
Thomas, Timmy 173, 206
Thornton, "Big Mama" 28
Three Dog Night 25, 44
Thriller (album) 61
"Tighten Up" 202–208
Tillotson, Johnny 211
Time Magazine 210
"Tiny Dancer" 116, 214, 223
The Tip Top Talent Hunt 118
T.K Recording Studios 173
"To Be a Lover" 98
"To Each His Own" 120
Today's Black Woman (television show) 15
The Tokens 154–157
Tommy James and the Shondells 23
Tommy Roe and the Satins 223
Tone Record Distributors 172–173
Tommy's Girls 180
The Tonight Show (television show) 14, 45
Tony Award 123
Tony Orlando and Dawn 13, 15
Top of the Pops (television show) 60, 115, 146, 216
Toussaint, Allen 160–163
Tower of Power 148–152
Tower of Power (album) 149, 150, 151
"Tower of Strength" 19
Townsend, John 102, 189–194
"Tracy" 52–56, 123, 127
Tracy, Spenser 54
Traffic 192
The Trammps 179
"Travelin Life" 39
Trexler, Donnie 39–40
Tri-Phi Records (label) 83, 85
"A Tribute to a King" 97
"Truly Yours" 85
"Try My Love Again" 140
"Tryin' to Love Two" 95, 99
TSOP (label) 206–207
The TSU Tornadoes 202
Tufano, Dennis 62–66
The Turbans 119
Turner, Sonny 195–201
The Turtles 69
"The Twelfth of Never" 120
"24 Hours from Tulsa" 39
Twenty Grand (Club) 89
"Twilight Time" 196
"The Twist" 202
"Two Faces Have I" 211
The Tymes 117–122

Uggams, Leslie 14
Ultra (label) 28
United Artists 80
United Sound 14
"United We Stand" 114, 214, 216
University of Alabama 190
The University of Georgia 101
University of Omaha Conservatory of Music 17
University of Southern California 202
"Untie Me" 143–144
Upchurch, Phil 79
Upton, Pat 41–46
Urban Renewal (album) 151
USA Records (label) 64

The Valadiers 93, 94
Valli, Frankie 58, 60, 114, 209
Vance, Paul 52, 54, 55, 125
Vanderbilt University 76, 78
Vandross, Luther 33
The Vatican 193
Vaughn, Frankie 19
Vee-Jay (label) 133, 134, 136
Vera, Billy 97, 98
Verne, Larry 161
Vetter, Cyril 103
Vietnam 58, 69, 86
V.I.P. (label) 83, 86, 88, 177
Virginia Beach, Virginia 129–132
The Vocals 29
The Volumes 92

"Walk Like a Man" 24
The Walker Brothers 104
Wand (label) 108
Warburton, Lou 114
Ward, Robin 119
Warner Brothers (label) 111, 146, 150, 151, 192, 193
Warnes, Jennifer 194
Waronker, Sy 17
Warwick, Dee Dee (Dee Dee Warrick) 97, 219
Warwick, Dionne (Dionne Warrick) 97, 181, 198,
"Washed Ashore" 200
Washington, Dinah 149
Washington University 67, 69
"The Way You Do the Things You Do" 73
Wayne, Sid 154
WDAS 118
"We Girls" 80–81
"Weep Little Girl" 145
"The Weeper" 76
Weigert, Dave 156
"We'll Have It Made" 88
Weller, Freddy 105, 227, 228
Wells, Mary 85, 198
"We're an American Band" 24
Weston, Kim 139

Wexler, Jerry 98, 192, 193
"What Is Hip?" 151
"What Kind of Fool (Do You Think I Am)" (Bill Deal version) 128–132
"What Kind of Fool (Do You Think I Am)" (Tams version) 130, 140, 143, 146
"What the World Needs Now is Love" 39
"What Would I Do?" 121
"What's the Use of Breaking Up" 134, 136
Wheatman, Heather 114
Wheatman, Yvonne 114
"When Julie Comes Around" 55
When the Lights Go Down (album) 14
"When You Come Back Down" 59
"Where Did Our Love Go?" 14, 85
Where the Action Is (television show) 69, 91, 140
Whiskey a Go-Go 65
White Plains 114, 215, 216, 217
Whitley, Ray 130, 144–146
"Who Stole the Batmobile?" 149
"Whole Lot of Soul" 80
"Why Can't We Live Together?" 173, 206
Wilbe (label) 10
Wild Cherry 7–11, 189
Williams, Andy 45
Williams, Ken 49
Williams, Lenny 149–152
Williams, Maurice 129; *see also* The Zodiacs
Williams, Tony 195–201
Willis, Carolina 59
Wilson, Brian 216
Wilson, Jackie 28, 49, 196, 197, 202
Wilson, Joyce 13, 15
Wilson High School (Virginia) 128
Winchester (label) 121
Wine, Toni 54, 124, 126
Wingate, Ed 90
"With a Little Help From My Friends" 114
"With This Ring" 198
WJR 12
Wonder, Stevie 50, 57, 59, 86, 87, 121, 188

"Wonderful Summer" 119
"Wonderful! Wonderful!" 120
Wood, Brenton (Alfred Jesse Smith) 107–111, 228
"Wooly Bully" 106
"Working My Way Back to You" 221
"Working My Way Back to You/Forgive Me Girl" 181
"A World Without Music" 206
"Wrap It Up" 206
The Wrecking Crew 44
Wright, Betty 173
Wyker, Johnny 190–191
Wylie, Richard "Popcorn" 198

Yes 178
"Yes I'm Ready" 176
"You Are the Sunshine of My Life" 58
"You Better Move On" 140, 145
"You Better Run" 55
"You Can Call Me Rover" 50
"You Don't Miss Your Water" 96
"You Lied to Your Daddy" 145
"You Light Up My Life" 175
"You Little Trustmaker" 121
"You Ought to Be Havin' Fun" 151
"You Send Me" 57
"You'll Never Know" 144
Young, Colin 186, 187
Young, Neil 131, 209
"You're Good for Me" 169
"You're Still a Young Man" 150
"You're Too Young" 218
"You've Been My Inspiration" 48
"You've Got to Take It" 50
"You've Got Your Troubles" 114

Zillow 111
The Zodiacs 129; *see also* Williams, Maurice
The Zots 224
ZZ Top 165

www.ingramcontent.com/pod-product-compliance
Lightning Source LLC
Chambersburg PA
CBHW052058300426
44117CB00013B/2190